UNDER
A
PAINTED
SKY

UNDER A PAINTED SKY

Stacey Lee

G. P. Putnam's Sons

An Imprint of Penguin Group (USA)

G. P. PUTNAM'S SONS
Published by the Penguin Group
Penguin Group (USA) LLC
375 Hudson Street
New York, NY 10014

USA | Canada | UK | Ireland | Australia
New Zealand | India | South Africa | China
penguin.com
A Penguin Random House Company

Library of Congress Cataloging-in-Publication Data
Lee, Stacey (Stacey Heather).
Under a painted sky / Stacey Lee.
pages cm
Summary: "In 1845, Sammy, a Chinese American girl, and Annamae, an African American slave girl, disguise
themselves as boys and travel on the Oregon Trail to California from Missouri"—Provided by publisher.
[1. Adventure and adventurers—Fiction. 2. Runaways—Fiction. 3. Sex role—Fiction. 4. Chinese Americans—
Fiction. 5. African Americans—Fiction. 6. Slavery—Fiction. 7. Oregon National Historic Trail—Fiction.
8. West (U.S.)—History—1848–1860—Fiction.] I. Title.
PZ7.L514858Und 2015 [Fic]—dc23 2014015976
Printed in the United States of America.
ISBN 978-0-399-16803-1
1 3 5 7 9 10 8 6 4 2

Design by Marikka Tamura. Text set in LTC Cloister Pro.

PUBLISHER'S NOTE

For my number one fangirl, Avalon

1

THEY SAY DEATH AIMS ONLY ONCE AND NEVER misses, but I doubt Ty Yorkshire thought it would strike with a scrubbing brush. Now his face wears the mask of surprise that sometimes accompanies death: his eyes bulge, carp-like, and his mouth curves around a profanity.

Does killing a man who tried to rape me count as murder? For me, it probably does. The law in Missouri in this year of our Lord 1849 does not sympathize with a Chinaman's daughter.

I shake out my hand but can't let go of the scrubbing brush. Not until I see the blood speckling my arm. Gasping, I drop the brush. It clatters on the cold, wet tile beside the dead man's head. An owl cries outside, and a clock chimes nine times.

My mind wheels back to twelve hours ago, before the world turned on its head . . .

Nine o'clock this morning: I strapped on the Lady Tin-Yin's violin case and glared at my father, who was holding a conch shell to his ear. I thought it was pretty when I bought it from the curiosity shop back in New York. But ever since he began listening to it every morning and every evening, just to hear the ocean, I've wanted to smash it.

He put the shell down on the cutting table, then unfolded a bolt of calico. Our store, the Whistle, was already open but no one was clamoring for dry goods just yet.

The floor creaked as I swept by the sacks of coffee stamped with the word *Whistle* and headed straight for the candy. Father was cutting the fabric in the measured way he did everything. *Snip. Snip.*

Noisily, I stuffed a tin of peppermints into my case for the children's lessons, then proceeded to the door. Unlike Father, I kept my promises. If a student played his scales correctly, I rewarded him with a peppermint. Never would I snatch the sweet out of his mouth and replace it with, say, cod-liver oil. Never.

"Sammy."

My feet slowed at my name.

"Don't forget your shawl." *Snip.*

I considered leaving without it so I wouldn't ruin my exit. But then people would stare even more than they usually did. I returned to our cramped living quarters in the back of the store and snatched the woolen bundle from a basket. Underneath my shawl, Father had hidden a plate of *don tot* for me to find, covered by a thin layer of parchment. I lifted off the parchment. Five custard tarts like miniature sunflowers shone up at me. He must have woken extra early to make them because he knew I'd still be mad.

I took the plate and the shawl and returned to the front of the shop. "You said we'd move back to New York, not two thousand miles the other way." New York had culture. With luck, I might even make a living as a musician there.

His scissors paused. When he finally looked up at me, I raised my gaze by a fraction. His neatly combed hair had more white than I remembered.

"I said one day," he returned evenly. "One day." Then his tone lightened. "They say the Pacific Ocean's so calm, you could mistake it for the sky. We'd see so many new animals. Dolphins, whales longer than a city block, maybe even a mermaid." His eyes twinkled.

"I'm not a child anymore." Only two months from sixteen.

"Just so." He frowned and returned to his cutting. Then he cleared his throat. "I have great plans for us. Mr. Trask and I—"

Mr. Trask again. I set the plate down on the cutting table, and one of the fragile custards broke. Father lifted an eyebrow.

"Only men who want to pound rocks go to California," I snapped. "It's rocks and nothing."

"California's not the moon."

"It is to me." Though I knew I shouldn't claim the last word, I couldn't help it. I was born in the Year of the Snake after all, 1833. Father looked at me with sad but forgiving eyes. My anger slipped a fraction. With a sigh, I carefully scooped the broken tart off the plate and left the shop.

Five o'clock: Keeping my chin tucked in, I hurried down the road, kicking up dust around my skirts. The smell of smoke was especially robust tonight. Maybe the smokehouse had burned the meats again. The boys who worked there were not particularly gifted, plus they were mean. I already knew they would overcharge us for the salt pork we'd need for the trek west, and Father would have no choice but to pay.

I marched past uneven blocks of mismatched buildings, longing for the orderly streets of New York City. There were actual sidewalks there, and the air always smelled like sea brine and hot bread, unlike St. Joe, which reeked of garbage and smoke and—

I lifted my head. The sky had thickened to a hazy gray, textured with particles... like ash? Something sour rose in my throat.

It was not the smokehouse meat that was burning.

I ran, my violin bouncing against my back.

Oh please, God, no.

I flew past empty streets and turned onto Main, where suddenly there were too many people, some standing like cattle, others clutching squirming children to them. Noise assaulted me from all sides, people yelling, animals braying, and my own ragged breath.

The Whistle was a charred heap, an ugly inkblot against the dusky sky. The heat made the air look wavy, but the bitter reek in my nose told me the scene was no mirage. Ashes fluttered like black snowflakes all around.

"Father!" I pounded toward the remains, scanning the area for his distinctive figure. His dark hair and small build. The worn jacket with the patches on the elbows that he wouldn't replace because he was saving for my future. Maybe he had shed it, for surely he was hauling water along with the rest of the men.

Smoke filled my lungs, and burned my eyes as I rubbed my grimy fingers into them.

"Out of the way!" yelled a man carrying buckets. Water sloshed onto my skirt.

I trotted beside him as he carried the buckets to another man who threw them onto the smoldering ruins. "My father—"

The man barely glanced at me. "He's gone."

I uttered a hoarse cry. *Gone?*

"Lucky you weren't there yourself or you'd have been trapped, too. Now move!" He trod on my foot as he shoved by, but I hardly felt it.

My God, I didn't—I should have . . .

"How?" I asked no one in particular. Was it an accident? Father was the most careful person I knew. He always doused the stove after we used it, and strictly enforced our NO SMOKING PERMITTED signage. No, if it was an accident, it couldn't have been Father's.

Whoever was responsible, may he pay for it in a thousand ways, go blind in both eyes, deaf in both ears. Better yet, may he perish in hell.

I choked back a sob and tried to make sense of the fuming mess in front of me. There was nothing but jagged piles of charred fragments. I could make out a heap of ash in the spot where we kept our wooden safe. Though Mother's bracelet was no longer inside, it had held other irreplaceable treasures. A photo of Mother. Father's immigration papers.

A wall of heat stopped me from going closer than fifteen feet from our front door, or where it used to be. My eyes burned as I strained to find my father, still not quite believing the horror was real. But as the heat began to cook my skin, I knew as sure as the Kingdom hadn't come that he was gone. My father burned alive.

I shuddered and then my chest began to rack so hard I could scarcely draw a breath. Smoke engulfed me, thick and unyielding, but the awful truth rooted me to the spot: after I'd given my last lesson of the day, I'd dawdled along the banks of the dirty Missouri, throwing stones instead of coming home directly. I should have been with him.

Oh, Father, I'm sorry I argued with you. I'm sorry I left with my nose in the air. Were you remembering that when the smoke robbed you of your last breath? You always said, Have patience in one moment of anger, and you will avoid one hundred days of sorrow. *My temper has cost me a lifetime of sorrow. And now, I will never be able to ask your forgiveness, or see your kind face again.*

Another man carrying buckets barreled toward me. "Move back, girl, you're in the way!"

I stumbled toward an elm tree, and there I stood, even after the glowing hot spots had ceased to burn, and buckets were no longer emptied.

Still the black snow fell, bits of my life flaking down on me.

2

"SHE'S BEEN STANDING THERE OVER AN HOUR,"
a man muttered to another as they passed by.

"Place just lit up," said a woman from behind. "Everything burned, even the Chinaman."

"They sold the Whistle to a Chinaman?" asked another woman.

My face flushed at her commenting on this rather than on Father's death. We were never welcome here. Why should I expect people to care now, just because Father had died? I turned to glare at the two women, only now noticing the crowd that had gathered. The thick soup of smoke had thinned to a veil of black.

"Six months ago. Where you been? Well, that's the chance you take when you operate a dry goods. Places like that are tinderboxes." This first woman finally noticed me, my lips clamped tight and my eyes swollen. She elbowed her friend, then they hurried away.

Fly, you crows. My father was not a spectacle. He was the greatest man I ever knew. He was my everything.

I clutched at the elm tree before I fell over.

A child born in the Year of the Snake was lucky. But every so often, a Snake was born unlucky. Mother died in childbirth, a clear indication that my life would be unlucky. To counteract my misfortune, a blind fortune-teller told Father never to cut my hair, or bad luck would return. In addition, she said I should resist my Snake weaknesses, such as crying easily and needing to have the last word.

"'Tis a shame about your daddy," said a familiar voice. Our landlord, Ty Yorkshire, shook his head. His puffed skin made him look older than my father, though they were both in their forties.

I wiped my eyes with the back of my hand.

"My best building, too," he said in his rapid speech that caused his jowls to shake. His left eye winked, the lashes fluttering like moth wings. "Sometimes you roll snake eyes."

I gasped. He knew my Chinese lunar sign? It took me a moment to realize he was talking about gambling, not me.

"I gotta meet with some company men. You need a place to stay, wash that black off you. La Belle Hotel is one of mine. Betsy will get you a nice room." He tipped the edge of his hat, then hailed two men.

I blinked at his departing back. Despite his kind offer, the man always made me uneasy. Maybe it was the way his black suits hung over his too-wide hips, reminding me of a spade. Father said spades represented greed, because the first Chinese coins bore that shape.

One of the onlookers covered her mouth and recoiled when she saw me. A man put a protective arm around her shoulders, like I was a wounded animal that might bite. I couldn't blame him. I was unsure of my own reactions. The anger and horror poisoning my insides made every nerve sing in pain, made me want to scream, and weep. I was my violin bow, bent to the breaking point and on the verge of snapping in two.

But I did not snap. Instead, I shuffled toward Main, not even sure where I was going as I picked my way around horse pies.

Did he suffocate before the flames—?

I shook my head. I couldn't bear to think of it.

My adopted French grandfather called Father his scholar. Father could predict the weather by listening to birdsong. Knew which plants healed and which poisoned. Spoke six languages. Tipped his hat to everyone, even Mrs. Whitecomb, who regularly pinched buttons from us.

The moist evening air licked at my face and bare arms. Somewhere I had lost my shawl.

To my right, a line of wagons led down to the Missouri River. The town of St. Joe squatted at the edge of the civilized world. Folks came here to jump into the great unknown, starting with a ferry ride across the dirty Missouri.

Into the great unknown was where the grocer Mr. Trask took Mother's jade bracelet after Father inexplicably gave it to him. Now, nothing remained.

I pressed my violin case into my gut and stared at the river. The shimmering surface beckoned to me. I could be with Father, instead of in this unjust world, which never threw us more than a cold glance. With the strong undertow, death would be quick.

But Father would not want that.

Dazed, I stumbled away. My boot caught on a sandbag and this time I did fall, sending my case skittering in front of me.

"Look sharp!" yelled a young man from atop a horse. I covered my head with my arms. His sorrel stamped its print just inches from my head. White markings extended past its fetlocks like socks. The rider slowed.

"You okay, miss?" he asked in a soft but clear voice.

I nodded but didn't look back. Father always said, *He who gets up more than he falls, succeeds.* I scrambled to collect my violin before another horse came along and trampled it. The rider moved on.

I found myself staring up at La Belle Hotel, whose pink walls set it apart from its drab neighbors. Up close, I noticed the dirt overlaying the paint. Father and I avoided this street because he said the uneven surface brought bad energy. But I had nowhere else to go.

I swung open the heavy door. Behind an elaborately carved walnut counter, a woman in bright taffeta lifted her shriveled face to me. "Yes?"

"Good evening, ma'am," I said in a shaky voice. "I'm Samantha Young. Mr. Yorkshire said I might find accommodation here."

"Good Lord," she muttered, thin nose twitching like a mouse's.

Her cane dragged along the floor as she hobbled toward me, *shhh, tap, shhh, tap.* She raked a contemptuous eye across my face and down to my worn boots. After an eternal pause, she said, "Annamae, bring Miss Young up to room 2A and scrub her down."

A girl my age appeared in the doorway behind the staircase, skin the shade of pecans. She didn't wear chains, but the brand on her forearm gave her away: a square with six dots, raised like icing piped onto her skin. If it was possible to feel any sicker, I did. Negroes walked tall and free in New York. I wished for the hundredth time we'd never left.

"Miss Betsy, ma'am?" said Annamae in a quiet voice.

The old woman squinted, as if the sight of Annamae talking displeased her.

"Thought you wanted me to pick up the linens from the launderer tonight, like I always do. I was just on my way." Annamae pulled her shawl tightly around her shoulders and slanted her heart-shaped face toward the main door.

"Well, I've changed my mind, and how dare you question me." Miss Betsy's voice sliced through the air. "Now do as I ask, and don't be slow about it." She threw a hand at the girl as if to strike her, but Annamae was just out of reach.

Annamae regarded me with her deeply inset eyes. Chinese people believe that eyes like those indicate an analytical, practical mind. The look she gave me was not unkind, but there was a spark of something there—anger?—that compounded the guilt I was already feeling. With a last glance at the door, Annamae bowed her head and placed her hand on the banister. One by one, she ascended the stairs, as if every step were a labor. I plodded after her uniformed figure, keeping my eyes fixed on the cheerful pink bow of her apron.

Room 2A was grander than I thought could exist in St. Joe, with a slipper tub set at the foot of a feather bed. But the opulence sat like raw chicory on my tongue. I wanted to be back with Father, picking apart the Paganini concerto. Taking nature walks with our copy of *Fowler's Flora.*

Annamae filled the tub. A thick-handled brush and a cake of soap waited on a side table. The brush looked big enough to scrub a horse. Annamae finished pouring the water while I stuck to the wall and hugged myself.

"You's grimy. Get in," she said. A moment later, the door closed. She was gone.

Maybe I wouldn't be scrubbed down. I peeled off my dress with the tiny flowers, washed so many times the color had disappeared. It was sticky with sweat and reeked of smoke.

I stepped into the water, lowering myself carefully. The bath smelled of lavender. This was the first tub I'd sat in since coming to St. Joe, but all I could think about was whether it was deep enough to drown in.

Oh, Father! How could you leave me behind? I could not even bury you like you deserved. What a disgrace of a daughter. I'm sorry. I should've been there, shouldn't have taken the last word.

I submerged my head and counted . . . *Thirty-six, thirty-seven, thirty-eight . . .*

3

SOMEONE PULLED ME UP BY THE BACK OF MY NECK.

Annamae peered down at me as I sucked in air. "You can't kill you'self like that. It don't work. I tried."

I gaped at her. Ignoring me, she stretched her lean body over mine to unwind the two buns on top of my head. Her own hair was cropped short, accenting the swan-like curve of her neck.

She wiggled her fingers to loosen my tresses. I wanted to tell her not to scrub me down, but when she started kneading my scalp, I forgot.

"God makes our bodies want to live, no matter what our minds want to do," she stated in a quiet, deep voice. Her face was more handsome than beautiful, with strong cheekbones, a narrow chin, and clear eyes that didn't wander. She must have been born in the Year of the Dragon, since she looked about a year older than me and held herself with a certain quiet dignity. Father said you could spot Dragons a mile away because all heads turned their way.

Annamae poured the rinse water over my hair, then picked up the wooden brush. The bristles scratched my skin, but she didn't scrub hard.

"Now why you want to kill you'self?" Her sympathy broke me.

"I got home too late," I sobbed. "The place was ashes. My father died. He was everything to me."

The brush stopped for a moment. "I'm real sorry about that. I know the hurt you's feeling. Like you want to disappear into the nearest rabbit hole and never come out." She took my hand and gently ran the bristles under my fingernails. "He the one gave you that fiddle?" She nodded at the Lady Tin-Yin.

"Yes."

"That means he believed in you. Only men play the fiddle."

I stared at her. It was true that most folks considered the violin too difficult for a woman to master, but, as with teaching me the Classics, Father never gave it a second thought.

She helped me out of the tub and handed me a robe. "I'll fetch some tea." Out she breezed, taking my soiled dress with her.

Not two minutes later, the door opened again. I thought it was Annamae, and jumped when our landlord Ty Yorkshire appeared in the door frame. Though he stood just a few inches taller than my five-foot-three height, his presence filled the room like the scent of bitter almonds.

"I'm not dressed," I cried, pulling the robe more snugly around me.

"Had a good chat with the sheriff." Slowly, he rubbed his thick hands together.

He stepped closer and I backed away. My skin broke out in gooseflesh.

"No point in filing charges for negligence against a dead man." He turned to hang his hat on one of the wall hooks.

"Negligence?" If there was negligence, it wasn't ours.

"'Course, fires are expensive. Someone's gotta ante up. Not easy to insure a wood building like that, but I can be very convincing." He waved at the bed. "Let's sit down." The bed groaned as he made himself comfortable.

"It's not proper for you to be here. I'm not decent."

"Doesn't bother me." He patted the spot beside him, his manner friendly and almost cheerful. "I really should get some chairs in here."

When I still didn't sit, he added, "All I want to do is talk a little business with you. It troubles me to see your poor situation, and I would like to help. But we can't do business if we don't trust each other, can we?"

I may not have liked him, but he did lease us the Whistle, even installed a new window when we complained about the draft. But what could he want from me, I wondered. Not violin lessons.

I perched on one corner of the bed, keeping my distance.

To my surprise, he stood and took two steps back to the wall hooks. I thought he was going to take his hat and leave, but instead, he unstrapped his gun belt and hung it next to his hat. "Wearing a piece when talking to a lady is just disrespectful." Then he shrugged off his black coat, spun of the finest wool, and hung it as well. "You got any family around? Anyone to look after you?"

I shook my head.

The bed sank as he reseated himself. An oily smile spread across his face. "That's what I thought."

His moth eye started winking again, picking up speed with every beat. It might have flown right out of his head. "So here's what I propose. Out of respect for your dearly departed father, I would like to offer you room and board here. In exchange, you will provide services."

I stiffened. "Services?"

"Silken hair, ivory skin, eyes like a cat. Eyes that tell a man to come in and shut the door," he hissed out of the spaces between his teeth. His bulbous nose twitched as he sniffed once, twice.

Dear God, what now? I stood abruptly, casting around for a way out. There was only the door and the window.

He stood, too, blocking the path to the door. "Men will pay dearly for the pleasure of a woman's company. I already got a Spaniard, an Injun, and two Negresses. An exotic number like yourself could augment my fine stable. The Lily of the East, we'd call you. Bet you'd fetch more than the lot of them, maybe five dollars an evening. You can wear pretty dresses, take baths. You'd enjoy that, wouldn't you, Sammy?"

Only Father called me Sammy. My face burned at the unwelcome familiarity.

A too-warm breeze blew through the open window and rumpled the back of my hair. I could end things right now. Step out the window like Ophelia, who fell out of a willow tree after Hamlet killed her father. Two stories was about the height of a willow.

I kept him talking. "Why would I do that?"

He shrugged. "You got no choice. No money, nobody to look after you. You think the pittance you earn from those violin lessons will keep you? This way, the only thing you'd have to lift is your, well..." His eyes skipped to my lower half. "It'll help pay your debts."

"What debts?" I tried to still the tremor in my voice.

"A fire like that could've been started by that stove you kept, against building code for a dry goods." His voice oozed like ointment.

I stepped to one side, wishing to squeeze past him and the tub to reach the door. He shifted as well, blocking me again. "A glimpse of a lady's ankle is like the first sip of wine. Makes you thirsty for the whole bottle. Now before we make any formal agreement, I'd like to test the goods."

"Stay away from—" I began, but quick as a striking adder, he clamped one hand over my mouth and the other on the back of my head. I clawed at him, trying to scream, but he squeezed harder, smashing my lips into my teeth. I tasted blood.

"Scream all you want. Ain't no one here going to rescue you. I pay handsomely, see."

He shoved me backward onto the bed. My head recoiled off the mattress when I landed. Looking wildly around for salvation, I spotted the scrubbing brush on the side table. When he looked down to undo his trousers, I reached over and closed my fingers around the handle.

Scrambling up, I swung it hard against the side of his head. My leverage was not good, but he yelped and grabbed my throat.

"Whore!" he spat.

Wasting no time, I brought the brush up again and clubbed him in the face, causing blood to spurt from his nostrils. He jerked back to avoid another blow, but the movement threw him off balance and he slipped. His arms flailed, but his feet couldn't get purchase on the wet floor.

Backward he fell. With a sickening *crack,* his head banged against the edge of the tub.

And as Ty Yorkshire crashed to the floor, his fall sent out ripples I feared would chase me no matter which way I ran.

I dropped the brush. It clattered on the cold, wet tile beside the dead man's head. An owl cried outside, and a clock chimed nine times.

Moments after the last chime, the door opens again. Annamae enters, bearing a tray.

"Oh, Lord," she gasps, eyes doubling in size.

"I think he's dead," I whisper. "He was trying to—to—"

Annamae shuts the door and sets down the tray. She paces for a moment. Then she straightens the waist of her dress. "Move him to the bed before the blood soaks to the first floor," she orders.

The hysterics gather in my chest, making it hard to breathe, let alone move.

She appraises my trembling self. Then, to my surprise, she hugs me. "Pull it together."

The warmth of her touch quells some of my panic. "I . . . I'm going to hell."

She pushes me away from her, and bends down so our faces are even. Her determined expression stirs me to mimic it. "Only if we don't do something about him."

She's right. I can't come undone yet. She grips Ty Yorkshire's arms, and I take his legs—one leg anyway. The man must weigh two hundred pounds. Together, we haul him onto the bed. Our efforts leave a trail of blood, more than I've ever seen at once. No one loses this much blood and lives.

When we finish, I'm heaving with exhaustion.

"How old are you?" she asks.

I catch my breath. "Fifteen."

"Old enough for the noose. You'll get your death wish, then."

I wipe my eyes at this sobering thought. My father is dead, my home destroyed, and I just killed a man—at least, that's what they will believe. I have no business aboveground. Yet suddenly, I don't want to die.

I could return to New York. It would be dangerous, a wanted criminal traveling through populated areas. But without Father, New York would just be another faceless city, worse now because living there would constantly remind me of my disrespect.

No, there is no going back.

Father said he had great plans for us, and I owe it to him to find out what they were. Mr. Trask was Father's best friend, and now he is my only real connection to the living. I could catch him. He only left a few weeks ago. After all, there's only one road west.

"Annamae, I'm going to California."

4

ANNAMAE'S DARK PUPILS WIDEN A FRACTION, AND she begins to knead her scar with her thumb. "It's a long way to California."

"A friend of my father's is headed that way," I say. "I've got business with him."

She begins to pace again, but only goes back and forth once before stopping in front of me. Her gaze comes to rest on a bloodstain on my robe. "If we're going, we best get you something to wear."

"We?"

"I'm going with you. I should've left two hours ago to meet my Moses wagon. It's probably long gone now." Her mouth sets into a grim line.

She was planning to escape? While I never heard of a "Moses" wagon, Father told me wagons were used as part of the Underground Railroad movement to free the slaves. "But they hang runaways."

"Then we'll swing side by side. I asked God to send me the right wagon, and now I think you's it. Alone, people will think I'm a runaway. But with you, maybe I can fool 'em."

"It won't be easy. I just killed a man, and they will come after us." My throat goes dry at the notion. "And I don't know the way, exactly."

"Don't want safety, only freedom."

Before I can answer, she says, "Be right back. Have a sandwich." She closes the door behind her.

The tray holds two thick wedges and a pot of tea. If I tried to send anything down the hatch, my stomach would throw it back up again.

Blood oozes out of Yorkshire's nostrils like two earthworms. By now, the entire pillow beneath his head is soaked with blood, the same blood that covers my arms. I bend over the tub and scour it from my body, trying not to look at the red stain on the lip.

Pressing a washcloth to my face, I steam out my grimace.

No one will believe that Ty Yorkshire's death was an accident. Six months here, and people still refused to shake Father's yellow hand. They will send men after us. With luck, the sheriff won't discover my crime until morning. Leaving now will give us a good seven or eight hours before they sound the alarm. By then, God willing, we will be on the Oregon Trail, though first we need to cross the Missouri River.

Annamae returns, holding a basket of clothes and a saddlebag. She sets the basket on the floor.

"Two girls on the run. Not ideal," I mutter, jamming my feet into a skirt.

"I can't decide what sticks out more, you's yella face or my black one." She stuffs a sandwich into her mouth.

I shake out a blue flannel shirt. Too big. I throw it back into the basket. Then a thought wiggles into my head. I press a pair of trousers to my waist.

"What if we weren't two girls, but two young men, off to make our fortunes in the gold fields?"

Annamae puts her fists on her hips and frowns at the basket. Then she unbuttons her dress.

We layer up for warmth and to give ourselves some manly bulk. I don't have much going on upstairs. Thank God for small favors. Annamae, though, has bigger problems. She takes a knife from her saddlebag and cuts the two pink ties off her apron. The ties are trimmed with a bit of cream-colored lace. Yorkshire spared no expense in his unseemly operation. Jamming one of the ties and the knife back into the bag, she uses the other tie to bind her bosom. "Always thought these would be the end of me. There's been talk of Mr. Yorkshire replacing Ginny, his older Negress. She's already thirty-three."

I shudder at the thought of being conscripted into Yorkshire's stable, an employment that would be worse than death. Plucking the gun from Yorkshire's holster, I place it on the floor. It's a Colt Dragoon pistol, a handsome five-shot firearm with a sharp nose. Mr. Trask kept one just like it in a cigar box by his cash register.

"You know how to shoot that?" asks Annamae, buttoning her third shirt.

"Only how not to shoot my foot," I answer.

Even on its tightest setting, Yorkshire's belt drops off my hips. It needs another hole. I set it on the floor, then position the prong of the belt a few inches past the last eyelet. The black book on the bedside table might do the trick. "Could you get me that Bible?"

She fetches it and kneels down next to me. "Which verse you want?"

"God helps those who help themselves," I say, though I doubt that one's in the book. "Quickly, use the book and help me knock in a hole."

She clasps the Bible to her chest. "You want me to be struck down?"

"Oh, sorry. Here, hold the pointy part against the strap, like this." I show her. Putting down the Bible, she takes the belt, and pokes the prong into the leather where I want it.

I take up the Good Book myself, then in one swift movement whack it down over the metal prong, driving it into the leather. I pray that nobody heard.

"Sweet Jesus!" Annamae cries out. Her mouth opens in horror.

"Thank you, Lord," I whisper piously. My heart pounds hard enough to knock some of its own holes through my chest.

The belt still slings low across my hips, but maybe it will give me a boyish swagger. I reholster the gun, hoping I will never need to use it, especially since I don't know how to load it.

Annamae pats down Yorkshire's pockets. She recovers a few dollars and a powder horn, then pulls two gold rings off his pinkie fingers. Shoving them into her saddlebag, she stands back to examine me. Her eyes land on my wet hair. "We need hats."

"He doesn't need his anymore." I unhook Yorkshire's black hat and hand it to her. "Wide brim, it'll hide your face."

"There's more downstairs. Miss Betsy probably still watching the front so we'll go out the back. But hush, mind you. She got rabbit ears."

Annamae stuffs the last sandwich into her saddlebag, while I sling on my violin case, pulling the strap extra-tight. All the layers slow my movement, and the gun hangs heavy against my thigh, but I might as well get used to it. No longer am I Samantha Young, the curious-looking miss from Bowery Lane in New York City. I am a desperado.

I wipe my palms on my trousers and try to stop breathing so loudly. Slowly, Annamae opens the door.

After dropping the key into the laundry chute in the hallway, Annamae leads the way to the back of the hotel. Shadows thrown by sconces along the burgundy walls give the illusion that the hallway's on fire. I stick close to Annamae and try not to think about Father in the Whistle.

We tiptoe downstairs and through another burning corridor leading to the back entryway. A rack of antlers yields an assortment of hats and coats. Annamae slips into a wool frock coat, while I cram my hair into the plainest hat I can find, appalled at the ease with which I've gone from law-abiding citizen to wanton criminal. *Father, you raised me better, but I'm out of choices right now.*

I reach for a coat, but the *shhh, tap* of a scraping cane freezes my hand. Annamae grabs my wrist and pulls me to the door. She yanks it open. As soon as we both clear the doorway, she pauses for a heart-stopping moment to ease it shut without making a sound. Then we dash away toward St. Francis Street.

After half a block, my legs shake like a newborn foal's. Annamae is not even breathing hard. The fabric of her frock coat swishes rhythmically as she pumps her arms up and down. She has slipped into her disguise as easily as if she's been wearing men's clothes all her life, her shoulders forming solid bumps even under the many layers.

By contrast, my garments feel like they're wearing me, not the other way around. "I can't," I wheeze, pausing to catch my breath.

She grabs a fistful of my shirt and hauls me forward. "Oh yes you can."

The uneven roadway and my oversized trousers vie for who can trip me first, but I manage to make it to the street corner.

Annamae glances back toward La Belle Hotel. No one is following us.

On St. Francis Street, a line of covered wagons stretches as far as I can see, and then all the way back to St. Louis, three hundred miles away. People from as far away as Maine journey to St. Joe, the step-off point into the Wild West, which lies on the other side of the Missouri. Teams of four to twenty oxen or mules fidget and snort, rocking their "prairie schooners," as they are called. We hurry by men hunched over their cigarettes or sleeping on their wagon benches as they wait for their turn on the ferry.

We also pass men on horseback, most between the ages of

fifteen and forty. Like the Greek heroes who quested after the golden fleece, these "Argonauts" seek gold, following the Oregon Trail until it diverges south to California. They aim not to homestead, but to strike it rich before the gold runs out. Plenty of them stopped by the Whistle, on the hunt for last-minute necessities like rolling paper for their tobacco. Argonauts are not women.

Moving silently as fog, we reach the wagon closest to the water and duck behind a pile of sandbags, out of view. My breath comes in gulps, and I collapse into an ungainly heap on the ground. I know the distance between La Belle Hotel and the riverfront to be less than half a mile, but it feels as if I have run clear back to New York.

Annamae hauls me up with one hand. "Look." She points over the sandbags. To our right, the first wagon jostles about, its team skittish and alert. On our left, the wagon second in line seems to have shut down for the night, its driver slumped back in his seat, and his oxen still.

The shoreline lies ahead of the first wagon by ten yards. There, several men warm their hands around a bonfire, including the ferry master, a man in a naval cap. The flames burn bright enough to light the adjacent ferry building, which is little more than a shack with a counter and a clock.

The ferry's last run is at ten thirty. I hiss in my breath when I note the time: a whisker past ten.

"We need to be on the next ferry," I whisper, just as a bell clangs to signal the ferry's return journey. River current drives the ferry, which is really just a wooden platform, held on course by a cable running from one shore to the other. I've only seen it carry one wagon at a time.

"We better pray no one's inside," says Annamae, nodding to the first wagon. "I'll go see."

The bonfire crackles and spews out a few embers.

"Wait, hand me the powder horn," I say. "If we're going to stow away, we'll need a distraction."

Annamae rummages through her saddlebag, while I pull a handkerchief from my violin case. She leaves me the horn, then sneaks off. With her dark coat and black hat, the night swallows her in moments. I sprinkle gunpowder into my handkerchief, then knot it into a bundle.

Annamae hurries back to me. "Something blocking the back, so I couldn't see much. But I didn't hear no sounds."

I grimace. "It's either that one or wait until morning."

She shakes her head.

"Meet you at the back of the wagon in a few seconds," I say. Then I inhale some courage and walk toward the bonfire. All present peer out at the oncoming ferry, whose oil lanterns illuminate its inky path. Every inch of me wants to flee. I force my feet to a stroll, like I have not a care in the world.

When I get to the bonfire, a few of the ten or so men turn their heads but none of their gazes linger on me. I fake interest in the oncoming ferry, hoping the dark obscures my features. When no one's looking, I drop the bundle at the fire's edge.

Then I head back toward Annamae, taking long strides. After a few seconds, the packet explodes.

I sprint. Men grab their hats and hit the ground. Animals

scream, rearing up and trying to break out of their yokes. Whips and curses fly as their owners scramble to bring their teams back under control.

I reach our wagon, still heaving as its oxen try to flee. Annamae jams our gear through the back opening, then hauls herself in after it, squeezing by a large wooden object. I suck in my stomach and wedge in after her. Please, God, let us be the only ones aboard.

I spy farm equipment and feed, but nothing with a pulse. The wooden object that blocks the back opening is a clock as tall as the canvas ceiling. I exhale in sweet relief.

Our ruse seems to work. Annamae and I stretch out on top of feed sacks as the driver calms his team. His stout form shows through the front arch of the canvas that opens to the wagon seat.

"Settle down, boys and girls, settle down," our driver calls to his oxen. "Our turn's next."

My heart pounds like a tom-tom. Surely the beat will give us away. I slip my clammy hand into Annamae's warm one and feel her squeeze.

"Mr. Calloway, is it? You're up," the ferry master bellows. "Bring 'em down easy. Jackson will lead your team. Once you're on the other side, wait 'til the line's secure before you lead 'em off. Good luck."

"Thank you, sir," responds Mr. Calloway, before barking, "Giddap!"

Oxen bellow and the wagon rolls forward. A sharp farming

tool falls painfully against my thigh, but I don't dare push it off. A lever squeaks, followed by the rush of water.

As the ferry lifts us up and over each wave toward freedom, the contents of the wagon shift and settle. My stomach turns at the motion. The water chills the air around us and I hug my feed-sack cushion to keep from shivering. I smell alfalfa.

"Jackson, did a green wagon pass by recently?" asks Mr. Calloway.

Green? That's new. Most people don't waste paint on a wagon.

"Driver had a red beard? Train of twelve to follow, suh?"

"That's the one."

"Saw 'em two nights ago. Hard not to see 'em. You trying to catch 'em, suh?"

"Family's with them. We had twin calves born the same night, so I sent my wife and girls ahead."

"I see. If you travel day and night, you should catch 'em just after the Little Blue."

The Little Blue is the first river we'll hit, two or three days from here. I remember that much from our pioneer customers.

"That's fine. Thank you," says Mr. Calloway. He tips Jackson, I gather, from Jackson's grateful murmur.

The wait to get to the other side seems to go on for days, years. I count watermelons in my head—Father taught me this trick to stave off the imps of tedium that drive one mad. One watermelon. Two watermelons. I bite my lip to keep from screaming. Three watermelons...

When I reach seven hundred and one watermelons, the ferry finally bumps against the shore, and after more leverings and jolts, our chariot heaves forward. We slide back a few inches as the oxen lug us up a bumpy incline. After several head-banging minutes, the road levels out, only jolting us now and then when we hit a pothole.

I begin to pull myself up, when a thought occurs to me. Mr. Calloway intends to travel through the night. We might save our feet some trouble. If he does stop, it's dark enough that we could slip away, unnoticed. "Let's stay awhile," I whisper in Annamae's ear.

We cover ourselves with canvas sheets, and I find comfort in the rocking of the wagon.

Father, can you hear me? I'm so sorry. I shouldn't have argued with you. I should have shown you the respect you deserved, and listened to your plans.

The burlap sack of alfalfa catches my tears.

5

ANNAMAE SHAKES MY SHOULDER. MY EYES SNAP
open to the gray light of morning. The lines on one side of
Annamae's face tell me she also fell into the sleep trap.

I poke my head up. The rumbling of the wagon as we roll
along the gravelly path is giving me a headache. Mr. Calloway is
no longer in his seat. I peer through the gap between the wagon's
bonnet and the sideboards, and stifle a gasp. His red-checkered
shirt walks alongside us, to the left of the wagon, not three feet
away.

We better leave before he stops his team for breakfast and
finds us.

"Let's go," I whisper.

But the sudden clatter of horse hoofbeats freezes us in place.
I dive back under the canvas sheet and peek through the crack
again. A man on a spotted horse slows to walk beside us.

"Mr. Calloway?" he barks, causing his droopy mustache to
flap.

Mr. Calloway doesn't break his pace. "Morning. Do I know
you?"

"Deputy Granger." He tips his hat. Its domed shape is the
only round part of him. Sharp elbows, hooked nose, and an

Adam's apple that could rip holes in his bandanna. "I understand you took the quarter-past-ten passage aboard the *Whitsand* last night?"

"Yes, sir, I did. There a problem?"

"Seen any girls pass this way?"

I bite my tongue so hard I draw blood. The image of a noose dangles before my eyes.

"Girls? No. Why?" Mr. Calloway removes his straw hat and wipes his bald spot with his arm. An angry sunburn stains his cheeks and nose.

"A Chinese girl bashed in a man's head last night and ran off. You seen her?"

I cringe. Annamae blinks her hooked eyelashes once at me and grabs my hand. It's a simple gesture, but it's enough to keep me from fleeing in a hot panic.

"No, sir. The only Chinese person I've seen since Virginia was that fellow who owns the Whistle. Bought my canvas from him yesterday."

"She's his offspring. The whole place burned down last night, the Chinaman with it. People like that are careless." The deputy's voice drips with scorn.

Mr. Calloway pauses before answering. "Didn't seem careless to me, Deputy. Mr. Young was his name? He spotted a crack in one of my wheels and helped me fix it. Seems more a tragedy than anything." He replaces his hat and shifts his gaze to the front wagon wheel.

"Well, we ain't talking about the father, we're talking about his girl taking out one of St. Joe's finest. And what I say is, a body don't run unless the body is guilty." His black eyes seem to zero in on me, and I stop breathing. Then they roam the rest of the wagon.

"A slave girl ran away last night, too," the deputy continues. "Don't know if they're in league."

Mr. Calloway shakes his head. "Well, I haven't seen anyone, Deputy. Anyway, I can't see girls running in this direction. This is rough country. Without a mule, supplies, they wouldn't last three days. You're better off searching St. Louis."

"They sent out a group this morning. Believe me, I have better things to do than comb the weeds for a snake."

"Good day, then," says Mr. Calloway, reverting his attention to his grunting oxen.

I pray the man will leave now, and when he falls back, I unhook my fingernails from my palms. Then, the wagon hits a rock, and the clock belches out a chime.

Annamae hisses in her breath, then clamps a hand over her mouth.

The spotted pony brings Deputy Granger and his probing eyes even with us again.

"I'm going to need to search you. You're the only wagon on which they coulda hid. Might as well be thorough before I go home."

Mr. Calloway's shoulders slump, like he might be sighing. Then he calls, "Whoa, boys and girls, whoa now!"

I cast about for an escape, fear wringing my insides into a wet knot. The slivered openings on either side of the wagon reveal nothing but wide-open prairie.

I lean over and speak into Annamae's ear, so low that I cannot even hear myself. "I will turn myself in. Pull the sheet over you and hide." I squeeze her palm.

Our chariot, now our prison, staggers to a halt. Annamae pulls me back down as I start to rise, pointing to the crack on her side of the wagon. A weeping willow, one of spring's first bloomers, drips down its branches not ten feet away.

The deputy's boots thud on the grass as he dismounts.

"Going to take a moment to move my clock," says Mr. Calloway.

We don't hesitate. While Mr. Calloway pushes aside the heavy timepiece we scoot to the front of the wagon box.

"I'll go around to the head," says the deputy.

I nearly push Annamae out of the wagon in my haste.

"No need, sir. Here we are," says Mr. Calloway.

I drop from the driver's seat right after Annamae. In five tiptoes, we cover the distance to the shaggy green haystack. Its verdant curtain swallows us up.

Neither of us dares to breathe as we listen.

"Just doing my job, sir, thank you. Good luck to you," says the deputy.

"And you," says Mr. Calloway. "Giddap, boys and girls, giddap!"

His oxen moo in reply. The wagon groans as it pitches forward. Deputy Granger's horse snorts, then pounds away, easily bypassing Mr. Calloway. Only then do I resume breathing.

After a few minutes, we peek through the branches. The trail is empty now. Beyond the trees, a rolling carpet of knee-high grass spreads out before us, but neither Annamae nor I want to venture into the open yet.

"May that be the last we see of the deputy," I say.

"Amen." Annamae stares up at the dome of green. The leaves rattle *shhh* as the wind stirs them. "God planted this tree right here for us."

"Maybe it's better to think of it as fate."

She jerks back, as if I sneezed on her. "What do you mean?"

"I mean, sometimes I wonder why God would grant a favor if trouble's just waiting around the corner? It feels disingenuous. If it's fate, then it's written in the stars, and we can't do much to avoid it."

Her lips split apart, and I can see her opinion of me begin to plummet.

"I don't mean any offense. I just mean, if God is benevolent—"

"God *is* benevolent, and it ain't Christian to believe in fate, because He's in charge of the stars, too." She raises her eyes to the canopy and mutters, "Be merciful on the poor wretch's soul. She's going through a rough spell." With that, she rummages through her saddlebag.

I drop the matter, for I don't want her to think I'm a heathen. Though Father's knowledge of Chinese beliefs was limited—he was brought to the states when he was only thirteen—he was just as adamant about passing them on to me as his Christian ideology, which he got from Pépère, my French grandfather. If they were important to Father, they were important to me, too, despite their inconsistencies.

Annamae offers me a canteen from her saddlebag, which I

gratefully accept, though I refuse half a leftover sandwich. My stomach is still too wrung out to accept food. "You got a chamber pot in there? Because I could use one."

She frowns. Here I thought her opinion of me could go no lower. Tilting her head to one side, she taps a worn fingernail against her chin. Whatever she's going to say, I pray she says it soon since the river threatens to burst the dam soon.

Her frown fades into resignation. "I'll show you a trick that's cleaner than squatting. Pull down you's trousers."

I do it.

"Now, take my hands, and make like you's gonna sit." She pulls back, counterbalancing me, and in this position, I relieve myself without sloshing my boots.

"My turn," she says.

When done, we find another spot under the willow and hunker down. Christening the ground seems to diffuse some of her annoyance at me, and her manner becomes easy again.

"It's nice here. I been in St. Joe four years and never gone more than two miles."

"Where were you before that?"

"St. Louis."

"Your parents?"

"Barely knew 'em." She speaks without emotion. "Only got two brothers. Tommy, the baby, he died when he was seven." She shakes her head and glares at a shriveled leaf. "I tried to drown myself in the horse trough after that, but kept bobbing back up."

"I'm sorry."

She nods.

"What about your second brother?"

"That's Isaac. Ain't seen him in near five years, since I was eleven. He swore he'd get free before he turned twenty. That was"—she counts on her fingers—"five weeks ago. I gave up hope on seeing him, but then Ginny told me he'd meet me at Harp Falls."

I remember that Ginny was Yorkshire's Negress. My eyes pinch together. "How did she know that?"

"Isaac musta told someone to tell her. She's like our messenger, knows lots of folks. She's the one who told me I'd replace her, even helped me get my Moses wagon."

"Oh. Did she tell you where is this Harp Falls?"

"Somewhere between here and California." She wrinkles her nose. "So you's from China?"

"My parents were, but I was born in New York."

"Your mama?"

I shake my head. "When I came early, the doctor turned her away because he had never delivered a Chinese baby. By the time Father found us, Mother was dead."

And now he is, too. A tear breaks loose, but I bar the others from leaving. Father would be horrified if I gave in to all my Snake weaknesses. Annamae hands me a handkerchief, and I blow my nose. Then she pushes away the hair sticking to my face and frowns.

"You got looks that could trip a fella. This ain't gonna be easy." She pulls my chin from side to side. Her fingers feel cool against my hot skin. "Well, we can do one thing."

She pulls sewing scissors from what seems to be a well-stocked saddlebag.

"Turn around," she orders, pulling off my hat.

I recoil, remembering the fortune-teller's warning about warding off back luck. Yet I doubt my luck could get much worse than it is now.

Before I can speak, I hear a *snip*. I clasp my hands tightly together as the last shreds of my identity are shorn away.

Annamae holds up my hair like a tangle of seaweed she scooped from the ocean. I draw in my breath at the sight. By the time she finishes, my head feels lighter, airy even. I run my fingers through my shorn locks.

"It'll grow back," says Annamae, giving me a stern look. She pats her bound chest, well hidden under the folds of her frock coat. "So you know, we each have our battles to fight."

I nod. She was right to cut it off.

She purses her lips, not satisfied. "Still too pretty. Keep you's hat low even at night when we're around people. Nothing we can do about our colors, though, short of Indian paint."

"We could wear handkerchiefs over our faces. But then we're back to looking like criminals."

She grabs a handful of dirt. As she brings it near my face, I recoil. "You think that's necessary?"

"I know. I hate being grimy, too." She rubs the dirt into my cheeks. I try to hold still. My eye catches on a piece of twine around her wrist with a single bauble—a brown rock with a hole in it. "Just think, you's still clean under the dirt."

When I'm grubby enough to satisfy her, she pulls my hat

low over my eyes and cinches the cord. The wet dirt on my face smells foul and makes me sneeze.

I dab my nose with my handkerchief. Annamae watches me fold the hanky into a neat square and clucks her tongue.

"At least you got that fiddle. But you still gonna need to man it up." She pokes at my soft thigh.

I flinch and eye her athletic build.

"I must run ten miles a day on chores, that's why I'm so tough." She chuckles.

"Ten miles?"

She nods. "Female slaves gotta do what we can to keep outta trouble. The less wag in your wagon, the better. You just got a few girl kinks to work out. You's wrists, for one. Too bendy. You ready to go?"

Before we leave, she digs a shallow grave with the heel of her boot, deposits in my severed strands, then kicks dirt back over it. I haul a rock and place it on top for good measure.

Slowly, we part the willow curtain. I follow Annamae back onto the deserted trail, feeling naked despite all my layers. The morning rays begin to paint the landscape with pastels. Yesterday morning, the sight would have filled me with wonder. Now, my gut chokes with sand and all I see before me is a road with no end.

6

"**WALK STRAIGHTA. NOT YOU'S BACK, YOU'S** curves," says Annamae.

I march in the straightest line I can manage, trying to keep the pendulum from swinging, though I don't have much to swing. Still, even the slightest tick-tock could give me away.

"Strut more, like the pigeons do. Feet out, looser in the knees. Keep you's head down. Like a pigeon hunting a potata bug."

I spend the next few hours perfecting my gait, and by the time I lose my shadow, it almost feels natural. The ferry starts back up at nine, which means we might see Argonauts by this afternoon, and pioneers and their wagons after that. For now, it's just us and the prairie dogs.

I remove my hat and swab my face for the dozenth time. March mornings are always nippy, but wearing enough clothes for four people might kill me before the law does. I shed a few layers, then collapse on the grass underneath the shadiest tree.

Annamae strips off her coat. From her saddlebag, she produces a brick of cheese and a hunk of bacon, though she returns the bacon to the bag. "We'll save this for tomorrow's breakfast. Nothing says good morning like a streaky slab of po' man's steak."

"Isn't this breakfast?"

"Nope. It's closer to noon." She shaves off a slice from the cheese, says a quick prayer, then hands the morsel to me. I swallow it in one bite and wait for more.

"That's it for now," she says. "We gotta make it last."

My stomach grumbles in protest. I sigh and ball a fist into it. On any other day, I'd be having two eggs and rice porridge—and there'd be custard tarts on special occasions. My eyes begin to blur when I remember the last thing Father gave me was a plate of miniature suns. I shove that thought away. Annamae rolls out the bubbles in the waxy paper covering the cheese.

"So how'd you and Isaac get split up?" I ask.

"We were all sold off from Frogg Farm. Tommy and I went to the Yorkshires, and I don't know where Isaac went. He got picked up quick, he being strong enough to carry Tommy and me in each arm." She flashes me a grin. Her teeth are straight as a picket fence on top but crooked on the bottom.

"Why'd Isaac want to go west? Why not try a free state, or—"

"Free states don't make you free." She sniffs. "If the law catches you, they return you to you's owner. Not much law in this direction and the pioneers got better things to do than trouble over runaways."

May the pioneers have better things to do than trouble over me, too. I force my aching feet back onto the empty trail after Annamae.

If I'm going to catch up with Mr. Trask, Father's friend who has Mother's bracelet, I will need a speedier mode of transport than these legs. We could use Yorkshire's rings to buy a horse, assuming we survive long enough to make it to the next trading post. But what if they don't sell horses? Without a horse, not only will I never catch Mr. Trask, I'll be a lame fox on hunting day.

I up my pace. Negative thoughts pour gravel in your shoes and make your step unsteady. Instead, I think back to the last time I saw the energetic thirty-year-old grocer from New York. Father's best friend and a fellow musician, Mr. Trask showed up out of the blue last month. He'd come all the way from New York City. Father said to him, "Don't tell me you're here to reclaim your tuning fork, because I've grown quite fond of it."

"That's yours to keep, Henry." Mr. Trask's tawny eyes twinkled. "Sold the store, now I'm off to see the Pacific Ocean. That coast is ready to explode. Dreams are ripe for the picking in all that sunshine." He grabbed his red suspenders and straightened his back, always managing to look taller than Father, though they were both a hand under six foot.

"I'm leading a train of seven. You ever think about heading west, Henry?" he asked.

Father turned his gaze on me, sweeping up coffee beans. "I think about it a lot."

Mr. Trask and his wagon train stayed in town three more nights as they waited their turn on the ferry. He and Father went to Belly's Tavern every night after we closed up shop.

On the last night, Father removed Mother's bracelet from our wooden safe and fingered the many-colored jade stones in the circlet. It was so dear, we'd bought the safe especially for it.

I looked up from my Latin reader in alarm. "What are you doing?"

After a long pause, he dropped the bracelet into a velvet pouch. Then he held the pouch in his hand, his eyes far away for a moment.

When he tucked the pouch into his pocket, I protested, "You're not selling it? That's the only thing we have left. That *is* her. You're giving away Mother?"

He ignored my disrespect. "You will see it again one day. Your mother would understand."

"How would you know?" I huffed.

He buttoned up his coat, then collected his walking stick. Before he left, he said in a voice more sorrowful than angry, "It is not for children to question parents."

That was the end of February, eighteen days ago.

I tell Annamae about Mr. Trask.

"So what did your daddy want to do out there in California?"

"I don't know, exactly." I press my fingers into my hard head. "He tried to tell me, but I was still mad about the bracelet and wouldn't listen."

"So after you find this Mr. Trask, maybe he'll help you out. Look after you?"

"Maybe."

"That's a comfort. Girl like you shouldn't be out by you'self."

"Nor a girl like you." Something pokes my heel. I stop to shake a pebble out of my boot. She offers me her arm.

"Oh, I've been taking care of myself for a long time. Practically a man already." She snorts. "You don't have to worry about me. So what's this Mr. Trask look like?"

"A few inches taller than you. Head like a nest with an ostrich egg in the middle, mustache, and a beaky kind of a nose. He always wore red suspenders and a white shirt. Not exactly the kind of man who stands out."

"Well, my brother *is* the kinda man who stands out, tall as a lamppost, and good-looking, like his sister"—she smiles—"but unlike your Mr. Trask, he won't be just strolling pretty. You know the way to California?"

"Follow the Oregon Trail to the California Trail, is all I know." We trudge along.

"Maybe you'll find some folks who can help. I'll go far as I can with you. But soon's I find out where Harp Falls is, I've gotta be on my way. Could be tomorrow, could be next month."

"I understand." An anxious bubble forms in my stomach. I've known Annamae for less than a day, yet I feel bonded to her in the way common suffering can knit two souls together. Or maybe it's just my small spleen talking. People with small spleens are notoriously cowardly.

"You know any hymns?" asks Annamae.

"Sure. 'God of Our Fathers.' 'Glory Be.'"

"Don't know those. You know 'Chains of Mis'ry'? 'Moses Split the Tide'?"

"No."

She scratches her neck and her forehead crimps. I'm about to suggest we might have better luck with a secular tune when Annamae stops suddenly and puts her arm in front of me.

"Rattler," whispers Annamae. The dirt moves, only it's not dirt, but a yellow snake with brown and red patches, thick as my arm. The head rears as if to strike.

It weaves an S pattern, hissing. As I wait for my heart to start beating again, I notice its tail thumping the ground. "That isn't a rattlesnake. Though it wishes it were."

She doesn't take her eyes off the snake. "How so?"

I point at the tail, ringed with black markings. "No rattle. It's a bull snake, not poisonous. Father made me memorize all the poisonous things, berries, frogs—wait, what are you doing?" I exclaim as she inches closer.

The snake accelerates its thumping in its best mimicry of a rattlesnake.

"You sure it ain't poisonous?"

"I'm sure."

"*Sure* sure?" Annamae waves her left hand at the snake now, pulling its attention off kilter. She wiggles her fingers like a magician about to perform a trick.

"As sure as I'm a girl, though I wouldn't—"

Quick as a flash, Annamae grabs the snake with her right hand below its diamond-shaped head. It wriggles as she squeezes. Then she snaps her wrist like she's cracking a whip and cries, "Ya!"

I gasp and recoil, coward that I am. Being born in the Year of the Snake only means I dislike them less than the average person does.

The snake curls up its tail, then hangs limp.

She drapes her six-foot-long prize around her neck. "Bet you tasty on the flame." When the tail twitches, she yanks it like a bellpull.

"Just goes to show," she says as we start moving again, me keeping my distance, "you may not look like a boy, but as long as you act like one, most folks can't tell you's missing your rattle." She breaks into a toothy grin.

We scout for a place to camp. The plains stretch before us in a slight descent, studded with teardrop-shaped junipers that remind me of jurors, silent and judging. Irregular jags of sandstone form rough hiding spots. It occurs to me we may not be the only criminal element on the trail here. Which would be worse, outlaws or lawmen? Or bears, for that matter?

Something screams, and I nearly jump out of all my shirts, which in turn nearly scares Annamae out of all hers.

But it's just a blue jay jeering at us from the nearest juniper. Annamae gives me a hard look, then straightens her cuffs.

"Sorry. Er, how about over there?" I point to a craggy wall of sandstone smeared with lichen rising fifty yards beyond the juniper. "That might serve as a lean-to."

As I collect firewood, I pick dandelion greens and edible roots, freezing every time I hear a noise. Now that we've stopped moving, I worry again about Deputy Granger. What if he decides to double back? We'll be easy targets.

May night roost soon, so that she may cover us with her black feathers. He won't be able to search for us very well in the dark.

Annamae arranges stones to contain our blaze. She wraps a char cloth the size of a playing card around a flint, then scrapes it against her cooking pot. The ignitable cloth catches a spark and soon a fire roars before us.

After witnessing Annamae butcher the snake and rub it with salt from her saddlebag, I doubt I will ever eat again. But once the meat starts popping on the fire with the greens, my hunger pangs return. If I'm going to survive the prairie long enough to find Mr. Trask, I must get used to blood and entrails. Father always took care of the cooking—another hobby of his. Now we only have our hands and Annamae's saddlebag, which surely has a bottom.

I pick at the hem of my shirt as I wait for our dinner to finish cooking. My throat aches from thirst even though I just sipped from the canteen not five minutes ago.

I catch movement from the direction we came.

"Annamae," I whisper sharply.

She whips her head around. "Lord, not already." Quickly, she pulls on her coat and buttons it up.

"Maybe they're Argonauts and not the law," I say, trying to keep the doubt out of my voice.

"What kinda knots?"

"Argonauts. Gold rushers."

I feel for my gun as Annamae closes her hand around her cooking knife. I pray that the threat of the gun is enough to deter violence, for I do not know if it is loaded.

The moving cloud of dust is now a hundred yards out. Surely they saw our fire.

My breath comes too shallow so I inhale a lungful.

Annamae pulls her hat over her eyes. "Act tough. Remember, you's a rattlesnake."

If we weren't so short on time, I might have attempted to explain my complicated past with snakes. But horses and riders are already tumbling into view. Three men—two white and one Mexican—stare at us as their horses bear them forward. The Mexican pulls along a fourth horse, a bay, its rich mahogany coat dressed with black boots.

Ride on, I implore them with my mind. But the clopping slows, and the horses squeal as their riders rein them in right before our camp. Dust blows into our faces and threatens to put out our fire.

The men loop around us, their horses stepping in perfect synchronicity with their heads held high. The movement makes me dizzy so I focus on my lap. My stomach drops as I remember that Indians circle buffalo to confuse them before the slaughter.

7

AFTER THREE CIRCLES, THEY STOP. ONE OF THE riders, a man less than twenty years old, swings his leg over the saddle and slides off his pinto in a single swift movement. He adjusts the waistband of his trousers and cocks his head at me, smiling with half his mouth.

Despite my terror, I cannot look away. If eyes left footprints, this man's face would be worn as a welcome mat. He's both attractive and inviting with grass-green eyes and a light tan that makes his skin appear golden. Beneath his wide-brimmed hat, sandy-blond locks curl boyishly around his nape. He's younger than I initially thought, perhaps seventeen or eighteen.

The three of them study us, and Annamae returns their gaze, chin lifted and bottom lip jutting defiantly. I do my best to mimic her.

"We havin' a stare-out or something?" Annamae says at last.

The green-eyed man stops squinting and his half smile doubles, showing white teeth and a collection of well-placed dimples. "Something sure smells good. You kids expecting company? Old Zach Taylor maybe?"

He turns toward his friends for appreciation and gets a

snicker. "Looks like you have more than your pea pods can hold. We can lend a hand. What say you?"

If a posse were chasing two dangerous fugitives, would they ask for supper before the apprehending? Annamae relaxes her grip on her knife.

The Mexican hops off his gray giant of a horse and murmurs something to her in Spanish.

The last rider sizes me up from atop his horse, a sorrel with a flaxen mane and white socks. I put him at the same age as Green-Eyes. Something about him and his horse ring familiar. I drop my gaze from the man's dark eyes to the series of dime-sized scars on his arm that trail up to his rolled sleeve.

Annamae hitches one shoulder a fraction. These men, boys really, except for the Mexican who looks a few years older than his companions, both outnumber and outweigh us. If we refuse, they may take our supper anyway, maybe even our gear, light as it is. In the second it takes me to process this, I hear myself say, "On one condition."

My voice sounds too high so I tune it to my lowest pitch and add bluster. "If we let you share our supper, and a good one it is, will you let us double ride your bay to the Little Blue?"

Green-Eyes drapes an arm over his saddle. "Must be one helluva supper. But you'll have to ask the vaquero," he replies, nodding to the Mexican.

The Mexican does not speak as he tugs off his sleek riding gloves. The gray horse and the bay push their noses at him. He rubs each of their faces in turn, not acknowledging me.

The one with the scars on his arm watches me being ignored. "That means no," he says, his voice clear and smooth like freshly steeped oolong tea. His voice. It's the man whose horse nearly collided with me when I tripped yesterday.

"He doesn't let just anyone ride his *caballo*," he continues. "Gotta prove yourself."

I go still as a pinecone as his sorrel drifts around me. Does he recognize me? He only saw me from the back after I fell. Then again, I could have erred. I don't budge a muscle as he inspects me.

"Oh, come on, get a wiggle on, compadre," Green-Eyes says to the Mexican. "I'm about to die of hunger."

The Mexican takes out a brush and starts to groom the saddle-less bay. The Mexican has not looked at me once, though the bay casts me a gimlet eye. With her long legs and proud bearing, she moves as gracefully as a gazelle, clearly outmatching me.

Still conscious of the scarred man appraising me, I lift my chin and ask, "*¿Cómo puedo probar?*" How do I prove my worth?

Green-Eyes chokes out a laugh. Annamae's pupils slide from one side to the other, like she's not sure she heard right. Finally paying attention, the Mexican swaggers toward me like a Spanish bullfighter addressing a cow that has wandered into the arena: posture erect, nostrils flared, eyes bemused.

"*Hablas Español*," he murmurs. "*Si Princesa te quiere, entonces tenemos un trato.*" I translate in my head: If Princess likes you, we have a deal.

I sigh. So I must let this royal beast bite me before I can trade a ride to the river for our supper, which must be cold by now, not to mention dusty. I don't have much of a choice, seeing that I stepped into this pie to begin with. Plus, I'll happily take a horse bite over a hemp collar.

I shade my brow to sneak another glance at Annamae. She curls her pinkie at me and mouths the word *rattlesnake*.

Princesa pokes her nose into the grass. I have not moved more than three paces toward her when she lets out a scream so shrill that I fall hard into the dirt. Dear God, it must be the Snake in me. Horses dislike people born in the Year of the Snake. I scramble backward, and Green-Eyes slaps his knee and hoots, lighting my face on fire.

Annamae covers her mouth with her hand, then quickly drops it.

The Mexican rests an elbow on the gray horse's withers, the silver rosettes trimming his black trousers and jacket winking at me in unison. The scarred man peers down at me in the dirt.

I catch my breath and steel myself for another attempt. *Laugh at me, will you?* Then I have an idea. Earlier, I tucked my violin case in an indentation of the stone wall, and now I fetch it. Opening the case, I remove the tin I keep handy for the children's lessons. Palming the contents, I march back up to the snotty-nosed bay.

The mare stands an arm's length away. Annamae rises to her feet.

"Pretty horsey," I croon.

"*Princesa sólo entiende Español,*" says the Mexican in a low voice.

I sniff, doubting horses understand human language at all, Spanish or English. To be safe, though, I give a rough Spanish version of, "If you let me pet you, I will give you this sweet," and hold out my hand.

In my palm, five peppermint candies melt into one pink blob. Princesa whips her head up and squeals again, blowing hot grassy breath all over me. I shrink back and shut my eyes. Her mouth crashes down onto my open hand.

Princesa smacks her lips noisily. I snatch back my hand, which thankfully is still attached to my arm, and whimper in relief.

Princesa noses around for more sweets. I scratch her forehead and see her ears flick.

The men whoop, and the Mexican adds a cry of "Ay ay ay!" from somewhere in the back of his throat.

Green-Eyes drops next to our fire. "Well, I guess you boys got yourself a mount. I'm Cay, short for Cayenne Pepper. That's my cousin West." He nods at the scarred man. Then he waves a gloved hand toward the Mexican. "That's our wrangler, Pedro Hernando Niña, Pinta, and Santa Maria Gonzalez."

"He prefers Peety," says West.

The Mexican salutes us with two fingers.

"I'm Sam, and that's Andy."

Annamae nods solemnly. I must only think of her as Andy from now on, so I don't err.

"Pleased to meet you, kids. Let's chew."

The men grab skewers and are about to partake when Andy exclaims, "Ain't you gonna say grace?"

West cocks an eyebrow at Cay, who clears his throat. "Well a'course, we were." Cay closes his eyes. "Dear God, bless this snake to our bodies and please let it not be the one from your garden."

Peety suppresses a laugh, and West says, "Amen."

Andy glares at the brim of her hat but doesn't comment further.

The snake is chewy, dry, and full of bones, but I eat my whole portion. Andy and I copy the boys by blowing the snake bones into the fire. I drink from our canteen, but Andy pulls it away before I get a chance to slake my thirst.

"We got lots of water, *chicos.*" Peety hands me his canteen. "Drink up."

As I get my fill, it occurs to me these boys might make decent traveling companions. Not everyone would share his water with a Chinese person, or a black person, for that matter. Maybe we can get them to take us farther than the Little Blue.

Cay casts a doubtful eye toward Andy. "You a gold rusher? I ain't seen a black one before." A healthy dusting of gold whiskers bristles on his face as he chews, and there's a solid curve to his cheek.

"Well, today's your lucky day," says Andy, crossing her arms in front of her. "Haven't you heard of the Compromise? Lots of us goin' west."

She's referring to the Missouri Compromise, which forbids slavery in the north, save the exceptional state of Missouri.

"That so?" Cay's eyes hop to me. "What about you?"

"I'm an Argonaut, too. You?" I make my voice deep and hope I sound as confident as Andy.

"No," answers West in a voice laced with contempt. "We're cowboys."

I decide this West must not have recognized me after all. After his initial scrutiny, he barely casts me another glance, which gives me the chance to study him.

Though his perfect eyebrows and straight nose could have inspired Michelangelo, his flaws interest me more: the frowning mouth, the slouch of his lean and muscled frame. His triangular earlobes run straight into his face, indicating a troubled life, unlike his cousin Cay, whose earlobes are fleshy and unattached, meaning things come easy to him. His head tilts down often, his dark hair casting shadows across his fair skin, shadows that draw me in like a secret. When he catches me studying the constellation of scars on his arm, he rolls his sleeve back down.

Cay lifts his chin. "Just moved one thousand head to St. Louis. Pioneers can't buy 'em quick enough."

"So why you on the trail?" asks Andy.

Before answering, Cay glances at West, who frowns at him. Then Cay says, "We got a job in California."

"You two look a little young to be out this late," West cuts in. A lock of hair the color of black walnut falls into his eyes, which he takes care of with a flick of his head.

Andy crosses her arms. "We're old 'nuff. Sam's seventeen, I'm eighteen."

She overshoots a tad.

Cay and Peety react like someone poked them in the ribs.

"Guess they grow us bigger in Texas," Cay says, not bothering to erase his grin.

Peety looks back and forth from Andy to me. "Not much fur on your cheeks, *chicos*."

I start to touch my cheek but snatch it away when Andy gives me a hard look.

West sticks a blade of grass between his teeth. "Travel light, too."

"How come yer English is so good?" Cay cuts in. "Never heard a Chinaman speak regular-like. Matter a fact, never seen a Chinaman outside a circus."

"Same reason as you. I was born here."

"Born here? How's that possible?" He scratches his chin.

"My father was an orphan. French missionaries found him when he was thirteen and brought him to the States."

"And your Español?" asks Peety.

"Father owned a translation business back in New York."

"What's that?" asks Cay.

West leans back on an elbow and blows a fly that wanders by. "Don't be a dunderhead. It's like, the Spaniard tells the Frenchie, 'I'll trade you a barrel of olives for that bottle of per-foom, you snail-eating bastard,' and Sammy's daddy tells the Frenchie what the Spaniard said. Right?"

I'm distracted by the way West drawls out his long *e*'s to long *a*'s, changing my name to "Sammay." Cay does it, too.

I blink. "Right," I say gruffly.

"So what other tongues you speak?" asks Cay.

"Latin, French, Cantonese, and enough Portuguese to start a conversation."

"But not finish it?"

"Not with words." I pat my gun.

This gets a laugh. Cay squints his green eyes at me. "Say something in Cantonese."

"*Nei goh ha-pa yau di se.*"

He repeats it. "Well, poke me, I speak Chinese. What does it mean?"

"'You have snake on your chin.'"

Another laugh from all except West, who is chewing on the grass again.

Cay takes it in good measure. "All right, you goneys."

"Who wants the jaw?" asks Andy, holding up a stick with a razor-edged bone dangling off the end. "Snake jaw's a lucky charm. You might need it if there's no moon tonight."

Both Peety and Cay raise their hands, but West makes a *tsk* sound with his tongue.

Cay gets down on his stomach and elbows. "Settle by wrestle."

Andy covers her mouth with her hand.

Peety lays a horse blanket on the poky yellow grass in front of Cay. Hitching his trousers, he carefully lowers himself onto it.

"Oh, c'mon, prima donna, your pantaloons are already filthy," says Cay.

"*Pantalones,*" Peety corrects. "Pantaloons is what you wear."

The two clasp hands and start pressing. After a good half minute of evenly matched straining and grunting, Cay summons a burst of strength and pushes Peety's arm to the ground.

"I let you win, hombre," gasps Peety, rolling onto his back. "'Cause you need more luck than me."

"I get more lucky than you, you mean. Who's next?" Cay shakes out his arm and looks at West.

West snorts. "I make my own luck."

"Chicken," says his cousin.

West's jaw twitches. Then he tosses aside the blade of grass and shakes his head.

As he positions himself in front of the grinning Cay, I wonder at the power of a single word to goad males into doing things they don't want to do to acquire things they don't want to have. I would never fall for that.

Biceps bulge and in under five seconds, West slams Cay's arm into the dirt.

"If I didn't have to wrestle that buffalo that came before you, I'd a won for sure," says Cay.

Andy holds the stick with the jaw out to West. "Here you go, and good luck."

"Hold on, now," says Cay. "He needs to wrestle one more to make it fair."

His eyes slide to me. I nearly choke on my greens, knowing I will be eating my thoughts for my next course.

8

EVEN IF I REFUSE TO ARM WRESTLE, SOMEONE will issue the chicken threat, and I will have to do battle anyway.

"Sammy, c'mere," orders Cay.

I drag myself over. This is madness. Neither of us even wants the darn thing.

I get down on my stomach, opposite him. Andy smashes her clasped hands up to her nose, praying, I think.

A tiny dent appears in the side of West's cheek. I hood my eyes and try to look fierce. The others crowd around us for the final match, or mismatch.

"I'll try not to hurt you," I mutter.

A warm wind kicks up, throwing dust into my eyes. West folds his callused hand over my cold bony one. He has guitarist fingers, slender and strong, the kind that might be nice to hold under different circumstances. What am I thinking? I shake those thoughts from my head and focus.

"Your hand's kind of soft," he says.

"I'm a musician," I say scornfully. "Of course it is."

"Shouldn't you be out giving lessons?"

"Shouldn't you be out branding cows?"

His thumb twitches.

Since one of his arms equals two or three of my own, I will never win this on brute strength. So I keep my elbow as close to my side as possible to add my body weight to the fight. Might as well throw a twig in front of the locomotive.

"On the count of three," says Cay. "One, two, three!"

I pull down a fraction before he says three, gaining an inch in my corner right out of the gate by bending my wrist over his. But a second later, he flicks out the kink. When I look up, he is watching me, not his arm. I might as well be wrestling a hitching post.

"C'mon, Sammy," says Andy, at least playing along with the sham. "Send him home."

"I'm boring, West," says Peety, faking a yawn. "Why you want to play with babies?"

I redouble my efforts, crooking his wrist again. He gives me some slack, though I wish he would just ax the chicken already. When I've depleted all my strength, he crushes me.

"Ow," I whimper, as my shoulder grinds against its socket. I grit my teeth and roll it out. The boys take turns slapping me on the back.

"Ain't a square match," says West, tucking the jawbone into Cay's hatband.

"You noticed that, did you?" snipes Andy.

West cocks an eye at her, then shakes his head. He and the others spread their bedrolls.

"Time for ropes," he says.

"What do you mean by that?" asks Andy, glaring. We both feel the same way about ropes these days.

He unwinds a length of cord. "Rattlers don't cross hemp."

Andy sucks in her breath and stops glaring. No doubt West wonders how a couple of greenhorns like us expect to survive the wilderness.

"'Course, ain't many rattlers in the towns, if you're still on the fence..." He trails off.

Andy and I don't have bedrolls, just our extra shirts, so we bundle them into pillows and settle down on the hard earth. Despite my layers, I feel every blade of bluegrass, every lobe of sow thistle, to say nothing of the gravel. I chuck the bigger rocks aside, though doing so just makes the smaller ones more obvious.

To my right, West shakes out his bedroll, with Cay on his other side. I expect Peety to lie beside Cay, but he spreads his blanket right by Andy. West lays the rope in a circle around all of us.

A chorus of *yips* starts up, coyotes celebrating a kill, but even worse than the coyotes is the wind. It started as a dry breeze, but now it pulls at me, sucking the moisture from my lips and eyes. It blows through the cedars in a dissonant chord that rises and falls like the wheezing of croupy lungs. I resist the urge to scoot closer to Andy. She's looking straight up at a rift in the clouds where a red moon has appeared, a bullet wound in the dark skin of night. Father said the moon changes color when bad luck is near.

"Looks like the moon did show up," says Andy. "A red one, too."

"What's that mean?" asks Cay, sitting up.

"Never you mind. It'll scare ya."

"Oh, come on," says Cay. "The only things that scare me are hairy caterpillars. The ones that look like someone's mustache fell off and is crawling away."

Peety cranes his neck toward Andy. "You got a story? Please tell us."

Andy sits cross-legged. The boys arrange themselves around us.

"Anyone heard of Harp Falls?" Andy sweeps her gaze over each of us. No one has. She pulls her coat more securely around her, then begins.

"A prince was born with everything a man could want, good looks and wealth. Never had to work for much. One morning after a night of whoring, he wakes up lying in a haystack, not even sure how he got there."

"I hate it when that happens," says Cay, flapping the brim of his hat up and down.

West leans back on his hands. "Yeah, but you ain't no prince."

Andy ignores them. "He's thinking what a sorry sap he is, when he hears music so sweet it makes him weep. A woman's voice, out of nowhere, says, 'I'm the harp at the top of the waterfall. Find me, and you shall have everlasting joy.'

"'I don't see no waterfall,' he says. 'How do I get to you?'

"'Follow my music,' she says. 'The way will not be easy. But listen for my voice, and you shall have me.'

"So the prince sets off, but before long, a group of men attack—chain him up and throw him in the river. As he starts sinking, he remembers the harp. He hears her sweet voice again, and suddenly, the chains fall away."

Cay and Peety scoot in closer, but West's face is unreadable as firelight dances around it.

"On he travels. Next thing that happens, black birds swoop on him, pecking his skin and lifting him to the sky with their sharp claws. As they's about to drop him onto some rocks, again, he remembers to listen for the music." She pauses and holds her index finger up.

"When he hears it, the birds begin to fall away, one by one. Then there it rises: a great waterfall surrounded by golden rock, higher on one side than on the other, like a harp, with water pouring like strings. He lands on top, and the view is wide and handsome."

Cay's brow wrinkles and he glances at his cousin. West, not noticing, folds his legs and puts his elbows on his knees.

"There, he sees her, a harp clear as glass, like she's cut from water, and she's in the arms of a hooded monk. The prince never wanted anything so bad in his life. 'I'm here for the harp,' he says. But the monk ignores him." Andy pauses, letting the ghostly *whoo* of the wind take over for a moment. "So he repeats himself. Still, the monk acts like he don't hear. Angry now, the prince tries to pull the harp out of the monk's hands, but that monk won't let go. They wrestle for it, and finally the prince smashes a rock over the monk's head.

"Harp falls into the water. The prince is reaching for it when he feels something wet on the side of his head." Andy touches her temple. "Blood. He looks down at the monk, whose hood falls away . . ." She leans toward us, hands held out like she's going to cast a spell.

"And?" urges Cay.

Andy sits back. "And he sees his own face."

"He's the monk?" Cay exclaims. "I didn't see that com—"

"Shh!" West cuts him off.

With the image of the monk's staring face in my head, the wind sounds even eerier, raising the hair on my arms.

Andy goes on. "The prince dives after the harp, but it's too late. The harp goes a-tumbling down the waterfall, and the prince with it." Her eyes study us, but only the wind speaks. "Hear that howling? That's the sound of the wind passing through the broken harp and blowing the prince's blood to the moon." She leans back on her hands and squints at the sky.

"What's it all mean?" Cay asks.

"What do you think it means?" asks Andy.

Cay rubs his whiskers. "Never trust a monk?"

"Don't take stuff that don't belong to you," ventures Peety.

"That's not it, you dummies," says West. "He forgot to listen to the harp. The music was all around him at the end, but he got too greedy."

"What do you think, Chinito?" asks Peety, using the word for "China boy."

Everyone looks at me. "Well," I say, still mulling over the

story, which reminds me of Icarus, whose wings melted off when he flew too close to the sun. "It's a parable of caution. The story represents man's struggle with others, nature, and ultimately himself, which is the hardest one of all. The prince didn't understand he was fighting himself until it was too late."

No one's looking at me anymore. West crosses his arms. I'm close enough to see the gooseflesh on his skin.

One by one, the boys start to nod off. I wait until I hear them breathing deeply, then scoot closer to Andy. "Was that a story from your ancestors?"

"Nah. I made it up."

"It's a good one."

She smiles. "Tommy, my little brother, needed stories to help him get to the end of the day. Isaac and I took turns telling 'em."

"You followed classic Greek story structure. I'm impressed."

"Best stories are the ones everyone can see themselves in. But you explained that meaning real well."

I thank Father for that, and also Pépère, my Sorbonne-educated grandfather, who passed everything he knew to his adopted son, who in turn taught me. Such an education was typically saved for males from reputable families, but Father didn't care. Studying was one of the ways to improve one's station in life, along with doing good deeds. He schooled me in music, philosophy, history, language, and, of course, literature.

"You done real well today," Andy says softly, halfway to dreamland already.

My stomach turns in loops as I once again worry about the journey ahead. "The Little Blue's only a day away," I whisper. "Maybe I should've bargained for farther."

"We'll think of something." She sighs.

9

SLEEP DOES NOT COME EASY TO ME, BUT BEFORE I know it, I awake to the sound of male laughter and the tantalizing smell of bacon. Scrambling to sit up, I try to make sense of where I am. West's brown eyes pin me like a bug from where he sits two yards away near the fire, chewing a fingernail. I stretch my eyes back down the trail. If the deputy's still after us, he hasn't caught up yet.

At least the wind has died, leaving behind a morning crisp as a water chestnut.

"It's gonna be a good day," says Cay, wiping tears of laughter from his face. He gestures in front of him, then rests his hand on the top of his head. "Bacon in the pan and a Mexican fried egg."

Twenty paces away, Peety helps Andy off the ground, cursing loud enough for me to hear his Spanish. The great gray mare stands beside them.

"What happened?" I ask, my alarm raising the pitch of my voice to girlish levels.

"Our wrangler's introducing your friend to the remuda," says Cay.

I yank on my boots. "The remuda?"

"What we call our horses. That gray one he just fell off is Peety's Andalusian, Lupe, and she's the easy one."

West stops biting his nail and flicks his finger to the sky. "He ain't hurt."

Sure enough, Andy brushes off her trousers and says something to Peety. His curses stop abruptly. Andy marches back to us, arms swinging high. Peety takes a moment to rub Lupe's forehead, then trots after Andy.

I breathe out a sigh of relief, though a moment later a new worry starts up where the old one left off. How would Andy know how to ride a horse? I never considered the matter before now.

Cay pinches a slice of bacon from the frying pan and devours it whole. "He's a good coosie even if his caboose don't stay on his cayuse."

My nose wrinkles. "What does that mean?"

With his mouth full, Cay answers, "A coosie is who cooks for you, a cayuse is the animal that carries you, and a caboose is what you should never wave over a stinging nettle." He peers into the frying pan and glances up at West. "Wrestle for the last piece?"

"Sammy didn't get one."

West keeps his gaze trained on a spot around my nose. My first reaction is to demur. I've been taught to never take the last piece for myself, which Chinese people consider very impolite. But to these cowboys, such a gesture would probably go unappreciated. They would simply assume I wasn't hungry, which isn't the case at all.

Why stand on principle when it'll just give people the wrong idea?

I take the bacon, stuffing the whole strip into my mouth just like a boy might do. It is wondrously good.

As Andy and Peety draw near, I hear Andy say, "He understands Spanish, so don't think you can fool Him with that cussing."

Peety stomps around our fire. "*Chico* pretend he know how to ride horse," Peety tells us, waving his hands at Andy.

"Well, it was a long time ago," Andy shoots back, brushing off her sleeves.

"*Estas loco.* How are you going to ride Princesa?"

"Ain't I gonna ride her double with Sammy?"

Peety glares at her. "Princesa only takes one rider, and you are bigger than Chinito. Sammy, you ride with West and Francesca today."

By Francesca, I guess he means West's sorrel. It's a tough call as to who's the most disappointed—Andy, me, or West. The deal was for us to ride Princesa together, but if we protest, the boys might get suspicious. Andy picks her face up the quickest. "Fine," she says gruffly.

"You ever rode a horse?" West asks me.

I stop picking at the hem of my shirt and raise my chin.

"I know how to ride," I say coolly. I don't mention that my only steed was our compliant mule, Tsing Tsing, back in New York who only had two speeds: slow, and slower.

West tucks his lower lip under his top, like he drew the shortest straw. He busies himself tacking his sorrel alongside Cay and Peety. I kneel beside Andy, who is rearranging the items in her saddlebag. "You okay?"

"He's a stubborn man, that Peety," she grumbles. "I ain't got no business riding that frisky she-devil by myself."

I cluck my tongue in sympathy, remembering well how fiercely I gripped Father's hand the first time I sat upon our gentle Tsing Tsing. "You want me to ask if I can ride Princesa and you go with West?" I ask a bit too eagerly.

"'S okay," she says darkly. "They might change their minds about taking us if we fuss too much. You got more waist than me, tie a shirt 'round your middle to even things out."

I do it while Andy knits her fingers together, casting glances at the sky. Yellow clouds, backlit by the coming sun, trek over the horizon like cat prints.

"You're sixteen, which means you were born in 1832, right?" I ask.

She stops praying. "I guess, though don't ask me the day, 'cause I don't know. Why?"

"That's the Year of the Dragon, the most powerful of the twelve animals on the Chinese calendar."

"Most powerful?" She slits her eyes at me.

I nod.

"What animal are you?"

"Snake."

A wry smile touches her lips. "You don't say?"

"Each sign has its strengths and weaknesses," I say under my breath.

She tilts back her head, causing her hat to fall forward. "Tell me the bad news first."

"Dragons are sharp-tongued, stubborn, and overconfident—"

She cuts me off. "Move on to the good stuff."

"They're also creative and independent. And when they put their minds to something, they always succeed, which is why they're so powerful. Mother was a Dragon. She made Father speak only English to her so she could learn the language. Took her three months."

"I already figured you's mama was bright as a sunbeam," says Andy. "But she ever try riding a horse?"

"If Princesa starts fussing at you, just remember dragons eat horses for dinner."

She wrinkles her nose. "Doesn't strike me as Christian to be a dragon. The ones in the Bible were always up to no good. Now go do your business while I say my last prayers."

Princesa belts out a high-pitched squeal, almost like a human scream, as Andy approaches her.

"Princesa," says Peety in a stern voice, pointing his finger at the horse's nose.

The screaming dies down, and Peety helps Andy into the seat. Immediately, she grabs the saddle horn.

"No holding apple!" says Peety, gesturing at the saddle horn. "Trust your legs."

"I trust my legs, just not what's under them."

Princesa jerks her head back. Andy wobbles but instead of grabbing the apple, she grabs Princesa's mane, causing her ride to rock in irritation. She'll fall off for sure, maybe break her leg. Then what?

As Peety pries Andy's fingers out of Princesa's mane, I clear my throat. "Maybe I should ride Princesa today, and Andy can go with—"

"Come on," grumbles West from behind me. "Don't keep Franny waiting." He forms his hands into a sling and boosts me up onto his sorrel. Her back is cushioned only with a blanket since Peety moved her saddle to Princesa. Then West climbs on in back of me, while I scoot as far forward as possible. Franny accepts the arrangement with a snort and a sigh, and I swear West does, too. His tongue clicks and away we go.

When Peety and Andy catch up with us, she's still holding on to the apple, sitting straight as a bottle on a rocking barrel. Her face is frozen in concentration. I curl my pinkie at her in our secret sign. Even if she disapproves of dragons, she will hopefully still consent to being a rattlesnake. She barely lifts her eyes to me.

West lets Franny drift behind the others. The horses kick up clouds of dust, which hang in the air for us to pass through. I pull my handkerchief up to my eyes.

The land changes underneath our feet as we travel, first pebble and sand, now grass tall enough for me to graze my hand over. Every now and then, some animal, probably a prairie dog, disturbs the rhythm of the waving blades with a rattling sound.

If the authorities dispatched men to come for us, they will catch up soon. How big was the bounty? The sweeter the prize, the faster the flies will find it. My stomach bunches like overworked *bao*, the little white buns we fill with sweet beans. If you knead the dough too long, the *bao* shrivel around the filling and become paperweights.

My back cramps, so I unbend it, placing my heels on the fat pads of Franny's shoulders. West tries to keep his distance from me, aiding my efforts to keep my waist away from him. We might as well be trying to run up opposite hills of polished jade in our socks. When we bump in the middle for the third time, he mutters, "Dang it."

Ears burning, I scoot forward again. Why do I offend him so much? Is it because he doesn't want to sit so close to a boy—or because he doesn't want to be too near a Chinese boy? He does not act jumpy and irritable around Andy, or glare at her. That must be it. A yellow man bested him at cards or took his best hat in a gamble, and so he hates us all. Fine, I think, steamed now.

Franny yelps as West, scooting back again, heels her in the kidneys.

Peety notices. "Don't hurt *mi tesoro* Francesca. West, you are a *bruto*. Apologize."

"Sorry, Franny," West mutters.

West is forced to slide closer to me. I pin my elbows to my sides and scoot forward again. Andy's still holding her posture erect, but at least one of her hands has let go of the apple.

A dust mote flies into my eye, and I dig it out with a knuckle. "Might we move up alongside the others? I can barely see."

"Franny and I always ride the drag." He offers no further explanation.

"The drag?"

"The back."

"Why? It's filthy back here."

He snorts. "It's got the best view."

"If you like looking at horse derrières."

"Dairy what?"

"Derrière, from the Latin root, *de retro*, meaning 'of the back.'"

"In Texas, we just call them butt-tocks."

My ears begin to cook once again.

"When we're moving a herd, riding drag lets me scope for problems, like coyotes," he says, real low and hissy-like. "You'd be surprised how many freeloaders are out there, trying to catch a meal."

That last part strikes the final match under my collar. Last I checked, they were the ones sharing our snake. I slide forward as much as I can and do my best to shun him.

An hour later, we pass two caravans. Each wagon train is a lively mix of people and livestock—mostly mules and oxen with the occasional pig or flock of chickens. The pioneers generally wear the same getup: bonnets and full-sleeved dresses for the women and plain shirts and trousers with suspenders for the men.

Mr. Trask is too far ahead to be part of either of these caravans, but I still find myself combing the crowds for him from the shadows of my hat. Brown thinning hair and mustache could describe half of the men I see. At least his red suspenders might stand out. I also keep an eye out for Andy's brother Isaac, even though finding him means I will lose Andy, a dismal thought.

"How many miles do you go a day?" I ask the grump at my back.

"At this turtle pace, we'll be lucky if we break fifteen," he says in a surly voice. "Usually it's twenty or thirty."

I ignore his unpleasantness. "How do you know?"

"Experience."

I clamp my lips together. How very helpful.

After a moment, he adds, "People leave mileage markers, but you have to look for them."

"Where?"

"On tree trunks, rocks, whatever they can scratch on."

"Does your *experience* tell you how many miles to California?"

"Nope. But Cay's map does."

I grind my teeth.

"Which road you taking to California?" he asks.

Doesn't everyone use the same one? I could kick myself for not listening more when the Argonauts shared their travel plans with Father at the Whistle.

"The usual one," I answer coolly. "What about you?"

"Ain't decided yet. Which one's the usual one?"

I glare at Princesa's backside. Despite his mild tone, he is obviously mocking me. I attempt to lie. "The one . . ." Oh, what's the use? "Fine. How many roads are there?"

"Half a dozen at least."

What? Once I clear my lungs, he adds, "California's big as Texas. Not everyone's going to the same place."

My shoulders slump. "How long before the trail divides?"

"The Parting of the Ways? About nine hundred fifty miles from here."

I sit up and all my blood seems to collect in my feet. The trail suddenly got shorter by a thousand miles. I should've known the path would fork at some point, but did it have to be so soon? I'll have to find Mr. Trask before it forks, or I won't know which way he's gone. He'll be lost to me forever.

I check to see if Andy heard. She's clutching Princesa's mane and trying to hold the reins at the same time. I want to ask if she's okay, but she doesn't look like she wants to be bothered.

Instead, I calculate how fast we'll need to travel to catch Mr. Trask. We'll have to go faster than fifteen miles a day, a wagon's maximum speed, not to mention, we want to put as much distance between us and whoever might be chasing us. Since Mr. Trask left twenty days ago, he could be at the Parting of the Ways in as few as forty-five days. If we upped our speed to at least twenty-two miles a day, we could arrive before him.

I chew on my lip as the situation becomes more desperate. Since riding double means we can't go faster than a walk, we'll need to get a horse for each of us. We'd need two horses anyway once Andy moves on.

I slump, but just as my back touches West's front, I snap back to attention.

Cay pulls his pinto back to walk alongside Andy and Peety. "Hey, Andy. What'd you mean last night when you said the view was wide and handsome? Never heard of a view being handsome before." Then a grin appears and he angles his chin so we can all see his profile. "Well, besides this view."

West groans.

"Wide and handsome is more a feeling, like the world is his to take," says Andy, finally relaxing her shoulders.

"I feel like that every day," says Peety, stretching his arms over his head. "You tell a good story."

She hazards half a twist in her saddle and casts me a sly glance. "That's not all I can do. I used to be a cook, too."

"Cook, huh?" says Cay. "I miss our coosie on the drive. He was a magician."

"Cobbler's my specialty."

"That so? You hear that, West?" says Cay.

"I don't have a sweet tooth," West mutters.

Cay flicks a gloved hand at West. "You don't got a sweet anything."

"What else can you do, Andito?" says Peety, scratching a red welt on his neck.

"I know how to take the itch out of a mosquito bite." She points to Peety's red spot. "Rub some dry soap on it. You have soap, don't you?"

Peety passes the question to West, who shakes his head, then barks, "Cay! Franny wants to shade up."

We park under a dogwood, a stately tree with a wide canopy of white cross-shaped blossoms that resemble a flock of butter-flies. Dogwoods mean that water is close.

Cay opens his trousers and anoints a bush. Peety and West do the same.

"Don't you gotta make water?" asks Cay, looking over his shoulder at Andy and me.

Andy elbows me.

"I saw a patch of something we can eat over there," I fumble.

We head off to a high-grass area with dense shrubs where we can do our business in private. My thighs ache and Andy's, too, judging by how she walks. Once we're hidden, Andy quickly opens up her coat and flaps the side panels like wings. "I've got to do something about this coat," she mutters. "I'm baking myself into a dinner roll."

"Good effort back there offering up your skills," I say, "but West clearly does not care for our company."

"He's a tough nut to crack. A good-looking nut, though." She tweaks an eyebrow at me. "Maybe we could pay them with one of the pinkie rings to take us farther."

"I think West would rather pay *us* to go away," I grumble. "Still, those are quality horses." If I had a horse like one of theirs, I could catch up to Mr. Trask in no time at all.

After we finish, we're left with the problem of what to bring back.

Andy points to a shrub with tiny red fruit. "Chokecherries. Good eats but sour as horse piss.'"

I don't ask how she knows this as we fill our pockets. Then we start to leave the cover of the bushes.

"Sammy!" hisses Andy from behind me at the same moment I see four men on horseback. They peer down at the boys, their somber dusters slung over with rifles. Cay leans back on Skinny, his hands gesturing.

My breath catches in my throat. Before we can dive back into the brush, West beckons us over.

I gulp as the four newcomers turn their heads in our direction.

10

"OH, LORD," SAYS ANDY. "I HOPE THEY AIN'T looking for us."

We drag our feet back to the boys.

"How fast can you run in case we need to split?" she whispers.

"About as fast as I can walk." I wipe my sweating palms on my trousers. "And anyway, we can't outrun horses. We'll just need to play it by ear."

"You mean, we need to pray," says Andy.

I iron out the wrinkles in my brow as we approach.

One of the men touches a black-gloved hand to his forehead by way of greeting, his mouth puckered as a belly button. His bullet eyes hone in on Andy, then me, wilting beside her. They linger on my dirt-streaked face.

Cay sweeps his finger at the men. "These are federal marshals."

I square my shoulders and try to stop hiding in my clothes. Too suspicious.

"Nate Early," says the one with the bullet eyes. "Names?"

"Andy."

"S-s-sam," I stutter, even with just one syllable.

"You kids runaways?"

Andy flinches.

"No," I answer. "We're Argonauts." I puff out my chest, then quickly deflate it when I realize that even the suggestion of a chest could do me in.

"Argonauts." Early draws out the word. "Where you coming from?"

Not St. Joe. No. "New Yorkshire," I say, nearly choking when Ty Yorkshire's surname falls out. Dear God! Who ever heard of New Yorkshire? My shoulders slump with the weight of the invisible rope I just threw around my neck.

Early squints at me.

I'm swimming in a pool of my own sweat. Shoot me now. Make it quick.

"Sam from New *Yorkshire*, that your slave?" He jerks his head toward Andy. She's gone still as a music stand. A fly lands on her shoulder, then crawls around her back.

The thought of even pretending to own a slave makes me sick. "No. He's a free man."

"You got papers?" Early asks Andy.

Papers? I want to kick myself. I should've said I owned her. That was the original plan, the reason I was her Moses wagon. But would he have asked for ownership papers? Before either Andy or I can speak, Peety says, "No need for papers out here. This is no Missouri."

"Who exactly you looking for?" Cay asks, fanning himself with his hat.

Early finally releases Andy from his stare. "Gang of five

negroes who robbed a bank a few months back. We call 'em the Broken Hand Gang. Big as gorillas."

"That's a funny name for a gang," says Cay.

Only Early's lips move. "They smashed the clerk's hand with a sledgehammer."

Cay shakes out his hand. "Ouch."

"Indeed. Word is, they're somewhere on the trail, terrorizing the pioneers."

"Wouldn't they be halfway to California by now?" asks West.

The man shakes his head. "Could be. Or not. We split up at Fort Laramie and me and the boys here doubled back."

"What do you mean 'terrorizing'?" asks West.

"They can't get what they need at the forts, so they steal from the lone travelers."

"Well, as you can see, we ain't a gang of five negroes. Our black fella's scrawny as a dill weed, but we wish you luck anyway," says Cay.

Early switches his gaze back and forth between Andy and me. "Lots of criminals out this way, you know. Think they can escape the law by running west. Never works."

I swallow hard. "No, sir."

Early reaches down and hooks hands with Cay, pumping once. Then the horsemen dig in their spurs and clear out like a passing storm cloud.

I spill most of the berries as Andy and I transfer them from our pockets to the sack that used to hold our cheese.

West watches me pick up berries. "Bank robbers. Bet they're

armed and dangerous. This is wild country, boys." He hangs on that last word and flicks his hair. Then he adds under his breath, "Maybe you oughta go back to your mamas."

Before I can talk to Andy, Cay calls for us to mount up and *vámonos*. I spend the next few hours both wishing we could go faster and worrying I might do permanent damage to my back if we don't stop. Was Early just blowing smoke when he said running west never works? And just how many criminals head west anyway? I never thought I'd be on the same side of the fence as anyone known as the Broken Hand Gang. May Andy and I stay out of their reach. At least the odds are in our favor. They say the frontier's bigger than all the states put together, with less than one percent of the population.

Unfortunately, that also means I may never find Mr. Trask.

What were those great plans you had for us in California, Father? You must have given him the bracelet for good reason. Lots of pioneers carry gold instead of money because it doesn't fall apart if it gets wet, and it's easy to hide. But you said we'd see it again, which means you weren't planning for him to sell it outright. I wish I had listened to you instead of being so dead set against California. Now, only Mr. Trask knows your intention.

Andy no longer sits ramrod straight, though she still hasn't learned to control Princesa. The horse barely heeds her orders, only stopping when the others stop, and going when Peety slaps her rump. When the bay pushes its way closer to the front, Peety pulls her back in line.

"No holding apple, Andito," orders Peety for the dozenth time.

We pass a third caravan. Cay chats with everyone we pass, especially the girls. He sweeps his hat to a young woman carrying a cat.

"Afternoon, miss. Cay Pepper, cowboy, whip shot, ace roper, and—"

"Windbag," says West.

Cay ignores him. "And gentleman." He bows low. "Who might you be?"

She lowers her smallish eyes, then lifts them for a fraction of a second. "Gladys." Her lips push out like a bing cherry.

"Why, I like the shape of your wagon," says Cay.

She giggles, and tickles her cat under the chin.

After we pass the caravan, Cay can't stop looking over his shoulder. Finally, he circles his pinto around. "I'll catch up."

"You're headed for trouble," West tells Cay. "I ain't running again from your mistakes."

"I just wanna ask if she wants a ride on my pony, ain't that right, Skinny?" He pats the pinto's neck.

"That's what I'm afraid of," mutters West, though Cay is already gone.

A flush creeps up my neck as I guess at what Cay intends to do. I will need to train that unmanly reaction out of me. It figures that he is a womanizer. If he's seventeen years of age, he was born in the Year of the Rabbit, meaning he has a tendency to overbreed.

His cousin softly whistles behind me. West is probably an overbreeder as well.

By the time Cay catches up to us, we've reached the Little

Blue, a winding stream that runs in a north–south direction. The sun sits two hands from the horizon, still high enough to heat the moist air. Though the horses are thirsty, shallow trenches made by stuck wheels convince us not to cross the muddy earth to the river yet. Instead, we plod onward through the waving clumps of grass.

My body aches from holding myself up on the horse all day long and my eyes are burned out from the sun's unforgiving glare. I am watching Andy trying to release the saddle horn again, when West's gloved hand brushes my waist. My back cracks as I snap to.

"You're slipping," he says. To the others, he calls, "Shade up, before someone gets their head stuck in the dirt."

My face grows hot, but I let that one go, remembering what Andy said about fussing too much. I still haven't figured out how to get the boys to take us farther. I doubt money, cooking, or any of the skills we could offer will change West's mind.

After another half mile, the earth dries up and we cut a path to the shoreline. Pawpaw trees with their dark leaves, big as my foot, shade the bank, linked by clumps of pussy willows and sprawling hazelnut.

We stop at a bald spot of earth shaded by a cherry tree with glossy leaves. I dismount and walk around bowlegged, trying to rub feeling back into my limbs.

Cay pulls a lumpy sack off his saddle.

"What's that, amigo, you got some rocks for your collection?" says Peety.

Cay opens the sack and pulls out an onion. "For our last

supper together. The sparrow liked her pony ride." He flashes a smile.

West groans. "Always a beggar."

"Hope there's more in there than onions," Andy says with a grimace.

Cay waves the onion in front of Andy's nose. "What do you have against onions?"

She shrinks away so fast she stumbles on a rock. "Just don't like 'em."

"These put hair on your chest. An onion a day cured my daddy of gout," says Cay.

"Also good for hangovers," says Peety.

Andy recovers her balance. "I also don't like talking about them."

"Why?" asks Peety.

"If I told you that, I would be talking about 'em, wouldn't I?" she says in a huff, stomping off to the river.

I trot after her. If she doesn't want to talk about onions, then neither do I.

We find a break in the screen of pussy willows lining the shoreline. Andy places two pawpaw leaves on the damp earth and kneels on them.

I do the same. "We need to ask them if they can take us farther."

"Especially now that we got bank robbers to worry over." Andy rubs water onto her shorn head.

"Agreed. I'd like to keep my hand in one piece. I just don't think a ring's going to be enough." Gathering water into my hands, I rub it around my hot neck and face. I sorely want to drink, too. But I will wait until we can boil the water to be safe. Of all the trail dangers, cholera worried our pioneer customers the worst, which is why Father always stocked his special mix of rehydrating salts.

"That's good money," says Andy. "What about both rings?"

"They don't care much about money. They brought us here on a practical joke," I mutter.

"It won't hurt to ask." Andy mops her forehead with her handkerchief. "Thought we were goners when those marshals showed up."

"Me, too."

"I just hope Isaac don't come upon that gang. He'll be traveling by himself, I reckon, which means he's easy pickins." She scrubs her arms with ferocity and glares at the water. "Plus, he's so good, he'd probably say a prayer for them after they break his hand."

"Is he as good as you?" I ask.

A smile tickles her lips. "He makes me look like a sinner." She stops scrubbing and pats her arms with a rag. "If he sees you hungry, he'll give you his portion and make sure you don't know it. Not even the birds fly away when he comes 'round. Don't even think he like to eat meat, but a'course he never complained."

"He sounds like a real gentleman."

"That he is." Her grin fades. "Some days I worry I'll never see him again. It's a big country." A mosquito lands on her hand and she slaps it.

"There's a Chinese principle called *yuanfen*, which means

your fate with someone else," I say. "Two people with strong *yu-anfen* have a greater chance of meeting in their lifetimes, and can become as close as family." I hold up my socks. "See, they're like socks. They may travel different places, but at some point, all the socks end up in the same drawer."

"Socks, huh?" She twists her mouth to one side. "Well, I hope that it is true, though I told you it ain't Christian to believe in fate."

"My father believed in it, and he was Catholic. He liked to say, just because you don't believe it doesn't mean it's not true."

"Like ghosts," she says. "I don't believe in 'em. But you'll never see me stepping on no one's gravestone."

"Me neither."

I finish washing my face and hands. Before I powder my nose with dirt, I peek at my reflection, which turns horrified when I see the boy squinting back at me. My complexion, once fair, is freckling, and my ears look enormous without hair to cover them. A grimace thins my lips, which were never pillowy to begin with. I relax and the curve at the bottom reappears, sweetening things farther up my face. My eyes lose their squint and become watermelons seeds again, shiny, black, and evenly spaced on my oval face. I must be careful to avoid smiling, though I wasn't planning to do that for a long time anyway.

Cay and West set down a few yards away and begin washing. Peety tends to the horses.

"Hey, kids, how 'bout you start a fire while we go hunting?" Cay calls to us.

"Okay," I answer. Andy swats dirt from her trousers, then off we go to collect firewood. We set our camp fifty yards from the river so we don't get caught in mosquito clouds. I break sticks over my knees and add them to our growing pile, while Andy gathers bunches of dried grass for kindling.

When we're done, we flop onto the ground. The moist air feels like a pack of panting dogs hanging over my shoulder. I fan my shirt layers up and down to air myself out. Humid is my least favorite weather, but today I am just thankful there is no rain.

Andy squints as Cay and West return from the river. "That was fast," she says. "Don't look like they got anything."

"Forget hunting." Cay removes his hat and runs a hand through his damp hair, which forms golden ringlets at the ends. "It's too damn muggy. Let's spear a fish instead."

"Whittling a spear will get you just as hot," mutters West.

Cay fans his face with his hat. My eyes catch on the lucky snake jaw in the band and an idea begins to hatch in my head. Perhaps we'll see how lucky my lunar animal's jawbone is after all.

Before the moment flies away, I say, "I have a wager for you."

The cousins cast their eyes at me.

"What's that?" asks Cay.

I tamp down my nerves and make my voice sound hale. "I bet we can catch a fish before either of you. And we won't even use a spear."

"Unlikely," West grumbles. "What happens if we lose?"

"You take us to the next trading post where we can get our own horse," Andy says, dipping her chin at me.

West spits. "Fort Kearny? That's three weeks of playing nursemaid."

Three weeks? I mask my delight by boring my eyes into the tiny cleft in his chin.

"And if we win?" asks Cay.

"What do you want?" I ask.

West dips his eyes at me. "Don't look like you have much to offer."

I cock back my tongue for a snappy response, but Andy steps in. "Neither does a stick, but that don't stop it from being useful if you got imagination," she says evenly. "And if you don't, we got a ring."

"What kind of ring?" asks Cay.

Andy pulls one of the rings out of her bag. "A heavy one."

Cay rocks forward on his feet to appraise it, then whistles. West makes a sucking sound with his tongue and finds a piece of sky to glare at.

"Not afraid, are you?" I challenge him.

He snorts and rakes his gaze over me.

Cay drags West over to Peety, who's a few yards off, combing Skinny's tail. Whatever Cay says makes Peety laugh and West kick the dirt. After a moment, they rejoin us.

"We accept," says Cay. "If you win, we'll take you to Fort Kearny, but you have to cook for us. Plus, I want some Frenchie lessons."

"And I want Chinese lessons," Peety chimes in. West mutters something to Peety, who shrugs.

Cay continues. "If you lose, ya gotta sing 'Yankee Doodle,' unshucked. And we'll take the ring."

Not exactly what I expected, but it's a shot. I wait a few seconds before replying, so as not to appear too eager. Since I don't know what *unshucked* means, I add, "Only if you do it, too— sing, unshucked—if you lose." I figure, if they agree to it, it can't be so bad.

"All of you," adds Andy, looking at Peety.

"*No hay problema.*"

Cay curls his mouth into a lopsided grin. "With pleasure."

I straighten my back and step up to Cay, close enough that I could tug one of his curls. "I'll need your hat."

11

CAY DOESN'T PROTEST, SO I LIFT OFF HIS TOPPER.
Then I work free the snake jaw and rehat his head.

I plop down beside Andy. She takes out a needle and thread from her saddlebag as well as the sack of chokecherries. I get to work unlatching my violin case. Inside is the Lady Tin-Yin, a member of the family for four generations.

The cousins peer down at us, both holding their elbows.

"Last time I checked, fish prefer the harmonica to the violin," drawls West.

"Yeah, and they'd take a good mutton over chokecherries any day of the week," Cay says around a smile. "I want the jawbone back after you lose."

They swagger off, laughing. They're so confident of victory, they think they can take their time. I eye the chokecherries, doubts creeping in. "Maybe this wasn't my best idea."

Andy threads a berry with her needle. "Don't worry, this ain't the bait, long as that ain't the pole." She nods toward my violin.

"Not in a blue fog." From my violin case, I remove the spool I keep in case of a broken string. "Catgut is the strongest fishing line I know of." Not to mention the most dear.

I unwind the string and attach the snake jaw to one end, careful not to stick my fingers. By the time I finish, Andy has threaded several more chokecherries, which she ties along the catgut.

"Isaac taught me this trick. These make good bobbers," she says.

I find a flexible branch for the pole, and Andy cuts up slivers of bacon for the bait. We hurry the contraption down to the river.

"I ain't got no patience, so you holds the pole while I run down the good spots," she says. "You do know how to fish, right?"

"Sure." I don't disclose that Father usually handled the actual fish. A pang of sadness hits me again but I suck it up before we reach the boys.

We hear them talking behind some cattails.

"Gentlemen..." I draw out the word, thinking I have time to play with their heads. Then I realize that Cay and West are shirtless, stripping leaves off their branches. When West carves a point on a branch with three slashes of his knife, I forget what I was going to say.

"Good luck," I squeak out, dashing off after Andy.

She scrutinizes rocks and underwater plants where fish like to hide. A jumble of mossy stones peeking through the surface of the water catches her attention. She points toward them and I cast my line, then she scampers off to scout out other likely spots.

Downstream, Cay and West wade into the water.

"Over there!" Cay drags himself to a fallen tree that breaks the river's flow.

My catgut drags on something, and I pull up. Springing onto my toes, I make out the silhouette of a fish.

"Yes!" I cry, hauling it in just as a breathless Andy returns to my side.

"*Rápido, amigos,* the boy caught something," yells Peety, standing on a rock to oversee the action.

But it is just a pawpaw leaf.

"No," I wail, untangling the leaf.

The boys laugh.

"We're just waiting on the right one," Andy hollers back.

West pulls back his spear, poised to strike. Cay holds his stomach with one hand, still laughing. "Hey, Sammy, how ya say 'loser' in French?"

"Chinito," Peety yells at me. "You gonna let that ugly bum boss you?"

"Pick a side, vaquero, and stick on it," yells Cay.

"Follow me," says Andy, trotting back toward the boys and pointing again at the river. "That brown mess."

I recast just short of a tangle of brown plants so my line doesn't snag. *Come on, fish!*

Now Cay jabs his spear into the water. He curses. "That was just to scare ya. Next time, my arrow's going in."

"You're catching fish, not sparrows," yells Peety.

"Girls never leave my mind, even when I'm fishing. That's why I'm such a crack hunter."

"Pervert, you mean," says West.

A shadow ventures out of the tangle and hovers over my bait, weighing whether the salty intruder is friend or feast. I glance at West, who is focusing on a spot. He is close, too.

"Chum the water," Andy says, tossing a handful of bacon at my line.

The pretend worms float for half a second before fish lips poke at them from below. I feel a tug. The second tug comes a lifetime later, and I jerk my wrist up.

The fish fights now, which means I hooked it, but I don't want my line to break. So I wait until it stops resisting before I reel in. Instead of giving up, my prey fights harder. If my line snaps, I lose.

"You gonna have to get wet," says Andy, already pulling off my right boot.

"Do I have to?"

"Yes," she barks, yanking off the other one.

With a farewell grumble, I step into the river. The icy water laps at my calves, but I grit my teeth and forge ahead. The fish leads me into the brown tangle, slimy and probably full of disgusting leeches. I glance back at Andy, revulsion pulling my face in different directions. Still clutching one of my boots, she gestures with it, *go on already.*

Just thinking about the leeches trips me and I find myself up to my chin in slippery brown strings. I bite my tongue to keep from screaming. Everyone must be watching my spectacle. I choke my pole with a death grip and pick myself back up.

Soon, a catfish the size of Texas blows me a cold-blooded kiss.

"Hallelujah!" Andy hollers.

Cay hollers, too, as West holds up his prize, a flounder still flapping at the end of his spear.

I stick my finger up my catfish's gill so I don't lose it and try to stop thinking about wet cow nostrils. The fish slaps my arm with its tail.

Peety tilts his brown face from the boys to Andy and me, his chin wedged between his thumb and index finger as he decides which of us caught our fish first. Andy raises her clasped hands toward heaven, her eyes squeezed shut.

Then the vaquero looks back at the boys. "Chinito wins by half a nose!"

12

DESPITE MY DISGUST AT THE FLAPPING THING AT the end of my arm, I can't wipe the grin off my face when Andy and I parade by the boys toward our campfire.

"*Un perdant,*" I tell Cay.

"What?"

"The word you asked for in French. 'Loser.' It's a good one to start with, don't you think?"

"*Un perdant,*" repeats Andy. "Slides off the licker."

After the flounder and the catfish are getting to know each other in our pot of simmering water, Andy and I park on a patch under the canopy of a pawpaw, me in my two dry shirts. It's showtime.

Peety starts pulling off his trousers right beside us, sending our eyebrows soaring. He wears red long underwear. Andy's face explodes with hilarity though she slaps a hand over her mouth before any sound escapes. With a flick of his wrist, the vaquero shakes out his fancy jacket and hangs it on a branch. The rear flap on the seat of his long underwear sags a bit.

"He could carry parcels in there," Andy says out of the side of her mouth, and now I have to cover my face as well.

Then Peety peels off the long underwear and folds them into a neat pile, sweeping away the last vestiges of my composure.

"Unshucked," I choke out, planting my face in my lap. I can't hide like this. Boys don't hide in the presence of naked male bodies, but I can't help myself.

Something almost knocks my topper off. West and Cay just threw their trousers at us, and now stand naked as two zucchinis wearing hats.

"Well, that's one mystery solved," says Andy, who manages to face them straight on while an invisible harness pulls my face back into my knees. "But now I wanna know, if they don't wear unders, how they stop the chafing?"

"Stop whispering," says Cay. "This is some serious singing we're about to do."

Andy elbows me. "C'mon, pull it together. They's just bodies."

I force myself to look up. The three fine specimens of the male anatomy line up. The cousins, a shade under six feet each, bookend the huskier vaquero, like two bolts of cotton twill with a shorter bolt of broadcloth between them. The bolt on the left might gain another inch if it stopped slouching.

The boys belt out the lyrics to "Yankee Doodle."

"Looks like we have three full moons tonight," I observe.

"And one of them coffee-colored."

When Andy says this, I know I'm going to have to fight down another laughing attack. I cough, spit, and hold my breath in. It never works. The floodgates burst, and all my fifteen-year-old giggles come snorting out while Andy whacks me. By the word *macaroni*, I'm teary-eyed, and her handprint is stamped on my back.

As I swear to myself I will never again wager without knowing what the terms mean, to my horror, the doodlers lumber toward us, their faces twisted with evil intent.

"No one laughs at this mountain of muscle and lives to tell," says Cay.

West flicks a mosquito off his arm. "The babies need their bath."

"Water's warm, *chicos*."

Truth be told, the sight was not so horrible, but never mind. Andy and I jump to our feet. Since we're boys, we cannot scream or faint, those being the things that a female does when naked men pursue her. So we do the next best thing.

We scoop up their clothes and race to the water. You might think being unclothed would put you at a disadvantage, but those boys run like cheetahs after a pair of bunnies. They catch up as we reach the shoreline.

Too late for them, though.

"It's a cold night to be unshucked," I tell the closest, Cay, as we dangle our bundles over the water.

The wind goes out of their sails.

"Hand them over and we'll leave you nippers alone," grumbles West.

Andy pretends to drop her bundle, and the boys all gasp. "Swear it on a stack of Bibles."

The boys shield their privates with one hand and hold up the other.

• • •

After Andy says a proper grace this time, we feast like kings, though we have to eat out of the pot with two spoons. Using the vegetables from Cay's sack, Andy turns out fish stew with chokecherry relish, no onions. At her request, I put the onions into one of the boys' saddlebags so she won't have to see them.

"My brother taught me this recipe," Andy says proudly. "It's called Snap Stew."

After we lick every fish bone clean, Cay wipes his mouth with his bandanna and announces, "Now ain't you glad we brung the nippers along?" He turns his gaze on West, who has the grace to flush at being called out.

I weigh the snake jaw in my palm. *So, Snake, you did me a good turn after all, though one lucky turn does not a lucky person make.* I tuck the bone back into Cay's hatband, then replace the catgut in my violin case.

Lady Tin-Yin's polished maple shell gleams under the sun's final rays. An Italian built the instrument, but Father gave her the Chinese name, which means "violin from heaven." She is the most precious thing I've ever owned, and now the only thing I own besides my boots. I lightly pluck the G, thinking again of Father, whose philosophy followed the open strings. *G* for grace. My throat constricts at the sound of the lone note floating up to heaven.

Next, the D-string, *D* for discipline, the note of empowerment. That one always comes out a bit cranky, like it doesn't want to wake up. Then the A-string, *A* for acceptance of the way God chose to outfit us, skin color and all. And *E,* not for excellence, but for exquisite, the standard by which I play.

When I come out of my thoughts, everyone is watching me.

"You gonna saw for us?" asks Peety.

Andy nods at me.

Discipline, I think, sniffing up any mistiness on my face.

Two flat boulders form a step under the shade of a junior-sized dogwood. I plant my bottom on the higher boulder and rosin the bow. I start rolling up my left sleeves, but the sight of my reedy arm makes me roll them back down. Definitely not manly.

Blowing off the excess powder from the rosin, I run the bow over each string and wind the pegs as necessary. Then I play the D-flat scale, my favorite. Sounds good, so I get to my feet. My audience falls silent.

My showmanship only comes out when I hold the violin—with Lady Tin-Yin in my arms, I don't care who watches. A peace comes over me, something I call my violin calm. I become someone else, someone quite entertaining, I like to think.

I compose myself with a deep breath. I put the wood to my chin, and launch into Paganini's Caprice no. 24.

When Father first showed me the sheet music, I told him I couldn't do it.

"You're right," he said, chopping vegetables with his cleaver.

"What?"

"Whether you think you can or you can't, you're right. Have a pea shoot."

By the end of the week, I had mastered it.

The piece features crisscrossing strings, which look more difficult than they really are. I work in several triple stops, three strings played at once. Mr. Trask, a clarinetist himself, brought tangerines just to hear me play those triple stops. I would've played them anyway, but I think he brought those rare treasures to show me what he thought of my playing.

When I finish, no one claps. They all stare at me. Andy swipes her sleeve over her eyes and turns her face away from the boys.

"Ain't never heard a fiddle like that," says Cay, his jaw slack.

Peety's head bobs up and down. "You got some skills."

West glares at his boots.

Time to lighten things up. *This one's for you, Father, because banjo was your first love.* Then I tear into "Oh! Susanna," which no one can hear without dancing, especially Cay, who does a polka.

Our spirits are high as we ready for sleep. We arrange ourselves like cigars again in the same order as last night.

We hear another howl tonight—this one not a chorus of *yips* but a single lone cry. A wolf. Wolves grow twice as big as coyotes, and can take down large animals like moose. I sit up and shiver. The howl repeats, this time closer.

"Holy moly," says Andy.

West rolls over on his side, away from me. "They don't bother people. Probably crying over his sweetheart."

"It's the bears and the mountain lions we worry over," says Cay, who's still sitting up, looking out into the dark.

"What we do about those?" asks Andy.

"You gotta learn a few cowboy tricks," he replies. "Sharp-shooting. Roping. We'd show you, but you ain't worthy." He tilts his face toward us. The firelight makes his teeth gleam.

Andy snorts and elbows me.

Peety starts to snore, and then the rest of them tumble off.

Andy turns toward me, and whispers sleepily, "I'm happy they's gonna bring us to the fort," she says. "You's in good hands."

"Me? You, too, right?"

"Yeah, me, too." Her breath gradually deepens.

I lie awake longer. What would I do if she did leave? Would I be able to pull off a boy act of one? Probably not if I cried. Then the curtains would fall for sure.

No sooner do I get Andy out of my mind when Yorkshire's lecherous winking eye moves in, along with bank robbers and lawmen and Father. *Oh, how you must have suffered.*

My grief shadows me into sleep, but then shakes me awake several times during the night. Father in a bonfire, or a prairie blaze, always holding his hands out for me. I cannot pull him free because I am always too late.

13

I AM THE LAST TO WAKE, BESIDES THE SUN, WHICH still hides beneath cloud blankets and makes them glow like embers. I cannot move. Every muscle in my body screams with pain, even the ones I didn't think I'd used, like the ones in my toes. Groaning, I gently ease myself up and peer toward the east. Several wagon circles lie two or three hundred yards farther down the river, small as bracelets. There's no movement on the trail.

A few feet away, Andy pulls her needle through the hem of her coat. She doesn't notice me yet. Her top teeth clamp down on her tongue as she works. Cay and West sit with their backs to me. In front of them, the horses graze on their breakfast as Peety wanders among them, murmuring assurances and rubbing noses.

West writes in a journal, though by the flicks of his wrist, I think he's actually sketching. Craning my neck, I make out an incomplete drawing of his horse, the sorrel, Franny. A quarter horse like Princesa, Franny wears a blond coat with no dark spots and a flaxen mane. Assuming they do sell horses at Fort Kearny, they won't be as fine as these. West's drawing is remarkably true to life, and full of motion, the muscles and sinew rendered in complicated hatch marks and shading. Only an artist could reproduce an animal so convincingly.

Peety scratches Franny's withers, causing her to nicker and blow out her lips. *"Mi reina, eres la fuente de mi ser. Te quiero con toda mi alma."* My queen, you are the fountain of my being. I love you with all of my soul. He kisses Franny on the nose.

West looks up from his journal. "I'm a jealous man, Peety." He closes his journal and slides it into his shirt pocket, then gets to his feet. "Come here, Franny." He clicks his tongue, but she does not budge.

Peety's full lips thin into a grin. "Can I help it if the ladies love me?"

"'Cause ya smell like horse, that's why," says West.

Peety smirks. "Oh no, *mi* amigo, not smell like a horse. Built like a horse." He taps his pelvis and then notices me. *"Mira,* Chinito's not dead after all. You need some help, my friend?" He walks toward me, arm outstretched, but I wave him off.

"I'm fine."

Despite the vaquero's initial aloofness, I find him to be the most warmhearted of the three boys, one eye always watching out for Andy or me as if we were part of the remuda.

I try not to wince as I start to stand. Quickly, Andy replaces her needle in her saddlebag. "We've got to come up with something better than berry-picking," she whispers as she helps me up.

All three boys are watching us. I clear my throat. "It is not custom for Chinese and, er, Africans to make water in public. In fact, it's disrespectful to... our ancestors."

Andy nods as she holds herself tightly.

West glances at Cay, who looks at Peety. Just when I think

my teeth are going to crumble from clenching them so long, Cay, chewing a carrot, says, "Where you wet the weeds is your personal business, boys. Me here, I just try not to stand by Peety. He drips on his boots most the time. It's disgusting."

I follow Andy to the river. Unlike mine, today her gait is even, with no hint of saddle soreness. Either she's good at hiding her pain or she has legs of iron. We duck behind a cluster of high grass tinged purple on the ends. The air no longer feels damp, but the morning is already warm, even with no sun out.

"You did well yesterday on Princesa," I say. "I think you're catching on."

"You mean hanging on. That was like riding a witch's broomstick. But look at what I did with my witch's cape." She unbuttons her coat and holds open the flaps.

Vent holes have been cut under the arms and finished with a whipstitch. She turns around. "And the back." I run my hand along the center of the rough fabric and find more vent holes hidden in the seam. There's even an opening underneath the collar.

"Ingenious," I say.

"What's that mean?"

"Very clever."

She snorts. "If I was real ingenious, I wouldn't get back on that four-legged death trap."

"Once we get to Fort Kearny, we can get horses of our own."

She nods. "Be even better to keep on with these boys *and* get the horses. That Cay's gonna keep you well fed as long as there's girls on the trail."

"You can't be thinking about leaving so soon?"

"No, not yet. But Harp Falls might come up sooner than later." Her mouth twists into a smile and she knocks her hand against mine. "Don't worry, Sammy. I won't go without telling you."

That doesn't reassure me much. We've only known each other a few days, but I can't imagine life on this trail without her. I chew on my lip. Maybe I'll find Mr. Trask before Harp Falls. He'll share Father's plans with me and return Mother's bracelet, freeing me to help Andy search for Isaac.

"Besides, that waterfall's probably not for miles and miles," Andy says lightly. "You might have to put up with me longer than you think."

Cay and West have already mounted their horses by the time we return. Peety's straightening the blanket under Princesa's saddle. The bay slides back and forth, seeming eager to get on the move. "You ready, Andito?" asks Peety.

"That horse is twitchy as a pair of thumbs," says Andy. "I think Sammy wants a turn."

I nod vigorously, not wanting to repeat the battle of the saddle with West. "Everyone wins."

Peety shakes his head. "Andito and Princesa are good for each other. You're a tenderfoot"—he points to Andy, then steers his finger to the bay—"and she has tender feet."

Andy throws me a dark look and I give her a fierce nod of encouragement. She pushes up her coat sleeves, not seeming to notice when they fall back down. Then she marches right up to the horse. "Okay, she-devil, let's do this."

The bay emits her customary scream when Andy approaches. Peety holds the horse's harness as Andy, grimacing, hauls herself up. Princesa tosses her head a few times to snap at some flies, but Andy stays seated.

Today I ride with the leaders, Cay and Skinny. The bossy pinto marches like a drum majorette, head high, steps as measured as a clock's *tick*. Cay focuses more on what's around him than who's in front of him, and that, together with Skinny's longer barrel, means a less tense ride for me. I almost enjoy my view up here in the front.

We walk along the Little Blue, whose rivulets run in all directions like veins. Despite my sore backside, I fidget in my seat, again wishing we could go faster. But when we ford the river to follow the trail northwest, I'm simply thankful Andy and I don't have to splash through the muddy water on our own. Even at its shallowest spot, the water oozes up to our soles, and I keep my feet high so my boots don't get soaked.

By midday, the land begins to stretch upward like a roll in the fabric of the flat prairie. A glade of pine trees gives the hill some extra height. Besides a few shadowy clouds lurking behind the pines, the sky is clear. It's the exact sky Father and I left behind in New York, such a deep blue, if you reached high enough, you could lose your hand in it. If only we hadn't left, Father might be drilling me on my Latin verbs under a sky such as this, and I wouldn't have nerves like a jackrabbit.

As one of only two Chinese families in New York, which though few, was at least twice the number in St. Joe, Father and I were more a curiosity than a threat. People mostly left us alone. Sure, we met our share of bigots, casting their eyes in our direction every time something went amiss, like when cherries disappeared off someone's tree—never mind all the crows in the area. But for the most part, people respected Father. He could speak their language, and he made it his business to bridge differences.

I always dreamed about us returning to New York, opening up a music conservatory. I would teach violin, he would teach the other strings, like the cello and banjo, and we would get someone to do the woodwinds. Without Father, the thought of going back to New York leaves me hollow.

The sound of thunder shakes me out of my thoughts. But it can't be thunder with that placid blue sky. West comes up beside us, staring hard at the pine trees. Earthquake?

I rub my eyes. Pouring out from the forest before us are dozens, maybe hundreds of livestock, tearing down the trail at top speed. The bovines and equines lead the charge, trailed by goats and a few pigs. They're stampeding right toward us.

"Holy Moses," cries Andy, wobbling in her seat.

I grab the brim of my hat and bounce up and down. "Let's get out of here. What are we waiting for?" I twist around to face an unusually quiet Cay.

Peety grabs Princesa's reins. "Princesa never done stampede before. *Vámanos.*" He quickly leads Princesa and Andy to a column of limestone ten yards ahead of a lone oak tree on our left. The limestone column rises up sharply like a shark's tooth.

"Why aren't we following them?" I ask.

"Cowboys never run from a stampede," says Cay.

"Says who? I say we get the hell out of the way, too," says West.

"We'd be doing someone a huge favor by catching their animals," pleads Cay. "Maybe that someone has a daughter and some friends."

"That ain't a good reason," says West. "We got a few of our own *friends* to worry on." He glances at me.

"They're tough," says Cay. "Come on, the remuda needs some practice." Without waiting for a reply, Cay taps Skinny with his heels. She moves toward the solitary oak.

"This is your stop," Cay says to me, halting Skinny.

"I can't outrun them," I wail, poking a tenuous toe toward the ground.

Cay locks his knee under mine. "Not down, dummy, up." He looks up at the branches. "You can climb a tree, can't you?"

If I can't, I am not going to tell him. "Shouldn't I wait by Andy?"

"They'll run you over if they get behind that wall."

"But what about Andy, what if—"

"Don't worry, stampede won't run down a horse. Usually. Let's go, they'll be here soon!"

He grunts as I step off his thigh, and then onto his shoulder, reaching up to catch a branch. Cay helps boost me up, but desperation gives me a final push. Soon I'm swinging like a trapeze artist. I hook my legs around another branch, grab the trunk, and scramble up even higher, toward the oak's sturdiest arm, my muscles straining. Finally, winded, I lie flat along the branch and look down below.

To my left, behind the limestone column, Andy sits stiffly atop Princesa, tugging the reins as Princesa tries to follow Peety and Lupe. West peers up at me. Franny fidgets underneath him. "This ain't one of your brightest ideas," he tells Cay. Then he curtains his frown with his bandanna.

"Let 'em run," yells Cay.

My perch twenty feet above the ground, while not comfortable, at least gives me a good view of the action.

"Heeyaw!" yells Cay, leading the boys off. They wheel back in the direction we came.

The din of charging animals increases until they finally tear by under me, mooing and shrieking. Their frenzied stomping causes my tree to shake and kicks up a cloud of dirt in my face, but I cannot spare a hand to wipe it off. I clear my vision by blinking and twitching.

With panicked livestock hot on their heels, the boys lead the chase down the prairie. West flanks Cay on the left. Some of the fleeter animals nose past, but the boys dig in and gain the ground. Then West swerves Franny farther left to slow down the animals in front, cutting close enough to give each animal a shave.

I glance at Andy, who's still tucked behind the limestone column. She waves at me.

A pair of longhorn cattle charges toward West. Sunlight glints off the wicked curve of their horns.

"Pull out," I cry, though he is too far off to hear me. West's hat twists. He sees them. Incredibly, he edges Franny closer.

"No!" I moan. "The other way." Another moment and—I squeeze my eyes shut. Then I pop them open again.

The longhorns veer off! Franny screams in victory, winner of the battle of the nerves.

Peety runs down a pack of animals in a flat-out race west. He overtakes them, then pulls Lupe up hard, waving his arms and yelling to bring them to heel.

Meanwhile, Cay zigzags Skinny in front of a hot press of confused livestock. The lead ox matches Skinny in length, its compact body like a barrel of brown fur. Devilish spikes protrude from its head.

It will gore him for sure. I can't watch, yet now I can't close my eyes.

Cay lengthens the distance between his turns, and eventually, the animals slow. Those behind must also decelerate. Then he begins circling the herd, and Peety and West do the same. Together, the boys cinch the animals into a tighter bunch.

Soon, the whole herd's moving like a merry-go-round, save for the animals in the middle, who've come to a standstill, rolling their eyes and bellowing in bewilderment. I rest my cheek on the branch and let out my breath.

As the cowboys continue ringing the herd with an invisible line, Peety begins to sing, his rich voice carrying across the noise of the herd. Cay and West feed the lines back to him after each stanza.

Hey little missy,
Little missy,
With the waddle.
Tell me if you wanna
Little pony with a saddle.
Wait for me
Until I make it
Back from the battle.
Bring ya back
The horns of the
Longhorn cattle.

I stretch my neck to look for Andy. Princesa's getting friskier and has crept to the edge of the limestone. The horse flicks its head and Andy sways. She recovers her balance, but nearly loses her hat.

Clouds have started to collect above us, blocking out the sun. They stick together like dirty snow by the side of the road. A flash storm must be on its way, which might have caused the stampede. Father says animals can sense weather before humans. I inch backward. If I can reach the trunk, I can shimmy down, then stand by the limestone with Andy. The animals graze calmly as the boys serenade them. No one's going to run me over.

A sudden jolt of lightning turns the sky hot white, freezing me in my tracks. Father used to tell me that lightning was the flash off the drunk man's whiskey bottle as he stumbled across the sky. I brace myself for the arrival of his angry wife wielding her rolling pin. Moments later, thunder roars across the prairie. I quake against my branch, four years old all over again.

The livestock scream in panic. And like that, like the saying goes, all the cats explode out of the bag. The animals run in every direction, sometimes falling over each other in their hurry to escape.

As Peety and Lupe gallop past us, Princesa surges so abruptly that Andy drops the split reins. She grabs on to the apple. "Stop! Whoa!" yells Andy. The horse ignores her and starts off after Peety.

Holy moly. Princesa is joining the stampede.

"Whoa, Princesa!" I yell. "Peety!" I yell at his departing backside. But he doesn't hear me through the din of animals.

"Peety!" I scream. Cay and West are too far away to hear or help. "Peety!"

Princesa enters the fray, tail and head held high. Approaching traffic slows her, but she continues to thread her way to Peety, still twenty feet ahead. The reins drag in the dirt, and Andy can't fetch them without falling off. She slides too far one direction, and I draw in a horrified breath.

At the last second, she corrects her saddle position. But now she's sliding too far the other way. Princesa snaps at a passing mule. The mule turns around and kicks at Princesa, who dodges the kick, and suddenly, Andy's in the dirt.

A longhorn charges from Andy's left, its horned head waggling up and down with each loping stride. She doesn't notice it.

With one hand on the ground, and one hand over the top of her hat, Andy looks wildly about her at the animals flying by.

"Peety!" I scream again, using every bit of air in my lungs.

At last, Peety turns his head. He sees the riderless Princesa tailing him, then finally spots Andy trying to get to her feet. Quickly, he pirouettes Lupe on one hoof, and they sprint toward Andy. Frozen in place, she stares, open-jawed, at the longhorn barreling toward her.

The vaquero reaches out and scoops up Andy by her belt, somehow managing to hold on to her with one arm until the great Andalusian has cleared most of the animals.

I let out a shaky breath of relief. Andy can't ride that unpredictable horse anymore. Maybe Peety will let her ride Lupe instead. I watch them move away from me until the throngs of animals swallow them up.

Cay and West pick up their pace, forcing the animals to stay on the merry-go-round.

Again, I start inching backward, tired of this tree and wanting to get down before I fall.

Another flash of lightning blinds me. My legs start shaking, then my whole body. But it's not me, it's my tree. Something crashes to the ground: a burning branch. I look up and behold hell where heaven should be. Dear God, my tree is on fire.

14

ANOTHER FIERY BRANCH DROPS RIGHT PAST MY head. I open my mouth, but I've already used up all my screams.

The first branch burns out, but flames from the second begin licking at the trunk. Now my tree burns on both ends. A fresh wave of panic makes my hands slick with sweat. With a shock, I realize that if I don't clear out, I'll be burned alive. Like Father.

My mind cries for my body to drop. Broken legs still beat burning alive. Maybe I would just twist an ankle. *Move!* I free one leg, then the other, and now I hang from the branch like laundry. My fingers grip the rough wood as tightly as I can, but they're slipping. Splinters pierce my flesh, and holding on is torture.

The boys yell something I can't make out over the roar of the fire. Smoke steams the tears off my face as they form. I shorten my breath to keep the smoke out of my lungs, but that makes me thirst for air.

With my body dangling, I've reduced the drop to fifteen feet. Still, I cannot let go. The burning branch spews out a swirling mass of black smoke that obscures the ground. I break into a cold sweat. God, not this way.

Something moves below me. A hat.

"I'll catch you," West calls up to me.

I try to release my branch, but fear paralyzes me. Stubborn, stubborn body.

"Trust me."

My arms weaken, and my fingers begin to slip. Another branch falls, singeing my sleeve.

I plummet like an anchor. West snatches me out of the air, hooking me around the chest with his arm and hauling me onto Franny's back.

Soon we are squeezed into the same saddle with me in front. I shudder against his solid warm body, biting my lip to keep from crying. Though I dearly want to collapse back into him, I remember myself. So I dig my arms into my stomach to calm the spasms racking my chest. He *must* have felt my shape when he grabbed me.

"You're okay," he says.

He wheels Franny around to face a longhorn that charges toward us. "Got to tie up a few strands." Franny engages the steer in a kind of mincing dance, matching it step for step until it tires of the footwork and rejoins its brethren. "Thatta girl."

West starts to whistle. In my fog of exhaustion, whistling strikes me as absurd. Still, the simple tune works at my mind like a carding comb through wool.

I look back at the burning tree, which is starting to burn itself out. Thank God the ground underneath is dirt and not grass, otherwise the whole prairie would be aflame by now. As I'm thinking this, the thunder and lightning end and here come their dawdling children, plump droplets falling from the sky. The blessed rain douses the final embers of the tree fire and dampens the livestock's spirits.

West stops behind a cottony ox thrashing at a bush. "This one's bushing up. They get confused, and you have to dig 'em out before they hurt themselves."

West wings his lariat under the ox's hind foot, then snaps his wrist up. Franny digs in her heels, and West reels in his catch, helping the ox remember it can go backward. In one smooth motion, West dismounts. Then he picks his rope off the ox's leg and slaps it on the rear.

As the sun reappears, the rest of the livestock begin foraging like nothing ever happened. Whoever they belong to hasn't come to claim them yet.

Peety, Andy, and Cay trot up to us. All the mirth has left Cay's eyes. A shaking Andy lets out her breath and raises her hand to the sky, like she's giving thanks.

Peety claps my shoulder and says in a gentle voice, "Hey, Chinito, you never be boring with us, *sí?*"

I nod, trying to switch my mask of terror for one of calm.

"God must think you're a good one, he don't let the lightning touch you. Is miracle." He reaches over to rub my face with his gloved hands. The waxy leather smooths the last of my tears away. "I will give Him extra thank-yous tonight, for you and Andito."

West winds his rope, pulling the loops taut with more force than necessary. He glances at Cay. "You're a fool, and one day you're going to get us all killed."

"Don't worry, I already got an earful from that one," says Cay, flicking his gaze to Andy. He hits me on the other shoulder and pushes my hat down on my head. "You okay?"

"Shouldn't have treed him," West says, taking Franny's reins. He says *him* so casually, I convince myself he did not figure me out after all.

"Oh come on, how was I supposed to know?" protests Cay.

"Half the stampedes we see are caused by thunder." West holds Franny's reins while I slide off, trying not to fall in the mud.

"It's okay," I say. My voice is scratched and raspy from all the screaming.

Cay glares at the underside of his hat brim, then glances down at me. "Sorry, kid, I owe you one. You can kick me in the nuts if you want, or I can give you all my money."

"I'd go with the nuts," says West. "He only has four dollars."

I hook an arm around Franny's neck and will my legs to stop trembling. "Thank—"

"Why don't ya walk her off?" West interrupts me. He kisses his horse on the nose, then hands me the reins.

"Well, thank *you* anyway," I tell Franny, patting her neck.

Andy dismounts. "I'll come with you."

Franny leads us toward the pine forest.

Andy nudges me with her arm. "Lord almighty, I almost bit off my tongue when I saw that tree catch fire. You's tougher than I thought."

"Just keeping up appearances. And anyway, I wasn't the one on the bronco. You held on real good, like a professional."

"Yeah, up until I fell off," she says, looking at me out of the corner of her eyes. "I'm just glad Peety heard you screaming. Thanks for that. I got so turned around, I didn't know which way was up or down."

"You don't have to thank me. Peety did all the work."

"Yeah, well, I guess we both needed a bit of rescuing today. At least Peety said I don't have to ride her anymore if I don't want to."

"He said that?"

"Uh-huh, right after I almost chucked up on the back of his shirt."

When she looks at me, her severe expression softens, and soon we're both laughing. I glance behind me. West is watching us.

The wind scrubs the slate clean once again, leaving behind not a single cloudy smudge in the turquoise sky. The walk unwinds me, and soon I'm taking deep lungfuls of pine-scented air. Like Father often said, *Breathing is underrated.* On our Sunday nature walks, he would stop, close his eyes, and inhale so deeply, his spine would flex backward like a violin bow.

Something pink shoots out from a hydrangea shrub and bumbles toward us. A piglet.

"Aw, where did you come from?" Even in my weariness, I can't help myself in the presence of a baby.

I pick her up and kiss her on the head. "Isn't she sweet?"

"Sure. She'd be even sweeter with a side of applesauce."

"Andy!" The piglet shivers, so I put her inside one of my shirts. Nothing soothes the soul like a warm piglet against your stomach.

She frowns at me. "You'll live longer if you don't get attached to your food."

My bundle wriggles, and an ear peeks out between my shirt flaps. Andy's face relaxes. "My little brother, Tommy, had a piggy just like this one, pink with white spots that looked like soap bubbles. Isaac gave Soapy to Tommy as a reward for cleaning out the stables without crying. He was terrified by the horses." She scratches the piglet's velvety head. "You's hands bad? Let's see 'em."

I open them. A cut runs across one of my palms and there's debris stuck all over. Andy takes off her bandanna and lightly whacks my palms to get off the larger particles. "Good thing we got a needle. But this one, I'll take care of right now." She pulls out a larger splinter with her fingernails.

I look toward the sparkling forest to distract myself. Surviving a burning tree didn't make me any braver. From out of the shadows, I am startled to see four men emerge, twenty yards away.

"Andy!" I whisper loudly.

The men stare at the scene before them. The biggest of the lot sports a crop of red hair and is scratching his matching beard. I put him at fifty. He beckons to us, waving both arms above his head, as if he was not visible enough.

Andy passes me a weary look. They already saw us. We can't just ignore them.

"Just keep thumping your tail," she says as we make our way toward them.

Someone whistles sharply: Peety, calling to West and Cay. The boys ride over to the men and arrive just before we do.

The redhead introduces his companions. "This is Mr. MacMartin and his boys, Ian and Angus—from Scotland."

The MacMartins share the same stocky build. The sons, in their twenties, wear twin scowls and matching hair styles, blond hair clipped close to the skin. Yellow stains bloom around the armpits of their once-white shirts.

The wrinkles in Mr. MacMartin's forehead crimp. "If it weren't for yer quick actions, we'd be in a right fine mess, nae, boys?" His thick brogue requires time to wade through.

Cay snaps his fingers in my direction. "Translator! You speak Scottish?" I can tell by the twinkle in his eye that he is teasing, but Angus's and Ian's blue eyes frost him from either direction.

"Fluently," I say.

Angus clenches his fists. A scar running down his cheek blanches when he scowls. "Any eejit can catch a bunch of cows and pigs." His voice grates my eardrums like a rusty fork raked across bone China.

"And any eejit can lock down the cows and pigs instead of nipping the bottle," counters Mr. MacMartin. "Hell slap you and your bruv. What these boys did was pure brilliant."

"All these bogging tumpshies did was snatch some glory they've nae earned. Stupid animals always come home to what feeds them, nae?" huffs Ian, taller of the two with a piglike snout and a rash of red pustules across his cheeks. A tattoo of a ram prepares to leap off his biceps as he flexes his arms. He rocks forward onto his toes, maybe to reach Cay and West's height. I can smell his spirits from where I stand.

"Well, I never heard of no tumpshie," says Cay, "but a child owes his daddy more respect than that."

"Child?" Angus snaps. "Compare to me, lad, you're a baby, and what you did was baby work. Try catching cougars or bighorn. Until you can trek real animals, shut your geggies."

Cay's good nature dissolves. "My what?"

West is giving off his hard look with the twin arches of disapproval and a tight mouth, the one he usually reserves for me. This time, though, his top lip curls for half a second. I notice the rope under his crossed arms.

"As wagon leader, I want you to take your sons back to their wagon for a splash a' cold water," says the redhead, drawing his bulk up to full height, which I guess to be well over six feet. "There will be penalties for their negligence and rudeness."

Angus spits in the dirt. Cay and West glower like they wouldn't mind enforcing some penalties of their own. Andy's nose wrinkles in disgust.

Peety's the only one with half a smile left on his face. "Hey, amigos, you need help tucking your sons in, you let us know."

My piglet decides she's had enough of the bickering and squirms free. She drops to the ground with a squeal.

"Son of a bitch," says Ian. "That chink tried to steal your pig."

The slur and the accusation hit me like a double slap on the cheeks. "Did not," I lash back. "I was keeping her warm."

Andy elbows me, a warning.

Mr. MacMartin's face colors. "Angus, Ian, mind now! Go on back."

The piglet goes to sniff at the ground, bringing her too close to Angus. His eyes glint. When he steps back, I know what he plans to do. I throw myself on top of the piglet.

"No!" I cry.

Angus's boot bites me in the ribs. I gasp and curl up like a pill bug. The piglet squeals as she races off.

"Sammy!" yells Andy, running to me. She helps me up as I try to draw air back into my lungs.

"Peety," says West. He puts a short length of cord between his teeth.

"*Sí.*"

Quick as a blink, West pitches a loop over Angus and jerks hard. Before Ian can help his brother, Peety lassoes him, too. In less than twenty seconds, the MacMartins are kneeling in the mud, arms roped to their sides. West spits the cord from his mouth and pulls it across Angus's thick neck.

The redhead opens his hands at Mr. MacMartin, who in turn, holds up his. "All right, lads, I thank you for your help, but we'll take it from here."

"Say you're sorry," says West through clenched teeth.

Angus spits again. West pulls the cord even tighter. "I didn't hear you."

Angus glows bright red now, his blue eyes popping out at me. "Sorrea," he says, which might be the worst word he had to use all day.

West turns Angus to face his father. "And to your daddy."

"Sorrea," Angus repeats, lacking sincerity.

"Anyone else need an apology here?" asks West, forcing Angus's head to look around at us.

No one says anything. Ian scowls.

"Aye, then," says Mr. MacMartin. "Boys, let's go."

West and Peety pull their catches to their feet and free them. The young men stumble after their father. As they leave, Ian slits his eyes at West and spits out something that sounds like a hex.

"You okay, son?" the redhead asks me.

My clothes are muddy and my face is probably covered with black smudges. I can't think of a part of me that doesn't hurt, but I say, "Yes, sir."

"Those boys been in and outta prison all their lives back home," says the redhead. "The father brung 'em out here to get a fresh start. But the iron hardened on them long ago."

"Well, sir, they can't be blamed for the lightning," says Cay. "Bovines will stampede when you say boo."

"'Tis true, but theirs was the job to secure the rest of the live-stock. The oxen would not go far by themselves, likely, but when everyone starts running, 'tis a race to the death."

He lifts his heels then rocks back onto them, his large hands folded in front of him. "Again, much obliged for your work. I shudder to think what could've happened. You shall be paid for your troubles. We have twelve wagons up about a mile. If you could do us the last favor of moving our animals back, we would appreciate it."

Cay touches his hat. "Will do, sir."

"This one's dragged out," says West, glancing at me. "You might want to take him with you."

No doubt he is thinking on how much work I am and once again wishing they had left us—me—behind.

"Andito, you go, too, bring Franny and get her some oats, okay?" Peety says. "We'll join you later." Andy runs to fetch her saddlebag, while I retrieve my violin case off Princesa's back.

"I didn't catch your name," says West to the redhead. "I'm West Pepper."

"Olin Bartholomew, wagon leader," says the man. "Most people call me Sheriff."

15

"I WORE THE STAR FOR EIGHT YEARS," SAYS THE
sheriff as Andy and I reluctantly follow him back to his wagon
train. "Boone County, Missouri. I know trouble when I see it, and
those MacMartin boys are it. Thinking about casting their wagon
out. Sure, they're good trackers. Skills like that come in handy on
the trail when you're looking out for bears and such, eh?" He hits
me on the back, hard enough to set off a fit of coughing.

"If it weren't for the Broken Hand Gang—well, I just couldn't
do that to their father." He casts Andy a suspicious eyeball. "Say,
those gang members aren't friends of yours, are they?"

"No, sir," she says adamantly, glaring at the ground.

"Well, that's good."

"Lotsa black people in this country," she mutters to me, then
picks up her pace. The sheriff and I step it up, too. Maybe she's
trying to wind him so he can't ask us further questions. It doesn't
work.

"So, you boys got family?" he asks.

"Nope," we say simultaneously.

"Neither of you?"

We shake our heads at each other, realizing this is suspicious.

126

"What a shame. Where from you traveling?"

"Texas," I say, as Andy says, "St. Louis."

We struggle to keep our poker faces while he scratches his beard. Andy stoops extra low, looking for potato bugs, deciding I should be the one to talk.

"I started in Texas and sh—" I catch myself with a cough. "He started in St. Louis."

"Either of you boys know how to tie a Texan overhand knot?"

"Sorry," I say, even though I'm the one supposed to be from there.

Just as I'm ready to throw off my hat and plead for my life, at last we clear the forest. The open plains sweep before us cut by a swathe of the Little Blue.

"Aha, here we are," he says.

The pioneers have daisy-chained their wagons into a circle, a dozen in all, except that two of the wagons are overturned, probably from when the animals broke free. Some folks collect spilled contents, while others repair damaged wheels, their tools rapping out a noisy symphony. Inside the circle, the rest of the emigrants buzz around the canvas hive fixing dinner.

The sheriff wraps a heavy arm around each of our shoulders and steers us toward a wagon painted bright green. Who was it who mentioned a green wagon? I stop in my tracks when I remember the rosy-cheeked gent who stole us across the Dirty Missouri.

Mr. Calloway was trying to catch up with his wagon train, a train that included a green wagon. Of course, it's just my Snake

luck that I ran into it. Thanks to Deputy Granger, Mr. Calloway knows that there's a slave and a Chinese girl on the run. If
he sees us, he'll raise the alarm.

Andy is already tipping her hat farther down her face. My
eyes careen around the campsite in search of the man, with his
red-flannel shirt and stout form.

The sheriff shades his eyes. "There's my missus." He booms,
"Melissa! We got some guests."

A woman in a calico dress twists her head away from a group
of people and squints at us. The pioneers drop what they're doing
and gather around, some smiling, others frowning. Fifty pairs of
eyes scrutinize my boy act as the late sun glares its disapproval.
My shirts stick to my body like layers of a winter-melon pastry.

At least Andy and I are covered in soot and mud, which may
help to disguise us.

The sheriff introduces us, then recounts the stampede. When
he finishes, everyone starts clapping and praising God. I stick
my hands in my pockets and grunt to discourage people from
coming too close. One grateful fellow reaches out his hand to
shake mine and I give him a curt nod. No one tries to shake
Andy's hand.

The sheriff's wife, Mrs. Bartholomew, bows her head. "Thank
thee Lord for sending Your angels to help us."

"Mrs. Bart will get you cleaned up for dinner," says the sheriff. "Joseph, give this horse some oats."

Mrs. Bart pulls us by the arms away from her husband and
toward the green wagon. Her bonnet disappears into its canvas
cover.

So far, no sign of Mr. Calloway. Dare I hope more than one green wagon roams the prairie?

Mrs. Bart hands us two sacks. "Clean rags, soap."

My throat closes when I spot *Whistle* marked on the sides of the bags. Father had the blacksmith make that stamp for us. Every Monday afternoon, I pressed in the marks while he held the fabric taut. I stiffen my lips to hold back the sob that wants to escape.

"Thank you, ma'am," says Andy, taking the sacks.

I stumble after them, trying to empty my head. I can't think about Father right now. Curious eyes follow as Mrs. Bart marches us through the circle to the farthest wagon.

Mrs. Bart stops in front of a woman hanging clothes on a line. This new woman wears her faded brown hair in a long braid. Smile lines mark the corners of her mouth and eyes. "Why, who's this, Mrs. Bart?"

"Andy and Sammy. They and their friends saved our livestock."

"Praise be," says the woman, clasping her hands to her bosom.

"I wondered if you might lend them some of Thomas's clothes until theirs can be washed. Three are to follow shortly."

"Of course."

To Andy and me, Mrs. Bart says, "Mrs. Calloway's husband has not yet arrived."

Andy's eyes widen as she finally puts the pieces together. "When you's husband gonna get here?"

Mrs. Calloway puts a finger to her sun-dappled cheek. "Tomorrow, I hope." She glances at two younger versions of herself scrubbing clothes on their washboards. "Though he hates to be separated from us. If he's been traveling day and night, he might arrive tonight."

My gut tightens and I clench my toes to keep my feet from making tracks away from here.

"Then again," the woman muses, oblivious to the hot poker she's waving around Andy and I, "the poor man is just not as young as he thinks he is. No, he'll be here tomorrow."

We'll be gone by tomorrow, but it won't matter either way. Mrs. Calloway will tell her husband about the Chinese boy and his negro friend and he'll figure it out. He'll tell the sheriff, who will put out the word, and the news will spread like a traveling hobo.

I'm about to drop dead of anxiety when the two girls leave their tubs to join us, drying their hands on their aprons. Apple cheeks flecked with freckles and frizzy hair reined in by braids, they angle themselves for a better look under our hats. Teenage girls. The worst kind of trouble. They will sniff us out for sure.

I square my stance and put on my fiercest grimace, lips curled back and nostrils flaring. My arms lock tightly in front of my chest.

"Go wash yourselves by the river," Mrs. Bart tells us. "Would you mind taking a few buckets to haul back water for Mrs. Calloway? She only has Mary and Rachel to help her." The girls dip a half curtsy as she calls their names.

"'Course not, ma'am," says Andy.

Mary cups her hands to her cheeks and says in a wispy voice, "Oh, a Celestial!"

I wince at the irritating term for Chinese people.

"You're a cowboy?" asks Rachel in a voice laced with doubt.

I nod curtly, then swivel my face left and right to avoid the trap of her gaze.

Mrs. Calloway puts a gentle hand on my back, as if we are kin. "There was an Oriental man at one of the stores in St. Joe. Do you know him?"

I swallow hard and my face falls. "I—" My voice catches in my throat. "Yes, I knew him. He was a fine man. The finest." I'm revealing too much, but I can't help it.

"Was?"

I glare at the ground. "He died."

"I'm sorry to hear that." Her voice is soft as a baby's breath. "Well, that part of the river is most private, hidden by lovely cedars." She nods toward a patch of green a hundred yards away.

The girls fetch us two sets of their father's clothes, one for each of us, and we head to the river.

Father always said, *If you cannot be brave, then imagine you are someone else who is.* So I imagine myself as him, my optimistic father, whose step never wavered, whose face never hid in shadows. Lifting my chin, I march after Andy as if my cares were few and my outlook, golden.

16

WE ROUND A HEAP OF FOLDED CANVAS AND SPOT the MacMartin brothers squatting in the dirt constructing tents. Their father's tongue lashes them in his thick speech.

"You want to gang back to a life of tracking?" asks Mr. MacMartin, shaking a stick back toward the trail. "Slupping through the muck for pennies a hyde? That what ye want?"

As we hurry by, I can feel Angus's and Ian's cold gaze following us, lifting the hairs on my neck.

"I bet those boys bit their way out of the womb," Andy whispers.

Once we reach the cover of the cedars, we place the saddle-bag and my violin case by a rock and quickly strip our clothes. The water runs clearer here than where we won our fishing bet, but it's just as cold. I count that as a good thing for my stinging hands, which quickly go numb.

"Maybe I should leave my face dirty," I say.

"Too suspicious. They sent us out here to get clean."

I scrub myself of dirt with one of Mrs. Calloway's rags, powered by nervous energy. With Mr. Calloway's pending arrival, surely the end is near. "Maybe we should make a run for it. The more distance we put between us and people who know our past, the better."

Andy rubs water from her eyes. "I know what you's saying, Sammy, but they already saw us. What's going to happen will happen, and when it does, I'd rather have those boys by our side."

She disappears under the water, leaving me frowning. She has a point. The boys wrapped up the MacMartin brothers as easily as if they were bakery boxes. But even the thought of West's quick reflexes doesn't chase away the calamity imps flying around me.

Father said all imps must be controlled through the mind. One watermelon, two watermelons...

Andy breaks through the water and clears her eyes. "What you's gut telling you?"

"I don't know."

"Well, mine is telling me I'm hungry, so let's go with that."

The bleating calls of the returning herd remind us to shake a tail feather. The boys will be taking their own bath soon.

I'm about to lift myself out of the water when the sound of giggles stops me in my tracks. I sink back down and motion for Andy to do the same.

Rachel and Mary emerge from the cedars toting buckets.

"We ain't finished yet," growls Andy in a voice much deeper than mine.

"You forgot the buckets for the water," says Rachel brightly. "Just set 'em down."

They put the buckets on the bank, but instead of leaving, they stand there, twirling their skirts back and forth like feather dusters.

"You want something?" asks Andy. To me, she whispers without moving her lips, "We ain't got nothing you don't already got."

Mary pulls at her braids. "Mother says to fetch your dirty clothes."

"Oh," Andy says, letting her breath go. "Right there."

The girls gather up the laundry at a snail's pace, holding up the shirts one at a time. I groan. What could be more uninteresting than seeing another shirt after an afternoon of doing laundry?

The boys will be here any minute. Sweat collects on my brow while the rest of me turns blue from the frigid waters.

"Why do you wear so many shirts?" asks Mary.

"'Cause we's cold, and we's getting colder the longer you take," snaps Andy. Mary pulls down her Cupid's-bow mouth and snatches up the last shirt.

"What's this?" asks Rachel, stooping down to pick up something.

"Looks like an apron tie," says Mary, as Rachel waves the pink scrap of fabric in front of her. Andy's lips come apart.

"I use it to bind my leg boils," says Andy. "So let it be."

With a look of disgust, Rachel drops the tie and hurries away, followed by Mary.

"Finally," I mutter.

We hear the boys' voices. Andy's face crumples.

I wade toward the shore. "Quickly!"

The boys saunter forth from the trees, coming head to head with the girls. The boys' faces are lit with laughter. Cay's shirt hangs open. Mud covers his chest and one side of his face.

Mary drops the bundle she's holding. Her hands flutter around her face. "Oh!" Another sparrow just flew into the cat's mouth.

Cay and Peety bend to help her collect the clothes while Rachel faces off with West.

I look at Andy and jerk my head toward the shore. *Now.* We dive for Mr. Calloway's bright plaid shirts, yanking them on faster than minutemen. Thank God the shirts are long enough to cover our bottoms. Facing the river, we hitch up our trousers, then twist around to assess the damage.

The girls, now in the presence of real cowboys, can hardly contain their delight. No one's paying attention to us. I blow out a shaky breath as I finish buttoning my shirt. Andy secures her apron tie. We fill our buckets and head back to the circle.

Not a hand lies idle when we return to our hosts. One group of pioneers chops turnips while others stir bubbling cauldrons of stew. Yet another group pulls hot buns off the skillets with iron tongs. After we bring Mrs. Calloway the water, Andy and I huddle together around her fire.

As an honored guest, the only fingers I lift are the ones Andy plucks splinters from. Her own nimble digits prick and dislodge oak bits with efficiency, not hesitating to stab when necessary. To comfort myself, I think of West, and how secure I felt when his arms caught me.

"Twenty-two," says Andy finally. She squeezes my shoulder. "You dulled my needle."

I pat the blood off my hands with a wet towel. "Thank you. I don't know what I'd do without you."

Her mouth presses into a soft smile. "Soak you's hands in a little tomato juice. The splinters come right out. It's messy, though."

"I don't just mean the splinters."

"I know." She slowly cleans her needle. "We watch each other's back, don't we?"

"Yes, we do."

She stares through a stack of napkins weighed down with a stone. When she notices me watching her, she smiles. "Now don't give me that long face. It's gonna be all right. You's gonna find your Mr. Trask, and then you won't have to worry about things like splinters and burning trees."

"What about you?"

"I won't have to worry about your splinters, either." She bumps me with her elbow. "That was some fancy roping back there. Might be useful on the trail. You think the boys would teach us if we ask?"

I snort. "We have to be worthy, first. Some of them are still getting used to the idea of playing nursemaid."

"You's sweet on West."

"What?"

"Mmhm," she says, not suffering fools.

"Is it obvious?"

"Yep, but only 'cause I know you don't have a rattle. Don't worry, men catch on slower. You might want to thump your tail a little harder, though."

Soon, we are sopping stew with skillet bread. The darkening sky drapes a helpful veil across our faces. Someone pours me a mug of hard cider, which fizzes on my tongue. I down the sweet brew and ask for another, remembering to thump my tail. The Calloway girls delight in serving us, or rather, they delight in serving the boys who've grown into their manly physiques. Naturally, Cay basks in the attention.

Talk turns to the Broken Hand Gang. "That poor man lost two of his mules and half his supplies," says an older fellow who wheezes every time he breathes. "Surprised they didn't just take the whole wagon."

"They break his hand?" asks Cay.

"No, but they shook him up good. Man wouldn't talk for a week."

"You think Father will be okay?" Rachel Calloway asks her mother.

Mrs. Calloway musters a smile. "Yes, I think so. The Lord watches over His sheep."

"Yesterday we passed federal marshals combing the trails back to St. Joe. I wouldn't worry too much," West tells Rachel. She nearly levitates under his gaze.

"We'd be happy to look for him, if you'd like," adds Cay.

My neck cracks as I raise my head. *Look for him?* Maybe we'll have to run away after all.

"Oh!" cries Mary Calloway, feasting her adoring eyes on Cay. She presses her fist, still clutching a biscuit, to her bosom.

"That is so kind of you to offer," says Mrs. Calloway.

I don't breathe. Calamity imps, anxiety imps, all of them descend upon me at once, flapping their wings and screeching.

"However, that won't be necessary," she continues. "We cannot think with our emotions, or let hysteria guide our decisions."

Andy puts down her napkin, and her spooked eyes recede into their sockets. I drown my relief in cider.

Mrs. Calloway pulls the lid off a pan of cake. "Mary, pass around the cake. Let's speak of lighter matters."

"You got any stories about your adventures?" Rachel gushes, scooting closer to West.

"Er, well," he says, backing away a fraction.

"Oh, please," she begs.

From under her hat, Andy sticks her tongue out at me and rolls her eyes.

I flash her a smile and finish my second glass of cider. Then I pour myself another.

"I ain't much of a storyteller, miss," West replies. "But Cay's got a head full of them—some are even true."

As Cay regales them with a story of the cousins' first cattle drive, the girls hang on his every word, gasping and sighing in all the right parts. Rachel keeps cutting her eyes to West, and I cannot blame her. He also takes my breath away. The shadows of the fire play over his face and catch the glitter in his dusky eyes. I envy his old shearling coat, wrapping his sturdy shoulders in a furry embrace.

I stare at the bottom of my tin cup, which I can see again.

"That steer eyed me right in the peepers, horns so close I could swing on them. I had no horse, no rope, hell, not even a hat. So you know what I did?" Cay asks in a hush, leaning in.

"What?" ask the girls, also leaning in.

Cay waits. Not even the fire dares to crackle. Then, "I told it to shoo with my mind." He touches his cup to his temple.

"No!" the girls gasp as one.

"That steer turned tail and walked off." He walks his fingers through the air. "Power of the mind. It's a real thing."

West sucks the tip of his finger, then flicks it up. "That one ain't true. You think he'd use his mind if his mouth still worked?"

The girls giggle. Mrs. Calloway, her face crinkling, allows the yin and yang of male bravado and female adoration to ebb and flow.

"Does it ever get lonely out there?" asks Mary in her spider-webby voice.

"Sure it does," says Cay in a rare moment of gravity. "But those times make looking on the fair faces of our gentle sex more meaningful."

West chuckles.

Cay turns to him. "What about you, wisecracker?"

All eyes shift to West, who is drinking a cup of milk. He puts down his cup and studies his crossed boots. "Well, sure, it gets lonesome. But I don't mind. I find cattle"— he pauses as he searches for the word—"simple. Nothing tricky or mysterious about a single one of them. That's more than can be said about certain folks, and if that means I'm lonesome some of the time, 's all right by me."

Rachel releases a girlish sigh, almost in West's lap by now.

I think about the deceit I've already practiced upon him and hang my head. Even if I do outrun the law, I will always be a trickster and a liar in his eyes. And after he saved my life, too. I hug my knees to my chest to stem my insides from pouring out.

"You ever shoot anyone?" breathes Rachel, fluttering her eyelashes at West.

I snort loudly through my nose. The biscuit's on the plate, sister, not sitting next to you. Maybe West likes a little buttering, however, because he shows her a dimple. Oh, brother.

I pound my empty cup into the dirt and raise my finger. "I shot shum-one." Why is my tongue so sluggish? All eyes turn to me.

"Thaj right. My licked wanlord." Wicked landlord, same thing. "Yup. I dijit 'cause he's in my way. Like a big moosh."

Cay screws up his eyes at me.

"Moosh," I repeat more emphatically. Doesn't he know what a moose is? "Mooshes can't just knockem the squirrjels on their wayj to the berry-bushels. So I shot 'im." I make my fingers into a gun and pretend to fire.

Andy splays her fingers out in front of her, eyes held wide in suspense. I do tell a good story. But now I need some fresh air. The heat from the bonfire smothers me.

"Ma'am, please scooz me," I say to Mrs. Calloway.

I rise, too fast, for my head spins. Someone must have filled my boots with water; I can hardly walk straight. I step over the tongue of a wagon and stumble toward the river, but then my feet take another turn and lead me into a copse of conifers. Above me, yellow and purple clouds puff out above the tree line, like someone punched the sky in the face. My knees wobble, and I grab on to the puzzly bark of a pine.

Now my insides really are pouring out. I retch out my pioneer dinner.

"Sorry," I choke out to Mr. Pine Tree.

My stomach feels better now, but my head still spins. The sky has charcoaled. I doubt I can make it back on my own two feet. I wander around for several minutes among the pine trees until I realize I'm going in the wrong direction. When I finally move back into open space, the wagon circle appears as one bright blur, even farther away now.

A noise freezes my blood. There in front of me, two goblins with bad haircuts are cackling. Someone's bent over on the ground between them. I recognize the way her coat drapes over her form. It's Andy.

17

"ANDY!" I CRY, FORCING MY LEADEN FEET TO MOVE.
I make it a step, then two.

Both Scots straighten when they notice me. Ian tosses whatever he's holding—a bottle?—from one hand to the other. "Chinkies, they're the easiest to trek. They got a reek, like vomit, for they can never hold their drink." He wiggles the bottle at me.

"Or you can just watch where their blackies go. They follow them like dugs. Here, blackie," says Angus, making sucking noises with his tongue and holding a coil of rope toward Andy. "Got a leash for ye."

God help me. I can't unravel what these Scots are saying, but it isn't good.

Andy gets to her feet and hurries over to me. I fumble for my gun. Not again. I can't. But that survival thing stirs me to lift it and point.

"Shtay awray from her," I order. Andy's eyes go wide and nearly glow. She shakes her head at me. What? Heaven help me, did I just call Andy "her"?

They laugh and close in. And I must do this thing that will

cement my place in hell, but I have no choice, once again, for the others are too far away to hear or notice us. The flames lick at me already.

Damn! Why am I moving like molasses down a sheet of ice? They separate, and I don't know which one to shoot first. How do I work this? My unpracticed hands shake visibly.

"Such a bonny wee thing, so dear when you cry," says Angus.

When I cock back the hammer, they stop moving and look at each other.

"I's syr-ius," I slur out, then burp.

Ian bursts out laughing and now so does Angus. So I growl menacingly, which only makes them laugh harder.

"Give it to me." Andy whispers to me. "You's gonna kill you'self."

She wants the gun? "Need to shoots jem first." They draw closer. I set my jaw. You dumb eggs. I am wanted for murder. Come on, then.

Angus approaches us with his rope held out. "C'mere, you dugs."

I pull the trigger.

Pow! Who knows where the bullet goes? The cockroaches scatter, so I must not have hit them.

Now someone yells from behind. I twist around. The sheriff runs toward us, wielding a shotgun.

My head hurts. Someone glued my eyelids shut. I force them open and behold a silver hairbrush, swinging from the center hoop next to a bucket of tools. Hoop? I struggle to get up as a dark face appears above me.

"Time for you's medicine," says Andy.

"What happened?" I ask, as the details of last night return to me, most of them at least. I didn't hit the Scots, though I did manage to blow a branch off the same pine tree I retched over. Guess trees can have bad luck, too. "Did they hurt you?"

"Just cuffed me on the head. Thank the Lord it's pretty hard. You just worry about you."

"Why?" My head feels twice as heavy as usual and my ears ring. Mrs. Calloway's face eclipses Andy's, her faded brown tresses loose around her shoulders. The woman combs her fingers into the back of my hair and presses a tin cup to my lips. I spew it back out just as she pulls her head out of the way.

"Everyone does that," says Mrs. Calloway. "It's willow bark plus a few other things. It does tend to smell like ripe diapers."

She tips the cup into my mouth again, and I swallow the foul drink, which reminds me of Father's bitter-melon tea.

"Mrs. Jeffers always makes her cider too strong," she says. "Of course, girls shouldn't be drinking so much anyway."

"What?" gasp Andy and I at the same time.

"I'm a midwife. I can tell these things even if the others can't. You mind telling me why?" She tilts her kind face toward me, then Andy.

Andy looks at me. I shake my head no.

"I will answer that question," I say. My tongue still lags behind my thoughts, but it's improving. "It's cuj, we're slaves-es."

Now Andy's inspecting the stuff swinging above us and shaking her head, though she should be paying attention.

"Well, *we* are abolitionists," says Mrs. Calloway. "And last time I checked, Chinese people aren't slaves here in the U.S."

Andy goes still. "You know a man named Obadiah?" she asks slowly.

Mrs. Calloway's gray eyes sharpen. "Yes, he's a cooper, though he's missing a thumb."

I'm not sure I've heard correctly and try to sit up again, but Andy pushes me down.

"I'll be." Andy chuckles. "Your husband was supposed to be my Moses wagon. Lord, You's almighty. See, I was running away." She turns to me: "Obadiah's our code word. She's part of the Railroad."

Dimly, I recall how Andy was planning to run away on her own before Miss Betsy made her scrub me down. Andy tells Mrs. Calloway everything, starting with when she found me with Yorkshire on the floor. The woman listens with her hands folded, not interrupting.

After Andy finishes, Mrs. Calloway presses her cool hand to my cheek. "You're not a murderer."

My breath falls out of me. "I'm not?"

"If that man tried to abuse my daughters like that, I hope they would have smacked him, too." Mrs. Calloway's soft voice takes on an edge.

I sag back against the wool blanket, head still dizzy.

Two cackling goblins wait behind my lids, stampeding me

through a maze of pine trees. I scramble up a tree, but they torch it. I climb until I can go no farther, and wait for the flames to take me.

When my eyelids finally snap open, I am alone, my head drenched in sweat. Dawn spills through the cracks of the wagon.

Andy sticks her head into the wagon. "Oh, good, you's up." She passes me a dipper of water and I drink up. It's so cold, it makes my head throb.

"There's someone here to see us."

"What? Who?" I ask as my stomach rumbles with nausea. At least my tongue is starting to work again.

I stumble out the back of the wagon, blinking in the thin light of morning. The campsite has been tidied, the crates and pots put away, and trees cleared of laundry. Twenty yards away, a mule is chewing on dandelions. Mr. MacMartin is holding her reins. He looks so remarkably like Angus that I hesitate to go any closer.

But Andy jerks her head toward him. "Come on. And just in case you forgot, you's still a boy."

As I draw near, I realize that instead of the icy eyes of his sons, Mr. MacMartin has sad eyes, with puffs of flesh underneath that Chinese people believe are caused by too much worry.

"Boys, I beg both of yer forgiveness on account of mah sons' behavior," he says. "We're leaving the train. A'm taking them back to Iowa."

"Oh. I'm sorry," I say, a sentiment that Andy does not echo.

"Nothing tae be sorry for. Methinks 'tis fair th' best. I wid lik' ye ta have this mule. A present from me."

I lift my hand to stifle a surprised gasp. The mule lifts her head and blinks her long eyelashes at us. Twelve hands tall, light gray in color like Tsing Tsing, but with a downy mane and snow-white tail.

"You's giving us a mule?" Andy exclaims.

He nods. I offer the mule my hand to sniff. She kisses it, and I fall in love.

Ten paces behind, Cay, West, and Peety watch us as they pack up the remuda.

"I think she likes ye already," says Mr. MacMartin, handing me her reins. "Good luck to ye and yer friends."

"Thank you, sir. And good luck to you, too." Andy and I take turns shaking his hand.

After he returns to his wagon, Peety, West and Cay approach us.

Peety rubs the mule's face. "*A Esme le gustaban las mulas. No la has visto, ¿no? Bueno, está bien. Bienvenida a la familia.*"

I translate: Esme loved mules. You haven't seen her, have you? No? Welcome to the family.

Who is Esme?

Andy draws her eyes from the vaquero to me. "You better think of a good name before someone else fixes her with one I can't pronounce."

"Best names are always Mexican," says Peety.

"Then how about Paloma," I say, the Spanish word for

"dove." "She's a gift from heaven." Now Andy won't have to ride Princesa.

"Not bad," says Peety.

"I think you should ride her," says Andy. "I'm gonna give the she-devil another try."

I fix my astonished eyes on her, but she doesn't look at me. Her lips press into a resolute bundle.

"Sure about that, Andito?" Peety asks.

She squares her hat. "I'm sure."

His broad face breaks into a smile. "*Bueno.* Mules got stronger hooves than horses, and more stamina. Paloma might be small, but she's perfect for a lightweight like Sammy."

Lightweight?

"Plus, they're smarter," he adds in a whisper, as if the other horses might overhear.

"I wouldn't get too close, vaquero—a little apple juice makes him deadly," says Cay. He holds out a gloved hand for me to shake, though I'm not sure why. I press hands and pump once, man-style.

Now West claps me on the back and extends his hand. Another pump. "You showed those tumpshies."

Before we leave, the sheriff's crew loads us up with food staples, including Cay's favorite, coffee. We also get bedrolls for Andy and me, and new saddles. The pioneers are generous, but we can only carry so much.

As I feed Paloma a turnip, Andy steps close to me and says in a low voice, "Mrs. Calloway wants to talk to us."

We climb into Mrs. Calloway's wagon again and seat ourselves on chests doubling as benches. The wool rug where I lay this morning pillows our feet.

Mrs. Calloway hands us each a bundle. "You might find these useful without revealing your secret. I made these for the girls to make riding the mules more comfortable. Mary and Rachel have some roundness on you, but they should fit."

Unfolding our bundles, we each find a matching set of camisole and white drawers, trimmed with a bit of eyelet lace. I draw in my breath.

Andy rubs the camisole against her cheek. "No more chafing."

There are also several six-by-three-inch rectangles of tightly quilted flannel. I turn one over in my hand, marveling at the tiny stitches.

"Pads for your monthly cycles. They'll fit right into the drawers," says Mrs. Calloway, beaming at us.

I am overcome. "Thank you, ma'am, for your kindness."

"You're welcome."

Andy and I hurriedly undress and put on the new undergarments.

"Ma'am, you ever heard of a place called Harp Falls?" Andy asks. "S'posed to be on the trail somewhere."

"Harp Falls?" The woman taps a fingertip against one of her rosy cheeks. "Can't say that I have. But if it's a waterfall, it'd have to be in a mountain range. And it's pretty flat until Fort Kearny. Maybe your boys can ask when they get to the fort," says Mrs.

Calloway, straightening Andy's collar. "They have trail experts, there."

"Thank you, ma'am," says Andy. "Tell you's husband I think there was an angel sitting on his wagon that night he saved us."

"I think you are right. Good luck, girls. No road is ever safe but the one you walk with the Lord. I will pray for your safe deliverance." She kisses us both on the forehead. That feels even softer to me than our new underthings.

We ride out at the front of the caravan, and soon leave it far behind. Our new steed means we can pick up the pace, since we no longer need to ride double. Paloma is more than able to keep up with the horses, sometimes frisking way ahead. I worry that Andy won't be able to handle Princesa at our accelerated speed, but she proves me wrong. Though the bay is just as deaf to Andy's commands as yesterday, I sense a fierce new determination in the way Andy holds herself in the saddle, less stiff in the bottom half, more upright in the top.

After we round the head of the Little Blue, we start climbing northward across the high plains that lead to the Platte River.

I cannot stop thinking about those Scots. Did they hear me slip up last night? No. They would have told someone. Anyway, Mr. MacMartin said they're headed to Iowa, which is a different trail from the one that goes to St. Joe. What are the chances they'll run into Deputy Granger or hear word of my crime?

A chill snakes up my spine as I brood over what they might

have done if I hadn't pulled the trigger. How did they plan to use that rope? Tie us up like the boys tied them, or worse?

My skin is clammy and I rub my arms hard to bring life back into them. I still don't know how to reload my gun, let alone shoot straight. Andy doesn't even have a gun. Who knows what other criminals we might encounter? We might not be so lucky next time.

I distract myself by searching out markers to tally our mileage. I find them in tree trunks and rocks and sometimes on paper staked to the ground. Two weeks until Fort Kearny, one-third of the way to the Parting. So far, I have spotted five men with firecracker-red suspenders. By the time I reach the Parting, I will be an expert.

The air thins, so we camp early to give the horses and ourselves a chance to acclimate. We settle near a narrow finger of blue on a sandy area scattered with bundles of switchgrass.

That night around our campfire, I unholster the Dragoon and hold it before me. My face flushes even before I speak. I stand tall and clear my throat.

"Um, does anyone know how to—er—load this?" I stammer. This will cost me their newfound respect, but I have to know.

West's mouth tucks back on one side. Cay whispers to Peety. Peety whispers to West. Andy, scrubbing a pan out with sand, starts to scrub harder, scratching the silence.

I hide my embarrassment under a scowl and reholster the Dragoon. Maybe I'll go jump in the river now. I turn on my heel.

"Sammy." Cay calls me back.

"What?" I ask in a gruff voice. Now all three boys are grinning at me.

"How'd you like to learn to be a cowboy?"

I stare, openmouthed. Andy stops scrubbing her pan.

"You, too, Andito," says Peety, licking the last of Andy's cobbler from his spoon.

18

FIRST NIGHT OF COWBOY TRAINING: FIREARMS.

After a day of dusty travel, we are camped in a clearing surrounded by wild plum trees. Clusters of pink and white flowers already show tight buds of fruit, which Andy used to spice up the pigeon stew. All around us is a flaming sky, reflecting a recently departed sun. Ten paces from the fire, Peety brushes Princesa's teeth with a corncob.

Cay stands in front of us, spinning his Colt around his finger so fast it blurs. Andy, picking burrs out of her new horse blanket, rolls her eyes at me.

It should've been obvious a long time ago that Cay was not born in the Year of the Rabbit like West, but in the Year of the Tiger. The Chinese New Year starts later than the Western calendar year, which means Cay must have been born in early January, when it was still the Year of the Tiger. He's fearless, but a show-off, which leads to recklessness. Yet he could charm the spots off a leopard, so people will follow him regardless. It doesn't hurt that the beauty of Tigers makes them difficult not to watch.

West leans against one of the trees, stripping the leaves off a slender twig. "Stop playing to the gallery. You're going to teach them bad habits. No one spins his gun if he values life and limb."

"Sourpuss." Cay reholsters his piece. "Now kids, the two rules of cowboy brotherhood are: keep your sense of humor, and leave the meddling to women. We had a boss once who liked to stick his nose in everyone's business. You try to cut out a steer and he takes up half your time showing you he can do it better. Or, he'll try to stir up trouble by telling you that your girl was kissing Hank What's-his-face. That kind of person just gets his teeth knocked out, and I'm not sorry I did it, either."

West slices his branch through the air with a snapping sound. "Even if it turns out your girl *was* kissing Hank What's-his-face."

Grimacing, Cay dismisses his cousin with a wave. "Now, Andy, you choose first, because I guess life didn't hand you a lot of first chances. Who do you want to have as your teacher? Sourpuss, or me?"

Andy looks from West to me and her eyes become sly. "I guess I'll go with the teeth knocker." She gets up from her spot next to me. "Don't have too much fun," she drops in my ear. Then she and Cay are making tracks away from the campsite.

I erase all signs of delight from my face. West gives me a hard look then tosses his stick away. Kneeling, he loads his rifle as easy as a reflex, then slings it over his back. He cocks his head to say, *Follow me,* and sets off in the opposite direction from Cay and Andy.

Peety nods at me. "Good luck."

The soft chatter of foraging birds and squirrels replaces the thick Scottish brogue of curses in my head as I pad after West. He walks with the ease of someone with places to go but time to get there. I'm entranced by the fluidity of his movement, like the way he bites on his finger and then flicks it skyward to make a point, to test the wind, to show he's thinking. How he plucks a stem of grass and places it between his teeth.

Yellow doesn't blend with white. "A single drop of yolk can ruin a meringue," the headmistress of a music conservatory in New York told Father when she denied me admittance. Still, I can't help wondering how it would feel to walk a little closer to West, so that our shadows touched. Chinese people believe Rabbits and Snakes make for a propitious union, since the word for happiness, *fu,* looks like the two animals intertwined.

A tree with a fallen branch blocks our path. West sets a hand on the branch, then hops over in one easy motion, barely pulling his chambray shirt out from his trousers. I scale it with a lot more effort, then scamper after him.

We hike through a wooded area tinted violet. The humidity has lifted, and the cool breeze feels as lovely as a fresh sheet against my cheek.

West looks up. "This is the best time to hunt, when the animals are out looking for their suppers. 'Course, with a painted sky, light's not always good."

I never heard anyone call the sky painted before, but it's the perfect word. Clouds outlined in gold streak across the firmament, casting uneven shadows over the landscape.

"My father said that artists see the world differently than normal people. I see a tree where you might see a collection of lines, shapes, and shadows."

"I see a tree, too."

"So it's not true?"

"It ain't true that I'm an artist."

An unladylike honk bursts from my nose. "I've seen—" I halt, wondering if I should be admitting that I peek at his pictures when he draws.

His eyes slide to me. "Drawing's my way of keeping a diary. It don't mean anything else." His voice is gruff, almost defensive.

"If you say so. But artists don't really have a choice in the matter. They create because they have to."

He grunts. "Ain't a proper way to make a living."

"Tell that to Michelangelo. He got more than three thousand ducats for painting the Sistine Chapel in Italy. That's about twenty thousand U.S. dollars."

West blinks as if splashed by water, but doesn't lose his stride.

"The Tudor monarchs would hire a royal painter to follow them around, drawing pictures of them. Sometimes the king's painter was given a fancy title like Baron or Viscount."

Leaves crunch, though I realize I am the only one stepping on them. West carefully avoids the tree litter without even looking at the ground.

"Of course," I prattle on, "the king's minstrel was given a fancy title *and* a pretty wife."

To my surprise, he chuckles, a strangely intimate sound that makes my heart flutter. "So I shoulda taken up the harmonica after all." Stopping, he rests his hands loosely on his hips and sweeps his gaze around me. Then his amusement gives way to something more serious. "That stuff you said about not having a choice. Is it the same way with your music?"

"Yes. My father said I was born with a song in my fingers. I don't know who I'd be if I didn't make music. It's the only thing I ever wanted to do."

"Besides gold rushing."

"Of—of course . . . besides that," I stammer. Then I shut my mouth, hoping I have not inadvertently given myself away.

Thankfully, he does not seem to notice my discomfort. His gaze drifts upward where a hat-shaped cloud is slowly stretching apart. "We best get started."

We park on a bald spot of ground. He tugs the bandanna off his neck and spreads it between us. All we need is a basket and a bottle of wine. As I entertain my picnic fantasy, I don't notice him hoisting his eyebrows at me until he reaches over and lifts the Colt out of my belt. I have been struck stupid.

"How many times you fire this?" He lays the gun on the bandanna.

"Once." I wish I still had hair to hide behind.

"So you didn't shoot a 'moosh'?"

I grimace and shake my head.

Suppressing his amusement, he draws a pouch and two tins from his pockets and lays them next to the gun. His sleeve pulls back to reveal the first two scars on his arm, like two white fingerprints on the back of his wrist. The marks are not raised, like Andy's scar, but they share a neatness of form, as if they were made deliberately. I quickly look away before he notices me studying them, and add Yorkshire's powder horn to the assembly.

He opens the chamber of the Colt and starts filling the five slots with the objects on the bandanna. "First, pour the powder, then wad, bullet, ram it, grease, caps."

I fill the last three slots. My hands shake, though I'm not sure what makes me more nervous, his close scrutiny of my fingers, or the possibility that I could kill us by mishandling the gunpowder. Finally, he takes the gun from me and puts it on full cock.

A mourning dove flutters about a bur oak forty paces to our left. He lifts the gun and sights.

"Don't shoot the bird!" I cry.

"Don't shoot the bird?" he repeats in disbelief, lowering the gun.

Somewhere in the distance, Andy fires Cay's gun, scaring off the dove. West drops his head back and closes his eyes.

"I'm sorry. I favor doves," I babble, wincing at how girly that sounds.

He shakes his head. "Sammy." Then he gives me the gun and pushes my hands toward a tree.

"What?"

"You favor trees?" he mocks.

I suck up my stammering and summon my gruffest voice. "Which leaf?"

"Start with that knot." He points to a depression, wide as my hand, in the same bur oak.

The first shot goes wide and the second goes wider in the other direction. But now I have a feel for the iron, and by the third shot, I hit the knot right in the middle. Shots four and five follow right on its heels.

As long as I don't have to kill anything with a pulse, my hand is steady.

West squints at the tree and then at me.

I blow out the smoke that rises from the barrel. "What do you know? It works."

Second night of cowboy training: riding.

Through a grove of sugar maples, Peety shows us how to turn on a half-dime, and how to handle a horse that bucks.

"Pull head up and move forward. It also helping if you give her compliment before you get on. Tell her she got nice smile, something like that."

"You's kidding me?" says Andy. She draws her arms across her chest, then thinks better of it and drops them to her sides.

"Trust him, no horse ever threw Peety," says Cay.

My mule loves to gambol even after a day of travel and an evening of riding exercises. After I tie her to a pink dogwood, she pulls the whole tree out of the ground chasing a butterfly.

While I spend my time trying to keep Paloma out of trouble, Andy works on overcoming her nerves with Princesa.

"Come on, ya horse, giddap already, can't you feel me kicking?" pleads Andy, giving Princesa another tap with her heels. Princesa drifts to one side, chewing the bluegrass near where Paloma and I are practicing our turns.

Peety wags his finger. "No begging. Order her to giddap."

"I *am* ordering her," says Andy.

"You are conquistador marching into battle, is that how you

command your troops? Horse needs strong leader to feel safe."
He bats his hand at Andy and says in a girlish voice, "Please, if
you do not mind me asking, let us go now."

Andy's mouth falls open.

"I am just a little girl, so scared of my pony," continues Peety
in his high voice, pinching the sides of his imaginary skirt and
tippy-toeing around. Princesa throws back her head and screams,
a scream that sounds uncannily like a shriek of laughter.

That does it. Eyes bulging, Andy pulls back her shoulders. "I
said, giddap!" She stabs in her heels.

Princesa cocks an ear. A moment later, she gits.

Peety drops his act and nods once. "*Exactamente.*"

After more drilling, Andy and I walk our mounts to cool
them down. Peety strolls beside us. "Princesa came to rancho one
day after her owner no want her. Says too much horse for him,
too wild. But he's wrong. She's not wild, she's spirited. 'Wild'
means 'I no care about what I do.' But 'spirited' means, 'I love
what I do.' Big difference."

Third night of cowboy training: roping.

We settle at the top of a grassy embankment, with basswood
trees to our backs, and the trail below us. A ring of wagons lies
on the other side of the trail, their oxen mowing down the scen-
ery all around them.

Andy and I hunker side by side on the grass and watch Cay
jump rope in front of us. Peety and West sit five paces away,
playing poker and half watching Cay. West fans his cards with

one hand, then refolds them by knocking them against his knee.

Cay stops jumping and ties a lariat. "Ropes come in all sizes but cowboy lengths are twenty or thirty feet." The lariat makes a musical whipping sound as it spins.

Cay handles his rope as skillfully as if it were a lady, spinning it with either hand, even crawling through it without letting it touch the ground. After he finishes playing to the gallery, he shows Andy and me how to make six kinds of knots, including a sweetheart knot, which is strong enough to connect two ropes together as if they were one.

"When do you use that?" I ask.

"When you need an extra length, like when you need to catch a wild horse. Or a sparrow." He wiggles his eyebrows.

Finally, he demonstrates how to make a honda by tying an eye splice. Weaving the thin strands of hemp soothes my mind.

"C'mon, Sam, let's throw already." Andy nudges me with the toe of her boot to hurry me up.

"Almost done." I keep my eye on my rope so I don't mix up the strands. This reminds me of how I used to braid my hair. If we had not cut it, I could have spliced my hair around my head as practice.

I get to my feet and dangle my eye splice in front of Cay.

"Not bad. Now, kids, hold the coils in your left, twisting half a turn for each coil so things don't get kinky. Lariat in your right."

We do it. Cay stands between Andy and me with his own rope.

"Since we don't have any good stumps, West will be yours," Cay tells me. Then he turns to Andy. "And you do Peety."

"What?" Andy exclaims.

West and Peety look up from their card game.

"I can't do that," I gasp, taking a step back. "I might strangle my stump."

West dares me with his eyes. "Catching me ain't as easy as it looks."

"Yeah, it is," says Cay. "Pretend he's a mute post, which ain't far from the truth."

He winds up and casts his lariat over West. West shrugs out of it and tosses it back.

Cay hands it back to me. "Your turn. Let's see if Chinamen can do more than bow."

I narrow my eyes. "You offend me."

"Oh-fend? You mean like rile you up? I thought Chinamen never get mad."

Steam trickles out of my ears. That fox wants me to prove him wrong, but I won't play his game. I unclench my jaw and toss my nose in the air.

"Could my stump turn around? He's making me nervous," I say, as coolly as I can.

West throws down his cards and turns around. Stretching out his legs, he leans back on his hands and mutters, "Good luck."

That's it. I will show those hot shots just what Chinamen can do. I crank up my arm, sure someone tied lead weights to my rope given how much it drags.

"You call that an arm? I call that spaghetti," Cay yells. "Put some game into it—you're throwing like a girl."

"I ain't a girl," I growl, stomping the ground a few times to prove it.

"Why you got spaghetti arms, then?"

"At least I don't have spaghetti brains." My eyes catch on one of the blond locks that springs out from behind his ear. Even his curls are mocking me. I stop winding to glower. "We Chinese like our spaghetti arms, which allow us to balance better when we, er, cross bridges."

I apologize to Chinese men everywhere, most of whom don't even know what spaghetti is. Andy pulls the brim of her hat over her ears. With a grimace, I throw as hard as I can, watching in horror as my loop heads toward our blaze, many miles from West. It lands in the nest of flames. Cay jerks back my burning lariat as I pray for a twister to suck me up.

Cay stamps out the rope. "Uh, Sammy, you noodled the fire."

The stumps are shaking with laughter. Even Andy.

I suck in my gut, then cuss and spit a few times. "Why must I learn this?"

Cay flinches like I slapped him. "Don't say that. How you gonna catch anything if you don't know how to rope?"

"Charm. My spiderweb." I chafe, stewing in my own juices. But as the laughter continues, I deflate.

Cay pushes my hat down over my eyes. "No one does it on the first try. Andy's turn."

Gladly, I step aside.

"Hit me with your best shot," Peety says. When Andy winds up, he starts heckling her. "Hey, Andito bandito, I know you wish you can touch this Mayan pyramid, this buffalo body of *músculo*—"

She casts. Her rope does not spin but whips Peety on the side of the head.

"Ow, *chico*."

One glance at Andy's shocked face sets me off. I fall to my knees and let my laughter tumble out.

Each night after cowboy lessons, I drill the boys and Andy on language. I use pages from West's journal to write out Chinese characters for them to memorize, and give them throat and tongue exercises so they can push out the French *r*. Cay likes to turn phrases like "Nice to meet you" into "Nice to meet your lips," but I don't mind as long as he remembers the vocabulary.

The boys take turns requesting songs from the Lady Tin-Yin, and she is always happy to comply, the show-off. Then we lie in our line, surrounded by rope. Most nights, I fall asleep last. The stars are too irresistible, and I don't want to close my eyes. Every time I do, fears start racing through my mind, led by a couple of Scots driving a rabid posse against me.

Eventually, though, I convince myself the MacMartins do not suspect us. Then there's only Father to consume my thoughts. I try not to dwell too much on what he suffered in the fire. That will set off girly tears for certain, and I have not cried since our first day on the Trail.

A hand touches my shoulder one night, and I wake with a confused gasp.

"Sammy."

I am curled in a tight ball, and my face is wet. I gulp and wipe my eyes with my sleeve. West hangs over me.

"I'm sorry," I whisper, unfurling myself.

"Don't be," he says, his voice compassionate.

The stars fade in that exquisite time between night and day, when neither the sun nor the moon shows its face. He settles back down beside me as I grab at the wisps of my dream. I don't remember it now.

"Something happen to you?" he asks.

I long to answer him. But I can't. "Why are you going to California?" I ask instead.

"Cay wants to go there." He takes his time. "He fooled around with the ranch owner's daughter. She said he got her pregnant. He was going to marry her, but then he found out she wasn't with child." He pauses to rub his neck. "Ranch owner wanted him to take his daughter anyway, but Cay didn't love her. So we cut out after we finished the last drive. Won't be going back to Texas for a long time."

"You left your home for him."

"He's family, just like Peety. Can't just give up on family, even when they act like fools."

"What about your parents? Brothers and sisters?"

"I'm an only child. Mama died when I was seven. With any luck, pa's in the ground, too." His voice cools, and I regret bringing them up.

I glance at his triangular earlobes, the telltale signs of a troubled life. "I'm sorry," I murmur once again.

He shrugs. "Ain't the first to have a mean daddy."

I get a pang in my heart, both at his suffering and at the reminder of my fortune in having had a kind father. "Every child deserves his father's love."

He sighs, then doesn't speak for at least thirty watermelons. I think he's fallen back asleep, but then he says in a quiet voice, "This one time, he cuffed me for painting the fence too slow. Blood got into the paint and turned it pink. No matter how much I tried mixing in more white, it still looked pink to me. I finished the fence, but I knew it was no good, even though people couldn't see it. There were certain things about me I could never change, no matter how I tried."

My breath stops short. Somewhere along the way, the subject changed from paint to himself. What things could he not change? A mean temperament? I have known West for less than a month, but I have not seen an ounce of spite in him.

"My father pointed out once that the violets with the deepest color grew from the dung heap." As soon as the words are out, I realize I have equated him with dung. "I mean, er—"

A puff of air curls out of his mouth, giving way to a reluctant smile and even a chuckle. "Sammy," he says in that way I've come to know as part exasperated, part resigned.

I regard his profile, his lips parted slightly, and his perfect eyebrows beginning to knit. It both scares and thrills me to admire his beauty from so close, like I am breaking some law against staring. My gaze wanders to the tiny cleft in his stubbly chin, like a fingernail mark. I clench my fist to stop my fingers from touching it.

He turns to me, but instead of looking away like he usually does, he lingers. Our eyes lock, mine still wet, his tortured, and I glimpse his soul.

They say time freezes, but I've never experienced it until now. I stay like that, lost in his eyes for that eternal moment, and then the dawn breaks, and we are Sammy and West again, boys on the trail.

19

BY THE TIME WE REACH THE HOMESTRETCH TO Fort Kearny, I've roped my stump half a dozen times, and Andy rides Princesa like a Nubian queen floating on a mahogany boat. Peety rewards Andy's improvement by giving her his kid riding gloves, fleece-lined, too.

Our trail soon converges with the one that starts at Independence, Missouri. The road grows thick with wagons and people plodding up to the fort on the hill.

The sun hangs low, so we settle in for the night a few miles past the junction in a sea of wagon circles, people, and animals.

Cay and West go hunting. They only have one rifle between them but hunting is their ritual together. Peety never seems to mind, in fact, I think he enjoys the time by himself. He told Andy he was twenty-one, which means he was born in the Year of the Rat. Though Rats are charming and sociable, they like to spend time in quiet reflection.

Peety leads the horses to a branch of the Platte River, talking to them conversationally in Spanish, while Andy and I collect firewood.

Only a few stringy willows grow among the sandy bluffs, not

enough to hold a flame. To solve this problem, emigrants are throwing buffalo chips onto their fires.

Andy pokes the toe of her boot at a pie-sized chip, then stoops down to collect it. She points her nose at the even bigger pile by my feet. "Get that one."

"Maybe one's enough," I suggest, not wanting to touch buffalo droppings.

But one tiny hitch of Andy's eyebrow tells me to stop being a girl, and pick it up. I pull my sleeves over my hands and retrieve it.

Turns out buffalo chips aren't so horrible. They're dry as skillet bread and scentless. Our two chips catch the sparks and hold them fast, and in no time, our water boils.

"Heard talk of a whetstone half a mile downstream. Think I'll go sharpen the knives." Andy rummages through our gear, collecting the miscellaneous blades: two pocket knives, a hunting knife, and her cooking knife. "You's okay here by you'self?"

"Yes. I'll sift the cornmeal."

She keeps her head down as she hurries in the direction of the river and soon is swallowed into the masses, more folks than I've seen since St. Joe. They're a diverse bunch with common dreams—land for the pioneers, gold for the Argonauts. Judging from the conversations, neither group can wait to reach Fort Kearny, the first trading post since we left civilization. Not me. The place is probably crawling with lawmen. Maybe they even keep a judge on hand so they can try and hang in one shot.

As if summoned by my worries, a trio of scruffy-faced men in navy-blue uniforms materialize out of the haze and skulk toward me. Army men. I drop the sack of cornmeal I'm holding and it spills into the sand.

"Hey, boy," says one of the men. His untucked shirt reveals a protruding belly, and greasy strands of his blond hair stick to his tanned cheeks.

I get to my feet, mouth gaping like a bass, but failing to produce any noise. The men's heads tilt and swivel as they try to make out my face from under the shade of my hat, like a band of coyotes routing out the throat hold. I notice that the cottonwood above my head is sturdy enough for a hanging and forget how to work my lungs.

There's no sign of the boys or Andy, only pioneers briskly going about their business, too far away to notice. I cannot flee since that would confirm my guilt. I step backward, willing the shade of the cottonwood to swallow me up. The men close in.

Blondie's eyes shift around our camp. "Here by yourself?"

All the blood in my body surges to my head as I ransack my brain for the answer to this simple question. I do not want to involve the remuda by saying no. Then again, plainly I have more supplies than one person needs. I sway, but catch myself before I topple over.

"We came to the right party," says another man with hair too gray for a soldier. "He's already full as a tick."

"Well then, I guess you won't mind sharing," says Blondie. "Come on, hand over some of your rookus juice."

A third man, smacking his tobacco, leans in toward me. "You wouldn't hold back from good soldiers protecting their fellow countrymen, would you? Share your stash and we might consider you a patriot." My brain trips over itself trying to keep up, but I can't figure out what he wants.

"Maybe he don't understand." The gray-haired man leans in closer. "Whis-key," he says slow and loud, as if I don't speak English.

A spark jumps out of the fire with a loud *crack* and wakes me from my stupor. "*Yo no—*" I begin in Spanish, quickly switching to Chinese when I realize my blunder. "*Ngoh mm ming baak,*" I say, which simply means, "I don't understand." I pray they will leave me alone now, but Blondie scowls and starts casting his eyes at our supplies.

"Maybe we'll check ourselves," he says. "Bet we find plenty of joy juice in those saddlebags."

I cannot let them put their grubby hands on our things. Perhaps I can scare them away. Father said people fear what they don't understand, and perhaps if I make myself very confusing, they will be very afraid.

Andy appears fifty feet away, slowing when she sees the situation. She begins to hurry toward me, but I shake my head at her. If the soldiers see us together, it might raise their suspicions. The soldier in the back, a thin man, turns to see what I'm looking at, and I quickly unleash in my harshest Cantonese, "For shame, you with the great blond belly. A bear knows better than to eat a porcupine!"

The tobacco-chewing soldier and the gray-haired one look at each other uneasily, but Blondie's face screws up. "Take it easy," he says gruffly.

I cannot stop now, or he will think I am weak. I throw my hands at all of them. "Do you not know that too much alcohol will make your bowels sluggish? Go away, you turtle eggs."

"Maybe we should ask someone else," suggests the gray-haired man.

"Yes, go pick on someone your own size, gender, color, and aptitude," I continue in my foreign tongue. "I am just as much a patriot as you. My skin may be yellow, but I am not"—I glance at my spilled grain—"I am not cornmeal, and you have no right to tread over me, as if I am mush." I kick at the cornmeal, spraying some of it onto the first man's boots. Blondie steps back and soon he is hurrying away after his compatriots.

I collect my breath, and Andy hurries toward me, her kitchen knife held low at her side. She eyes the scattered cornmeal. "What happened?"

"They were looking for whiskey."

Her worried expression turns wry. "Looks like they came to the wrong place."

I crumple onto the ground, my guts flooding with acid. "What if they had...what if—"

"They didn't." Andy makes brisk work of salvaging what cornmeal she can.

I stare at the fire, willing the panic imps to leave.

She bats at my hand. "Stop picking off you's buttons. You's

nervous habits drive me batty. Take off you's shirt." She whips out her needle and reattaches my sleeve button. "We's safe. Nothing gonna bug us tonight except a few stones in the mush."

I crane my neck in every direction, looking for more soldiers. "We can't go to the fort tomorrow."

"All right, we won't," she says solemnly.

Her words of solidarity soothe me. "You ever think about the noose?"

She snorts, then glances at me, though her fingers don't lose their rhythm. "I been thinking about the noose since I was born. You know, sometimes they use thirteen loops in the hangman's knot. That makes it go easy. Six or seven gets the job done, too, if it's hemp. Any less and you got you'self some powerful kicking to do when you swing."

I gulp, never considering this aspect of things.

She swats my arm. "As Isaac always says, no one ever injured an eye by looking at the bright side. We's making good time and flying under the wings of eagles."

I shift my focus to Andy's dark hands, and try to unbend my frown. Next to the stone on the twine bracelet she's worn every day since I met her, she's added a wood button, along with two furry seeds that she somehow punched holes through.

"Why do you collect those things?"

"One day I'm gonna see my little brother, Tommy, again. And I want to show him pieces of where I been."

"I thought he died?"

"He did. See, I figure if this bracelet's on my body when I die, it's going with me to heaven." She stops sewing and holds up her wrist. The baubles line up neatly. "Isaac tucked this rock with the hole in a boll of cotton for Tommy to find. He was always doing silly stuff like that to help the picking go by faster."

She removes the bracelet and lets me hold it. "Tommy said if he looked at a person through the hole, he could see the good in them." She points to the seeds with her needle. "These are from 'Yankee Doodle' night. They dropped on me when we were sitting under that tree. And this button is from Mrs. Calloway. I found it on the floor of her wagon and she said to keep it. Tommy's gonna like that one."

I loop the twine around my finger, remembering Mother's bracelet.

Father gave Mother the circlet of ten different-colored jade stones as a wedding present. A client in New York once offered Father three hundred dollars for it. It's irreplaceable, not because the jeweler only made one, but because it's the only thing that remains of my parents, besides Lady Tin-Yin, of course. Mother never took her bracelet off, which means she believed it was a part of her. She might not have lived long enough for me to know her touch, but if she had, I imagine it would feel like those jade stones: smooth and delicate and full of warmth.

I twist the twine around my finger but it springs away and unwinds. It's quality twine, the kind that has a mind of its own. "It's beautiful."

She puts down her sewing. "It's time to ask the boys if we can keep on with 'em."

I nod. "You don't think we should tell them about us, do you?"

She doesn't answer right away but squints as if divining the future in the smoke of the fire. "No. Those boys done nothing but good by us. The less they know, the better. If we's ever caught, then they's innocent."

"The law might not believe them."

"It's not the law I worry about. What if they swear on the Book but don't tell the truth? God likes his harps back nice and shiny."

"You think they would lie for us?"

"They might."

I loop the bracelet back over her hand, and she tucks it under her sleeve. If the boys did lie on the Bible, I hope God would not hold it against them. My harp isn't exactly shiny either.

"I'm also gonna ask 'em to find out about Harp Falls," she says in a softer voice.

"I remember," I say glumly. I try to lift up my frown as I sense her eyes upon me. "You can have Paloma."

"Thanks, but I wouldn't take her from you. I'll get another animal somewhere, don't worry about that. You's a real gem, Sammy, a gem to the core. Gonna miss you a lot."

She finishes with my button, snapping off the thread with her teeth. My own fingers somehow tied my shirt flaps into a knot, and now I try to work them free. I don't know which worries me more, lawmen catching us, or Andy leaving. How does she expect to find her brother in this wild country? The federal marshals could easily have taken her for a runaway, or even as one of the Broken Hand Gang. Without the protection of the remuda, she'll be an easy target.

As for myself, if the boys don't want us, *and* Andy leaves, I'll be all alone. It won't be easy, especially when my companions have become like family. The flames appear like bright blurry patches in front of my eyes.

20

WEST AND CAY RETURN EMPTY-HANDED. THE NOISE
of the crowds scared off the game. We huddle around our fire
with bowls of turnip-corn mash.

"Well, kids, with Fort Kearny a whoop and a holler away,
looks like we'll have to cut you loose soon," says Cay as we chew.

Andy nudges me. I open my mouth to speak, but Peety beats
me to it.

"We getting boring of you, *chicos*," says Peety.

Andy drops the nut she was about to put in her mouth.

"Bored. Speak English, vaquero," says Cay.

"We'll give ya rope you can use for the snakes at night," says
West. "But remember, it don't keep away bears."

"What do we do about those?" I ask, dreading the thought of
climbing another tree.

"Bears are funny," says Cay. "See, what they really want are
your boots. They like to chew on them. Something about our
feet smells good to them. Especially Peety's. How do you think
he got that hole?"

We look at Peety's boots. Sure enough, his big toe pokes right
through the leather. He wiggles it for us.

"You let a bear chew on your foot?" Andy exclaims.

"I'm not loco. I took off boot first. The bear chew on it for little while, then he give it back."

Peety's face does not crack. But when I look at West and Cay, they are doubled over with laughter.

"Bear say, '*Gracias, señor*, tastes like *chocolate*.'"

Andy stabs Peety with her glare. "Shame on you jackals and you's nasty toes."

"It's like this, boys," says Cay, his voice still hoarse with laughter. "We ain't going to California for another drive. We're going to dig for gold, too, and we want you to come with us. What say you?"

"Yes!" yells Andy, throwing up her arms and grinning at me. I muster a smile, though not much more. Despite our good fortune, the thought of Andy leaving still troubles me. It puts a hole in my mood, through which all other good feelings seep out.

Later that night, we pat down our pockets and pull together a total of twenty-four dollars plus Ty Yorkshire's rings. Nobody knows exactly how much those will fetch. I debate whether to tell the boys they're stolen, then decide they probably already know. We need enough supplies to last the month until we arrive at the next trading post, Fort Laramie. West tears out a sheet from his journal for me to write a shopping list and tally costs. Out of the corner of my eye, I catch Andy counting on her fingers, her lips mouthing the numbers. She loses her place and grimaces.

"We'll need about fifty for everything," I inform our group.

"Peety needs new boots," says Andy.

Peety tucks his foot under him. "No, new horseshoes more important."

"One day, Peety, we're going to find enough gold to shoe all the horses," says Cay.

"How they gonna walk, hombre?"

"They're not gonna need to walk. They can sit around and drink tequila. We just better get there before everyone else digs it all up."

West doesn't look up from his journal where he's sketching a picture of the fort on the hill. "We'll get there when we get there."

Peety uncaps a silver flask. Before taking a sip, he says, "I know you want to pan for gold, but I got another idea."

"What's that?" asks Cay.

"Mexican governors grant *mucho* land for ranchos to Mexicans. Miners going to need cattle and horses."

"If I wanted to drive cattle, I woulda stayed in Texas."

West puts down his charcoal. "That wasn't an option for you, remember? Peety's on to something. We'd be the bosses, instead of the beef herders. Do something respectable for a change."

"Maybe I like being unrespectable," says Cay, turning his socks inside out.

West sighs. "Why doesn't that surprise me?"

Before the good humor of the night is wasted, I summon my most casual tone. "So who wants to do the supplying?"

All the boys raise their hands.

"Great. Andy and I will meet you at the Platte River crossing."

"That's ten miles past the fort," West says.

"I know. I don't like supplying." I spit onto the fire. "Women's work."

Andy hoists her eyebrows at me but adds an emphatic, "Me neither."

West looks at Peety, who shrugs. I brace myself for questions, but to my surprise, Cay says, "Suit yourself."

Andy stops counting and knits her fingers over her knees. "When you get to the fort, you mind asking how to get to Harp Falls?"

Cay puts down his sock. "I thought that was a made-up place."

"Never said that."

West tips up his hat. "Why do you want to know?"

"Got some people going that way. Thought I might join them."

West's face is an unreadable page. "Okay, we'll ask."

Cay slaps his socks against his saddlebag. "All right, all right, too much business and not enough play today. Time for 'Miss Mable's Table.'" He can't get enough of that dirty ditty about two lovers who meet under the furniture.

I cough. I can't play that here with all these people around, or any other song for that matter. Folks always flock to a violin, no matter how rusty it sounds.

"My arm hurts from roping. But I can strum."

This, at least, I can do quietly. I remove my fiddle and place my hands, left on the fingerboard, right over the bridge. E *for exquisite, Father, even without the bow.* Tonight I play for three princes and one princess.

"'West Is Where My Heart Lies,'" I announce.

I usually let others take care of the singing, but since not many know this song, I croon the words in my soft singing voice and strum as quietly as possible. Even my normally cranky D-string gets along with the others this time. Andy hums along in a pitch-perfect alto.

West's shoulders relax as he listens, and his eyes follow my fingers. When I sing the refrain, *West is where my heart lies,* my eyes flit to his, though I drop them quickly before I tip him off to my longing.

Later, after everyone falls asleep, I take my violin and steal away to the water. I kneel on a patch of dry grass. The waxing moon casts just enough light to give me a reflection. My hair sticks out in different directions and I'm grimacing. I shiver, wishing I still had my shawl, the one Father had Mrs. Kurtz knit for me out of the softest lambs' wool. He tied it tight over my shoulders and told me not to mislay it, the way I did its predecessor and my bonnet with the daisies.

But I lost it anyway. The same day I lost him.

I cradle the Lady Tin-Yin to me, her warm wood as comforting as the touch of an old friend. Then I pick out Beethoven's Moonlight Sonata. Father loved any instrument he could strum—banjo of course, guitar, harp, even washboard if that was the only thing available. Lady Tin-Yin understands my sorrow like no one else, singing my pain through mournful triplets, filling my speck of the world with a poem of aching sound.

A tear breaks through my resolve, then another, and soon I'm crying hard enough to set off hiccups. I swipe my face with my sleeves and try to calm down.

Well, at least now I have nothing left to lose. I should have been a boy. A son would have been more dutiful and less of a watering pot—though maybe that's just the Snake in me. I wouldn't be such a mess under these stolen clothes. *And you, Father, would still be alive.*

Smoothing my hand over the water's surface, I rub out my reflection. Something rustles behind me, but when I look, there is nothing but wind in the rushes. With a last glance at the disappearing moon, I head back to the others.

When I get there, I find West's old shearling coat laid across my bedroll.

21

I WAKE TO THE LOWING OF OXEN. IN FRONT OF ME, West breathes softly, one arm tucked under his head. His shearling perfectly cocoons me.

I roll over slowly. Mist spreads out in fingers above us, like a drawer full of white gloves. Andy warms my other side. She grimaces, and then her face releases. Her hooked eyelashes tremble, and though she's not awake, her hand clutches at the hem of her coat, like it's a baby's blanket. She is old enough to be a wife, a mother, yet a remnant of her innocence clings to her.

I was wrong to think I had nothing more to lose. If anything ever happened to her, I would feel responsible.

Her eyes flutter open. Making fists, she stretches out her arms, then smiles sleepily at me. Silently, we go for our morning rituals. A handful of pioneers are already washing by the river, which is so cold, it hurts to touch.

We dip rags into the water and wring them out. After we wipe our teeth, I yank up some wild mint growing by the stream and hand Andy a springy leaf to chew on. "What if you came with me to find Mr. Trask? And after that, we'll search for your brother."

"Isaac's the only family I got. I can't leave him waiting."

"But Mr. Trask might give us proper supplies, another mule."

"Actually," she says slowly, "Peety said Princesa belongs to me."

"He did?" I say once I recover my voice.

"Yeah. I didn't ask for her, either," she says. "Last night, after they told us we could we go with them, he said she and I were made for each other. Said he can tell by the way we carry ourselves—something like that. And then he said, she's mine, as long as I promise to take care of her."

"Why didn't you tell me?"

"I'm telling you right now." She squeezes my wrist. "Listen, Sammy, you got you's path to follow, and I got mine. Even if I went with you, you think Mr. Trask gonna let you leave with me, a runaway, to find another runaway? Especially with the law already chasing you?"

"He's a good man. He'd help us."

"He may be good, but he ain't stupid." She frowns at the water. Fish nip at mosquitoes, marring the surface.

"I still don't think we should split up. What if you run into more criminals, like those Scots?"

She doesn't meet my gaze. "Ain't afraid of lawbreakers." Her eyes stick on something in the dirt. "How long you think this bead's been waiting on me to find it? Bet Tommy will like this one best."

She hands me the barrel-shaped bead to inspect. It's grooved along the sides and is smooth as glass. It looks Indian in origin.

I hand it back. "The Broken Hand Gang is still on the loose. Aren't you afraid of them?"

"They only attack folks who got something to steal. And I won't have nothing but myself. And now, this bead."

"And Princesa."

She gives me a stern look but doesn't reply. I decide not to push further. For now. If I nudge the boulder each day, eventually I'll get it up the mountain.

The boys are already up when we get back to camp. When West goes to wash in the river, I secure his coat to its usual place on the back of Franny's saddle. I pray he didn't see me bawling. Just in case, I pin a grumpy scowl on my face and gnaw on my bacon with extra gusto.

Soon, we join the endless stream of prairie schooners floating up the trail to Fort Kearny with their white canvas sails. I pull my hat as low as it can go over my head and fidget on my saddle as we crawl along. Dense grass on either side of the path means we can only go as fast as the wagon in front of us.

I glance back at Andy. Her eyes are unfocused, like she's lost in thought. I hope that means she's considering my proposal.

My attention returns to Cay, who's memorizing lines he can say to French girls without being slapped.

"*Je peux tu aider?*" he says. "That one's easy to remember. It sounds like 'sh poo two a day'?"

"Use *vous*. You can't be too familiar. A slap for certain."

"Aw, heck, I'm gonna be black-and-blue by the time I catch one." Cay steers Skinny toward a shallow stream that runs parallel to the main road. A screen of yellow grass grows tall enough to cut the wagons from view, except for their tops. The watery track proves cooler than the trail by a notch, and it's more private.

"Why do you want to catch a Frenchie so bad?" I ask.

"It's only natural, I'm part French. You gonna get yerself a China girl someday, right?"

I'd settle for just *being* a China girl again one day, but I nod.

"Long way to China," says Peety from somewhere behind me. "Maybe you can find a nice girl here. Lots of Mexicanas in California."

"You can't joke like that, vaquero."

"Not joking. I think Chinito can marry whoever he wants. If Europeans did not marry Aztecs, we would not have Mexicanos." He thumps his chest, causing his buttons to jingle.

Andy angles her face toward me, an amused expression bending her eyebrows.

"Yeah but that happened way back when folks didn't have choices," says Cay. "It was either take the señorita or row yourself back to Spain, and no one knew how to get back anyway. I think Chinito might be better off if he stuck to Chinitas." Cay throws a glance over his shoulder. "Ain't that right, West?"

West doesn't answer, and I guess he's too far back to hear. But then he says in a quiet voice, "I s'pect."

His response cuts a notch off my posture. Of course it's unrealistic to think he might feel differently.

"But that's the problem. There's no Chinitas here," Peety tosses back, keeping his tone mild.

"Well, how'd Sammy's daddy get a Chinese wife?"

"He had a matchmaker send him my mother from Guang-dong," I say.

"Like ordering a barrel of tea?" says Cay. "Is that legal?"

"No one complained."

"'Specially not you. So how much that set him back?"

"One hundred eighty-eight dollars. Eight is a lucky number because the word for eight, *baht,* sounds like the word for 'prosper.'"

West whistles a thin note that falls off at the end.

Cay scratches his hat. "Ain't that a mite risky, not sniffing the bottle before you drink?"

"Never stopped you," comes West's voice from behind me. Peety snickers.

"It wasn't risky. The matchmaker used a formula based on time of birth and alignment of the heavens, since we believe our fates are written in the stars." Cay cocks his head in consternation. I glance around. Andy frowns, probably saying a prayer for the preservation of my heathen soul. "It worked, too. Father said Mother was as lovely as the empress's teacup, with a temperament as sweet as autumn pears. He loved her very much. Every night, he placed a cup of her favorite drink, fermented rice wine, on the mantel."

"Sounds like he got his money's worth," says Peety. "But how was her cooking?"

"He was buying himself a wife, not a frying pan," mutters Andy.

"I don't know. He never talked about that."

Franny's step increases until West surpasses me, riding slightly ahead. The sound of the collective hoofbeats on the wet pebbles is as comforting as rain. His oolong-smooth voice pours out, "You want my take, there's nothing wrong with matching people up according to the stars, because at least someone gave a thought to it. Lots of deuces leap the altar 'cause they like getting sacked, and lots of girls agree 'cause they think they got no choice. Ain't fair to the human race, and that's the short of it." He crosses his arms, causing his shoulders to bunch under his flannel.

I lose my balance and grab the apple of Paloma's saddle. Still waters may run deep, but trying to understand West is like trying to see through a muddy river.

Cay nudges his pinto up alongside Franny. "You mean a nice piece of calico sits in your lap and you're gonna tell her to shoo?"

"She could sit as long as she wants," says West in an offhand way that puts a bloom on my cheeks. "But I ain't making promises I can't keep."

"I never made promises I couldn't keep," Cay protests.

"Don't recall ever mentioning your name." West clicks his tongue and Franny surges ahead, blond tail swishing fiercely.

By midday, our lick of stream runs into the Platte River forcing us back to the main trail. The Platte stretches over a mile wide, a coursing waterway cut with islands that give it a braided appearance. Along the banks, a line of tents extends out as far as I can see. Then we spy Old Glory, with her twenty-nine stars on a field of blue, rising out of a collection of timber-and-sod buildings. Fort Kearny.

Cay's shoulders slump and he scratches his hat. "That's not a fort." He perks up again when a redheaded girl in a polka-dot dress looks over her shoulder at him.

"We'll wait for you at the crossing," I call after Cay, who is already following the girl.

Peety goes next. "Don't get lost, *chicos.*"

West pauses in front of me. "You sure you don't want to come? Probably got some good things to eat in there."

"I'm sure." I'm touched by his concern, but even if a barrel of custard tarts waited inside that fort, I would not be tempted.

He opens his mouth like he's going to protest further but then closes it. "All right. We'll try to be there by sundown." He clicks his tongue and Franny takes him away.

Andy and I continue down the trail, which meanders along the Platte River. Along the banks, large cottonwoods stand ramrod straight like sentinels among minions of sagebrush.

"How much farther to the Parting?" asks Andy.

"Seven hundred miles—about thirty-four days at our present rate."

"How long will it take for Mr. Trask to get there?"

"At least thirty days." I peek at her, wondering if she's changed her mind about coming with me. "I just hope we can make up some time crossing the Platte." Unlike the pioneers, we will not have wagons to encumber us.

"How do you figure out those numbers so fast?"

"I could teach you."

She flashes me a view of her crooked bottom teeth, holding up its straighter brethren. "I'd like that."

We reach the Platte River Crossing when the sun sits low in

the sky. Though this crossing is both the shallowest and narrowest point on the river, we still cannot even see the other side.

Wagons crowd the shoreline, some with their wheels removed. The pioneers must float them across while the animals ford. But no one attempts the crossing this late in the day with the water level so high. Sometimes the shoreline disappears altogether as the brackish waters ooze over into the high grass.

"Maybe we should go farther up where there's less folks," says Andy. "We can come back here later when the sun sets, and we don't stick out so much."

We take our mounts another two miles upriver, then leave them to dip their noses. Saddles in hand, and the Lady Tin-Yin strapped across my back, we settle under the only trees in sight for miles—a group of three cottonwoods set back several yards from the river where the ground is harder.

Andy plops down under the center tree, then carefully tugs off Peety's riding gloves, finger by finger.

"I'd say someone's taken you under his wing," I say.

She twists her mouth to the side. "Peety do have some flake to his biscuit. He understands feelings. You can tell by the way he is with horses. Like he knows little things that bug 'em without them saying so."

"Not to mention, he cares about their feet more than his own."

She chuckles, then goes quiet, her eyes drifting to a spot on the river. Absently, she begins fanning herself with her gloves. The sun seems to have grown fiercer since we arrived, as if determined to go down in a blaze of glory. I take off my own hat and unbutton my shirts down to my camisole.

"You really believe all that stuff about choosing a husband by birthdays and stars?"

"It worked for my parents, though one case is not enough to prove a theory. By the way, Peety was born in the Year of the Rat."

One eyebrow hooks up. "How do you know that? He only *thought* he was twenty-one. He wasn't sure."

"I'm sure. He likes to talk, but doesn't share much about himself. He's a perfectionist, a tireless worker, and—this cinches it—he loves elegance." My eyes drop meaningfully to the lambskin gloves in her lap.

"Rat for certain, then. I feel like you's makin' a point, but I ain't feeling a prick."

"Of the twelve lunar signs, Rats are most well-suited with Dragons."

I swear she blushes, though her dark skin makes it hard to tell.

She slumps back against the tree, causing her hat to lift off her forehead. "A man like Peety wouldn't be interested in someone like me."

"You mean someone good-looking, smart, and an expert cook to boot? No, you're probably right. You're his worst nightmare."

She lightly slaps my arm with the gloves. "It ain't as easy as that, and you know it."

I lean back on my elbows, wishing I didn't understand so immediately what she meant. A wasp buzzes near my face, and I blow at it. There may not be laws against interracial marriages in California, but society still frowns upon the practice. It is no easy thing, living under the weight of public scrutiny day after day. Even worse to subject another to it.

I didn't know if Mexicans felt the same way about blacks as whites did—surely Peety was different. "Rats live by their own rules. You heard what he said back there about Chinito marrying whoever he wants."

He shrugs. "He might already have a sweetheart."

He never spoke of a sweetheart, though I recall him mentioning one girl, Esme. When we first got Paloma, he told her that Esme loved mules.

"Anyway, I been thinking I might not want to get married. Most men want children, but I don't want to bring a child into a world where he could be sold like a hog."

That makes sense to me. "But don't you want someone to look after you?"

She leans back against our tree. "I don't need nobody to take care of me. And you don't either. Though that first day on the trail, I didn't hold much hope for either of us. That look on your face when I caught the snake…" Her lips tuck in, as if trying to suppress a smile.

"Only because I do not like killing my own kind." I sniff.

"Your kind was pretty tasty, though, admit it." A grin breaks through and soon I'm wearing one, too. "What's West's animal?"

"A rabbit."

"As in bunny?" Her mouth hangs open and she looks so dumbfounded, I start to laugh. Soon, we're both slapping the ground in hilarity. Another wasp swoops by, and her teary gaze drifts toward the tree next to us. Something catches her attention. "So many wasps buzzing over there." She stretches her neck to get a closer look. "Is that a boot?"

Something brown sticks out of the earth near a heap of brush. The boot's only a shade lighter than the dirt.

She gets up and slaps her hands together. "Maybe this is Peety's lucky day."

I follow her to the boot. "Hope it's a pair. Chinese people say good things come in pairs because the word for 'two' sounds like the word for 'easy'—"

"Sammy," she hisses, stopping short.

"What?" Something in her voice makes me afraid.

She's staring at the brush. Tangled in the base of the plant is a negro man.

He's crumpled into a fetal position, facing us. Blood mats his hair, and the wasps are busy laying their eggs in his scalp. His eyes are nearly hollowed-out sockets and his skin is peeling in patches, like paint. Chunks of his arms are missing, maybe eaten by animals.

My mouth falls open, but no sound comes out. I try to pull Andy away, but she's immobile, staring fixedly at a spot on the tree at eye level, where a cross is carved into the trunk.

"Come on, let's go," I urge, yanking her by the arm.

We fetch our saddles and run.

22

NEITHER OF US SPEAKS UNTIL WE CAN SEE PEOPLE
again. This time, the sight of the pioneers comforts me.

Andy tugs at her collar, wet with sweat. "Someone sure don't
know how to bury a man, or maybe just a negro man."

"Maybe they didn't have time to dig deep. Or maybe they
didn't have shovels."

"He looked killed to me," Andy says. "Surprised they left his
boots. Maybe whoever did it thought they were dirty."

"Well, they were pretty muddy."

"I don't mean dirty that way. Some people think touching
a colored or his things will get 'em dirty." She removes her hat
and fans herself with it even though people can see us. Then she
relids her head and sighs. "I'm just glad it wasn't Isaac."

I nod. "Should we tell someone? Maybe he's part of the
Broken Hand Gang."

"Just 'cause he's colored don't mean he's part of that gang, you
know." Her tone is not accusing, but I still feel the sting.

She goes on. "Anyway, who would we tell? And why?"

I steer Paloma between a couple of tents and concede the point.
No one's going to care about a dead black man. Poor fellow. He
came all this way to end up under a tree. At least someone took

the time to carve a cross. That means someone cared about his soul.

We pick our way through the pioneers and are scouting for a good place to camp, when we see the boys flying down the trail. They draw up their panting horses beside us.

"Time to go, kids," Cay cries, straining his eyes behind him. His shirt is buttoned wrong.

West curses as he pulls up behind him. Cay holds his hands out to his cousin. "I'm sorry, okay? How was I supposed to know she had six brothers?"

"You gotta chase every skirt you see?" says West, glowering.

"I don't chase 'em. They just fall into my lap."

"That's the last time I'm doing that," says West, pulling Franny to the water's edge. We all follow him.

"How deep goes that water?" Andy squints at the inky lane.

"Don't worry, Princesa likes *agua*."

"I ain't thinking about her."

Cay stands up on his stirrups for a better look down the trail. "If it gets too deep, stand up."

Andy crosses her arms. "I knows you's joking with me."

"Ain't joking. C'mon, c'mon! Let's wiggle."

"Fine," says Andy. "You go walk on water first."

"All right, I will." Cay digs in his heels. "This is what we call a Skinny dip."

Andy goes next, followed by Peety and West.

Paloma paces the shoreline, not sure if she wants to do this after all. The remuda—both horses and riders—peers back at me. "Come on, girl, it'll be an adventure, you can tell your children about it one day," I plead to her.

"Mules no have children, Chinito," says Peety. "Let's go, Paloma."

But she will not go.

West tugs his rein to signal Franny back, but Peety holds out an arm.

"Trust me, Paloma, you can do it," says Peety. Then he spurs Lupe onward, and the remuda follows. The distance between us increases until the sound of the rushing river drowns out the horses' splashing.

The faint sound of yelling reaches my ears. Six men on mules clamber down the trail, six matchsticks with their flame-red hair flying in all directions. The brothers.

One yells and points in our direction. Fear blows her icy breath down my neck. I'm not the one being pursued, but when six angry men run at me from behind, I don't fuss with details.

"Giddap!" I cry, digging in my heels hard. Paloma charges forward. The remuda stops again to yell encouragements as Paloma and I slog toward them.

Finally, two hundred feet out, I glance back to see all of the men pacing the shoreline. One shakes his fist at us.

"I'm okay," I gasp when we catch up. I try to affect an air of reckless indifference despite my heaving chest.

"Move," West barks at Cay. We move.

The water's surface shifts the rays of the setting sun like hands sifting through cut jade stones. Five hundred feet out, the depth increases, and water seeps through my boots. I hiss in my breath at the chilly temperature, but my brave steed plows on. Good girl.

The boys sling their saddlebags onto their backs. I do the same with Lady Tin-Yin, wishing I had had time to wrap her in blankets. A single drop of moisture can ruin the sound completely.

A few hundred feet remain. When the water comes to my thighs, I realize the boys have climbed up to standing, their steeds not even pausing as they ferry them across the depth. I rub my eyes, hardly believing their ability to balance.

"You kidding me?" exclaims Andy.

"Real men stand," Cay ribs her.

Andy looks back at me and bumps her forehead with her fist. Idiots. I show her my palms and shrug.

"Don't worry, I would never do that," I mutter to Paloma.

Andy hauls up her legs and crouches on her saddle. What is she doing? She must have misread me as being up for the challenge. I groan, realizing I must once again eat my words. When will I learn never to say never? Andy can chop her own turnips tonight.

In front of me, West hooks his thumb inside his trousers pocket, one foot in front of the other at a slight angle.

"Maybe it's not as hard as it looks," I tell Paloma, more to convince myself.

West cocks an ear back toward us. "I think you should stay put."

Now I have to do it. He did not say that to Andy.

I hoist up my anchors, then kneel.

"Sammy," says West in that stern, exasperated way he has of saying my name.

This is as far as I go. I can save my face by not soaking my behind. I hug Paloma's neck, my tail hanging somewhere in the air. Who cares? I'm in the back anyway. Peety approaches the other shore.

Paloma takes a wrong step and screams. She staggers under me, and I cling to her neck. With jerky movements, she tries to regain her footing, but she cannot find solid ground, and I'm unbalancing her further.

She lurches too far to the left. Oh! The freezing waters immerse me up to my shoulders. I have to let go.

"You can do it!" I cry out. "Stand—"

My mouth fills with water, and I spit it back out. A bolt of terror stabs through me. The current is wrenching me away, thick and unyielding like a layer of blubber. I kick, paddling my arms, but something weighs me down. Lady Tin-Yin. *No!*

I flail with all my might to reach air.

But I waited too long. The violin's strap is tangled around my neck, so sink with her I must. As the river's icy fingers drag me down, I almost laugh as I realize I'm managing to drown myself after all.

23

WEST IS KISSING ME. I'VE DREAMED ABOUT THIS for weeks, how his mouth would taste and feel. Except in my dream it always happens in the moonlight, and he does not pinch my nose.

Andy pushes my chest, which has been covered with a blanket. Smart girl.

Oh, West, you are so dear up close. My eyelids shut, and I wait for him to kiss me again.

"Sammy," he says with a note of desperation. *Hm?* My eyes flutter open again, and I notice he is all wet. Even his eyes drip, splashing my face every time he blinks. *Were you swimming?*

Suddenly my chest caves and I suck in air like a newborn. I turn my head into his lap and empty my insides.

The next time I open my eyes, Paloma is drooling on my face. I'm wrapped in shearling, lying on a bed of horse blankets. Shaking out the fog in my head, I prop myself onto my elbows. I'm resting at the top of an embankment, shaded by the long branches of a hemlock tree whose leaves hang like green sleeves on bony arms. A hundred paces out, the boys are helping some pioneer men drag their wagon out of the water.

Beside them, two other wagons dry in the mid-morning sun, their contents neatly arranged along the grassy shore. I don't see Andy.

"Oh, Paloma," I gush as I remember our near drowning. "You are an exceptional creature." I hold up my hand for a kiss, and she gives it to me.

The lifting sun erases the last tangles of morning fog, though the wetness remains, invisible and heavy.

Andy appears, holding two of my shirts, dried stiff. She must have had to take off my clothes, dry them, and re-dress me. She drops to the ground next to me. "You almost died. But you didn't. You remember what I said about body over mind?"

I nod weakly, then run a hand through my shorn locks. "They didn't find out, did they?"

"Almost. West wanted to rip off your shirts when we pulled you in, but I stopped him. Told him you'd catch lung fever if he did that."

"Good thinking."

"I'm just glad you didn't leave me all alone here. What would I do with three cowboys who can't carry a damn tune?" She falls silent and puts a fist to her mouth.

I put an arm around her shoulders and offer my sleeve. "Oh, sister. I'm sorry to have worried you." She pushes away my sleeve and blows a few times into a handkerchief from her saddlebag. Though I dread the answer, I finally ask: "Is Lady Tin-Yin gone?"

"Lady who?"

"My violin."

"Yeah, she's gone."

I press my sleeves into my own eyes.

Andy clucks her tongue. "Come on, we gotta keep our canteens watertight," she says gently.

I nod, but can't stop my chest from quaking. Lady Tin-Yin was almost sixty years old. My grandfather—Pépère, as I knew him—carried her through the Battle of Montenotte, Napoleon's first victory in Italy. There, she soothed the minds of the wounded and mourned the passing of the dead. Father played her to quiet his colicky Snake baby. Objects have pasts that cling to them, which means she was filled with positive energy.

Now she is gone, and only one thing remains of my past: Mother's jade bracelet. Of course, I may never see that again, either. By the time I find Mr. Trask, he might have already sold it.

Andy's warm eyes are wide with concern. She pats my knee. "I'm sorry, Sammy. If you's daddy was here, he wouldn't give that violin another thought, he'd just be happy to see you alive."

She is right, but I can't help feeling I let Father down, once again. Taking a deep breath, I wrestle my tears back into their corners. "Tell me what happened after Paloma fell."

I brew the coffee as she talks. My head feels light and my hands shake as I measure out the beans.

"We all saw you sink. Cay and West dove off their horses and swam after you like a coupla otters while Peety and I brought in the remuda.

"They found you on the bottom with your strap 'round you's

neck like pigging string. Pulled you up, but you was out cold. Didn't breathe water, though, you held you's breath good. West breathed for you. Hope you were awake for that," she teases. "Then you spat up on him."

"You don't think he could tell?"

"Ain't sure." She holds her chin and watches as the boys shake hands with the pioneers. "I bet he's sipped nectar from more than his share of willing flowers, but unless one of them flowers also had a sipper, nah. Lips is lips, 'specially if they's blue with cold and fulla river slime."

I wipe my mouth on my sleeve.

"Though, if he does still think you's a boy, maybe he'll feel like a plucked rooster for a bit."

"He'd have done the same for Peety or Cay," I say quietly.

She leans her head to one side and squints. "You's right on that. These are some fine horses we found."

I pour the coffee, then add sugar to all but West's cup since he doesn't favor his sweet.

The boys return from the river.

"Good to see you above snakes," says Cay.

"Snakes?" I ask with some alarm.

"Alive, kid," he replies.

Peety drops down next to me, his eyelids heavy and the corners of his mouth pulling down. "*Lo siento. Es mi culpa.*"

"How is it your fault?" I gape.

"Not looking back for you... like Esme." His shoulders begin to twitch.

Esme again. Andy slides her eyes from Peety's to mine. Before I can puzzle Esme out, Cay slides in on my other side. "It's not his fault, it's mine. I parade too much."

West glares at Cay, then grabs his cup and leans against a tree. "That ain't it."

Cay drops his chin to his chest. "And sometimes I lead with my horn instead of my head. You understand, right?" he pleads with me.

My nose wrinkles as I try to make sense of what he's saying.

West answers for me. "Of course he don't understand, he's a"—he glances at me, then angrily looks away—"a kid. You ain't a farmer, you can't go planting your seeds every time you see a field, or you're gonna get us all killed."

"You plant more seeds than me," says Cay.

"Not in the fields with the no-trespassing signs." West stabs his finger toward the river.

A vein pops out of Cay's neck. I try to chip at the ice that's formed between the cousins. "It's no one's fault but the river's. You both saved my life, and I'm nothing but grateful."

Peety sniffs loudly. A hug would be too girly, so I punch him in the arm, which I quickly realize is also girly. I punch him harder.

"Ow, *chico*," he cries, still not smiling.

I do the same to Cay.

"That's all you got?" His face relaxes.

"And West," I say, "I also—"

He takes a sip of his coffee and spits it out. "You call this coffee?" he snaps at me. "It ain't coffee, it's wagon grease." He dumps the brew on the fire and heads back toward the river.

"Plucked rooster," Andy whispers in my ear, then gives me a solemn wink.

After we finish our coffee and bacon, I find a quiet spot by the river to say good-bye to Lady Tin-Yin. *You were my first friend. When none would pick me for their rounders team, you kept me company, giving me a voice that made people laugh and cry. I'm sorry we won't be opening that music conservatory together after all.*

My fingers twitch, already missing the feel of her smooth contours in my hands.

Andy comes up beside me. I wait for her to say something, but she doesn't. She simply stares with me at that bloated body of blue.

My violin is not the only thing we lost. Half our food supply also lies at the river's bottom. However, all of our hats washed ashore earlier this morning, to everyone's amazement. It is easy to get attached to a hat.

Before we saddle up, West unties a sack and tosses a book at me. "Got this at the fort so you don't have to keep taking my tally book," he says brusquely.

"Thank you," I say to his back.

"No one sounded very sure about Harp Falls," he tells Andy. She nods. "Thanks for asking."

"But we did get a new map," he says, handing her a folded bundle of paper. "It's pretty detailed. Maybe your waterfall's on there." He fishes something out of his pocket. The gold rings. "The cash covered everything. Got these appraised, though. Two hundred dollars each. Pretty sum."

While the boys collect the horses from the river's edge,

Andy and I pore over the new map. Instead of the simple lines of Cay's old map, this one has shading and other topographical renderings. It also includes sketches of landmarks like Independence Rock—the halfway point on our journey.

Andy traces her finger down the trail, then stops at a mountain range north of Independence Rock, two hundred miles in the opposite direction from the Parting. "What do these words say?"

"Haystack Mountains."

She points to a wavy line that runs through the mountains. "What about this one?"

"Yellow River."

After pulling the map close to her face and then away again, she taps her finger at a spot. "That looks like a waterfall to me."

I squint at the series of squiggly lines that intersect the river. "Or maybe it's just how the mapmaker drew the river. It's unreliable. There's not even a name."

"You see any other markings like that?"

I examine the page in detail. "No, but that still doesn't mean it's a waterfall."

"Uh-huh. And what's that say?" She points to the pass that leads to the Yellow River.

"Calamity Cutoff."

"You's pulling my string."

"No. Now tell me that's not a sign you shouldn't be going that way."

She snorts. "Probably someone's favorite cow died there. A real calamity."

• • •

In the late afternoon, we enter a lush playground with dense thickets of American plum. Giant dogwoods drop their petals on us as we pass and golden currant dabs the landscape with a honey-like scent. I inhale greedy lungfuls, letting the scent soothe the ache from my lost violin.

West hasn't spoken to anyone since this morning.

Peety spots muscadine grapes ripening alongside a babbling stream and cuts off the vines most heavy with fruit, attaching them to the saddles so we can eat as we ride. They dangle like tiny green bells. When the juicy orbs explode in my mouth, I swear I never tasted anything as good.

Maybe life just tastes sweeter after you've licked death.

24

APRIL MARCHES INTO MAY. THE DAYS GROW LONGER
and the weather loses its wet-dog feel. We gain more ground in
the winding hills that slow the wagons to the speed of sap. The
emigrant men brace the carts so they don't tip over as they zigzag
down the slope. We haven't seen any more dead bodies, smashed
fingers, or law enforcement in the two weeks since we left Fort
Kearny.

The more I try to dissuade Andy from pinning her hopes on
the map's squiggly-line markings, the more convinced she becomes that they're her waterfall. So I stop pushing. If Dragons
are pushed too hard, they will fly away.

The boys scare birds out of the trees and throw up pinecones
for us to shoot. Moving objects are much harder to hit than tree
knots, but we improve slowly. Andy practices throwing her rope
around any oblong shape she can find, but since most of the terrain
is grassland, she usually just ropes Peety riding in front of her.

In the evenings, West hunts by himself.

The night after my near drowning, he set off with his rifle
while Cay was still airing his shirts.

"Hold on, don't you want me to come?" asked Cay.

"No," said West, striding off.

When Cay noticed me, he shrugged. "Sourpuss. He'll come around tomorrow."

But he didn't, setting off alone the night after as well, and soon Cay stopped asking.

Lately, West avoids being alone with me, too. He always arrives last for language lessons, and sleeps with his face turned away from me.

Three more days until Fort Laramie, and seventeen days until the Parting. We've upped our pace to twenty-five miles a day, aided by a flat terrain and a wider trail. At this rate, we'll make it to the Parting before Mr. Trask, assuming he hasn't upped *his* pace. Though I don't know how he would do that without leaving behind his wagon and team and buying a horse. Once at the Parting, I will examine the faces of those who pass by, one by one, until I spot him.

I restart my campaign to convince Andy to come to the Parting, re-treading old arguments and presenting new ones. "If Isaac gets there first, he'll wait for you, right? You said yourself neither of you know when the other's going to show up," I say on one of the rare occasions where she and I lead the remuda. "What's another few weeks?"

Her answer is always the same. "You's got your path, and I got mine."

Maybe I have met my match in the war of stubborn.

We camp in a clearing surrounded by thick coyote brush. A bare film of clouds veils the ripening moon. After dinner, West and I both draw straws to scrub the plates.

"I'll do 'em myself," West tells me. "Work on your sharp-shooting."

"I can already hit nine out of ten."

"Then work on your knots," he grumbles, collecting the dirty dishes.

"Still a plucked rooster," Andy whispers.

When we've spread out on our bedrolls, Andy announces, "Tonight we's got a romantic story."

"Oh good," says Cay. "Come on, hold my hand, West. That'll make it extra-special."

West snorts and scribbles harder in his journal with his wrapped charcoal. From where I sit, I can make out swirly lines that look like water, and the jagged edges of a tree line.

He feels me watching and looks up. I pretend to study my knees.

Andy begins. "Once there lived a princess name Bonita."

"Finally a story for the brown man," says Peety.

"Bonita was the daughter of King and Queen Snake, who ruled the Land of Noble Sunsets in the west. They liked it there because snakes do their best slithering at night. In the east, lived their enemies, the rabbits, in the Land of Splendid Sunrises. Being early risers, living in the east suited them. The rabbits' king and queen had a son, Zachariah, whose hare coat was black and shiny as flint."

A rabbit and a snake. That sly girl. I cut my gaze to Andy, but she's wrapped up in her storytelling.

"A lake separated the two countries, which worked out good, since rabbits thought snakes were nasty, foul-mouthed things, and snakes thought rabbits were dim-witted fluffheads. But the two countries agreed they wouldn't truck in each other's business as long as they kept their own boundaries."

"What's luckier, a snake jaw or a rabbit foot?" Cay asks.

With a look of supreme patience, Andy folds her hands together. "Depends on if you're the snake or the rabbit. Now if you don't mind. One day Bonita and Zachariah both go down to the lake at the same time. As they dip their heads, they see the other's reflection.

"'A rabbit!' Bonita cries, a little trembly.

"'Darn't if that ain't a snake,' Zachariah says back." Andy makes her voice growly and rough for Zachariah, and I try not to giggle.

West stops drawing. He rolls his piece of charcoal between his fingers.

"Their eyes meet across the water. Unlike the rabbits Bonita had seen, this one did not look dim-witted, but held himself with his back straight, ears poked straight up and alert. He looked rather princely, with a finely brushed coat and white fur in his ears.

"Unlike the snakes Zachariah had seen, Bonita wasn't slimy or foul. She had wrapped herself around a branch and looked as elegant as a cord of yellow silk.

"For three nights, they met at the lake, not speaking, just watching each other. But on the fourth night, she asked him, 'How did you get so big eating nothing but grass?'

"He answered, 'I s'pect it's the same way you stay so slender, eating all that meat.' His ears flopped to one side. 'Say, you's not going to eat me, are you?'

"She laughed, and then he did, too. Every night after that, they met at the lake. Sometimes she wrapped herself around him, and they hopped through the forest. She would never dream of biting him. And he carried her gently, so her tail never dragged in the dirt."

Peety works a hand over his chin. "I do not think snakes have tails."

"Or necks, come to think of it," says Cay.

Andy glares at them. "You want to hear the story, or not?"

"Sorry, please continue," says Peety.

"Sometimes he would jump real high, and to Bonita, who'd never been off the ground, it seemed they were flying to the moon. But soon, folks got wind of the rabbit-snake lovers, and their parents forbade them from meeting. The punishment for not listening was death." She lets that word sink in, and now we're all staring at her in rapt silence. "So, Queen Snake begged her husband to give Bonita one last chance. Queen Rabbit begged her husband to give Zachariah one last chance. Their husbands say, fine.

"But again Bonita and Zachariah meet at the river. And they was as close as Saturday night and Sunday morning. He loved how pure was her heart, and she loved how steady were his shoulders.

"They got ready to hop away, this time for good. But the snake guards and rabbit soldiers waited for them behind the bushes. They threw their nets and caught the pair as they tried to escape."

She clasps her hands in front of her heart, pausing for a dramatic beat. The only one moving is Cay, whose knee starts to shake.

Andy lowers her voice. "But neither side could kill their own kin. So the parents decided to separate the lovers forever." She lifts her hands to the sky. "Zachariah asked to live on the moon so that Bonita could look up and see him, wherever she was. Bonita begged her parents for a good strong rattle, so Zachariah could hear her, wherever he was. Now, when the moon is full, their love shines brightest. One day, they hope they can be together again, maybe in a land both noble and splendid."

Andy's smile reaches from ear to ear, like she licked the cream off the milk.

"Well, I'll be damned," says Cay. "I never thought a rabbit or a snake could have such a powerful effect on me. So what is the moral of this story, Sammy?"

"Beats me," I say gruffly, though I know it is that nothing cannot stop true love, not even putting it on the moon.

West is scowling at his closed journal, his charcoal now hidden in his fist.

Peety sits up and wraps his arms around his knees. "I think if everyone stayed on their side of the fence, this tragedy would never have happened."

"That ain't it," Cay protests. "Bonita and Zachariah shoulda split when they had the chance. Go have a couple snake-rabbit babies."

"That is impossible, fool," says West. He gets to his feet and walks off.

Andy winks at me. Her simple gesture chases away some of the bad taste in my mouth. Somehow, she always understands how I feel, watching out for me not just in body, but in mind. I don't know what I would do without her.

This thought crosses my mind so often that I finally think: What if I went with her? What if I abandoned my quest to learn why Father wanted to go to California? I would have to give up Mother's bracelet. It's just a piece of jewelry, yet, I thought if I could touch its positive energy one more time, if only to say good-bye, some of the broken pieces inside me would mend. But Andy has already healed me in many ways, not just my fingers, but my emptiness, bolstering my fragile stance in the world with her own solid shoulders.

Father, fate has dropped another stone in the stream, forcing new choices, new paths to follow.

Later, after the boys fall asleep, I scoot closer to Andy. "I'm coming with you to Harp Falls."

"I already told you—"

"You were wrong when you said Isaac was the only family you had. You have me, too."

The fringe of her eyelashes flicks up and down as she studies me. "I feel the same way. But you can't give up on you's daddy's dream after all this way. What kind of life would that be for you, living with a couple of runaway slaves? Listen, Sammy. You's a smart gir—er—person, someone of the first water, as Cay would say. Ain't nothing you couldn't do. But me, I'll always be marked by my face."

"I'm marked by my face, too."

"Not as a slave."

I swallow my words, because I can't argue with her there.

"Once you find Mr. Trask, you'll be with decent folk. People who can help set you up with the life you deserve."

I prop myself up on an elbow. "I *am* with decent folk. Would you let me go by myself to some mythical waterfall in the middle of nowhere?"

She snorts. "Of course not. But the difference is, I know how to survive. You never had to run ten miles a day on chores." She flops onto her back and purses her lips.

"Last I checked, you can't outrun bullets, or bears for that matter." Dragons are known for being overconfident and unrealistic, but I decide against mentioning that since Dragons do not take criticism well. I lie back down. "I can make my own choices. And I choose to stay with you."

Maybe what matters is not so much the path as who walks beside you.

25

DURING OUR AFTERNOON BREAK, ANDY AND I stretch out under a dogwood. While she calculates sums in our journal, I mentally work out how many miles Mr. Trask has traveled and estimate him to be a couple hundred miles ahead of us yet. A warm breeze blows some of the cross-shaped blossoms into our faces. One tree over, the boys study their map, with the remuda grazing nearby.

Princesa screams.

"I saw that, Skinny," scolds Peety, shaking his finger at Cay's horse. "Keep teeth to yourself."

The chastised pinto turns her snapping jaws on West's horse.

"Get your hellcat off," West barks at Cay.

Cay jerks Skinny's harness to one side. "Bad girls have more fun, don't they, Skinny?"

But now the whole remuda's thrashing and lunging like they're crawling with fleas.

Peety throws his hands in the air. "No one's proper ladies right now. They need to go stand in cold river."

Andy peers at Princesa's rump and pinches her nose. "I say a run will do them better." To me, she whispers, "That, and a hot-water bottle for the cramps."

When Peety nods at her suggestion, I look twice to make sure I saw right. He never takes horse advice from West or Cay without objecting first.

"Choke your hat strings," orders Cay as we remount.

He leads the charge, like the speed-loving Tiger that he is. We run at top speed through a wide open plain fuzzy with sagebrush, a flat line of purplish bluffs far off in the distance. A year ago, I was barely comfortable ambling down the cobblestones with Tsing Tsing. Father didn't want to buy a speedier horse because he thought I'd break my neck if it went too fast. But now I fly like I'm riding Pegasus. Maybe we can hit thirty miles today.

After the horses expend their cranky energy, we park in the shadow of a low-lying bluff with a baby stream at its base. The water runs clear and glassy, but too shallow for fish.

I uncinch Paloma's saddle, and drop beside her at the stream's edge to wash my face. West waters Franny farther down the stream. Our long run took us a few miles from the main trail, but at least we're away from prying eyes.

The air shivers a fraction, like the barest rumble of a bear you cannot see but only suspect might be there. All my thoughts halt as I snap my head up. Only a few white clouds smear the sky. The stampede springs to mind, and I frantically search the landscape. When I locate the sound, I freeze.

Three horses tear across the prairie straight for us, manes and tails flying wildly. They wear neither riders nor saddles.

Wild mustangs.

Peety and Cay are carrying their saddles toward the shade of a cottonwood when they notice my alarm.

"H-h-hors—" I babble, pointing.

Everyone starts talking at once. Peety unleashes a stream of Spanish, too fast for me to understand, so I tune in to Cay instead.

"Skinny, come back, you stubborn hussy!" he yells as Skinny hot-trots toward the oncoming horses. "You let that son of a bitch bang you, and I'm leaving your ass in this weedy wasteland."

Skinny snubs Cay by continuing her spree toward the stallions. Lupe runs a step behind her. Cay and Peety drop their saddles and race after their mounts.

"Where you going?" yells Andy.

"Can't have pregnant horses!" Peety yells back. "Tie Princesa!"

As Andy attempts to tie a frisky Princesa to the cottonwood, Franny darts away from West and starts kicking up her heels, too. The only member of the remuda who wants nothing to do with the stallions is Paloma, who plunks her bottom down in the middle of the stream.

While Andy secures Princesa's lead, I distract the horse with some raisins.

Two stallions reach Skinny and Lupe, hungry for the pretty mares. The mares stop prancing and let the stallions nudge and sniff at them.

Cay reaches the horses and raises his riding whip. "Shoo, you horny rascals, before I quirt you!"

Not thirty feet away, a black stallion, drooling with desire, attempts to mount Franny. West pulls her harness in a circle so the stallion can't get good purchase.

I wring my shirt hem at the sight of that poor stallion,

begging for relief. Franny, too. It's not their fault. It is spring, after all.

The stallion snaps its teeth and lets out a scream that chills my blood. Rearing up, it plants its forelegs on Franny's back. West lays his quirt hard upon the stallion's flank.

Now the stallion recognizes West as the source of its frustration and it screams again. I scream, too, as the monster bangs its front legs right in front of West, almost stepping on him. Then the stallion's great head crashes down, and it bites West on the shoulder. West clutches his arm and curses, stumbling backward into Franny.

That horse could kill him. The realization hits me like a punch to the gut. I may be a nuisance to him, but to me, he is one of the few people who matter in this world. My own survival depends on his.

I grab Andy.

"The tree!" I cry, pointing at a bur oak. "Your rope!" I circle with my finger.

Andy understands perfectly. She unhitches her rope from Princesa's saddle as well as the one from Paloma's saddle. One twenty-foot rope won't be long enough. I pray she remembers the sweetheart knot.

I charge toward West, pulling my gun from the holster, knowing I cannot yet shoot the stallion for it stands too close to Franny and West. I aim it in the air and fire.

The stallion whips its head around, slinging saliva from its mouth. It rolls its eyes at me.

"Leave them alone, or I'll geld you in one shot," I yell, willing the stallion to hold still so I can get a better aim. Instead, it charges me.

Though I race across the plains faster than I ever expected these legs could go, you cannot outrun a stallion on foot. This is common knowledge, though I imagine many a man has lost his life trying to disprove this theory.

Running is not my forte, though neither is being a boy. I tear over to the oak, which suddenly seems very far. But the sight of Andy and her lariat spurs me on.

Just as my lungs feel like they will burst, Andy casts. Her rope catches the stallion around the neck. Yes! Andy hastens to fasten the loose end around the oak. I don't watch this part as I'm running like crazy around the tree. If her knot isn't secure, it won't hurt to tie things a little snugger.

Finally after several wide circles, I think the stallion has cinched the noose tight enough. I dash away and fall to the ground with Andy, heaving lungfuls of air. I doubt I will ever move again, but the sound of a gunshot brings me up onto my knees.

In the distance, two stallions crash to the ground. Skinny and Lupe skitter, agitated, but their virtue remains intact.

Andy and I scramble to our feet and over to West, who leans upon Franny.

I must be crying because West groans, "Sammy," in his exasperated way. Andy ties up Franny, and I help West to the ground. We prop him up with blankets and unbutton his blood-soaked shirt.

I dry my eyes. The wound curves over his shoulder and down

to his chest on the right side. My stomach cramps at the sight of so much blood, but this is not the time for girlish vapors. I mop up the blood with West's bandanna so I can inspect the wound. I see bone.

"Your needle," I say to Andy.

She rushes to get her saddlebag.

Another shot explodes from behind me, and I jump. The black stallion drops to the ground under the bur oak.

"No." I groan. Peety kneels by the stallion and bows his head.

West moans, and I slide my arm around the back of his shoulders to listen to his breathing, coming in short gasps.

"'Breathing is underrated.'" I repeat Father's words. Then I draw in deep breaths for him to mimic.

He turns his face in to my neck and inhales.

Andy returns with her sewing kit and rags. She offers Peety's flask to West, but he clamps his mouth shut and returns to my neck. After she cleans the wound, she sews, her hand steady and fleet.

West gasps at the first poke, his nose grazing my ear. Then he falls silent. When she finishes, my face is wet on the side where I hold him. He has gone limp, and I gently set him back to the ground.

The other boys settle the remuda and now stand over West, Cay with his hands in his pockets, and Peety staring down, his face tight.

"We can't stay here," says Cay. "The vultures will come soon, and they'll spook the horses."

"We can't move him," I protest. I won't risk losing him now.

"We'll move him farther upstream, away from these dead stallions." Cay squints at the dark heaps in the distance. "No one can sleep with a dead horse nearby. Trust me on that."

Everyone looks at me. Andy bobs her chin ever so slightly.

I let out my breath and nod.

"Maybe we say something for those *caballos* before we going," says Peety, wiping his brow.

We all remove our hats.

"Dear God, we're sorry we had to return your stallions to you earlier than you expected," Cay says. "They couldn't help being who they are any more than we can, I s'pect. Ashes to ashes, dust to dust, and all the rest."

"Amen," adds Andy. "Let's go, then."

Peety strings up the remuda while we carefully position West on a blanket. Then we each lift a corner.

We carry him up the stream until the stallions are out of sight, then camp under a pair of cottonwood trees that lean toward each other, providing a green canopy. Andy helps me remove West's bloody shirt, then she takes it to the stream. I press some rags to his chest, still oozing blood. He may require more stitches. But not now.

Peety sets about the currying, staring at nothing. Cay also falls silent. The one who takes charge is Andy.

"You, blondie, you thinking of growing roots? Pick up some sticks. And you, brownie, you's brushing those horses bald. Haul some water."

Cay decides to ride out to Fort Laramie that night. We need a doctor, medical supplies, and food. His green eyes shine too bright against his ashen face.

"Wait until morning," I say in a low voice as he packs up Skinny.

He digs a knuckle into his temple. "We've done night rides before."

"You're tired, and so is Skinny." I hope I don't sound too motherly.

He gives me a lopsided smile and kicks off.

26

I FALL ASLEEP BY WEST'S SIDE BUT WAKE WHEN-
ever he moans. Finally, when the sun travels over my face, I
rise. The prairie is a shadowed landscape clotted with shrubs
like giant mushrooms. With the trail out of view and no one
around, the world seems foreign, as if we've arrived at a country
where we are the only inhabitants. It relieves me to be out of the
scope of lawmen, but it is a fleeting comfort. We cannot hide
out here forever.

Peety takes West's rifle to go hunting, and Andy accompanies him. Before they leave, I ask them to look out for wild yarrow. Father always applied the cooling yarrow to my bumps and
scrapes. Maybe it will bring West some relief.

When I start to change his dressings, he winces. I show him
the whiskey but he presses his mouth into a line and turns away.

"Okay. What about a story while I clean your scratch?" He
does not protest so I press on.

"Father and I were about the only Chinese people in the state
of New York when I was growing up. Mr. Wong owned a bakery
down the street from us, but he did not have family. So whenever
we went out, people paid attention.

"When I was six, someone brought a menagerie to town." I pause as I realize that was almost ten years ago to the day. I turn sixteen next week. "I begged Father to go, but he didn't want to take me, probably fearing we would become another exhibit for people to point and stare at. I was born in the Year of the Snake—"

I pause when the ghost of a frown flits over his face. "It's not a bad thing," I add. "A Snake brings good luck." I don't mention that I'm the exception. "Anyway, I wouldn't be so quick to judge, you were born in the Year of the Rabbit."

He chokes on his disbelief, I suspect most men prefer to think of themselves as something more ferocious than a rabbit, and I let him finish his coughing before continuing. I muse that, despite their lovable appearances, Rabbits are uncomfortable talking about feelings, and if matters turn personal, tend to hop away. Of course, West can hop all he wants, but he won't be getting too far in his condition.

"Snakes don't like to be told no."

More throat clearing ensues, which I ignore.

"So Father gave in and took me. While I was counting zebra stripes, a crowd of children gathered, but they didn't care about the zebras. They were staring at me.

"'I bet it feels like rope,' said one little girl. She was talking about my hair, which had grown so long I could sit on it. Father always combed it so gently before braiding it, like Peety does the horses' tails."

West lifts an eyebrow and a zing of panic shoots through me.

I sweep my hand through the air in what I hope is a gesture of indifference. "All Chinese boys wear long braids, you know. It's just the style."

His eyebrow settles back down and I hurry on with my narrative. "The girl's father told her, 'Nope, it ain't like rope, it's like a snake, and it will bite you, so leave it alone.'

"She could not resist. She edged toward me, but I didn't turn around. And then, when I could almost feel her hand reaching for my hair, I spun around real fast, and yelled, 'Boo!'

"She screamed and ran away. Everyone laughed at her, instead of me, especially Father."

West starts to chuckle, but the movement triggers a spasm of pain. His face screws up, and I put a cool towel on his head until he relaxes again and closes his eyes. I wish for him the kind of sleep that Homer called a 'counterfeit death,' delicious and profound.

A while later, Peety and Andy bring back a prairie chicken. Peety and I follow Andy to the stream after watching her plunge the bird in boiling water.

She hands the chicken to Peety. "Go."

"Ay, too hot, Andito," says Peety, bouncing the bird in his hands.

"Don't juggle it, just pluck it. A deal's a deal," says Andy. She winks at me. "*I* caught it, so he's doing the cooking today."

Then she pulls out a bouquet of feathery gray leaves from in the back of Peety's belt. "Here's your weeds."

I thank them and rinse the bunch in the stream. "He's hurting," I say as I pound the yarrow into a poultice with a rock. "What do you think about slipping him some of your whiskey, Peety? I know he does not want to drink it, but this is an emergency."

"No, *chico*. You cannot do that," he says, ripping out feathers.

"Careful! You's gonna take off the wings," protests Andy.

"Ees okay, chicken no using them no more. West had *uno problemo* with the spirits, the whiskey."

"West?" I repeat, as if we could be talking about someone else.

"He was only ten, maybe. His papa don't like nobody, blacks, reds, yellows, not even his own son. Even after Cay's family took him, papa still hurting him in here." He taps his heart with his fist. "Maybe he don't want to live no more. Maybe there's too much hurting inside and can't be fixed." He stops plucking. "So, he runs away many times. Cay always find him, passed out somewhere with a bottle. Not always good stuff either, you know. Sometimes, very bad stuff. Puts demons in your mind. Maybe those demons easier than ones papa put there."

My chest burns, like someone poured in poison. Andy takes the chicken and finishes plucking it.

Peety wipes his hands on a rag. "This happens until he's fourteen and old enough to work at El Rancho. West finds peace with animals. But those demons are always there in the bottle. So he don't go near it. You understand now?"

I nod, then return to West's side with the poultice. He seems to be stable for now, no fever that I can tell, though his face is pale as death. I watch his eyelashes flicker in deepest slumber, and wonder at the wounds that tear at him from the inside.

Peety doesn't want an audience when he makes dinner so Andy and I sit by the river. The water tumbles by, blissfully unaware of the suffering upon its shores. Yellow grass and tangled reeds gain footholds on the opposite bank where the ground is less rocky.

"You's gonna freeze like a gryphon statue hanging over West." Andy cuts her eyes to me. "Don't look at me like that, I know what a gryphon is. Lion body with an eagle head that's always stuck out like it's gonna pounce. Ungodly things. Miss Betsy had a statue of one she made me clean every day. It got real dirty between the claws, even though it never caught anything."

We dip our toes in the water. "What kind of demons do you think West's father put in him?"

"The worst kind, is my guess. Child's supposed to depend on his parents. Better to have no daddy at all than one that hurts you."

"But his daddy's been gone for years."

She kicks up her foot throwing water across the stream. "Your head's like a room and when you's forced to stay in it, you gotta deal with all the trash that's left in there."

Andy reminds me of you, Father, and your infinite wisdom. "You think everyone has trash?"

"Yep, I do. Even the ones whose head you think is empty, like Cay. Bet he's full of it." She grins, and I feel my cheeks lifting, too.

Peety calls us back to the fire, where the horse blankets have been folded in three neat squares for sitting. Between two of the squares, a bouquet of purple blazing stars blooms from one of West's empty boots.

Andy eyes the floral arrangement with a bemused expression. "You got a lady friend in town?" She makes a show of looking behind herself at the miles and miles of empty prairie land.

Peety chuckles. "I got no lady friend." With his handkerchief, he whacks at the folded horse blankets, then gestures toward them. "Please sit in my best chairs."

Andy and I plunk down, and he proudly hands us steaming mugs of soup. "I put in a surprise for you."

"What do you mean by that?" asks Andy.

Peety grins. "If I told you, it's no surprise." He kneels beside us and digs into his soup, even though it's still steaming.

I watch him carefully blow his spoon, then I ask, "Who is Esme?"

The vaquero lowers his mug to his lap. "Esme." He stares into his soup as if seeing a memory. "She is the youngest of my four sisters. They're all trouble, but Esme worries me the most. The other three, they will make good Mexican wives one day, but not Esme." He looks up from his lap, lips curved into a sad smile. "Please, enjoy your soup."

I stir my cup, wondering about this youngest sister, and something round comes to the surface. As Andy brings her own mug to her lips, she looks at my spoon. Abruptly, she sets down her cup, nearly scalding herself. She runs to the river.

Peety's broad face splits open in confusion. "He don't even try it."

I show him the onion on my spoon. It still wears its papery peel, like he just dropped it in recently. "You put onions in the soup."

"I found in my bag. Three of them for three of us."

I remember the onions I put there from Cay's lumpy sack back at the Little Blue. Sure took him a long enough time to find.

"He doesn't like them," I explain. "It's not your fault."

I hurry over to Andy, with Peety on my heels. She hugs her knees to her as she glares at the river.

"I'm sorry, Andito," says Peety. "I ruin your dinner for you."

She waves us away, so we return to the fire. I try my best to finish my soup, raw onion and all, just to make Peety feel better.

The next day, West's temperature spikes, and I alternate bundling him up with fanning him down. Andy simmers a new soup, this time with no onions. A layer of fat swims on top. But West has no appetite for it and only takes a few sips of water. When he slips into sleep, his pain follows him and he cries.

"She didn't do it," he gasps during one nightmare.

I take his hand, clammy and trembling. The two scars on his wrist peek out from under his sleeve, gleaming like the eyes of a ghost. I match my fingertips to them, and they feel hot under my touch.

He opens his eyes and squints at me, like he is trying to remember who I am. "Sammy?"

"Yes."

Then he fades back into unconsciousness.

Every hour I put the cup of broth to his lips, but he will not take it, not even with me spooning it to him. Eventually he stops sweating and his eyes lose focus.

"West," I call to him. His eyes slit open for a moment. "You need to drink something, or you will…" I can't say it. "Please?"

Still, he does not drink.

Later that night, I beg sleep to open her doors to me. She leads me to a barren field. West and I face each other dressed as two knights, wearing armor too heavy to shed. The earth opens and swallows him. I clutch his hand just like that day we wrestled, but he is slipping from my grasp.

When he refuses to drink again the third day, I want to shake him in desperation. "Come on, drink, or I might do something reckless."

Nothing.

Peety and Andy took the horses out to graze and will not return for another hour. The late-morning sun hides in a tepid curdle of clouds.

I shuffle to the water. A random trail of stones lines the shallow stream. I roll up my trousers and step out of my boots. I remember Father walking a path of stones. He said it helped him sort through problems. *A balanced body balances the mind.*

I step up onto a steady rock with my right foot and hold my left in back of me.

Problem one: the faraway Mr. Trask.

I had accepted the possibility that I might never find him when I decided to go with Andy, even if she still hasn't accepted my company. Yet I held out hope that I might cross paths with the grocer before Calamity Cutoff, especially now that we are so close. With every passing moment, however, he slips farther from my grasp. And with Lady Tin-Yin gone, the loss will be doubly bitter.

A twinge of sadness stirs me again as I remember Father, his face full of hope as he told me, "I have great plans for us. We might even see a mermaid!"

I grimace and pass to the next stone.

Maybe Mr. Trask has experienced some delays of his own. We can't be the only ones.

Water laps at my foot. I cannot stand here forever. I move to the next stone, one that requires me to leap and catch my balance again.

Problem two: West will die if he does not drink. I nearly fall into the stream but hold out my arms to steady myself and hop onto a larger rock. Pain, not just physical, seems to have stolen his sense of self-preservation. I felt the same way, not long ago.

I wobble too far to the right and step onto the next stone. Balance. Think.

Angry tears prick my eyes as I remember the assault that pulled me out of my despair. Ty Yorkshire's hand over my mouth. I inhale and pass to the next stone, a sharp one that wobbles.

Forcing Ty Yorkshire's moth eye out of my head, I replace it with West's handsome visage. *We all have secrets, don't we? Secrets that can destroy us, one way or another. Yours are buried deep, too deep for me to reach.*

I pass to the final boulder. There I stand on both legs and close my eyes, not easy, I realize, when I almost fall forward. I sway again but grip the boulder more firmly with my feet.

I have kept secrets from you, and still you saved my life, twice. And now that your secrets threaten to kill you, it is my turn to save you from the fire, even if it means you will learn the truth about me.

I open my eyes and drop from the boulder into the cool stream. Time to make good on my threat.

Once I get back to camp, I kneel next to West and comb the hair off his face. His eyelashes flutter. "May you forget this, or at least forgive me if you do not."

Then I fold my hankie into a square that I use to press down his chin.

I sip the broth and hold the salty warm liquid in my mouth. Lifting his head, I press my lips to his, not lifting my mouth until he opens his to take the broth. His moan catches in my throat as his parched mouth warms under mine. I don't care if he finds it distasteful, only that he swallows the broth.

He does.

Then I do it again.

This time, when my lips slide over his, his mouth parts easier. I release another sip, a tiny amount so I don't choke him. When I lift my head, he is gazing at me. He drops his eyes to the cup in my hand. More.

Though I think I can revert to the spoon now, I don't want to.

My pulse beats fast as a hummingbird's. Did he recognize the truth when it kissed him on the mouth? The way he looks there now, his eyes soft and searching, tells me maybe. My body floods with warmth, and all my boyish resolve melts away.

Two more mouthfuls, and then three. As I feed him the last drop and begin to pull away, his lips follow mine for a fraction of a second.

The empty cup drops from my hand and lands with a tinny *thud* beside us at the same as time he collapses back onto his bed-roll. Still close enough to feel his breath on my face, I open my eyes to his, shrouded in pain. He turns his head away.

27

CAY RETURNS IN THE LATE MORNING AS PEETY, Andy, and I drink our coffee. We crowd around him as he slides off Skinny. His bloodshot eyes take in his cousin, sleeping again, this time peacefully. Shortly after Peety and Andy returned, West drank another two cups of soup by himself.

"They don't got a doctor, but they gave me a boatload of stuff," Cay tells us. "How is he?"

"Better," I say. "His fever broke."

We unload Cay's supplies: bandages, soap, and food.

"Come here, Skinnita *bonita*, your *papi* will give you a nice brushing now. Clean your pretty hooves, too." Peety kisses Skinny on the nose and leads her to the river.

Cay collapses by the fire, his face drawn in a way that ages him. Looking at him now, I catch a glimpse of the man he will be, still sweet, but more subdued, even reflective. A tinge of sadness dampens my mood as I realize I will not be there to see his older self. Andy pulls off his boots and socks while I beat out his bedroll. Soon, he joins his cousin in the land of nod.

"Cay must have moths in his boots. Look," says Andy, poking her fingers through his socks.

"Or mice."

Andy pulls out a ball of yarn from her saddlebag. "Real men wouldn't darn socks for each other, but I can't help myself."

"The boys might if they knew how." I wring out a warm cloth to use on Cay's dusty face and hands. Andy wants to scrape out the dirt from under his fingernails with her knitting needle, but I stop her.

Cay is still sleeping when West awakes mid-afternoon. I wrap West's arm in a sling while Andy prepares biscuits down by the stream. He flinches at my touch, though I'm uncertain whether the pain comes from his shoulder or from being near me. At least his color has returned.

After I finish, he mutters, "Don't you have anything better to do than wait on me?"

I stiffen as the sting brightens my cheeks. Andy slaps her dough loudly, then starts kneading it. West is giving off his hard look again, the one with the eyebrows of doom and the frowning mouth. He won't look at me.

I go to shower my attentions on one who has no reservations about accepting them: Paloma.

We race down the riverbank, but I can't erase West's glare from my mind.

It wasn't that horrible, was it? No one was there, and I don't have cholera or worms. So what if another boy's mouth touched yours. It kept you alive, didn't it?

Or maybe he did figure out my secret. My thighs grip Paloma too hard and she slows. Maybe he knew all along and never said anything because kissing a Chinese girl would be as indecent as kissing a boy. I can't help remembering the story West told about painting the fence. He said there were certain things about him he could never change. No matter how hard he tried, he could not get the blood out of the paint. Was he talking about his father's bigotry? West couldn't be a bigot himself, not with a Mexican as such a close friend. Not with the way he defended us against the MacMartins.

But who knows what lies beneath the glass? Father said people are like bottles of rice and water, which need heat to transform into a fine rice wine. Too little heat, and the wine is sour and weak. Too much, and the fermentation stops all together. But with patience, the mix will ripen into an exquisite drink, and only the winemaker knows when that time will come.

I pat my mule's neck and find comfort in the silky tufts of her mane. Father told me not to brood when people judged me for my wrapper, not my filling, or I would spend my whole life in the steamer.

When we arrive back at camp, West is standing with one hand on Franny's saddle. The others watch him from under the shade of the cottonwoods.

He's back on his feet again. Can I catch Mr. Trask after all? With each day that we rest, the man gains fifteen miles on us, which means we're forty-five miles farther behind. West won't be well enough to travel for another few days, which means roughly... a hundred miles behind.

With a heavy heart, I dismount and join the others.

Franny whinnies in reply to something West says. He removes his hand from her saddle and takes a small step forward holding her lead rope. Franny also steps forward. Then West steps backward, to the right, and to the left. Franny follows in perfect synchronicity. My mouth opens at this small miracle, despite my irritation.

"Horse is man's best friend," says Peety, noticing my surprise. "And I got lots of best friends. That one, her mama kick her in the head when she was born. Nobody want her anymore." He sweeps the air with his hands. "But she is the smartest one in whole remuda. You know *caballo* is for you when she reflects your soul. That is why Franny and West move like magic."

Cay nods, his face serious.

Later that afternoon, Andy and I walk a quarter mile down the river with a pile of grayish rags for what we now call our minute-baths.

"Never doubted West was gonna make it," she says as we undress. "He got all the angels pulling for him. Some people's like that." She smells one of her shirts and wrinkles her nose. "Eh. Don't like grimy things."

I smell my own shirt as she continues. "You's mind's busy lately, but you know you's still on schedule, right?"

We hop into the water and make short work of scouring ourselves. "Cay told Peety wagons got to wait their turn into the fort 'cause of all the folks twiddling their thumbs, trying to decide if they want to climb the Rockies. You gotta wait at least a week if you got wagons." Her teeth begin to chatter.

I go still as hope seeps through my veins. Maybe I can catch Mr. Trask after all. "Thanks," I say carefully. If Andy knew how pleased I was, she'd be even more reluctant to let me go with her.

"You's in good hands with the boys," she says, reading me perfectly anyway.

"I already told you I wasn't going to let you go off on your own," I grumble. "Even if it is a waterfall, what if it's not the right one?"

"Then I'll keep looking." She steps out of the water and dries herself while I move more slowly beside her. After she presses the water out of her head with a rag, she binds herself with a clean apron tie. The tie is still bright pink despite all of Andy's vigorous beatings. I guess certain qualities are more stubborn than others.

My frozen fingers fumble with my buttons. "There could be hundreds of waterfalls around these mountains. You'd be wandering forever."

She chews her lip as she tucks in the ends of her tie. "Well, that Calamity Cutoff ain't for another two weeks. Don't let it trouble us right now."

She dismisses me, and I'm afraid to argue with her. Now that West's health is improving, Andy might feel free to fly away.

We beat out the rags with stones and clean them with a bit of soap.

"Take these wet things and dry 'em in the pot while I hunt down miner's lettuce," Andy says.

As she proceeds down the river, I stare after her as if she might decide to bolt right now. She stoops and sifts her hand through long bundles of reeds, yanking out lettuce. With a sigh, I scoop up our wet rags plus Andy's second apron tie, then trudge the quarter mile back to our camp.

When I return, the boys are standing in the river. I throw the rags into a dry pot Andy left heating on the fire. She says the heat gets them cleaner, not to mention, dries them faster. I stir them around with a fork and let them get toasty. The lacy apron tie stands out amongst the grayish rags.

One by one, I hang the rags on a length of rope strung between two branches of the cottonwood. I will have to take Andy's apron tie somewhere else to finish drying.

Peety walks up, carrying his holey boots. He's rolled the hems of his trousers past the knee. The river has matted the black hair of his legs. "Hey, Chinito. Still hard at work, eh?"

"You work harder than me," I say truthfully.

"It's not work to me." He grins. His sunny disposition immediately lifts my spirits. "You and Andito take good care of us. I want you to know we appreciate it. We're like a big *familia*, eh?"

"Yeah, we are."

He carefully sets down his boots, then settles on a blanket. I toss him one of the warm rags.

"*Muchas gracias*," he says, using the rag to wipe his feet.

Familia. Family. Peety would never let Andy go by herself to Harp Falls if he knew she was a girl. He cares for her, maybe even as much as I do. If he knew she was a girl, he would feel a lot differently about the *chico* to whom he gave a horse.

Without thinking, I reach into the pot for the apron tie, that scrap Andy uses to suppress her female form. If Peety saw this, he would wonder at its bright pink sheen and lace edges, so incongruous amongst our weedy surroundings. Questions would give way to suspicions and then realizations.

"What you doing there, Chinito?" asks Peety, studying me with my hand in the pot.

What am I thinking? Quickly, I let go of the tie. I can't betray Andy, no matter what. "Oh, nothing. Do you know where the map is? I want to look it over." When he twists around to fetch Cay's saddlebag, I quickly stuff the tie into my pocket.

28

TWO MORE DAYS PASS, AND WEST RALLIES HIS
sand, as Cay puts it. On the sixth morning, when I open my eyes,
West is sketching something in his journal. I try not to make
any noise as I lift my head off the crook of my arm to glimpse
what he draws.

It is me as my six-year-old self. He did the braid perfectly.
There are my eyes, my nose, and now my lips. But then his charcoal stops, and he crumples the paper and throws it in the fire.

When he hears me stirring, he declares loudly, "I'm going
crazy sitting here doing nothing. I want to get back on my taps."

So we pack up. West drapes his arm over Franny's saddle and
walks. We take up our usual positions and head back to the trail,
all of us on foot. Nearly a week has passed since the stallion bit
West, which means we're back on track with Mr. Trask, given
the week-long delay for wagons at Fort Laramie. With luck, we
might catch up soon.

Andy starts singing "Amazing Grace" with her warm gospel
voice, in the low key she uses to avoid suspicion. No one joins
her. Andy's gospel solos always make us weep for our mothers.

I rub my neck, sore from hours of sitting and taking care of
West, and think about his drawings. Maybe he doesn't hate me

for assaulting him with my mouth. In fact, maybe he liked it, and that's why he pushed me away. The thought goes to my head like champagne bubbles. I sit up straighter.

Not for the first time, I think about telling West that I am a girl. At least that might clear up one possible source of confusion for him. He might never trust me again, but at least he could put his head right about himself. And if his distaste for me stems from the fact that I'm Chinese, then I will know for myself what kind of man he is, and that will clear up some confusion for *me*. I glance back and catch him looking at me. He scowls and stares gloomily into the endless sea of amber grass.

If I told West the truth, then Andy and I would have to reveal the whole truth to everyone, since I could not burden him with that secret. Then they would knowingly be harboring criminals. Would the boys feel enough of a kinship to us that they would be able to lie to protect us?

We may never find out.

We only travel a few miles the first day, stopping frequently to let West catch his breath. After another sunrise, he is back on Franny for the full day.

Soon, we rejoin the queue of emigrants bound for Fort Laramie, and Andy and I are back to keeping our chins tucked in and our hats low. We travel as one long snake toward the white adobe walls of the fort, rising like a giant white bread box set atop an outcropping of bedrock. All around us, tents, tepees, and wagons spread out as far as the eye can see.

Just as Cay reported, the wagons grind to a halt in the middle of the trail at least a mile before the fort. The remuda weaves through the wagons, stepping high with short strides. Heads turn as we pass. Paloma does her best to follow along with me crouching against her neck.

When the fort is about the size of a wagon in the distance, Andy calls for a halt, and we dig in at a spot by the swift-moving Laramie River. Thanks to the river, the grass grows a deep shade of green.

"More folks here than we seen in the last month put together," says Andy.

I take in the debris littering the fields: barrels, wheels, a loom. I even spot a piano. "And they left their junk everywhere."

"I think those are from them who brought too much and need to lighten the load."

Andy and I untack the remuda, and the boys walk the last quarter mile to the fort. They'll use one of Ty Yorkshire's rings this time to pay for our supplies.

Pulling off saddles and brushing coats is hot work, and soon we're both glistening with sweat. Andy rolls up her sleeves. The boys have seen her square brand with the six dots by now, but they've never questioned her about it.

I work a brush between Paloma's ears. "You think it's time to tell the boys the truth? Maybe they'd even come with us to the falls."

"Sammy." She gives me a look of supreme patience. Unbuckling Princesa's saddle, she hauls it to the ground. "You don't give up easily, do you?"

"Regretfully, no. And so you know, even if you did leave,

you'd just be giving Paloma and me more work to do looking for you."

Scowling, she shakes her head. "I just hate to think about you giving up on you's daddy's dream, 'specially after losin' you's violin."

I don't let on how much I hate it, too. "I'm not giving up. I'm just taking a detour. My father would understand. He always said people come before things."

She lifts her eyes to the heavens and consults with a cloud. Not dropping her gaze, she says, "I'm gonna feel guilty about this the rest of my life, but . . . okay. You can come with me."

I throw my arms around her. She lets me stay for a moment, then pushes me off. "About the boys . . ." She bends down and rubs Princesa's leg. "They've done nothing but good by us." Still squatting, she looks up at me. "So if you want to tell them, it's okay by me."

I smile. "I wonder what Peety will say when he finds out we're *chicas*, not *chicos*." I stomp down the dried grass, then kneel beside her.

Her face breaks into a grin. "Maybe he won't say anything for a change. Cay will probably want us to unshuck to prove it. But what about West?"

I blink in the bright sunlight. "Sometimes I think he knows. But then, why wouldn't he say anything?"

"Well, the other day I swung Peety's fifty-pound saddle onto Lupe. He didn't even blink. I'd say we've gotten pretty good at being boys. I bet I could even fool Isaac."

"You think he's changed much?"

She shrugs. "It's been five years since I seen him." A shadow passes over her face. She begins to knead her scar, her eyes unfocused and troubled.

Gently, I say, "You know you can always tell me about your trash."

"It ain't right to track my dirt in your house."

"Father told me that sweeping the Whistle three times a day would improve my bow strokes."

"Did it?"

"I don't know. But I got really good at sweeping."

She groans, but I see the glimmer of a smile before it quickly disappears. "When Isaac was sold off separate from us, Tommy began to cry real hard. He was seven at the time. Isaac wiggled his ears at him—that was our sign that everything was going to be okay—but that just made Tommy cry harder."

"Poor thing," I murmur.

"So the auctioneer plugged Tommy's mouth with an onion. I started screaming when he did that, and then I got an onion, too."

"Oh, Andy."

"Isaac went crazy. Normally, he's gentle as sunshine in April, but when he's pushed, he's more like a hurricane. He threw off the two men holding him, and started toward us, like maybe he's going to get us free, but of course, he's no match for a rifle. They forced him to his knees, made him put his face in horse droppings"—her voice breaks—"made him eat it, to show him his place." Her face squeezes tight, but two tears still escape and I pass her my handkerchief.

"I am sorry for that," I say, my own eyes watering as well, and she nods. It occurs to me that maybe God is in charge of the stars, after all. Maybe He has been saving Andy from the horrors of her life, little by little each day, and perhaps the trouble ahead isn't so bad as the trouble she left behind. I sure hope that is the case.

Together, we watch the horses several yards away. Andy's breath gradually begins to lengthen. She nudges me and jerks her chin toward the deserted piano. "You know how to play?"

"Yes," I say cautiously, glancing around. This is the worst time to draw attention to ourselves, with the fort a holler away. The place is probably crawling with soldiers, same as Fort Kearny. Yet, I can think of no better way to cheer up Andy than with that cure-all that knows no cultural bounds: music. A few people are setting up tents in the distance, but they're probably too far to hear.

"Ain't every day you come across a piano on the prairie."

I hesitate. "All right, sister."

We drag discarded barrels over to the piano and hunker down. My skills with the ivory keys are not great, but I pick out a tune, one of Father's favorites about a cat and a banjo. Soon, Andy starts humming along. I play the final note, and someone clears his throat right behind us.

We jump to our feet and turn around to find a man, his face grizzled and sweaty under an unusual cap with a flat top and visor. I have seen such a cap before, in our safe at the Whistle. It belonged to Pépère, a relic from his days in the French Army.

I gulp. I've heard of foreigners hiring themselves to police the frontier, since no one else wants to do it.

"Jean Michel," he says a heavy accent.

Definitely French. I lick my lips, casting sideways glances around for an escape route. Surely if he were a soldier, he would have immediately stated his rank. Plus, he is not wearing a uniform, but tweed trousers and a linen shirt.

The man's cap dips toward the piano. "Zat was my mother's."

My ears redden, but the rest of me sinks back into my boots. He is only an emigrant, not a soldier. *"Pardonez-moi."*

He smiles, showing us the space between his top teeth. *"Pas de problème.* Ees good to hear her sing one last time."

He throws out a few more questions in French, which I answer using manly grunts and some of his native tongue. Andy goes mute.

"We are here for one week already," he says, waving toward the nearest wagon circle. "Half want to go, half want to stay. Dinner ees for our last night as one group. Big fun. Would you join us? Bring your friends." Jean Michel heads back to his caravan.

French party. Dare we attend? It would be a dream come true for Cay. Those French lessons would finally pay off. It would just be a few hours, and I owe him. Andy's kneading her scar again, her gaze far away. Maybe a celebration would be good for us all.

29

THE BOYS RETURN FROM THE FORT WITH NEW SUP-
plies. They visited the barber and now look more like *chicos* than
hombres, especially with Peety whirling around in his new boots.

Cay paws at his cheeks. My eyes cut to West's fair complexion, which, now stripped of its shadow, seems to glow. I can't
help smiling at how healthy he looks. His eyes immediately shift
elsewhere, like two billiard balls moved by my cue.

Andy pulls out her journal. "So how much we spend?"

"Twenty-seven," says Cay, handing her the change.

We tell the boys about our dinner date, but for Cay, we might
as well have told him the circus was in town. "Real Frenchies?"
He puffs out his chest and checks to see that his muscles still
work. "Sammy, Andito, I owe you big."

I help him review some phrases he thinks might be useful
like *Entre deux coeurs qui s'aiment, nul besoin de paroles* ("Two hearts
in love need no words"), and *Voulez-vous m'épouser?* ("Will you
marry me?").

Within the French wagon circle, our hosts have arranged
chairs and tables with wildflowers and candles, even toile table-
cloths.

"They do things up fancy here," Andy murmurs to me.

While Jean Michel introduces us to the other French families, I try to stand in the back with Andy, but the boys need me to translate. So I tuck in my round parts and cross my arms over my chest like a seasoned boy. Half the families do speak some English, and we gravitate toward these folks.

My presence does not cause the stir it usually does, a fact that puzzles as much as relieves me. People are friendly to Andy, too, shaking her hand, and clapping her on the back. The boys drift toward a flock of girls.

A round woman with a chunky braid wrapping her head hands us wet cloths scented with lemon. "Madame Moreau," she introduces herself as we wipe our hands on the cloths. The ruffles on her blouse flap as she switches her attention between Andy and me.

She settles on me. "In France, we had lots of Chinois."

"Why did you come to America?" I ask.

"After Napoleon, our farmland ees destroyed. We heard about ze good chances here." She raises her hand toward two girls sitting with Cay. "My Mathilde, her cousin Sophie, zey like everything *américain*."

Both play with their hair. Mathilde strokes her own thick braid and her cousin Sophie slings around the dark ringlets framing her face. Crocheted caps droop over the girls' eyes and frilly lace adorns their pinafores. Like Cay and West, the only physical similarity lies in their smile.

While Madame Moreau engages Andy, I watch a man in a buckskin coat converse with West nearby. West's eyes drift to me and then snap back to his company. But the man waves me over.

"Burl Johnson," he says, as his meaty hand swallows mine. The lapels of his buckskin are trimmed with thick beaver fur. "You people put me out of work."

"Oh?"

"You and your Silk Road," he says, tapping tobacco onto a square of paper and rolling it into a cigarette. "Beaver used to be fashionable."

Finally, I catch on. "You're a trapper."

"Was. Now I work here. Lots of us became wagon leaders 'cause we know the terrain."

West rubs at his face, probably desperate to escape this conversation and, more important, me. I twist at my shirt hem. I will tell him tonight, when I can catch him alone.

Johnson lights the quirley, then hands it to West. "Real men smoke Virginia leaf, none of that Mexican weed."

West studies the cigarette for a moment. I've never seen him smoke, but he takes it and inhales a long drag, blowing the smoke to one side.

Johnson rolls another, but I don't notice until he strikes the match. "Here you go, China boy."

"Oh—no—I couldn't," I stammer as he pokes the cigarette between my lips. I try not to breathe.

He frowns at me and my frozen mouth. "Inhale. You gotta taste it."

"Those Virginians sure know how to spank a man," says West, watching me from behind the film of smoke stinging my eyes. He sucks hard on his quirley, then throws it to the dirt half-smoked and crushes it with the toe of his boot. I hiccup in a bit of the smoke. The fumes fill my lungs like hot vinegar, and I cough them back out in a panic. I might as well stick my head in an oven full of old boots.

Johnson laughs and claps me on the shoulder. "Welcome to America. Truth is, I don't blame you too much for your silkworms. Beaver population just ain't what it used to be. Now all you find in the Haystacks are criminals."

"Haystacks?" I ask.

"The mountain range of the Yellow River."

My hacking masks my alarm. I look around for Andy. She's still talking with Madame Moreau.

"Hey, translator, get your tail over here!" Cay yells at me from the opposite direction.

Still coughing, I hurry away from Johnson and West.

Cay pulls me closer by the sleeve of my shirt. "Don't smoke in front of the girls." He plucks the quirley out of my fingers and takes a drag of it himself. Then he stomps it out. "I wanna tell *les filles* about our little adventure with the stallions. *Comment tu dis* 'sausage'?"

"*Saucisson.*" Too late I realize his intent.

"*Saucisson?*" repeats the curly brunette, Sophie. "*L'étalon a un grand saucisson?*"

The girls scream with laughter, and I frost Cay with my eyes. I turn to leave.

"No, wait," says Cay. "Tell 'em the rest of the story. Come on."

"Why doesn't your mother translate?" I ask Mathilde. She gives me a blank stare.

Sophie digs her nails into my arm, which I yank away.

"*S'il vous plaît,* please." She bats her heavy-lidded eyes imploringly.

I snort, caught in the trap of my own making. I wish I could summon up a burp, but the best I can do is make a loud slurping sound with my nose.

Then I summarize the story in French, including the part about West's injury. When the girls cast their eyes in his direction, I kick myself. At least I dimmed the light of Cay's candle. He deserves that, the cad.

Before I lose my appetite altogether, I march over to Peety and Andy, who are holding up their plates to be filled. I want to tell Andy about the Haystacks, but not here.

We feast on the same things we have eaten before, but with those classically French touches: a sprinkle of rosemary here, a whole lot of butter there, and lots of wine. I steer clear of the latter, remembering my experience with hard cider.

"You can't just eat butter plain like that!" says Andy, pulling Peety's arm down as he tries to put a whole gob in his mouth.

"Is not butter, is potato." He licks it off and holds it in his mouth. "Mm, it *is* butter. Try it." He pushes a spoonful at her face. With a scowl, she bats it away.

I glance over at West, now drinking wine with Cay and the French girls. Maybe wine does not feed his demons. Children drink it, after all. He laughs, and the sound brings me a strange kind of agony. It makes my heart glad to hear him so carefree, but I wish it was me he was laughing with.

Sophie leans her head against his shoulder. Maybe all those curls under her cap get heavy, especially with an empty head. She speaks to him, and he barely looks up as someone refills his wine glass.

"Zey go nice together," says Madame Moreau, appearing beside me with a basket of rolls. She angles her face toward West and Sophie. "He is handsome, she is beautiful. Sophie's father is an important judge back in France. Is good marriage, maybe?"

"Surely her father would want her to marry an aristocrat, *un noble.*"

"Her sisters marry well already. He just wants Sophie to settle down."

Trying not to think, I rotate my peas from one o'clock to nine, one at a time. The noise of the crowd pummels my head. There must be more people here at Fort Laramie than in all of St. Joe.

The words *le main cassé* catch my attention. The man beside me is talking about the Broken Hand Gang. I elbow Andy.

"Pardon me, but I heard you mention the Broken Hand Gang. Have you seen them?" I ask the man in English.

He wipes his mouth on his yellow scarf. "A woman came to ze fort a week ago, carrying dead baby. She say ze Broken Hand Gang attack her wagon and kilt her husband."

Andy sits up straight. "Oh, my Lord."

"Is she certain it was them?"

"Black men, she remembers. Who else can it be?"

Peety notices Andy and I giving each other big eyes. He pushes his hat brim up with his butter knife. "No good to worry, chicos," he says grimly. "God has special place for men who hurts children."

After dinner, I stretch my restless legs, while Peety takes Andy to bring in the horses. Tiny cakes with whipped cream form neat rows on a table for people to help themselves. Seeing them cheers my spirits. Father loved to bake. I take one and save it.

Later that night, we spread our bedrolls in the wagon circle. Cay and West are off somewhere, so we lay theirs down for them. I plan to wait up for West, but the fire is so warm and the rhythm of Andy's breathing finally lulls me to sleep.

Sometime later, I awake, confused by a dream, and realize West is not beside me. Andy and Peety snore in concert, and Cay sprawls out with his hat on his face. I lift it off to give him some air.

The last time I saw West, he was drinking wine. I push away the thoughts of him in a ditch somewhere. Surely he is fine, I tell myself. Probably sleeping with his horse.

I sit back down to pull on my boots. *I always hated when you woke me up at midnight to celebrate my birthday, Father. You knew I'd be grumpy when I awoke, but you did it anyway every year. Why do I miss it so much now?*

I hold a candle to the fire, then lift the flame to heaven. *See? I made it to sixteen without falling off a horse.*

I poke the candle into my cake and wipe my nose on my sleeve. No wishes this year.

Debris from the revel litters the grounds. I skirt bodies and wine bottles and head toward the nearest opening between wagons. I find our horses, but not West. Paloma nudges me in greeting, and I scratch her neck.

A girl moans, and I freeze like a jackrabbit. It chills my blood to hear her gasp and gasp again, like someone's hurting her. Forcing myself to breathe, I unholster my gun.

I stumble toward the noise. A rock trips me, and I nearly drop the cake, but the candle remains lit. The moaning grows louder as I round the wagon circle.

I see her on the ground wrestling a man.

I aim my gun, but cannot see well enough with only the glow from my cake.

"Let her go, you filthy cur," I shriek, steadying my grip, "or I will put a knot in your trunk!"

Her head pops up from over the man's shoulder.

"Oh! *Ton ami Chinois, il me protège. Qu'il est mignon!*" she trills, her voice sickeningly familiar. A very flushed-looking Sophie just called me sweet.

My cheeks blaze, bright enough to power a universe.

The man rolls off her, his chest heaving under the folds of his open shirt. The bandage I put there has torn, soiling the white gauze with spots of blood. When West's burning eyes meet mine, the shock of our connection knocks both the cake and the gun from my hands. The flame from the candle draws a golden arc on its descent, and when the gun hits the ground, it roars.

I cry out and drop to my knees.

"Sammy!" yells West.

I clutch at my chest but only to still its jolting. *No, West, my wound is not from a gunshot.*

Sophie clutches at West but he pushes her away. Before he comes any closer, I scramble to my feet and run.

I find Paloma, climb onto her back, and ride out of the camp, not caring if my candle burns up the whole fort. Let West handle it, I think, clenching my jaw. He is good at starting fires; maybe he knows how to extinguish them, too.

I cannot see through my tears, and let Paloma do the driving. I find that soft spot right behind her ears and stick my face in it. She takes me just down to the river, though I long for her to take me far away, to another continent, to the moon.

30

A DEVILISH SUN STRETCHES OVER THE LARAMIE
River, and pokes me in the eye. I curse it. I curse the clouds that
spring out like ringlets around it, and while I'm at it, I curse the
moon and the traitorous rabbit that lives there. To see that. And
him. It stabs me a million times over.

Mostly though, I curse myself. I share the blame for this by
causing too much confusion for West. Still, I cannot reconcile
that with my hurt.

Tumpshie. Idiot. Why couldn't I just focus on my mission? It
could never work out between us. Like beef and tomatoes, one of
Father's favorite dishes, we have nothing in common except that
we wound up in the same wok. Our paths have crossed, and soon
we will head off in different directions.

I sit with my head in my hands, my brain circling over the
sickening image of Sophie and West like a vulture over a carcass.
How could I be so stupid, Father?

My chest rises and falls as I take a deep breath. I must act
nonchalant. Another act of survival.

When I return to our camp just after dawn, I head off Andy's
questions by telling her I went for a morning ride. I don't meet
West's eyes. Instead, I see right through him, like he is a ghost.

I do not notice his anxious glances, nor the way his shoulders slump even worse than before. When Andy asks if he needs her sewing kit, I turn my back.

By late morning, I am snoozing over Paloma's snowy mane as she carries me. A hand pulls my hips back onto the saddle, and I snap to attention. West has brought Franny up beside me.

"You're slipping," he says.

My face heats up, and I tighten my grip on Paloma. Nonchalant. I clear my throat.

"I'm sorry about my intrusion last night. I did not"—my voice cracks—"realize..."

"Forget it." The hint of a blush appears on his cheeks, but he quickly pulls Franny back to the drag.

He tucked my gun back into my holster; I can feel the weight of it against my thigh.

Useless thing. Perhaps it still carries the negative energy of its past owner, and that has made it unlucky. Or perhaps *I* was lucky it didn't shoot anyone this time. All the variables in Chinese luck make it difficult to keep track.

Cay casts a mischievous grin toward West. "So did you curry the kinks out of Sophie?"

West doesn't answer.

"Mathilde said Sophie's father sent her here to settle her down," Cay prattles on. "Guess she's a bit of a bangtail." He looks over his shoulder at Andy and me. "That's a wild horse, boys." His eyes stretch wide for a fleeting moment.

I snort and then I cannot stop laughing. They must think I'm one strange kid.

I can feel my laughter quickly turning to tears so I shove my hat farther down on my head. I urge Paloma to a trot, out of the group and down the trail.

Andy rides Princesa up to join us. "What happened?"

"Didn't sleep well last night."

"Did you tell him?"

"I changed my mind," I say, maintaining a look of equanimity.

She sneaks a look back at West, but I keep my eyes fixed on the road ahead. No more looking back into the drag.

I switch the subject by telling her what that trapper Burl Johnson said about criminals in the Haystacks. "So it's a good thing I'm going with you."

She blows a short breath out of her nose. "Yeah, because sometimes, you's real fierce."

In the late afternoon, we camp in a grove of birch trees.

At dinnertime, I don't even notice Andy is frying up something special until she starts knocking her spatula against the pan.

"And now y'all, it's time for our special celebration in honor of Sammy. Come on!"

I shake my head furiously at Andy, but she smiles and summons me with her hands. I didn't think she remembered since we talked about it long before we even met the boys.

She does not pick up on my mood. "Sixteen years young and a hundred years smarter than all of us put in the same bag."

How wrong you are, I think, shuttering my eyes for a moment.

"I thought you said you was seventeen," says Cay.

"You the only one who believed it, hombre," says Peety.

We each get a flapjack in the shape of a violin. Cay and Peety clamor for a speech. I put down my pancake and pick myself up. My ears ring like a pair of hot horseshoes under a hammer, but I ignore them and summon up my violin calm.

I hold my cup of water to Andy. "If you had not saved me from the bathtub, I would not have made it to this old age."

The boys puzzle over this.

"And to the rest of you, you raised me three feet higher at a time when I needed the boost. I'm ever grateful to you."

"Oh, you mean by giving you a horse," says Cay, beaming. I dip my head at him.

As I put down my cup, I glance at West's boots, and again picture Sophie tangled up in him. Everything turns bright and blurry as I fail at being a boy once more. My violin calm vanishes.

"Thank you for this, Andy, but I'm not hungry." My voice is suddenly too high.

"What's biting you, Sammy?" Cay asks.

"Nothing."

"Then why are you—?"

"Go mind the bees in your own bonnet," Peety cuts in.

I spy a fortress of sagebrush a hundred yards out, perfect for hiding dark thoughts. "Chinese boys like to be alone on their birthday."

Halfway to the sagebrush, a voice startles me.

"Chinito," says Peety. The man moves as quiet as a sunset. People born under the sign of the Rat are known for their extreme stealth. He hands me a bow and a quiver with ten arrows. "We got this at the fort for your *cumpleaños.*"

I swab my face with my sleeve and take the gift with both hands, as is the Chinese way to show respect. Father never received a gift without giving something in return, a bag of candied ginger, or an étude on his cello. I have nothing, and even if I did, it would not be enough. I owe these boys more than I will ever be able to repay.

Peety shifts from foot to foot and rubs the stubble on his cheeks. Though I want to fling myself at the vaquero and sob into his solid shoulders, I just hug the quiver.

"Peety, this is the nicest—" I can't finish my sentence. I wipe my eyes and take a deep breath to get the tremors out of my voice. "*Muchas gracias, mi amigo.*"

He nods. "You want to try it out?"

The landscape around is arrayed in black and gray shadows, though the sky is putting on a light show for us. "It's too dark, but we could shoot the stars."

His face pinches, and he slips his hands into his pockets. Then he blows out a lungful of air. "Someone stole *mi hermana* when she was only five."

His sister? Esme. "Oh, Peety."

"I taking her to buy sandals, getting mad 'cause she so slow. I let go her hand, and when I look back, she not there. They took her because I no looking back, and she had no shoes."

"Who took her?"

"*Salvajes.* They steal children away to sell them." He shakes his head as if to clear it of bad thoughts.

"I'm sorry, Peety."

He nods. "She love horses, always say she want to be a horse when she grows up. So, I decide to become wrangler, because I always looking for her."

Suddenly, the vinegar pickling my heart loses its bite.

We glance upward. Everywhere I look, there are stars and more stars, coalescing like white dust.

"Sometimes I think she is gone from this world. If it's true, that means she's a star now, because that's what happens to the innocents. That is why you cannot shoot the stars."

Over the next week, we pass hundreds of wagons grinding deep ruts into the soft sandstone outcroppings. Andy asks me why I'm so mopey, and when I don't tell her, says, "When you're ready, I'm all ears."

I try to forget what happened with West by concentrating on finding Mr. Trask. Andy keeps a lookout as well. Who knows? He might be right under my thumb. I examine everyone who wears trousers, perfecting the art of moving my eyes without moving my head. Mr. Trask, as captain, will likely lead the caravan, but I don't overlook anyone.

When the trail empties, I rest my eyes on the prairie grass. It shimmers as we wade through its waves, each blade tossing back the rays of the sun. We pass white-tipped Laramie Peak, an orange sunset at its crown.

"Dig in for a second, boys," breathes Cay. "My eyeballs are full."

We stare at the splendor in silence.

Lately, after giving halfhearted language and math lessons in the evenings, I wander off by myself. I keep my hands busy, shooting snails with my bow and arrow, and splicing Andy's baubles into a stronger bracelet made of rope.

When I return to our fire, West is usually gone, which makes things easier for me when I curl up.

But I am always awake when he drops quietly beside me, not realizing I excel at feigning dead. Another survival instinct, I imagine.

31

AFTER THREE MORE DAYS OF TRAVEL, INDEPENDENCE Rock towers before us, a giant sandstone shoe that got stuck in mud and was left behind. Clusters of sagebrush ring the landmark, and wagons sprawl over the landscape, at least two hundred schooners amassed at the midpoint of the Oregon Trail.

Farther up the trail, the boys play follow the leader, a game they use to keep the remuda sharp.

Andy rides beside me. She shows me the neat row of numbers she wrote in our journal. "Ten more days 'til the Parting, in case you changed your mind."

"I haven't changed my mind. According to my estimates, the pass to the Yellow River lies at least two days' ride from here. You recall, the one called Calamity Cutoff, in case you want to change *your* mind."

She snorts, then jams the journal back into her saddlebag. "Nope."

The boys spin their horses around and walk backward. They are out of earshot, but I can sense West's eyes upon me.

"You ever gonna tell me what happened with West?" Andy asks, watching me.

Ten days have passed since La Disgrâce, what I've started calling the French party. My wound has healed, partially. I can at least recount the mortifying events without shedding a tear.

After I tell her, Andy tilts her chin toward me and *tsks* her tongue. "Lots of things surprise me, but that ain't one of them. And so you know, what West did, it don't mean a thing. You just confused him, so he had to test his rooster in the ring."

She might be right, but it still fails to cheer me. I don't understand the constant need to prove one's manhood, as if it is always on the verge of slipping away. We never need to prove our womanhood.

"You miss being a girl?" I ask her.

"Not as much as I thought I would. Just feels like when I'm being a boy, I can cut a wider path."

I nod, knowing exactly what she means. Cay spins around on his saddle so he's riding backward. "If we were them, we could cut the path in reverse."

Andy's face grows serious. "Yeah, though I'm done with wanting to be *them*. I was done with that a long time ago."

"What do you mean?"

She doesn't speak for a long time, and I think this might be more trash in her mind she's not ready to dump. But then she glances at me. "After Tommy died, I cursed God for giving me this body, for making us slaves."

I wonder if I heard right. The notion that Andy could curse God for anything puts grease under my heel.

"What good's a black face if it means I'm just someone's

property? Why give me these arms and legs just to carry some-one else's load, not my own?" She stares through the road, as if watching a memory. "Just like that prince, I struggled, wanted to be something I wasn't, even though the answer was here all along." She pats the spot over her heart. "See, God gave me this harp, which is my soul, along with the promise of sweet redemption." Her posture is as poised as a feather on a cap, flexing in time with Princesa's gait. "I don't need anything else. Never thought about being white again after I figured that out."

I smooth a spot on Paloma's mane, sobered by her words. Fa-ther always made me feel proud to be Chinese, that ancient race who roamed among dragons, who exploded gunpowder into the air to make flowers of fire. We might be a rare breed in this country, but I never wished to be white. Then again, I was also never a slave.

The boys begin walking their horses back to us.

Andy flicks the reins at a fly. "You ever wondered what West's face would look like if you pulled off all you's shirts and yelled, surprise?"

"No!" I protest too loudly. I swear West straightens up in the saddle at my outburst.

"Well, I have," she says around a smile. "Not West, a'course." She flicks her eyes toward my hands. "Now take that out since we're still rattlesnakes."

I let go of Paloma's mane, scowling. Somehow, I managed to braid my mule's hair from her crown to her withers.

Tonight is one of my last chances to look for Mr. Trask. If I don't find him in these two days before Calamity Cutoff, I must accept that he is lost to me.

A celebration to mark the trail's halfway point starts even before the sun dips. Cay accepts an invitation to join the largest wagon circle, seventeen schooners in all. Andy and I tag along after the boys, hats low. I watch them with an ache in my heart, grieving the loss even before it happens.

Peety accepts a plate of stew with a hardy *muchas gracias* and compliments for the woman serving him. Andy must feel the same as me because she sits closer to Peety than normal, and even lets him steal one of her corn cakes.

Cay chats up a doe-eyed girl with a cloud of white-blond hair. All she needs is a halo. How fitting that my last memories of him will be of charming the ladies.

Somewhere behind me, West fields a volley of questions from a lad who admires our horses. I cannot watch him. Just the sound of his voice makes me giddy and tearful at the same time.

Before I turn stupid, I lean over toward Andy. "You finish," I whisper, setting down my untouched bowl of black-eyed peas. "I'm going to start combing the crowds."

"I'll go." She begins to rise, but I pull her down by the sleeve. "You barely touched your food. I'll be fine."

"Lots of people here," she says in a low voice.

"We haven't seen a marshal since the Little Blue."

"That's 'cause we've been trying not to."

Peety catches wind of our whispering. He moves his mouthful to his cheek. "You no like your food, *chicos?*"

"I was just telling Andy I need to walk off a dead leg. I won't be long."

I adjust my hat over my eyes and pretend to limp off, leaving Andy frowning after me.

As I finish examining a neighboring group of diners, the strains of a violin float toward me. I follow the sound.

In the middle of a circle of adults stands a girl, six or seven, fat braids like yellow bellpulls on either side of her head. She is sawing on her violin. "Twinkle, Twinkle Little Star." I drop to my knees. I have only heard one little girl play the fiddle before, and that girl was me.

The simple strains of the lullaby return me to the world I used to live in, each bow stroke conjuring a memory. Father with his ear cocked as he tuned Lady Tin-Yin. The two of us flapping like herons to help me loosen my arms. Father telling me not to rush the second movement of the Vivaldi if I wanted my audience to cry.

The crowd claps, rousing me from my stupor.

When the little girl bows, I head back to the remuda. But moments later, someone tugs on the back of my shirt. The girl pans her freckled face at me, her violin tucked under her arm.

"Are you Chinese?" she asks.

"Marianne," reprimands her father from behind her, his eyes darting about like blue minnows under the glassy pools of his spectacles. A stiff gray hat trimmed with a blue jay's feather sits primly atop his head.

"It's all right." I kneel so that I'm her height. I shouldn't socialize, but I cannot turn my back on her sweet face. "You play that fiddle quite well."

She beams, her eyes lighting up in that way that comes natural in children.

"I bet I could give you a few pointers," I say before I can stop myself.

The father holds out his hand. "Dr. Raymond Highwater. I think Marianne would love some instruction. She has been on her own since we left Boston."

We sit on milk stools. Lifting my chin, I align my posture, and she copies me. One glance at her eager face puts a lump in my throat. Suddenly I'm back with one of my pupils, waiting on the edge of my seat for a flawless G to reach my ears.

Since that dark day, I have been scurrying around like an ant with no purpose after someone has stepped on its nest. *Father, you told me music is a world that measures virtue by grace notes, and truth by the vibration of pitch against your soul. Will I ever find my way back there? Or is that world gone forever, now that you are no longer a part of it?*

Marianne begins to play, drawing me out of my thoughts.

"Straighten your wrist. Walk on the tips of your fingers," I instruct. "You're making the nightingales jealous."

I teach her "Mississippi River," and she plays it perfectly after two tries.

"One more, just one more," she begs.

"It's past your bedtime," says her father. "Mind now, and I will let you comb Jory's tail tomorrow."

She wraps her arms around my neck and I kiss her head. "I

see you one day performing in the great concert halls of Europe."

As Dr. Highwater settles her into their wagon, Andy appears by my side, her face crimped into a frown. She jerks her head, *Let's go,* and I follow her.

The doctor calls after me. "You obviously have much skill." He holds up the instrument. "Mind if we impose on you?"

There's no way I can do that. "I'm sorry."

He tucks the violin under his arm. "I understand. Quite a crowd here, probably everyone will want to come hear you. Not everyone likes the stage. Well, thank you, again."

"Wait," I say, my mind spinning. Mr. Trask, a clarinetist himself, heard me play on several occasions. Do I dare?

"We're s'posed to be laying low," Andy grumbles in my ear.

"Maybe the mouse will come out to see the cat play," I whisper back.

Andy shakes her head. "What if the mouse turns out to be a dog?"

She is right, as always. Who knows what law enforcement or mercenaries lurk about? Even if there are none, I would not like to make a lasting impression. Still, I am so close to Mr. Trask. I can feel it in my bones. And maybe just this once, for Father, fate will look the other way. "We'll never get to everyone," I press. "It's like a mass migration of buffalo here. I can knock out the pins with one ball."

She still doesn't look convinced. Dr. Highwater's gray eyebrows push together.

An awkward moment passes, and I clear my throat, knowing

I must give this up. If Andy knew how much losing Mr. Trask pains me, she might change her mind on letting me go with her to Harp Falls. "All right, I won't," I say at the same time as she throws up a hand and grumbles, "Fine, do it."

I smile at Dr. Highwater. "I'll do it."

Dr. Highwater grins and hands me the fiddle. It's too small, but I can work with that. *If I had you in my arms again, Lady Tin-Yin, we'd rip up the prairie. How I miss you.*

Andy stands back and crosses her arms. "I don't like it," she mumbles, "but I'll keep watch." Then she slips back into the crowd.

"We have a fiddler, folks! Make way for the fiddler!" cries Dr. Highwater.

I breathe deeply to release my butterflies, then hitch up my trousers. This is the biggest group I've ever performed for, and I don't just mean the violin. But I have the boy act down by now. I stalk out toward the main bonfire where most of the pioneers are assembled.

"Look, a coolie!" someone yells. Ripples of curiosity follow me. Fingers lift like hunting rifles tracking a duck as I pass. I keep moving.

Twenty feet from the fire, I stop by a barrel, my back to an overstuffed Conestoga wagon with fruit trees poking out the rear. The violin calm washes over me, and I poise the bow.

"Hold on there, yella," says a man's voice. The crowd parts to let a pair of red suspenders through, the color of firecrackers. My bow slides off the strings.

But it's not Mr. Trask, not even close. This man is West's height but brawnier. What could he want from me? He grins like he knows a secret. Dear God, a mercenary. Andy was right. A dog's on the loose. Why didn't I listen?

I collect myself as he draws near. Then I notice the suspenders are not suspenders at all, but straps securing a banjo to his back. I nearly moan in relief.

Pulling his instrument to the front, he quirks an eyebrow. Nothing draws a crowd like a duel between a banjo and a fiddle. Father and I dueled often back in New York, especially when we were short on rent money.

The man shows me the crown of his head with its combed waves of chestnut hair, and I return the bow. His copper eyes take in the child-sized violin, and he says in a silky voice, "I'm Jack. That baby fiddle mean you play like a baby?"

The men in the crowd call out, "Hear, hear!" to egg us on.

I size him up and set my jaw. "Why don't you stay and find out?" I challenge, leaving off my name, as I did with Dr. Highwater.

He grins rakishly from beneath a neat slash of mustache. The rest of him is neat, too, not a single wrinkle on his shirt or his face.

The crowd cheers. Familiar cat whistles pierce the noise, and a real smile replaces my fake one. The remuda's only a stone's throw away though I can't make them out among the masses.

"What do you have in mind?" I ask.

Jack's muscles bulge under his rolled-up sleeves, the skin

tanned and flecked with copper hair. "Been a while since my banjo ate a fiddle."

I put on my rooster comb. "Well, I know where it can get a good slice of humble pie."

The crowd laughs. Jack places his banjo pick between his teeth and tunes his instrument, not lifting his eyes from me. As soon as he hits the first four C's, I recognize "What Shall We Do with a Drunken Sailor?" A crowd pleaser.

The emigrants, already in high spirits, jump to their feet. More people gather 'round, and soon Jack has the whole caravan's attention.

He nods the signal, and I pick up where he leaves off. To begin, I make my playing sweet and easy. I scan heads for Mr. Trask, but cannot see much beyond the front row, where a line of girls stand pining over Jack, their mouths forming little O's of adoration.

So I jump up on the barrel.

The song picks up pace, and now my fingers are a blur. I use the momentum to ricochet bounce off the top of my bow and add several triple stops—three strings played at once—the move that Mr. Trask paid fresh tangerines to hear. Come on, Mr. Trask.

I rest, and now Jack's fingers go fuzzy. His female fans multiply and start screaming. One even cries, "Marry me!"

Shielding my eyes from the bonfire, I scan the crowd from my higher perch. I don't see the grocer from New York, but I do make out the boys under the oak tree, and they whistle and whoop when I find them. I salute my bow their direction, then rip out my solo. The remuda's cries spread like wildfire and soon the whole crowd's cheering for me.

Something's wrong. My head feels too light. Damn, my hat! I must have knocked it off with that last triple stop. The show must go on, but not under present circumstances. I drop down off my perch.

Jack stops playing and takes the baby violin out of my hands. I scramble after my hat. One of the pioneers picks it up and hands it to me. I grunt out a thank-you.

When I return, lid in place, Jack is positioning the baby fiddle under his chin. "Don't mind if I do."

Though he scratches the bow and falls off pitch, his screaming fans don't care.

"You gonna let him boss you, Chinito?" yells a familiar baritone.

I groan under the weight of two hundred eyeballs, all expecting a good fight. If I don't get back into the ring, I might as well ditch this hat and tie on a bonnet. The boys start chanting my name, and now everyone takes up the chant. "Sammy, Sammy!"

I cringe. If he is here, Mr. Trask will find me now, or I can assume he's gone deaf. I snatch up Jack's banjo, and jump back onto my barrel. I strap Father's favorite instrument across my shoulders, and a hush descends over the crowd. The banjo's bigger than Father's, at least fourteen inches in diameter with a heavy rosewood fingerboard, and it probably looks like it's wearing me rather than the other way around. But I've got hot coal in my firebox and I'm ready to go full steam.

I don't have a pick, and my nails are ragged, so I bite off my sleeve button, then set it on the strings. Andy's going to kill me.

Some of the screaming girls now clamber over to my barrel. Maybe I look tall and dashing up here. Eat your heart out, Jack.

I finger out a simple roll. Sounds good, time to move the show along. When my turn comes up for the solo, I double the tempo and punish that drunken sailor to within an inch of his life. My right hand works the strings like a spider in its death throes. I might even sound better than Jack, judging by audience reaction.

By the time the song's over, my clothes are damp, but I am glowing. My barrel vibrates under the noise of the pioneers' cheering and clapping. Remembering my task, I sink back on my heels and survey the crowd one last time.

No Mr. Trask. It was a long shot.

I climb down from my perch.

"You ride your strings hard," says Jack. "How 'bout we take a sip of lemonade together?"

His eyes brush over me like maybe he would rather take a sip of something else, and that something is not the girls gawking at him.

"My—my—friends will be looking for me," I stammer, pushing the banjo at him. "But thank you anyway." His gaggle of admirers swallows him up.

Andy trots up to me, holding a stack of tin cups. "That was genius. You almost caused a fire up there."

Dr. Highwater walks up behind her, hand extended toward me. "Best music we've had on the trail since setting out." His warm two-handed handshake reminds me of Father, who shook everyone's hand as if it were an honor. "Even better than the clarinet-and-harp duo we saw last week at Fort Laramie."

"Did you say clarinet?" I ask.

"Yes. It's not my favorite instrument but—"

"The man, was his name Tucker Trask?"

"I only caught his first name, but it wasn't Tucker." He kneads the knuckles of one hand with his thumb.

I bow my head to hide my disappointment. "Well, it was nice meeting you and your daughter."

"Theodore," he says. "That was his name."

I snap my head up. Theodore, of course! How could I forget such an important detail? Tucker was just a nickname.

"Did he say where he was going?" I ask, not breathing.

"I didn't speak to him directly. But he did tell the audience he was going to teach at a conservatory."

Conservatory? The barren west coast offers no such thing, at least not to my knowledge. He might as well have stayed in New York for that. Unless he—

I stare at the blue jay feather in the doctor's hat as the pieces click together. Mr. Trask played woodwinds: clarinet and some flute. I dreamed of opening a school of music one day where Father and I would teach strings, but we needed someone to cover the woodwinds.

I sway and feel Andy's arm bump me back into place.

"You okay, son?" Dr. Highwater asks.

I nod and dig the nails of one hand into the palm of my other to shock my face into holding still.

The doctor continues. "Do you know him? He set out before

us by at least a week so my guess is he might be at the Parting of the Ways by now, unless he detoured. On horseback, you could probably catch him. He did have a few wagons on his train."

After thanking the doctor profusely, I stumble after Andy to a table assembled from a length of wood and two stumps. She ladles lemonade into a cup and puts it in my hands. "What's a conservatory?"

"A music school," I tell her quietly as the tears well in my eyes. "I always wanted to open one. Father was bringing us to California for *me*."

She clucks her tongue. Behind her, the crowd parts to let through Cay, Peety, and West. Cay pushes Peety, laughing, and Peety pushes him back.

"I'll hold 'em off," Andy says, shooing me away.

I scamper away, seeking out a quiet place to think. Behind a dark row of wagons, I collapse onto a saddle-shaped boulder. Independence Rock floats like a white whale on a dark sea.

What a pig-headed, ungrateful daughter you had, Father. My sorrow pours out in a deluge of tears and stuttered gasping. I clutch myself and rock back and forth. When the storm finally passes, I stick my face in my lap and blot my eyes with my knees.

Feverish now, I remove my top shirt, the faded blue flannel, and drape it across the grass.

Oh, Father. I will make it up to you. I will open that conservatory like you wanted for me, for strings and woodwinds. Did you hear me play tonight? I still have my fingers. But I may need to take a detour first. You understand, don't you?

Yuanfen. Fate between people. Perhaps it works between

people and objects, too, since objects carry a bit of their former owners, just like Lady Tin-Yin. Maybe one day, Mother's jade bracelet will find me, and we can all be together again.

I unbutton my next shirt, and since I can't take that one off, I fan myself like a seagull winding up to fly.

"Well, well. 'The wicked flee when no man pursueth,'" says a voice from behind me.

32

I NEARLY JUMP OUT OF MY REMAINING WARDROBE.

Cay holds out the front of his shirt like a basket as he approaches.

"'But the righteous are as bold as a lion.'" I finish the Biblical proverb for him, willing my heart to slow down.

The scent of tangerines lifts my spirits.

Cay plops down and hands me one from the pile in his shirt.

"Where did you get these?" I gasp. I haven't seen a tangerine since we left New York. If it weren't for Mr. Trask, we would never have been able to afford those fragrant orbs, which are considered lucky by the Chinese, since the word for *tangerine* sounds like *luck*.

"Angelina."

Naturally, a girl. I skin my fruit and block out the prying moon. When it comes to tangerines, I do not care if the treasure was won through ignoble means. Little sacs of sweetness burst like liquid sunshine, and I chew very slowly to make mine last.

The moonlight plays with the blond tendrils at the nape of Cay's neck. They beg for fingers to wrap around, the way certain vines need to be swung on.

"When's your birthday?" I ask.

"January sixth, 1830."

Just as I suspected. Tiger. "So what happened to the doe?"

"Angelina? I brought her back to her mama. You see, I'm learning."

My eyes catch on a red mark on his neck right above the collarbone. A love bite—fresh, too. A flush travels over my face.

He catches me looking and winks. "Didn't say I was perfect." After swallowing his last wedge, he sucks the juice off his fingers, one by one. "You know, I think God does an okay job evening things out with his people. Sure, some folks draw a bad lot. But the average person has about the same amount of tricks and troubles."

"Seems about right."

"Take you, for example. God gave you arms of twine."

"Thanks again," I mumble.

"But then he gives you the power to move people."

"People are born to dance."

"No, I mean, *move* them. West's been daunsy all week, dandered up, probably at me. When you picked up Jack-a-Dandy's banjo and put him back on the shelf, suddenly West starts laughing. None of us knew you could play the banjo. But then he starts crying. Oddest thing."

A rush of longing stirs my soul, crowding out my breath. The memory of our brothy kisses tears at my resolve. I put the peel to my nose to ward off the heartsick, and to stop my mind from wandering in a direction it should not go. "Banjos are deeper than people think. So what are Cay Pepper's tricks?"

"The good Lord gave me the power to catch sparrows. I know you think my head's too big, but I'm speaking plain. West has the same gift."

"I noticed."

He catches me in his green eyes, and I quickly don my mask of nonchalance, but I cannot seem to break away. It is like being caught in Narcissus's mirrored pond.

"Trouble is, finding a girl is still a tricky situation, like choosing a hat." He flips off his hat and sweeps a finger along the edge of the brim. "Like, maybe you've had your eye on a fine-looking French number, but when it finally falls onto your head, it loses its appeal."

Poor French Mathilde never had a chance.

He rehats his head. "Or maybe you've been told all your life that bison felts are the only hats worth wearing. And when something different comes along, say alligator suede, even though it's the most worthy thing you've seen in your life, you might leave it in the window"—he taps his chin—"until you realize no other hat will fit just right."

As I try to figure out who could possibly want a hat made of scaly alligator hide, I don't realize he's staring at me. A grin lurks under the neutral line of his mouth. What exactly is he saying? "Er, so you're through with the French girls?"

He laughs and rolls out his neck. "What I'd really like is a girl with fire. The kind you can warm your hands on without getting burned. Mischief must be her middle name, so things don't get dull. That's all."

"A little fire and mischief. That can't be too hard."

"You would be surprised." He rolls over and lifts his apple-bright eyes to the stars burning above.

Early the next morning, Andy and I tidy up behind the dense sagebrush.

I hold her coat while she whacks the fabric clean of dirt with a broom of dried sage. "Isaac taught me this one. The herbs take out the odor, see?" She finishes whacking her coat, then starts on my shirt, with me still in it.

"Wait, let me take it off, first!" *Whack.*

Her mouth tightens. "I decided to go with you to find Mr. Trask."

A lump forms in my throat as fast as if I've swallowed a pebble. I leave the shirt on. "What? Are you sure?"

"Uh-huh." She shakes the branches at me. "Wouldn't sit right with me if we didn't try to catch him. We'll fetch your bracelet, then double back to the Calamity Cutoff."

"Thank you, sister." I can't resist hugging her.

She tolerates it for a moment, then pushes me away, as she always does when I show her too much affection. "What are we going to tell the boys once we get to the Parting?"

A pang of sadness leaves me speechless for a moment. "They already know you want to go to Harp Falls. I'll just say I'm going with you."

"What if they want to come?" Again, she starts whacking my shirt, this time faster and harder until a piece of sage goes flying.

"They've got gold to find."

Andy snorts at my non-answer. If the boys do want to come, we'll have to tell them the truth, a truth that has grown many heads like the chimera. My concern over the boys' welfare wars with my own cowardice and my feelings for West, which persist even after I've tried to convince myself I do not have feelings for him. I don't know what to do, and apparently neither does Andy.

Sighing, she tosses her whole bundle of sage into a bush.

"Africans and Chinese take a long time to build their log cabins," says Peety, sneaking up on us with his stealthy Rat feet.

"Lord, give me patience," mutters Andy, and she stalks out of the brush.

After a morning of riding, Cay leads us off the main trail up a narrow road. "This will save us a few days of travel. That means we'll get to the gold sooner."

Andy glances at me. I shrug. Cay has never steered us wrong before so we dutifully follow.

"How do you get one of these land grants in California, Peety?" asks West from the drag.

Peety glances back. "Not sure. I think you go to the governor in Monterey and just ask."

Cay swivels around in his saddle and rides backward. "We ain't going to Monterey. We're going to the first river we find and digging in a pan. Besides, we got no money for land."

"I think it's free," says Peety.

"There ain't nothing free in this world except bad ideas." Cay crosses his arms over his chest and leans slightly back, a defiant twist to his mouth.

No one speaks for a moment. Then West's voice casually breaks across the silence. "We'd have to build a fence. If we work hard, we could get our first herd out by next summer."

Cay crushes his hat to his head. "Dang it now, that wasn't the original plan."

"What do the *chicos* think?" Peety slows Lupe to walk alongside Andy. "Andito?"

"Well . . ." For a tense moment, I think she's going to tell them the truth, that we won't be going with them to California. Instead, she says, "I think we'll know when the time comes."

The answer sounds so sage, Peety doesn't even ask my opinion, for which I am grateful.

The path begins to cut into the side of a mountain stuck with tall pines. Loose gravel makes the trek slippery. Peety suggests we dismount to make the passage easier on the horses, so we do it. Everyone fastens his rope around his waist, holding the lariat in a ready-throw position. But not me. I rub my shoulder, which aches from playing a too-small fiddle. Roping throws my arm out of joint, and so I have no future there, especially if I hope to be back on my instrument someday.

"My arm hurts, and I'm just as likely to hang myself as save myself," I tell Andy when she asks me where my rope is.

She purses her lips and I see her eyes catch on something behind me. Probably just West glaring at my hard head. I pick out the pine needles caught in Paloma's mane.

Not two seconds later, the hiss of a lariat cuts through the air. It lands right on top of me. Now I'm the stump. I wriggle my arms out, face burning, but I don't acknowledge him. Hitching my shoulders, I soldier on after the others.

The narrow passage ends, and we start to remount. Then Cay's voice echoes in the canyon. "What the hell?"

A man Father's age sits on the ground, leaning against a fallen chair on one side of the trail. He clutches a wooden cross. The sun-blistered skin of his face and scalp practically glows against the white of his Sunday shirt, and he's soiled his trousers.

Cay kneels by his side. "Your friends leave you here? That ain't right."

"Oh my Lord," says Andy, rushing to the man's other side, me on her heels.

"How 'bout some *agua*?" says Cay. The man's canteen is slung in the dirt, unlidded and empty, so Cay gives the man a sip from it.

"Wait, Cay," says West. He rushes up to knock the canteen from his cousin's hand. "Back out. Don't touch him."

We all gape at West. "He has cholera," he says. "Look at his eyes."

The man's orbs are sunk into his skin like two olives dropped in vanilla pudding. They stare into space, glazed and green. He is not going to make it.

Cay freezes. West yanks him back to his feet. "Let's go." His mouth presses into a grim line.

Cay and Peety remount, but Andy and I hesitate.

"*Vámonos*, God will take care of him."

"Ain't you got some whiskey, Peety?" asks Andy.

Peety shakes his head. "All dry."

Andy touches her palms together. "God bless you, and take away you's hurt."

I should follow Andy back to the horses but I'm caught by the man's blanching fingers, grasping at his cross like it is the only thing holding him to this world. His lips quiver as he moans.

He knows we are leaving him. I clasp my own throat, though I'm not the thirsty one.

"I am sorry," I tell the man in a shaky voice, dropping to my knees.

"Let him go, Sammy," Andy murmurs.

West tugs on my rope. "Sammy."

I ignore them. The man speaks to me. "Shhh."

Cay and Peety turn their horses around to watch.

"Sir?" I breathe.

"Shhoo."

"Shhoo," I repeat hoarsely, hoping he wants my shoes, but dreading the other thing he might be asking for. His eyes drop to my belt, and I gulp. "Shoot?"

Andy gasps. The man blinks.

"Blink once for yes and two for no," I say, my breath coming faster.

He blinks once.

"Are you sure?"

Another blink.

"Really sure?"

Another blink.

I cover my mouth with my hand.

My hand shakes as I take out the Dragoon. I put it on full cock and raise it to his head, the place where Peety showed me how to put down a horse. What if it is not the same place for a human? The man closes his eyes. A white band of skin circles his finger where a wedding ring should be. I bite down on my trembling lip and wrap my left hand over his.

Then I let him go, and stand back. All I need to do is shoot once. No one survives a bullet in the head, right?

But I cannot do it. That would be murder. My eyes find West's. I have not gone there since—

I shut them and my tears jump off the slope of my cheek. When I look again, West is winding the rope around his arm as he approaches me. His eyes do not leave mine until he takes my gun, aims, and fires.

33

"DON'T SEE WHY HIS FOLKS DIDN'T SHOOT HIM themselves. Woulda been kinder," says Andy as we sit around our fire.

We spent the day traversing the foothills of a vast mountain range that stretches to the north. Tonight, we nest in a valley of pink granite rock shot through with black veins. The rocks crop out in odd formations like giant knobs of ginger.

"Could you do that to your daddy?" asks Cay.

West stares at nothing. "I could."

"Me, too," says Andy. "If it meant he didn't have to wait there and suffer in the sun like that. Just downright cruel."

I hug my knees tight to stop my hands from wringing themselves dry.

"In my religion, you go to hell for doing that," says Peety.

"Which? Leaving him or shooting him?" I ask.

"Murder is a mortal sin. Still, mercy killing probably okay."

"Speaking of murder, I got an interesting bit of news for you," says Cay, squinting at me as he pulls something from his pocket. I go still as a forest animal hearing a twig snap. He unfolds a piece of newspaper. The firelight allows me to see through it and read, backward: WANTED.

My stomach clenches. He knows.

Cay zeroes in on me again. "One of the pioneers at Independence Rock gave me this Wanted Bulletin. It's kinda interesting. Guess who's on it?"

I put my head between my knees, not wanting to guess. Andy grabs the paper. She does not read much, but she scans the pictures. She gasps and the paper crinkles in her tight grip.

"It's the Broken Hand Gang," says Cay, reaching for the paper again. His hand hangs in the air for a moment before Andy realizes it's there. She hands the paper back, then clasps her hands together so tightly her fingernails blanch. Her wide eyes hop to mine.

"They finally drew a good picture of them," says Cay, turning around the paper and holding it up for all of us to see. "Three of them, at least."

The top of the page reads: BROKEN HAND, $200 EA, DOA. He points to the first man, who has a broad forehead and hawkish eyes. I put him around twenty years old. "This one's the leader, which makes him the index finger." He taps the next picture, a boy who couldn't be more than twelve, with a long face and a nose like a miniature butternut squash. "This one's the pinkie, 'cause he's the wee one."

Cay taps his finger over the third picture of an older man. "This one's the thumb, all wrinkly, the kind of man who always gets the odd jobs. You know, like opening pickle jars."

The fourth and fifth ones are blank squares.

"Just read the caption, dummy," says West.

Cay turns the paper back toward himself and reads: "'Wanted

for murder of two innocents: Amelia Dearborn, a baby, and Cedric Dearborn, 37 y.o.; AND, seven counts of aggravated assault and robbery. Last seen at Fort Laramie, Wyoming. Armed and dangerous.'"

"Could I see that?" I ask. He hands me the paper and I study the pictures up close. A series of smaller photographs checker the rest of the page accompanied by one-line captions. My eyes hastily sweep the pictures, but I don't recognize any other face. Then the last entry. There's a photo of a Chinese woman.

I don't hear the rest of the conversation as I read silently: "Young San-Li: wanted for MURDER in the first degree of Mr. Ty Yorkshire of St. Joe, Missouri, and THEFT of a slave. 15–25 y.o., Chinese, long black hair, black eyes, dangerous. Reward: $500."

I'm gasping in air now, and I put my head between my knees again to calm myself. The only saving grace is that my "picture" is not my picture at all. It seems no one had a picture of me to print so they pulled one of some Chinese woman in her twenties smoking a cigarette. She poses in a clingy dress with a slit, a cheongsam.

Picture or not, they're after me. Now, thousands of pioneers and Argonauts know to be on the lookout for a Chinese girl. Mercenaries will be clamoring for a shot at the prize, which is easily enough to sustain a living for the next few years. I won't be able to go to the Parting. It's too risky. Mr. Trask will be lost to me, and so will Mother's bracelet.

Father, I was so close. I held the butterfly in my hand, but a gale swept it away.

Andy nudges her knee against mine. West, on my other side, takes the paper from me. I don't want him to see it, but I cannot protest without making things worse.

"That a friend of yours?" he asks.

I shake my head.

"No?" West starts laying out his rope. "Well, sleep with your irons cocked."

After the boys fall asleep, Andy and I head to a sluggish brook for a minute-bath. Afterward, we huddle together on a thick pile of pine needles, teeth chattering. The moon is an ivory sliver that barely emits light, so high and out of reach. I want to unhook it from the sky and hold it in my hand, where it might do some good.

"That picture didn't look like you."

"Chinese is Chinese."

"So what'd it say?" she asks.

"Wanted for murder and theft of a slave. Five hundred dollars if you can catch me."

She stares into space and her lips start moving. Then she tilts her face toward me and licks her dry lips. "You's almost worth the same as three of the Broken Hand Gang."

"Isn't that a comfort. Three for the price of one," I mutter. "We can't continue on the trail. We'll go straight to the falls. No one will find us there."

My head pounds so I pinch my left hand below the web of my thumb and index finger, the way my father taught me to take the edge off headaches.

Andy rests her chin on her knees. "I think we should separate."

"What?"

"The boys would help you. You could go with them to the Parting. They'd keep you safe. After you find Mr. Trask, you keep on with him to California, and then you's home free."

"He'd be harboring a fugitive. So would the boys."

"They already been doing that before the Wanted Bulletin came out."

"But now I'm being hunted in earnest. After all they've done for us, I can't put them in such danger."

She frowns as she fingers the Indian bead on her bracelet. Her bony elbow digs into my arm as she scoots closer to me. "When I was picking the fields back on Frogg Farm, the owner's sons thought they'd have some fun with me. Stuck me in a corn maze with a pair of rabid bloodhounds."

"Devils."

"I've never been so scared in my life. I could hear the barking and knew the dogs was coming for me. I raced down a row of corn. Sometimes I saw spaces between the stalks like missing teeth, but I didn't take 'em. Then my legs started shaking, and I fell. I saw a dog loping toward me, drooling 'n 'crazy."

Her face tightens and she shudders. "Only thing I could do was duck into one of the spaces. And then another. Soon enough, I got out to find Tommy's weeping face."

She twists her body toward me. "You see, I was running so fast, I passed up the spaces even though they was the exit. You's in that maze. You got spaces around you. You want to run until the dogs bite you dead?" She raises her voice, and I shush her.

"I am thankful the spaces saved you," I say. "But spaces don't have to worry about jail."

"The spaces can think for themselves, when they ain't making bad jokes. One space in particular would pick the seeds off a strawberry for you if he knew you's a girl."

I shake my head. "It could never work. Chinito should stick to Chinitas, remember?"

"Cay was the one said that."

"But West agreed with him. And anyway, I can't continue putting them in danger. Here's what I think. Once we find the trail again, we'll keep our eyes open for Calamity Cutoff. The night we find it, we'll leave the boys a note, then double back."

It's the coward's way to leave, but I don't see any other choice.

The next day, we continue riding over the floor of granite. We have not seen a major trail since leaving the cholera man. My eyes keep flitting to Andy, walking beside me. We've hardly spoken all day. She burnt the breakfast for the first time this morning and singed her sleeve in her haste to lift the pan off the fire.

Now she's lost in her own world, not steering much, just letting Princesa drift where she wants to go. After last night's talk, I can't help feeling I need to keep an eye on her, as if she might disappear at any moment.

She senses me watching and gives me a brief smile that fails to reassure me.

When Cay turns us into a rocky incline, West protests. "We need to be going west. This ain't right."

"I know," says Cay, holding the map before him as we continue to march forward. "We're still on the shortcut. Have I ever led you wrong?"

Andy and I exchange worried glances. Tiger personalities can make hasty decisions and have trouble backing down. Father always blamed President Van Buren's Tiger nature for the Panic of 1837 when he wouldn't recant a decision not to interfere in the economy. Still, I remind myself that like all cats, Tigers do have a good sense of direction. I wiggle around in my saddle and try to relax.

We travel all day without seeing a single person, let alone the Oregon Trail. The mountain range that started off on our right now seems higher on the left side.

In the late afternoon, we reach a running stream full of fish. We follow it to a dumpling-shaped clearing hidden by dense foliage. Cay orders a shade-up and consults his map again. Then he refolds it.

"You sunk us, right?" asks West in a voice that doesn't sound surprised.

"There's a first time for everything," says Cay, a little sheepishly. "Tomorrow we'll just turn around."

"We should make you sing 'Yankee Doodle,' hombre," says Peety.

"That would be more of a punishment to us," says West.

We release the horses to graze. I shake out my boots, one by one, and try not to take our wrong turn as a bad sign. Andy watches me as she glugs from her canteen. At least no one will find us up here. But what if we overshoot Calamity Cutoff? Though I've traced Cay's map into our journal, it won't help us if we don't know where we are.

Andy pinches me. "Go on, look. It's like the Garden of Eden." She crouches to inspect a bush of yellow flowers.

I peruse our slice of the world and grudgingly agree. The trees grow high enough to shield us from view. Were it not for the storm in my mind, I might sleep well tonight, pillowed by a lawn of pink clover and lulled by the tinkling stream. I draw in the fresh air and detect the smoky scent of cedar.

"No fig leaves and lots of snakes." Cay sniggers. "Wish we had us some hens for sinning." He looks at Andy and me when he says this, so we both grunt in approval.

Cay goes to lie down by the stream. "I could use a nap. I'm dragged out." He tilts his hat over his face.

The fact that we are lost does not concern the boys, skipping stones in the water, or the horses, happily chomping heads off the clover. I park my bottom in the shade of a solitary fir, the tallest tree in Eden. Father told me they use fir in railroad ties because it's so strong. I inhale its sweet piney scent and try to quiet the unrest in my mind.

Andy squats in front of me. "No one knows His plan but Him."

In the morning, Cay does not want to wake up. I put my hand on his temple. He stirs at my touch. Hot as a pepper.

Andy and I are about to fetch water when Cay starts to

heave. When he finishes, we help him to a spot by the stream, which will carry away his sick. I pour him a cup of water from my canteen and tilt it into his mouth.

Cay whispers something to Peety. Then Peety puts Cay's arm over his own broad shoulders and helps him over to a dense shrub dotted with white flowers, stretching as high as the horses. When they return, Peety is shaking his head.

"*Choro,*" Peety tells me, and when I don't understand, he translates "diarrhea."

All the blood leeches from my face. These are the signs of cholera, the deadliest disease on the prairie.

34

I CHECK EVERYONE ELSE'S HEALTH AND HEAR NO complaints.

But by midday, we realize Peety and Andy are not fine after all. They also come down with the fever, vomiting, and *choro*. As Andy vomits for the third time in an hour, I start to wonder if the shortcut we took *was* Calamity Cutoff, and if I caused this by shooting the cholera man, even though I didn't pull the trigger.

How could I ever think I would outrun my bad luck? It is like a plague, spreading its contagion to those I hold most dear.

Since West and I have not spoken for nearly two weeks, words no longer come easy, but we work together to pull the others' bedrolls closer to the river, next to Cay.

"We should dig holes," I say, rummaging around for spoons since we don't have shovels. We find a spot behind the shrub with the white flowers to dig our latrines. The flowers smell like oranges and freshen the air. We scoop up spoonfuls of earth. Father made a special blend of rehydrating salt for dysentery that he believed would also help the pioneers with cholera. No one ever returned to tell us if it worked or not.

"Cholera isn't always fatal," I say without much conviction.

"At least we got a stream," he says at the same time.

We pause in case the other has something more to add. Then we both start up again. West stops to let me finish.

"Father had a remedy—"

"What's in it?"

My digging slows as I try to remember. "Half a teaspoon salt, six teaspoons sugar, four cups water—"

West throws down his spoon. "Hell." He glares at the mound we've scraped together so far, the size of a grapefruit. Then he starts clawing the dirt with his hands.

An hour later, we have three holes and two broken spoons. We kneel by the stream to wash. When Cay moans and clutches his middle, West grimaces.

"For stomach pain, we used blackberries and pepper," I say. "There was a bush yesterday that Palom—"

"I think I remember the direction. I'll fetch 'em."

"The thorns can pierce your gloves." I dry my hands on a cloth. West picks up the other end to dry his. "Maybe use your fishing spear to knock them off."

"I know what to do," he says gruffly.

Now our hands meet in the middle of the cloth, and we both let the other have it. He plucks it out of the air before it drops to the ground.

"Might be gone for a stretch," he says, like nothing happened.

"They'll be okay. I'll help them use the necessary." I decide that is what we should call the holes.

"They got to use it a lot. What if you—"

"Don't worry about me," I snap, crossing my arms over my chest.

He closes his mouth and looks at Franny, standing next to us. Her ears start to pull back. We bore her. As he straps on his rifle, I hold Franny's reins, willing the remorse on the tip of my tongue to leap out of my mouth. But nothing comes.

Fixing my stare on his shirt buttons, I notice that one looks different from the rest, a replacement for the one Sophie ripped off. I drop my eyes to his belt buckle, an even worse place. *Shake it off.* How can I think of that at a time like this? I refocus on the only freckle he owns, a solitary speck on the smooth curve of his cheek.

I soften. "I know you are afr—worried." I switch words, remembering the chicken threat. Boys do not like to be seen as fearful. "But I'm stronger than I look."

His brow wrinkles as he takes in my fingers, hopelessly entangled in the leather straps and getting tighter the more I pull. Turning my back to him, I hiss out my irritation at my nervous habits, which lurk like uneven floorboards, waiting to trip me up.

"Sammy." That tone again, two parts exasperation, one part resignation.

I shake my head as I wiggle my fingers free and hand him back the reins.

"I know you are," he says. He swings his leg over Franny and clicks his tongue.

For the rest of the day, I alternate between patients, feeding them the mix, and helping them to the necessary. I throw dirt into the holes after each use. I mix the salt, sugar, and water, praying I got the ratios right. Then I steep pepper in the kettle.

Andy's so still and ashen, she looks almost dead. I kneel beside her and take her limp hand in mine. It's cool, but not cold, and I put it to my cheek.

I want to talk to her, but I can't with Peety and Cay here. They lie motionless, and it's hard to tell if they're sleeping or just resting. So instead, I say a prayer for all of them and hope God is listening.

By my estimates, we are at least twenty days from Fort Bridger. Even if we reached the fort, what could the people there do? Most folks stay as far away from cholera as possible. There is no cure. We must wait for the disease to run its course and keep everyone hydrated.

Cay wakes up shivering, his lips blue. I scoot in behind him and put his head on my lap. Then I hold his cold face between my hands.

Cay blinks up at me hanging over him. "My stomach..."

Another of Father's methods comes back to me.

"Want to try *tui-na*?" I ask, using the Cantonese word for a technique that uses pressure on certain points on the body. "I will need to touch your ears."

"My ears?"

I nod. Chinese people believe the entire human body is mapped on the ears. I don't remember where everything is, only the key points.

"Does it hurt?"

I smile. "No. You might even like it."

"Well, okay, but don't tell Peety."

Sliding my hands up to Cay's ears, I tug at his lobes, then circle my fingers around the edges toward the center. There, I find the spot that corresponds to the stomach and press in toward his head.

He closes his eyes. His face twitches at first but eventually relaxes. When I hear him sigh, I begin to knead his earlobes with my thumbs, the loose and easy headtabs that indicate a charmed life, unlike West's. Some charmed life, nose against death's door and only eighteen. Maybe earlobes are not the weatherglasses of one's life that I've always believed them to be. Wasn't it Cay who got the boss's daughter pregnant? And didn't West survive that stallion bite? Maybe ears are just ears.

Cay moans, "That... feels...so..."

West drops down beside us, startling both Cay and me. I let Cay's ears go.

Cay's eyes slit open and take in his cousin. "You always spoil the fun."

"Please, continue," says West dryly, sweeping his hands at us.

I pat Cay's whiskery cheek. "I think you're better now. I'll go fix the tea."

As I gently lift Cay's head, West slides in to take my place. Before I can leave, Cay says, "Why do you always smell so good?"

I choke. Maybe Cay's delirious. His eyes drift close. West watches me so I give him a helpless shrug and don't answer.

Cay's eyes pop open. "I don't have all day."

I smile, because he can make me do that, even in my misery. "I smell like horse shit like the rest of you." My face heats up at my vulgarity.

"Nope," says Cay. "You smell like jacaranda. Oddest thing..."

Jacaranda? Those fragrant purple blossoms were Father's favorite. He couldn't know that. I lower my head while I collect my composure. When I look up again, I'm pinned by a pair of brown eyes and a pair of green ones.

"Cowboys ain't meddlers, but you got me balled up. Why're you such a secret?" Cay rasps. "You ain't no Argonaut, obviously."

I open my mouth to deflect the question or give a cheeky answer, but close it again, suddenly weary. The boys have been nothing but honest with us, while I have lurked in shadows. Even now, with death knocking, the lies still flock to my tongue like ravens to a kill. What is the worst that can happen if I tell them a little of myself? This is not the time for a confessional, but the least I can do is be straight with him for once, maybe even take his mind off his suffering.

"I come from St. Joe," I begin.

"Missouri?" asks Cay.

"Yes. Father's Portuguese partner in New York lost the whole business with one roll of the dice."

"What'd he roll?" asks Cay.

"Four. That's an unlucky number for Chinese because the word for four, *sei*, sounds like the word for death. So Father decided not to rebuild the business and instead bought the Whistle in St. Joe, hoping we would join the pioneers one day."

I describe the cold welcome we received in St. Joe, then end with the blaze that took Father's life. "He did not have a proper burial."

My throat constricts, and I grab a fistful of dirt to distract my mind from the pain, letting it seep out like sand in an hourglass.

"We fought that morning," I hear myself say. "I didn't want to move to California. After violin lessons, I sat on the riverbank instead of coming straight home."

My shameful tears water the dirt as I bow my obstinate head. *I failed you. I should've been in there with you. I should've pulled you out.*

Cay breaks the silence. "So he's an angel, then. We'll adopt you. Go on, West."

West pauses a moment before reciting, in a gentle voice, "Welcome to the family. Keep your neck and hands clean, and scrape the shit off your boots before you come into the kitchen. And don't pick the crust off the pie."

I laugh a little at that.

We let Cay sleep. I spread out my bedroll by the fire, and West arranges his next to mine. The two lone blankets side by side bring a blush to my cheeks. I am thankful it's dark.

"I'll take bobtail," says West.

"What's bobtail?"

"First watch."

He does not wake me for my shift. Instead, I rouse myself at sunrise and find him kneeling between Peety and Andy. Peety lays comatose, but Andy twitches like she lies on a hill of ants.

Did West help Andy use the necessary last night? Surely he would have said something if he learned the truth. Or maybe it was too dark to see.

"Next time, don't let me sleep," I plead, carefully watching his reaction.

He drops down onto his bedroll without replying.

West wakes in the early afternoon. I hand him a cup of coffee, suddenly struck with the urge to smooth back his rumpled hair.

"Andy needs help," says West.

She is halfway off her bedroll and about to crawl over Cay. "I'll help him," I say, nearly scalding myself with coffee in my haste to get to her before West gets up.

She clutches me with more strength than I expect. Her fingernails dig into my arm. "Isaac misses us something awful," she croaks. "But we'll be with him soon, won't we, Tommy?" Her forehead knits and I can smell the bitter sickness in her breath.

She must be in the middle of a dream. "Sure, Andy. Of course we'll see him soon."

I pull her, half stumbling, toward the necessary. Once she finishes using it, I resettle her on her bedroll. West brings over a cup of blackberry tea, and I put it to her lips.

"Being still ain't good for the horses," he says. "They ain't fed enough either. I'll explore with them today. Maybe I'll run into some folks who can help."

He takes out his journal. I have not seen him draw since that picture he sketched of my six-year-old self. The book opens to the page held by a leather cord. While he rips out a blank sheet,

I catch a glimpse of the last picture he drew: a girl whose hair cascades over her shoulders, hiding her face in shadow.

It couldn't be Sophie, as she had ringlets. I recall his fitful sleep after the stallion bite, when he cried out, "She didn't do it!" Perhaps that "she" is the girl in the picture. Maybe a friend, or... There is so much I do not know about his life, and a part of me mourns that I never will.

He draws the route he will take so I know where to go if I need him. Paloma will stay behind with me. He tacks Franny, then leads the remuda out of Eden.

I rub each of my charges' legs and backs. Then I take out my bow and notch the arrow. Fitting the point into the arrow rest on the grip, I try to shoot fish in the stream. My aim is steadily improving. Last week, I hit a dandelion from thirty feet away.

I wound a trout, which I throw in the pot along with some wild parsley I found upstream. Maybe Andy's Snap Stew will comfort us. The fire releases plumes of gray smoke when I throw on a chunk of pine with too much sap, and I use a rag to clear the air.

Andy whimpers and I rush to her side. I find her with one arm linked through Peety's, her fingers kneading her sleeve where her scar with the six dots lies. The vaquero still slumbers. Andy's eyes are clear though her face is drenched with sweat.

She sighs when I place a cold rag on her forehead. "Go tell West the truth. You two go on before you catch what's-it we have. I'll take care of the boys. Ain't got nothing better to do."

"Shut it, Andy. I'm not going anywhere," I growl, hoping my harsh tone hides my distress.

I swear she rolls her eyes at me, then lowers her voice to a whisper. "When the master's son drowned Tommy's baby pig, Tommy didn't cry. He scooped that pink ball out of the rain barrel and gave it to Isaac. 'Bury him for me,' he tells Isaac. 'Soapy needs you to help him get to heaven.'

"Isaac buried Soapy by the craggy tree. Carved a cross on the trunk so God would know where to find him. Tommy sat by Soapy's grave all morning, looking through the stone with the hole." She pulls her arm out of Peety's and presses her palm to the rag on her forehead. "If I don't make it, I need you to tell Isaac one day what happened. I'd sure hate him to think I died a slave."

"Hush. We still have a lot of trail to cover before the end. You're not going to die up here. I won't let you." I hold her hand to my cheek.

"But here's where I always wanted to be. Free." The shadow of a smile crosses her face. "Promise it."

"I promise." I pull her hand away so she cannot feel the tears streaking down my face.

Sometime in the late afternoon, my skin crawls, like ants are marching up and down my legs and arms. I check my surroundings, but see only a lone falcon, wobbling on an air current. So I finish scooping the fish bones from the pot. But I cannot shake the sense that someone is watching me. I let it build for another moment then whip around.

Not twenty feet away, two black men stare at me, one from the top of a mule. The first, a young man of about twenty, has a good few inches on West, with hawkish eyes that don't blink, and lips that pinch tightly together, causing his forehead to bunch over his brow. He's wearing a buckskin coat only a shade lighter than his own skin, and underneath that, a white-and-blue-checkered shirt. The one on the mule leans forward over his animal's neck. He is more a boy than a man, with a long face and a nose like a baby butternut squash. I've seen their faces before. The index and pinkie finger of the Broken Hand Gang.

35

MURDERERS. AND WE ARE ALONE UP HERE.

How did they find us?

My heart sinks when I remember the gray smoke from our fire.

My legs lose all feeling, and my tongue petrifies. The only part of me capable of movement is my mind, which jumps like a cricket in the cage of my head.

They don't yet see the others lying by the stream. I have to lead them away. But I can barely work my lungs, let alone walk. I have solidified, as if I have looked upon the Gorgon Medusa and turned to stone.

Pull it together—the others depend on you. You are a rattlesnake and you have a bite. I unholster the Dragoon. The pearly handle slips in my sweaty grip, but I hang on. "Don't come any closer!" My voice comes out weak and raspy.

The man removes something from beneath the flap of his coat. A gun, long as his forearm, with a black nose. He points it at me with more conviction than I point mine. He steps closer. "And if I do?" he rumbles.

Good Lord, could I really shoot this man?

Step by step, death comes for me, steady as a plow. The twin sinkholes of his eyes trap me, rendering me motionless once again and I forget all about being a rattlesnake. All I can think about is how I am the easiest catch on the prairie, not even a moving target.

When the man stands only spitting distance away, the queerest thing happens. I see myself in him: hunted and outraged. Set upon a dishonest scale. They are runaway slaves, just like Andy. As bad as my luck has been, I know there is no worse life than one that is not your own to live. No, I could never kill a slave in cold blood.

But how can I protect us?

Father called himself a translator, but he was much more. He was a negotiator, a diplomat. When the German farmer and the Spaniard restaurateur were at loggerheads for the price of bratwurst, Father always moved the conversation to areas of common interest. What were the preferred methods for cooking? Did beer or wine best accompany the meat's richness?

Stop struggling, and you will find common ground.

I drop my gun, shaking, back to my side.

The man flexes an eyebrow. The nose of his weapon dips, then rises, like he's trying to decide where to put the hole.

Then, miracle of miracles, he uncocks his gun.

I nearly fall over in relief.

"Never seen a yella before," he says.

"You going to kill me?" My voice goes high. Curse my idiot's tongue. Might as well ask a bear if I should season myself up before becoming dinner.

"You got something worth killing for?"

"No," I say quickly, then curse myself again. Now he thinks I'm hiding something. "But my fish stew's half decent."

A puff of air blows through his nose and his chest twitches. Is he amused? Provoked?

The boy sniffs and runs his sleeve across his face. Only now do I notice his pant leg is torn and bloodied, and his teeth clenched. He looks younger in person than in his Wanted picture, with no facial hair that I can see, and no bump on his throat.

The man eyes my pot. "You by you'self here?"

If I say no, he might hurt the others. But I can't say yes, when it's obvious I've made enough fish stew for a pod of whales. While I root around for the best answer, it dawns on me: Just tell the truth. "My companions have the cholera."

"Where are they?"

"By the stream."

In five steps, the man overtakes me and peers down the length of the stream at the blanketed forms of Andy, Peety, and Cay, twenty yards away. Their heads are half covered with the wet rags I've placed on their foreheads.

"Well then, we won't be staying long," he says, returning to me. "How 'bout we have ourselves an understanding? We won't kill you, if you let us borrow your fire and some clean water. Do we have a deal?" He extends his hand for a handshake.

Even though I suspect he's just humoring me, I solemnly shake his hand, pumping extra hard to make up for my scrawniness.

The man helps the boy off his mule and to our fire. Blood glistens on the fabric of the boy's trousers near the thigh, soaking through at an alarming pace. Beads of sweat trace a path around his high cheekbones and trembling upper lip. He sucks in air through his nose, then hisses it out through the spaces of his gritted teeth.

The man carefully cuts away the trousers, exposing a large wound below the boy's hip bone. Quickly, I fetch clean rags and boiled water, plus the bandages and salve that Cay bought in Fort Laramie.

"Disease gonna set in if I don't get out that bullet," the man tells the boy.

The boy shakes his head, his eyes large with terror. "It hurts. Don't do it, Badge."

The man glances at me when the boy says his name. "Shh, it's gonna be all right."

Now the boy starts whimpering. "I says, don't do it. Just leave it. Ain't gonna help."

Badge starts sopping up blood with the rags. "What did Paul write to the Romans about suffering?"

The boy's eyes flick to me. "Don't remember."

Badge helps him out. "'Suffering leads to patience, and patience, to experience, and experience, to—'?"

"Hope?" The boy gasps.

"That's right, and without hope, we ain't got no business in this world." Badge sighs and looks at his right hand. It's nearly as big as my foot, the fingers wide and muscular. Then his eyes cut to my own hands, tiny by comparison. The boy begins to cry.

Badge fetches a bottle from his saddlebag and uncorks it. The sour scent of fermented hops stings my nose. Badge holds it to the boy's lips, but the boy pushes it away and covers his face. His tears leak through the cracks between his fingers.

The sight of his suffering, and his shame at crying makes my head throb, filling my own eyes with hot tears. It is indecent, grotesque even, that someone could shoot a child.

"I can do it," I hear myself say.

Badge narrows his eyes at me. Slowly, I show him my bow hand, wiggling what I always considered to be bony digits. "My fingers are nimble, and it will hurt less."

The boy uncovers his face. His eyes are so swollen they appear shut.

"I have a lot of experience with these fingers," I tell him. "The mayor of New York once gave me a whole silver dollar for playing 'The Peddler's Waltz' on my fiddle. Said my fingers were as nimble as spider legs." I smile and hope the story improves his confidence in me.

He bites down on his trembling lip, and looks at Badge. Badge nods at him.

The boy buries his head in his arm and bobs his head up and down.

I pour the spirits on my hands and rub them together. Then I pour some on a rag. "This will sting, but that's a good sign. It means things are getting clean."

When I touch my rag to the wound, the boy gasps.

Badge takes his hand. "Squeeze my hand, Jeremiah."

The boy squeezes, but when he sees me wiping my pinkie, he shrinks back into Badge.

"God bless us, a falcon!" Badge exclaims, lifting his head. Jeremiah lifts his own eyes, falling for the distraction, and Badge nods at me. "Falcons are a special bird, Jer. Ain't no one can catch 'em. Not even you with your bow and arrow."

My trembling pinkie probes the hole. I bear down on my own tattered nerves.

"Jeremiah made friends with a couple of Cheyenne and they gave him a bow and arrow," Badge tells me. "Made it special for him."

"Special, eh?" I push farther and Jeremiah hisses. Keeping my voice light, I ask, "Can you shoot a dandelion from thirty feet away?" Warm tissues close around my finger and blood runs along my arm. I force down the bile rising to my throat and soldier on.

Jeremiah nods, lip trembling.

"What about a dandelion seed?" I ask.

"Ain't tried," he rasps.

"Well then, I guess you'll have some work ahead of you."

As gently as I can, I probe the walls of the bullet's tunnel, past ridges and slick bumps, praying I'm not causing more damage. Jeremiah begins to whimper again, and Badge starts a hymn about Moses and the Promised Land. He has a bass voice with an even keel and a rich vibrato. It's meant for the boy, but it steadies my own jangled nerves.

Finally, just past my second knuckle, I brush the end of the bullet. I don't talk so my concentration does not break.

The boy's eyes roll. I don't have much finger space left, but I do my best to pull the bullet down by stroking it with my fingernail. There. It moves. Gently, I coax it backward.

Soon, we see the end glinting in the daylight. I pinch it between my thumb and index finger, and pull out the crushed piece of metal. Quickly, I finish cleaning the wound.

"You done good, Jeremiah, you done real good," says Badge.

Jeremiah stops crying and looks down at his leg as I clean it off. I roll the bandages around his thigh. Soon I've rolled enough so the blood no longer soaks through. Badge fetches him a fresh pair of trousers that smell like herbs. As Badge helps him into them, I ladle fish stew into two cups.

Badge bows his head over his cup. "Bless this food, dear God, and this boy, who helped your poor servants in their time of need."

Jeremiah eats with his left hand. Badge waits until the boy finishes half his bowl before starting on his own. I don't ask questions, since doing so would require answers in kind. Obviously, they're outrunning the law up here. The less I know, the better. Still, it seems odd not to converse.

"How long you played the fiddle?" asks Badge, saving me from having to think up a neutral topic. Now that the crisis has cooled, his face looks almost friendly with the high and protruding forehead that Chinese people believe indicates good fortune. His mouth still remembers how to smile, despite his hardship.

"Since I was four," I answer, not wanting to give out my age.

"You got one now?" asks the boy weakly.

"No, it drowned at the Platte River Crossing."

"We lost one of our own there, too," says Badge, staring into his stew.

I sit up, remembering the dead man we found at the base of the cottonwood. He was one of theirs after all?

Badge puts down his cup. "We needs to be going."

He gets to his feet. Gingerly, he lifts Jeremiah into their mule's saddle. One half of Jeremiah's face bunches into a grimace, while the other half tries to remain strong.

"Stew's fine," says Badge, shaking my hand, and putting his other hand on my shoulder. "Almost worth killing over."

A voice behind him suddenly yells, "Get your hands off him, before I blow your head off. I swear I'll do it."

Jeremiah's mule skitters out of West and Franny's way, knocking Badge into me. We fall into a heap on the ground. Badge mutters a curse, then scrambles to a crouch. He eyes his gun, lying on a blanket by the campfire, five paces away.

"No, West!" I scream. His horrified eyes fix on me and my blood-soaked shirt.

"Sammy," he cries as he slides off Franny. Then, to Badge, "You son of a bitch." With the butt of his rifle, he whacks Badge in the temple. But at the last second, Badge dodges, and the weapon does not deal a fatal blow, only glances off his cheek. I lunge at West, trying to grab the rifle from him.

As West and I struggle, Badge clambers toward our fire.

"It's not my blood!" I pant. "I'm fine, he doesn't mean to hurt us."

West doesn't hear me. He throws me off and aims his rifle at Badge, just as Badge raises his. Unlike when he pointed the gun at me, I know by his expression that this time, Badge will use it.

Hastily, I jump to my feet and stand between them. "No, no, don't shoot!" I babble as I look from one to the other, nearly crying in my panic. West's chest heaves as he stares through the sight line of his piece.

"Please, listen to me," I beg him.

"Move away, boy!" Badge orders, his voice now tight and angry.

West tries to move to the side of me, but I get in front of him again. "I swear, out of my way!" he growls.

The chicken threat. West won't back down as long as Badge doesn't. I cannot move them to common areas of interest for they won't even listen to me. *Father, are you listening? Tell me what to do.*

I once begged Father to rescue a cat stuck up a spruce. We dragged our ladder at least a mile and propped it against the tree. Once Father reached the cat, it ran up another ten feet. So Father climbed back down.

"We'll come back for the ladder tomorrow," he told my teary self. "Cat just needs a way down."

By the next day, the cat was gone.

"Badge," I say. His head bleeds where West hit him. "Think of Jeremiah."

"I said, move aside, if you value you's life!" yells Badge, causing spit to fly. I wilt under the heat of his fury.

"Jeremiah," I repeat, trying to keep my voice from shaking. "What we did today." I hold out my hands to him, still stained with blood. *Please take the ladder and climb down.*

Badge's eyes flick to Jeremiah, still huddled over his mule, then back to my hands. His body is so rigid, his muscles tremble.

At last, he looks up from his sight line. "A life for a life, eh?" he says.

"Yes, a life for a life." Behind me, West's breath escapes as a short gasp.

"Do I have his word?" Badge asks.

West doesn't say anything.

"West?" I call in a low voice, praying he will see reason.

Again, he doesn't answer. I count up my remaining options and realize I don't have any. Badge's pupils constrict, signaling the imminent squeeze of a trigger.

"Fine," he says coldly.

Badge puts down his gun. "But if I ever see your face again"— he stabs his finger toward West—"do not think I will be so merciful."

"Nor I," comes West's surly reply.

The two glower at each other for three more counts of white-knuckled panic, until Badge finally tucks his gun back into his coat. In a few strides, he's with Jeremiah and their mule.

West and I watch them depart until the mule's footfalls grow too soft to hear. Trees whisper silently to themselves, and shed tears of leaves.

36

TEA. WE BOTH NEED A CUP OF TEA.

Father and I drank chrysanthemum tea to calm nerves, but since we don't have that, I fill West's cup with our blackberry brew.

West kicks at the ground and yells in frustration, walking in a rough circle with his arms wrapped around his head. "That was the Broken Hand Gang, wasn't it," he states more than asks.

I push the cup at West. Then I stand back, wringing my fingers so hard, my joints crack.

He mutters a curse then, "I'm sorry."

Dropping the cup, he grabs my hands. My heart pounds at the intimacy of it. All I can do is gape.

"You're trembling. What happened?" he asks.

I pull away. "The boy had a bullet in his leg," I tell him in the calmest tone I can manage. "They needed help removing it." I look down at my fingers, still stained with blood, too much blood. Suddenly, I wonder whether I did the boy more harm than good.

West's shadow reaches out to me. Reflexively, I step back. Like Franny, I somehow connected with his motion.

"Don't," I say, unprepared for the moment, and in danger of falling for him again.

• • •

The next day, instead of going out, West sprints each horse across Eden, winding around pine trees and over shrubs. The sound of their hooves crescendos and diminishes as he takes them back and forth.

I examine the invalids closely for any signs of improvement. Their skin looks no less chalky, and I despair again of them ever leaving this mountainside.

Cay's eyes open and he blinks at me, trying to straighten his vision. After he swallows his salt water, he says, "I know why you smell good. It's okay."

"What's okay?"

His eyes study my face so intently I begin to sweat, sure that he's figured me out. "That you're a filly."

"A what?"

"A filly," he whispers.

A girl? Or the common term for a man who enjoys the company of other men? I don't breathe. It must be the latter or else why would he use the word *filly* and not *girl*?

"I am not," I say with mock indignation, playing along.

"I know it ain't my business. To each his own." He grins. "But you run funny, and you ain't hairy."

"Maybe you should save your air for breathing."

"Plus, you used to stick around West like a burr."

"A burr," I repeat as my face heats up for real.

"Don't hold it against him, Sammy." His eyes shift around like West could be hiding somewhere in a bush. "His father got soaked often and beat him oftener. Burnt quirleys on him."

The round scars on his arm. Shock replaces my mortification.

"Once, he caught West drawing pictures. Called *him* a filly. His daddy beat him so bad, West didn't remember his name when the sheriff brung him to us. Asshole." Cay's breath grows shallower.

"Shh. Stop talking." I swab his face. His locks grab my fingers like the tendrils of a sweet pea.

After Cay falls asleep, I seek out the comfort of Paloma's snowy white mane. My thoughts are a jumble as I groom her, fresh from her run. When I brush against the direction of her hair coat by mistake, she jumps.

"Sorry," I mumble, smoothing the hair back down. Then I rest my forehead against the slope of Paloma's back, letting my guilt pile up.

Did you think your father's words were true because of me? And you still saved my life twice, even killed the cholera man so I wouldn't have to.

Father always said, *Give a man a mask if you want to hear the truth.* But even with a disguise, I could not be honest. Now it is too late. *You will never trust me again.*

I swipe my eyes with my sleeve and busy myself with my patients, whether more for their sake or mine, I can't be sure. After giving them their salt water, I wash Andy's hair using our frying pan as a basin. She hates to be dirty. She falls asleep as I wrap her head in a rag I warmed by the fire.

In the late afternoon, West shoots a turkey that wandered near our camp. I avoided him all day but now get to my feet as he approaches.

Dark half-moons underline his eyes since he refused to wake

me again for last night's watch. There are a million things I want to say to him, but my stubborn tongue refuses to port them out of the tunnel.

"Let me," I say lamely, holding my hand out for the bird.

"'S all right. I'll do it."

"No, you should rest."

"I rested enough."

"Well, someone better cook it or I'm getting up and doing it myself," says Andy.

I gasp and drop down by her side. Her eyes are clear and her face, tranquil. She stretches her arms over her head and pats at her hair wrap.

"How come I got this woman's rag on me?" she asks in a loud voice, then slyly winks at me.

"Andy," I cry out.

Peety opens his bloodshot eyes and squints. "Sammy, you write my eulogy yet? I hoping you could say, 'Pedro Hernando Gonzalez, he rode his horse to the end.'"

"More like, 'He rode the end of his horse,'" mumbles Cay, though his eyes are still closed.

I touch both of their foreheads, which are cool again. *Oh, Father, I think your salt mix worked.* I choke back my emotion.

"You three are worse than a herd of acorn calves," West says.

Andy and Peety's appetites have returned. We spend the evening feeding them bits of turkey stew. Peety nods gratefully when I brush the crumbs off the front of his shirt with a rag. He likes to keep a neat table.

I sop a piece of skillet bread in soup and reflect on my Snake luck. Unlucky that I fell into the Platte River, but lucky I survived. Unlucky that the Broken Hand Gang found us, but lucky West wasn't killed. Unlucky about the cholera, but somehow, the people I care about are still breaking bread together. I suppose as long as everyone keeps surviving, I am up on my luck.

Cay, still queasy, just sips blackberry tea. "Now ain't you glad I took that wrong turn?" he asks in a weak but still playful voice. "Gave you a little vacation up here."

West doesn't mention the visit from the Broken Hand Gang, and I follow his lead.

After a few bites of his dinner, Cay falls back on his bedroll and asks me to pull his earlobes again, so I oblige. Peety rises unsteadily to his feet, then gives every horse a kiss and a back-scratch. After licking her spoon, Andy joins him. West tidies the campsite. He moves slower than usual and yawns every minute, but he won't go to bed until the last cup is wiped.

Finally, Peety turns in, followed by West, who drops onto his bedroll without even taking off his boots. Cay, his head in my lap, has finally fallen asleep—along with my legs. Andy beckons me over to her bedroll. I unhook my legs and rub feeling back into them.

Andy's face has the bright sheen of someone with fever, but her head is cool. "I feel grimy."

"Come on, I'll give you a bath." She bats away my proffered hand and gets up on her own. I find our soap and rag and lead her upstream. The night is warm, and the dirt on my own skin feels like an extra shirt.

We stop at a shallow part of the stream where the water pools, and toss our hats onto an overhanging branch.

Andy strips off her clothes and wades into the water, arms held out to the sides. I wash her frock coat. She can cover herself with a horse blanket tonight and by morning, the coat should be dry.

She carefully sits on a rock, and splashes water on her face and over her shoulders. "Feels good to get clean again. Thought the next time I got wet I'd be in the River Jordan." The six dots on her arm glow in the moonlight. She catches me looking.

"Does it hurt?" I ask, remembering the way she's been rubbing it the last few days.

"Itches now and then. But I think I figured out why God allowed Mr. Yorkshire to stick me with this nasty die."

"Die?"

"He loved his dice. Six was his lucky number, though it always set him back seven."

I stare at the square, wondering why I didn't realize it was a die before, especially considering how a single die figured so significantly in my own history.

"But I think six is *my* lucky number. Five of us, plus Isaac. I have a good feeling I'm gonna find him soon."

"I hope you're right." I plunk down next to her, hoping no fish bite my bottom. "You talked about your brothers a lot." I lather her hair with the soap and scrub.

"That's 'cause I was dreaming about them."

"What about?"

She smiles. "I was dreaming about the year before they split us up. Tommy was seven, He and Isaac used to play a game called Follow. Isaac would blindfold Tommy, and call, 'Follow,' and Tommy would have to trust that Isaac wouldn't trip him, or lead him into the mud. Tommy was a good follower, never even stumbled."

She churns the water with her hand. "But one day, Tommy asked to be the leader. He made Isaac wear the blindfold. Isaac only went two paces before he fell, though of course, there was nothing blocking his path but his own scaredyness." She chuckles.

"Did you ever play the game?"

She stares hard at the space in front of her, like someone's there, though all I see is the river. Finally, she answers, "I'm still playing the game."

As I puzzle out what she means, she says, "You and West took good care of us."

"You gave us a good scare."

"Serves you right for nearly drowning in the Platte. I guess we's even now."

She disappears under the water. When she surfaces, she blows a stream from her mouth. Her skin is sleek and glassy, like an exotic river dolphin. "If anything had happened to me, you'd have told the boys about you, right?"

"No."

"Why? They'd help you get to Mr. Trask."

"They've done enough for me. Besides, I think I can find my own way now." I start in on my own scalp, scrubbing hard.

Water drops off her thick lashes when she squints at me. "Maybe you could. But would you want to?"

I don't answer.

Her gaze drifts away, and I worry again that she's thinking about separating. I decide to tell her about our visit from the Broken Hand Gang. She listens, wide-eyed and motionless.

I finish my story. "We'll have to be careful. They may not mean us harm, but whoever shot Jeremiah might still be out there."

"Yeah, you's right. We gotta be careful."

Andy settles into her bedroll between Peety and Cay. We didn't move their bedrolls back in case they start feeling sick again. I heat our stew pot and turn it upside down to half-dry Andy's coat, then hang it on a branch to finish air-drying. By the time I fall on my own bedroll, I am utterly dragged out.

When I open my eyes next, night still wraps the land tight as a bud, unwilling to allow sunlight in just yet. I start to unfurl, when I realize West's arm is draped around my waist, and his face is buried somewhere in my neck. Is he awake? His arm feels too heavy, and his breathing too even. Each exhale kisses me.

My heart starts frisking about in my chest. If he awoke, would he be horrified that he's cuddling a boy? Or has he seen through my disguise at last?

The thought sends alternating cold and warm tingles down my back. Is *that* why Cay called me a filly? I stiffen, causing West's hold to loosen. He flops onto his back, releasing me, and I don't dare breathe. I turn around and my eyes trace down the dark feathers of West's eyebrows to the straight line of his nose, and then to his mouth, parted and inviting. His chest rises, then his breath *huhs* softly out. Still sleeping. Slowly, I exhale.

Cowboys ain't meddlers, Cay said. They must have been waiting for us to tell them. I bet they figured out we were wanted criminals as soon as they knew we were girls. Yet they stuck with us.

I bite my lip as a wave of gratitude blurs my vision.

West's breathing becomes shallower as if he senses me watching him. Slowly, I roll onto my back. I wish I could talk to Andy right now, though of course she'll be sleeping. Maybe I'll just check on the patients anyway.

Quietly, I get to my feet. When I pass by the tree where I hung Andy's coat, I stop short. The coat is missing. I know I put it on that branch. Maybe a wild animal got it, or—

I sprint to the river and my heart collapses in my chest. Between Peety's bulky silhouette and Cay's sprawling limbs, I find an empty space.

37

I STAND OVER CAY AND PEETY, REFUSING TO ACCEPT it. She couldn't have left. Maybe she simply laid her bedroll somewhere else because Peety was snoring too loud. But I don't see her anywhere.

Maybe she went for a walk. She stashed her bedroll, took her coat, and wandered off.

I kneel in the flattened grass of the empty space.

The ground is cold. My eyes catch on a fragment of metal on Peety's hand, glinting in the moonlight. He has a gold ring on his pinkie.

I scramble to where the horses are clumped together. Both Paloma and Lupe are lying on the ground, while Franny and Skinny stand facing each other, as if silently communing.

Princesa is gone.

As I stare at the horses, my mind jogs back to our conversation in the stream only hours before. *Follow.* She is still playing the game.

She has gone to Harp Falls without me.

I grab my head in frustration. *Andy! I was supposed to come with you. Curse your Dragon's overconfidence and rocky head.* The tears come, even as I know she had my interests at heart. She thought I'd be safer with the boys and Mr. Trask.

I hastily fill my canteen and stuff jerky and nuts into a feed sack. Then I tack up Paloma. If Andy runs into Badge, he won't know she was part of my group. And even if he did know, he might not care after what happened with West. And what of the other gang members? It would be easy to catch her, still weak from cholera and obviously deluded by visions of her brother.

After I attach the saddlebags, I fetch my bedroll.

At least the dark will slow her down. Maybe she's still close. I can catch her and bring her home. But what if she doesn't want to come back?

West fell back into a peaceful slumber. I try not to look at him as I fold my blanket. I can't bear to say good-bye.

My resolve weakens and I hide my snuffling in my sleeve. I take a deep, shaky breath to calm myself. I am tempted to wake West, to pour out my troubles and let the boys charge to the rescue.

But I can't. I owe it to the remuda to keep them from harm's way. And deep inside, I know West could have a better life, a luckier one, without me.

I finish packing quickly, taking the minimum I need to survive and leaving the rest for the boys.

I tear off paper from West's journal and spend precious minutes trying to figure out what to write. But even if I had a lifetime to compose the right words, nothing I say would be adequate. So I simply scribble: *Thank you—Sammy.*

I fold the now-wet paper, and carefully slip it into West's pocket. Finally, I allow myself a last look, trying to memorize every detail of him, every scar and dimple.

I wipe my eyes and force myself to my feet. I kiss him good-bye in my head, bidding farewell to the one I have loved in silence.

The sky has lightened several shades by the time I steer Paloma upstream. Our river must have a source, and perhaps that source is Harp Falls. At least, I hope that will be Andy's reasoning. I don't have any better route to follow.

I urge Paloma to a trot, thankful once again for the steady feet of my mule. She expertly steps over pinecones and fallen branches. The rhythm of her movement comforts me.

I pat her neck. "I'm sorry to make you leave your friends. But we will see Princesa soon. Help me keep a sharp eye out for her, okay? They have to rest sometime."

In the somber light of predawn, the pine trees take on the eerie silhouette of hulking phantoms with gnarled limbs and shriveled goblins, waiting to jump out at us. My legs grip Paloma harder and she increases her tempo.

I pat my gun for assurance. If these are the Haystack Mountains, criminals hide here, according to that trapper. I've already run into the remaining members of the Broken Hand Gang, haven't I? If these mountains are a lawbreaker's lair, it follows that mercenaries will flock here, too.

My mind winds back to my last conversation with Andy. Something she said about Ty Yorkshire troubles me. I begin braiding Paloma's mane. *He loved his dice. Six was his lucky number, though it always set him back seven.* He had a gambling problem.

Sometimes you roll snake eyes, Ty Yorkshire had said. *Snake eyes means you lose.*

I stop braiding. Though I hate to think of that dark night, I strain to remember what he said before he assaulted me. *Not easy to insure a wood building like that, but I can be very convincing.*

"Ty Yorkshire started the fire," I say aloud. The only one to hear is Paloma, who ignores my sudden outburst. He blamed it on Father so he could get the insurance proceeds.

My skin turns clammy as a seal's and my head pounds so hard I can hear it. Any remorse I felt for Ty Yorkshire's death vanishes like a puff of smoke.

But as furious as I am, fury won't bring Father back. The one responsible is already dead. And as the Chinese saying goes, every second spent angry is one less to spend on tranquillity. I can almost see him now, fishing out an eggshell from a bowl of cracked eggs with a patient, steady hand, practicing tranquillity during the small things so he'd be ready when the bigger things came along.

After an hour or two, my anger has abated a notch, but whether that is from mental discipline or sleepiness, I cannot be certain. The moon has faded and drizzly clouds outlined in white sprout at the eastern horizon. The landscape is easier to see now. The sight of a recent horse dropping bolsters my spirits in a way I never thought horse droppings could. We soldier on with renewed energy.

I can't help ogling this corner of God's museum. Red and

yellow flowers peek out of the spaces between the rocks. Softwoods stipple the landscape as far as the eye can see: bristled lodgepole pine, stately hemlocks with tops bent like sleeping caps and the white pines with their straight trunks that run unbranched on their bottom halves.

By midday, we shade up. Paloma dips her nose into the stream, which has widened and lost its bank. I eat a pull of jerky and a leftover biscuit, nothing fancy, but enough to take the edge off my hunger. Water fills the remaining spaces in my stomach.

As Paloma gets her fill of grass, I rub stream water over my hot face. The sight of my own reflection startles me. My face has thinned, uncovering cheekbones and making my eyes look bigger, almost startled. There's a tightness to my jaw that must have come from months of scowling. I make an effort to relax my face, and it disappears. *Would you recognize me now, Father?* I cover my reflection with a withered leaf and watch it float away.

I don't tarry long. Andy doesn't have a gun or arrows. How does she expect to catch game, let alone protect herself? She is resourceful, yes, but she didn't even take a pot. How will she boil water? I thank God that Paloma surpasses Princesa in both stamina and steadiness. We might even catch up by midday.

The river has grown so tumultuous that I cannot fathom crossing without a bridge, and the faint odor of rotting eggs stings my nose. I haven't spotted any more horse droppings and I hope that Andy didn't cross the river earlier. Soon a new sound catches my ear, lower in cadence and more pounding, like the beat of a kettledrum.

We crest a hill and a waterfall rises before us, a torrent of white as great as God's beard. It must rise at least two hundred feet. The yellow-streaked rock flanking the falls rises steeply on the left side, but not so steeply on the right, like the top of a harp.

My chest collapses at the sight.

Harp Falls. Just like Andy described.

38

THE FACE OF THE FALLS IS TOO STEEP TO CLIMB
so we veer right, passing the downpour completely until we come
upon a smoother route up the mountain. The *whoosh* of running
water intensifies as we track up a carpet of pine needles.

It takes the better part of the afternoon to scale the falls. We
have to rest several times to catch our breath. During the steeper
stretches, I dismount and lead Paloma through a zigzagging trail
of trees and rock.

"Almost there, Paloma," I pant once we reach a level area. I
climb back aboard for the final stretch.

From behind us, a herd of elk scales the mountain with more
haste and power than we just did. They storm past us in a blur of
gray fur and antlers, then dissipate like a cloud of smoke. A lone
figure appears: a bay, with sleek lines and slender legs.

"Princesa," I cry, spurring Paloma to a canter.

When we reach her, Princesa turns a baleful eye to me, but it
doesn't faze me. I hug her neck. "Where is she?"

The horse is still saddled, and damp with exertion, which
means they must have just arrived recently.

I don't see Andy anywhere, so I continue my upward trek,
leaving Paloma saddled next to Princesa out of caution.

"Andy? Where are you?"

Never have I seen so many pine trees in my life. They obscure the ascent, and I stumble when I crest the top sooner than I expect. My breath sweeps out of me at the view.

Below, a river stretches a hundred feet across, a rolling strip like a dragon's tongue. It stagnates toward the middle, but ruffles at the south end before the drop-off. On the other shore, more pine trees poke out of the earth.

I descend a hill of rock and find solid footing about fifteen feet down.

My heart nearly jumps out my mouth when I hear voices. I fumble for my gun. Forcing myself to remain calm, I creep in the direction of the waterfall. A bulging wall of rock partially obscures the drop- off. Cautiously, I round the bulge. The thin margin of shoreline isn't wide enough for a horse, and is slick with green slime. The voices grow louder. I close my eyes, straining for the words, and I hear her.

My foot slips on the slick surface, and I grab on to the wall to keep from falling into the river. But in my haste, I drop the Dragoon. I watch in horror as it clatters down, but thankfully it doesn't explode this time. The water reaches for it. Hastily, I bend down to retrieve the damn thing, willing the water to stay back. I stretch my arm way out, and my boots slide toward the river. I urge the gun backward with my finger and finally get it back in my grip.

One of the voices begins to sob. I hurry around the bend with my gun outstretched.

It's Badge! He's wrestling Andy in a sandy alcove, his face twisted with rage.

Badge sees me and pushes Andy aside.

"Don't you hurt him!" I yell, holding my gun with both hands to keep it steady.

When Andy sees me, she cries, "Sammy!" at the same time as Badge says, "You again."

"Put that thing down," Andy snaps. There are tears in her eyes, but the trace of a smile lingers on her face.

"He's part of the Broken Hand Gang!" I exclaim.

"Put it down before you shoot someone," she says.

I don't listen, and am reminded of West's standoff. Am I afraid of being a chicken, too?

"Sammy, this is my brother."

Her *brother*?

I stare at him, refusing to believe it. But as I compare the two, side by side, the similarity is hard to deny. The high cheekbones, the deep-set eyes and rounded hairlines.

The truth lines up like poker chips in a dealer's tray. The Wanted Bulletin. I thought Andy had gasped because she saw the picture of the Chinese woman, but in actuality, she had recognized her brother as a member of the Broken Hand Gang.

Only now do I realize the two were not wrestling but embracing. Badge holds a wad of cloth stained red on one side to the wound on his temple. West got him harder than I thought.

My hands drop back to my sides and my voice fails me.

Andy puts her arm around my shoulders, dragging me to Badge. He looks even more haggard than when last I saw him, with heavy bags under his eyes and a gash across his cheek.

"Sammy, this is Isaac," she says.

"I thought you were called Badge."

"Some call me that."

I glance at Andy and don't bother to hide my irritation. "How could you leave!"

"I'm sorry. But you shouldn't have come." She squeezes my shoulder. "Let's all sit down."

I now notice a canvas tent and a pile of supplies beneath the boughs of the massive fir that shades us. The tent sags in the middle and is ripped in several spots. Five paces away, a kettle hangs over a smoldering fire. At the far end of the alcove, a series of staggered rocks forms a natural staircase back up the mountain.

We settle onto the dirt floor.

"You musta known I was coming," Andy chatters happily to Isaac as she pours coffee from the kettle into three mismatched cups. "You got the coffee brewing. Now where's the honey?"

"Haven't had honey since the time I climbed that old magnolia." Isaac cracks a grin, and Andy begins to chuckle.

Isaac explains, "We found this hive, and Annamae gets it in her mind that she has to have honey." He makes his voice go high and wags a finger, "'Sure would be nice to have some honey. Don't you want honey? If we had some of that, we could make honeycakes.'"

"Oh hush, I only asked once."

"So I climbed the tree for her. Got stung so many times I thought I was gonna float away, I was so puffed up."

"It was just a few stings." Andy bats him on the arm. "They didn't stop you from having you's share of honeycakes."

The two converse easily, one starting up right as the other leaves off. They exchange a few more memories, and while they don't always explain the inside jokes, I enjoy listening just the same.

"So where'd they take you?" asks Andy.

"Georgia. We was all from Georgia." His smile falters. "But let's not talk about that right now."

I suddenly remember the boy with the bullet in his leg. "Where's Jeremiah?"

His smile fades completely. "Gone."

"I'm sorry," I whisper. Was it because of my crude operation? Did I make things worse? My eyes blur as I think about the boy forced to bear it like a man. "I'm sorry," I repeat, this time to Jeremiah, wherever his spirit lies. I hope he has become a star, with Peety's sister Esme.

"They all died...my friends...even the smallest, Jeremiah," Issac explains, more to Andy. "He reminded me of Tommy, asking questions all the time. Softhearted, too." His large hands wring his wadded-up cloth. "I told myself if I could save Jeremiah, God would make sure Tommy arrived safe, too. But I couldn't save him. He caught a hunter's bullet, and even after we got it out"—his eyes flick to me—"he was too weak to go on."

Andy takes the cloth from him and dabs his head. "It's okay, Isaac. You tried you's best, and God knows it."

"Well. At least the Lord gave me Tommy anyway, and for that, I praise Him. Don't make me wait any longer, sister. When's Tommy coming?"

Andy casts me a weary glance. She didn't tell him? She

refolds the cloth so she has a clean side and tries to press it to his wound again, but he twists out of reach.

"Tell me," he urges.

She makes an exasperated face and sits back in the dirt. "I'm sorry, Isaac. I didn't tell you everything. When I said Tommy's fine, I meant, Tommy's in God's hands now. I didn't want to tell you the bad news so sudden-like, but there it is."

All the air goes out of Isaac and he puts his head in his hands. "Oh, sister. Oh, no. God, no." He begins moaning and then he lets out an animalistic howl so filled with grief that the image of a burning building, ashes falling like black rain, springs to my mind.

Andy puts her arm around his trembling shoulders but he shakes her off. "It's all right, Isaac, we's got each other now. It's a miracle we's here—

He cuts her off. "You shouldn't have lied to me."

"I know. I'm sorry."

"Tell me how it happened." When she hesitates, he growls, "Tell me."

I jerk at his anger, sloshing hot coffee on my hand. His mouth cinches tight as button and his hands become fists, reminding me that the outlaw Badge still lives in Isaac.

She sighs. "You know he liked animals." She swallows hard and shakes her head. "The missus' son was throwing darts at a dog and Tommy got it in his head to rescue that bitch. So the son started throwin' darts at Tommy instead."

Isaac begins to rock back and forth. My head pounds at the awful image. I pinch the fleshy part of my palm.

"Careful, Isaac, you gonna start it bleeding again," Andy says as Isaac rubs his hands over his head.

"I lost my chance with Him," he says, drawing his gaze up. His eyes appear empty.

"We never lose our chances with God," says Andy. "You the one told me that."

"I'm a criminal, sister. Leader of the Broken Hand Gang," he says with irony.

"I bet a lot of that stuff weren't true."

He shakes his head. "We didn't break no one's hand, but we did scare people, I own that. The five of us, we were all desperate to escape. Couldn't think of any other way to get things. Folks were scared of us anyway without us even tryin'. But we never took more than we needed."

"I believe you. And I think if you talk it over with God, He's gonna understand."

He winces. "He won't. I killed a baby, Annamae. A baby. I didn't mean to do it. The man's gun went off and he shot himself by mistake. Then the woman kept screaming, and she dropped the baby and ran. And I was too scared to touch that baby, so I left it, thinking she'd come back." A note of hysteria creeps into his voice. "But she musta been too scared to come back, and that baby died. Matthew says whoever harms the children, better have a millstone around his neck and be drowned in the sea."

Andy rubs a hand over her mouth to hide her shock. When her hand falls back down, her features are smooth once again. "Well. I'm sorry about that baby, I truly am. But think about Paul. He killed all those Christians, probably some babies, too, but God made him an apostle." She cuts off her bracelet with a pocketknife. "Look, Isaac. It's Tommy's stone. Remember how he found the good in people just by looking through this hole?"

She holds it up to her eye. "I see lots of good in you. God wouldn't have let you come so far if He didn't believe in you. We traveled a thousand miles, and yet we're here, and now we can be free. That's a whole lot of something."

She hands Isaac the stone. His cheeks are wet but he doesn't wipe them dry. "You remember the time that duck left her eggs?"

"Sure. Tommy put warm towels on the nest so they would hatch."

Isaac smiles. "Changed the towels every few hours so they wouldn't grow cold." His lip starts to tremble and he bites down on it.

"You took over the night shift when he fell asleep."

"Don't remember that. Only remember thinking, this boy's heart is too big for this world."

"Well, that was true." Andy swipes at her eyes.

I want to ask what happened with the ducks, but now is not the time.

Isaac sucks in another breath and wipes his nose on his sleeve. When he looks up again, his face is devoid of emotion, almost placid. "You two best catch your horses before they run off. If you don't mind, I want to set here and think awhile."

"Okay." Andy touches his shoulder again, and this time, he doesn't shake her off. "We'll scrounge up something to eat. You brought your bow and arrow?" she asks me.

"They're with Paloma." I gulp down the weak coffee, then get to my feet.

Andy kisses her brother. Then I take her back the way I came, which I estimate to be a shorter route than up the rocky staircase.

"I'm sorry about what happened to Tommy. You think Isaac's going to be okay?"

"Yeah. He just needs some looking after. And time."

I'm about to scale the hill, when she calls back, "Isaac, set some water to boil!"

No answer.

"Isaac?" she yells louder. "Set some water to boil. You hear me?"

Again, no answer.

We double back around the rock and find that Isaac's no longer on the shoreline.

Instead, he stands, shirtless, at the top of the rocky staircase on a platform that overlooks the waterfall, two stories up. His back bears a tangle of tannish scars. Beside him, a pair of pine trees grows stubbornly from the platform.

Isaac steps dangerously close to the edge. Then he spreads his arms wide, like a black crane preparing to dive.

"What you doing up there?" cries Andy. But either he doesn't hear her against the wind, or he chooses not to listen.

She grabs the edges of her hat, then looks furtively around her. "I need rope."

Both of us search the supply pile, which is a disorganized

mess, like Isaac just dumped everything in a hurry. Blankets are unfolded and a sack of nails is half open and leaking its contents. But no rope.

I continue rummaging, and Andy dives into the tent, quickly emerging with two coils of rope.

As she forms her loop, a mocking voice freezes both of us in place.

"Ye going swimming, blackie?" asks a voice in a Scottish accent.

I don't see the person speaking. Isaac turns his head a fraction to the left.

"Always a good day when ye spot a blackie. They're always runnin' from something, nae?" says another voice, followed by a cackle.

With a sickening twist of my gut, I recognize the voices of Ian and Angus MacMartin, the trackers from Mr. Calloway's caravan.

"Where are they?" says the first Scot. "Tell me now a'fore I shoot you,"

Isaac finally turns, giving us a view of his profile. "Who you talking about?"

"The China girl and the Negress. We come a long way fer them."

They've come for the bounty.

39

MY UNLUCKY STREAK SHADOWS ME LIKE A BAD
conscience, taunting me, haunting me.

I catch Andy by the arm and pull her toward the tent.

She tries to push me away. "No!"

"They haven't seen us," I hiss. "Think!"

"But Isaac—"

"You're no good to him dead."

I feel as though I might drown in my own sweat, but she finally follows me.

The tent's canvas walls shiver at our entry and I worry they will give us away. My skin breaks into itchy tingling as I remember the time Deputy Granger nearly caught us in Mr. Calloway's wagon. Trapped in another canvas prison.

We use the rips in the tent's walls as peepholes.

Ian and Angus come into view at the far left end of the platform, weapons drawn as they slowly approach Isaac. A coil of rope droops from Ian's belt.

"Ah know they're here," says Angus. "We been trekking them for weeks now. And I seen me old naig a quarter mile back."

"I killed them," Isaac says defiantly.

"Kilt?" says Angus. "Why would you do that?"

"S'pect that's my business," says Isaac in a steely voice.

"Bruv, it's even better than we thought," says Ian. "I knew this blackie looked familiar. He's one of th' Broken Hand Gang."

"Weel, bruv, I think yer right. I guess we'll take you for oor troubles, instead," says Angus. "What'd that poster say? Dead or alive?"

Isaac remains silent.

"I prefer dead," says Ian. "Less trouble that way." He shows Angus a rotting-tooth grin, then his eyes catch sight of our tent. His grin fades. I stop breathing.

"Seems to me, you needs a body before you can collect a prize," says Isaac. Ian frowns and reverts his attention to Isaac, who adds, "And I'd prob'ly fall off this here waterfall, if you shoot me."

The Dragoon slips in my sweaty hand, and I quickly put it down to wipe my palms, inhaling deeply to tamp my burgeoning panic.

"I'll do it," says Andy, grabbing for the gun. "Quickly! They'll kill him."

I shake my head. "My aim is better." I'll have to fire two quick shots just like I did at the pinecones the boys threw up for us to hit. My targets stand forty or fifty feet away. *Oh please, God, I know I shouldn't be asking you for help in killing, but let these bullets fly true.*

I fix my sight line on Ian. Before he moves, I take a deep breath and squeeze the trigger.

It clicks.

Andy gasps. "What happened?"

I sight again and squeeze, but the gun clicks like the *tsk* of a tongue. My stomach sinks as I remember dropping it on the shore. It must have gotten wet and now the powder will not burn.

Raw terror freezes me in place. *Think!*

"Isaac carried a gun in his coat!" I hiss.

We search the tent. No coat. I peek out of the hole again. There it is, a folded buckskin near the pile of supplies. I point and move aside to show Andy.

"I'll get it," I say. "You stay here."

"No, I'm coming, too. Might be another weapon in that pile." She crooks her pinkie at me. "We're rattlesnakes, remember?"

Giving her a grim smile, I hook my pinkie around hers. Then, silent as moths, we slip out of the tent.

Angus and Ian close in on Isaac. They don't notice us.

While Andy rummages through the supply pile, I unfold Isaac's coat and feel around the pockets.

Empty.

I pat the rough buckskin a second time, though I couldn't have missed it, a gun as long as my forearm. My eyes rove the alcove, but I don't see the black iron anywhere. I shake my head at Andy. *The gun's not here.*

She drops a lantern and it jangles noisily. She hastily silences it. I creep to the opposite side of the supply pile and search the heap with her.

Isaac inches back. The sun outlines his silhouette with a golden halo. "You's cannibals. Living off the flesh of other men, because inside, you's souls are black as my skin and eating you's own bodies away."

"Now thet's no way to talk, nay, blackie?" Angus's voice turns soothing, putting ants on my skin. "We're offering you yer life. Ye ain't got noowhere else ta' go, noowhere ta' run. We'll pat in a good word for ye, make sure th' baillie don't go so harsh, if you come easy." He holds up two fingers of his left hand. "Scotsman's word."

Ian tucks his gun into his waistband and unhitches the rope from his belt. Angus keeps his gun drawn.

In my panic, I can't distinguish one item in the supply pile from the next. Slow down. Cord, saddle, shirt, feed sacks, turkey feather. Turkey feather. I pull it out as gently as I can. It's an arrow.

Jeremiah claimed he could shoot a dandelion from thirty feet. Where is his bow?

Andy squints at my arrow, then plows into the pile again.

"We don't want no trouble," says Angus. "We're peaceable lads. Just want tae do right by the law. We'll make sure your ride back is comfortable, and that ye get a fair jury, wouldne we, bruv?"

"Scotsman's word," Ian agrees, mimicking his brother's hand motion.

"You God-fearing men?" asks Isaac.

"Raight, we are," says Angus. "Church every Sundee."

"Then stand before me and swear it before God, and I will let you put the rope over my hands," says Isaac.

Ian slowly approaches his quarry until he stands in Isaac's shadow. "Ah swear it," he says.

Angus sidles up to his brother. The nose of his gun hovers just an arm's length from Isaac. "Ah swear it, too."

Isaac looks each man in the face. "Well, I hope you told the truth." Solemnly, he holds his wrists out to Ian. The Scotsman begins binding them. "That's a good blackie," Angus purrs.

"God bless us," says Isaac, suddenly lifting his head to the sky. "A falcon."

I don't see whether there really is a falcon, because at that moment, Isaac grabs both men by their arms and yanks.

Backward Isaac falls, pulling the brothers off the cliff with him.

"Isaac!" Andy screams, echoing one of the men's screams.

My horrified eyes take in the platform, now empty save for the leaning pine trees and the dust that still clings to the air. He *jumped*. He took his own life, to take the lives of those two hellions. Oh, my Lord, have mercy on his wretched soul. Have mercy on us all.

Andy's eyes are stretched wide. In her hands is the Cheyenne bow. She grips it so hard it might break in two.

She sobs. The sound squeezes a fist around my heart. I rush to her and put my arms around her quaking shoulders. It is a trick of the cruelest type that she came all this way, from a garish hotel to a mythical waterfall, only to have the reason for her journey vanish into thin air. Where is the justice in that?

Covering her head with her arms, she gulps in ragged breaths.

My own eyes grow moist, and I shut them to trap the tears inside.

Why, Father, do the angels fly away when we need them most? Left to ourselves, how do we wrestle with fate, a demon casting stones left and right, snuffing out fires before they grow too bright? If I knew the answer to these questions, I might be of use to Andy right now. But all I can do is hold her while she cries.

I open my eyes again, focusing on the place where Isaac just stood, still not quite believing what happened.

Something moves. I squint to block out the late-afternoon glare. Maybe the sun is playing tricks on my eyes.

There it is again. I gape as a hand comes up and then another, from below the cliff's edge.

"Andy," the word falls out of my open mouth.

She's still sobbing and doesn't hear me. I scramble to my feet, just as whoever's returned from the dead throws his leg over. In a moment, Angus is lying on top of the cliff, heaving.

"Andy," I cry, shaking her. She's rocking back and forth, fingers still gripped around the bow. *The bow.*

Angus rolls over and finally spots us, a crazed look in his eye. As I pry the bow out of Andy's fingers, the Scotsman gets to his feet, letting out a primal scream so full of anguish all the hairs on my arms stand straight up.

Where's the arrow? I quickly rush back to the pile and collect it.

Angus charges toward us, zigzagging down the rocky staircase.

My fingers move as thickly as if I were learning a new Paganini on someone else's violin. This Cheyenne bow is different from my bow, lighter. I notch the arrow, but where's the arrow rest? On the *other* side?

Isaac's words ring in my head. *Jeremiah made friends with a couple of Cheyenne and they gave him a bow and arrow. Made it special for him.*

Jeremiah was left-handed. In desperation, I calculate what's more likely to hit, an arrow notched correctly on the left, or an arrow notched incorrectly on my right? Thanks to Lady Tin-Yin, my left arm can do a thing or two, but an arrow? I switch to my left, but now I have to use my left eye.

Dear God, my fingers shake so bad, I can hardly hold the bow. It's too late to switch back—he's nearly upon us. Quickly, I notch, sight, and let it fly.

It misses.

But it nicks Angus's ear, stopping him for a precious moment.

He wipes his ear, smearing blood down his neck. I fling away supplies in my hunt for a second shaft.

Andy finally understands our predicament and rouses herself. Slipping off her frock coat, she runs at Angus, flinging the coat over his head and kicking him so hard she falls onto the shore clutching at her own leg.

Angus stumbles but remains upright. He frees himself of the coat, then jumps on her. His hands find her throat and squeeze.

I drop the bow and grab the closest object—a wooden spoon. Running to them with my weapon high, I'm reminded of the scrubbing brush I wielded a lifetime ago. As I swing the spoon at his wounded ear, Angus blocks it with his arm. Quick as a cat lick, he snatches my arm and yanks me down beside Andy.

I fight to hold on to my weapon, but he's bending my wrist so hard, he will break it. My bow hand. I let go of the spoon.

He crawls on top of me, pinning me down so heavily I cannot budge my legs. His sweat drips onto my face. I glance at Andy, who has stopped moving. Did he crush her windpipe?

My blood boils, my rage like a demon about to spring out of my chest. I lunge, tearing my nails down his cheek.

"Bloody hell!" His grasp on me weakens and quickly I wrench myself out from under him, calling upon strength I never knew I possessed.

I scrabble back toward the supply pile. If I could just—

The monster grabs me by the ankle and pulls hard. All the breath blows out of me as I land heavily on my front. I try to scream but blood fills my mouth.

Frantically, I claw at the ground but it's no use. He's too strong. He releases his grip on my ankle only to yank me up by the arm. I struggle with all my might. But now he's shaking me so hard, my teeth clatter.

"Yer fault! Ye kilt my bruv! Yer goin te' pay!"

After I think he's broken every bone in me, he stops shaking and hooks his eyes into mine. His empty orbs of blue ice are the eyes of a madman. I do not think he even has a soul.

"I knew it when we saw the bulletin. Where's your nellie boys now? They get tired of ye?" His sulfurous breath blows hot against my face. I'm so dizzy, I can barely stand.

"Almost gave up," he hisses. "But then we heard ye showing aff with yer fiddle."

Oh, my God, they were at Independence Rock.

"Five hundred somethin' fer you and your blackie sets me up good. Biggest quarry I ever—"

My heels slip from under me, cutting Angus's sentence short. I fall back, pulling him with me. I expect to feel hard stone as I land, but instead, bitterly cold water engulfs me, cutting off my breath. The ground has disappeared and my feet cannot get purchase.

Angus flails somewhere next to me. In a panic, I kick off my boots and swim away from him. Water clouds my vision and floods my ears. Soon, he catches my ankle once again.

But now something else has caught me, and I fear its rough hands more than Angus's. Hissing, snakelike, the river pushes me toward the falls.

40

I SCREAM, BUT WATER CHOKES ME.

Though I paddle as hard as I can against the current, the water is a sticky, living thing, playing with me before it will consume me whole. Angus sees the danger, too, and starts swimming up current, using strokes more powerful than mine.

I spend a precious few moments working off my clothes to reduce my drag, shedding the layers I have hidden under for so long. But in so doing, I slide even closer to the edge. Kick, stroke, focus. It's like climbing a giant bolt of fabric by pulling on the cloth. It unrolls and I get nowhere. I look wildly around for something to grab on to. But there is only the slick rock of the shoreline.

"Sammy!" Andy stands on the shore holding a lariat, which she has anchored to the great fir tree. *Oh, thank God she's alive!*

"I'm gonna throw it, and you better catch it! On the count of three!" she yells.

The drop-off inches ever closer, only twenty feet away now.

My arms are so tired, I want to give up. But that would mean fate would collect yet another prize today.

"One!"

Why should fate always have the upper hand? Passing out

luck, like mooncakes in autumn, then snatching them right out of your mouth. *Well, Fate, I reject you, from your gleaming jaw to your pale underbelly.*

"Two!"

From now on, I will make my own luck.

"Three!"

And this time, I will not roll snake eyes.

Andy hurls the rope and it lands a few yards ahead, but quickly starts moving toward me. I catch the rough hemp by the loop.

Angus notices and stops swimming. The current speeds him backward, and as he passes me, he latches on to my waist. I kick with all my might, but he pushes my head underwater. With one quick yank, he wrestles the rope from my hands.

And just like that, fate shows me who's still in charge.

I lift my head, eyes stinging. Angus flashes me a grin. His cheeks are red with cold except for the scar like a jag of lightning running down his cheek.

Oh, Father. I cannot fight fate. It is too great, and I am so tired.

You're right, I hear Father say. *Whether you think you can or you can't, you're right. Have a pea shoot.*

This is not the Paganini, I want to scream.

Right again, he tells me.

Fine, I tell Father, since I still need the last word. *I can stop a waterfall with my bare hands. I can sing opera, too. Fly, if I want, all the way to Mars. What I can't do is catch that damn rope.*

Andy screams something. Maybe good-bye? The story she told about Harp Falls rushes back into my memory. If only the prince had seen that he was holding the harp all along, he would not have fallen to his death.

Who am I struggling against now?

Nature? No gun, no rope, no feat of strength will stop this river from taking me.

Angus? He's more than an arm's length away—too far, even if I had the strength to fight him for the leash.

Myself. I am the monk. I am the prince. I have struggled with my Snake luck all along, and now, only at the end, do I understand this.

Fate casts its cold shadow over me, daring me to be afraid. In those last seconds before I go over the falls, I listen for the harp, the voice as familiar as the D-flat scale.

Stop struggling and you will find common ground, says Father's wise and gentle voice.

My arms go limp. As I stop kicking, suddenly my feet graze rock. I can touch the sandy bottom. In a last move, I push off, more out of instinct than any conscious effort. Like a giant bull-frog, I lunge. Angus is pulling the hemp over his body as my hands catch the rope.

Over the falls we go.

Father, I will see you soon.

41

MY STOMACH DROPS AND I FEEL GIDDY AND SICK all at once. I grip the rope as tightly as I can, wondering, as the river ejects us, how long is this rope, and will I have the strength to hold on if it doesn't break?

The rope runs forever, and when it finally ends, it nearly pulls my arms off. We swing under the falls like an anchor. Water pummels me so hard, I wonder if it's rinsing me of my skin. Somehow, even though all of my senses are engulfed with icy torrents and I cannot see him, I can feel Angus moving beside me.

The downpour ceases for a moment as we pass into a cave behind the falls. We dangle, two keys on a chain—thirty? fifty? feet above a dark pool. Angus kicks, making it harder to hold on. With a sickening clutch of my gut, I realize that my arms encircle his neck. After a moment though, he goes still, and we sway like a pair of lovers, slow dancing.

I draw back my head a notch and let out a gurgled shriek. Angus's eyes bulge, the black pupils like ticks on a cornflower. His tongue looks like a bitten plum with red juice running out the sides.

He was trying to pull the rope around his body.

But he only made it as far as his neck.

I am hugging a corpse.

Even in death, Angus manages to terrorize me. I recoil as much as I can. Every fiber in me wants to put as much space between myself and Angus as I can, but the only place to go is down. I nearly laugh at the irony. That the end of my journey should be at the end of hemp, but not hanged.

Even if my arms could hang on longer, the rest of me refuses. As my grip begins to slip, I know for certain that this is my moment of reckoning.

An image of Father holding out a plate of suns flashes through my mind. And Andy, crooking her pinkie at me. And West, with light from the campfire dancing around his face, who will never know how much I love him.

You may have me now, Fate. I am ready.

The world speaks no more.

My body hangs, suspended in some buoyant medium. It drowns out my senses until all that remains is a single note. An *A* for acceptance.

I cling to that silvery strain, following it to the source. A violin. But not just any violin. I know that voice—her highs, her lows, and her cranky D-string. My vision clears.

Before me, a man plays Lady Tin-Yin, doing the Paganini as easily as if he were whistling. His wrist trembles expertly as he draws out the last note. *Father!*

He puts down the violin when he sees me. I rush over and squeeze him tightly, for I can't lose him again. My tears pour out. He smells like I remember, of ginger and cedar shavings.

"I'm sorry, I'm sorry," I say, blubbering all over his small but sturdy frame.

He pats my back. "I know, daughter."

Then he pulls me away from him. I drink in every detail of his face. He looks younger than I remember, with neatly combed hair, a smooth forehead, and only a few creases at the corners of his eyes. His cheeks are tight, marked by one dot under his watermelon-seed eyes.

"Where have you been?" I choke out.

"I have been with you," he says in his quiet voice. "Remember what we learned about the fireflies?"

My mind drifts back to a warm July night, in New York. "You caught a firefly in your hand. You showed me that the glow is actually on the lower abdomen, where the firefly can't see it."

He nods. "We carry around the light of our loved ones who have passed. It is they who light the path for us."

"Passed?" I gasp, beginning to cry again. Father's really dead. That means I must be dead, too.

His own dark eyes grow luminous and he stretches his shoulders back. "I am proud of my Snake daughter."

He looks up, slowly letting go of my hand. Cirro cumulus clouds fan out, like a knife spread them across the sky.

I start to panic. "Father, don't leave me, I still need you," I plead. The threads of his worn gray suit disappear under my fingers like smoke. "Come back!" I scream.

The echoes of my cries ring in my ears. But Father is gone. And I'm alone in the world once again, only this world is not the one I remember. I am standing on a floor of white marble wearing the dress I wore that very dark day, the one washed so many times that the flowers had faded.

Have I died? I scream but no one and nothing responds now, not even my own echoes. Maybe I have gone to hell, for Ty Yorkshire, for Angus. Maybe hell is not fire and brimstone, but a place of loneliness.

I collapse onto the marble and sob.

Something warm and wet wedges itself under my cheek, pushing its furry face into mine and nuzzling until I open my eyes.

It's a rabbit.

He lies down beside me. The black of his magnificent coat invites me to pet him. I lose my fingers in his fur, stroking its silkiness until I feel calm again.

The rabbit rises onto his hind legs, regarding me steadily. He's as tall as a horse, with glittering eyes and sleek ears. I climb onto his back, and knot my fingers in his fur.

His muscles flex and release as he stretches out his legs. And then, with a mighty leap, we shoot into the sky.

42

I WAKE TO THE WARMTH OF BODIES BESIDE ME.
Something soft and warm is pulled up to my neck, like a knitted blanket. I force my eyes open. Two cowboys with the same dimples kneel on either side of me as if praying, one with brown hair, the other's, golden. On my right, West wears the haggard look of someone who hasn't slept for a week.

My friends! How did you find us? Where's Andy? I want to ask a million questions, but my tongue is too sluggish to even utter a syllable. I wander back to the sleepy realm.

"You did a good job knitting this up," says Andy. Her cool touch on my right arm is familiar and gentle.

"I know how to set bones. I do for animals all the time," comes Peety's low, reassuring voice from somewhere behind me. "Andita, it is time for you to rest. You've been up all night."

Did he say Andita or Andito?

"I promise to get you if Sammy wakes up," he assures her.

"*When* Sammy wakes up," she corrects.

Oh sister, go to sleep. I just need another moment here, myself. My whole body aches.

"That's what I meant," says Peety.

"Careful of that bump on her head," she says. *Her.* The word never sounded so sweet. "Put the shawl back on. She's freezing."

Something comforting and warm is laid across me, and though my eyelids are too heavy to lift, I know it is the shawl that I lost a lifetime ago, made of the finest wool. I can almost feel its positive energy cocooning me. In an instant, I understand. West found it, that dark day when I nearly collided with him in the street. He knew.

I hear a double set of footsteps as Andy and Peety walk away.

West lies down next to me and lays his arm securely over my chest.

"If you're going to start pitching woo, I'm making tracks," says Cay.

"So make 'em, then."

The gravel crunches as Cay walks away. Now I'm fully awake, but I don't move.

"Samantha?" West's voice is uncertain, almost shy. "That's going to take some work." His Texas drawl sounds more pronounced. It strikes me that he is nervous. I'm about to speak, but instead I let him continue. "I ain't good at talking about things like this. So maybe I'll practice so I get it right when you come to."

I relax my eyelids and stay limp.

"I could give you a heap of reasons for my bad behavior. I didn't have a smart daddy like you, or maybe where I come from, people like you don't mix with people like me."

A single drop of yolk can ruin a meringue. My cheeks flame as I remember his story about the blood in the fence paint. There were certain things about him he could never change, no matter how he tried.

"Or maybe I've just got stew for brains and couldn't see what was in front of my nose until it was waving good-bye." His voice takes on a more urgent tone. "You know when you were in that tree, burning? That was me whenever I looked at you. Stuck between heaven and hell, and not sure how I got there. All I knew was, I was gonna die if I didn't do something about it. Thought I could get my head on straight if I just—" His normally smooth tenor cracks, and he pauses long enough for me to notice a songbird calling. "I'm sorry for what I did. By the time I realized no other hat would fit me, I figured you despised me, and there was no way I could dig myself out of that hole."

I nearly open my eyes. Cay wasn't talking about himself that night we peeled tangerines at Independence Rock. He was talking about West. *I* was the alligator-suede hat left in the window.

He lifts his arm off me and tucks the shawl up to my chin. "You know, I never needed much. Worked out good since all I owned was the sand in my boots and Franny. But now I do need something," he says in a ragged voice, pausing to inhale. "I need you."

The words send a delicious tingle through my ears and down to my toes. I should wake up now. Though it would be nice to hear this all a second time.

I open my eyes. He blinks when he sees me and the tears that have collected on his dark lashes splash onto my face.

"Well then, come here and kiss me." I don't bother lowering my voice anymore.

His face lights up and he does it, a kiss as sweet as a serenade and achingly familiar. The smoke of a lonely fire and something wild fills my senses and lifts me from my ordinary existence. My sigh echoes in his throat.

He lifts his face from mine. His eyelashes flicker. "You killed me twice in one day—once when you left that note, and again when I come here to find you half dead."

"I'm sorry for so many things, for lying, putting you in danger, being a bur—"

"You're apologizing for the wrong things."

"What should I be sorry for, then?"

"For not trusting me." He tucks his mouth into mine, making me lose all sense of who I am, and how I got here. All I know is, the snake's aboard the rabbit again, and we're flying to the stars.

43

ANDY WEARS ISAAC'S BLUE-AND-WHITE-CHECKERED shirt. We're standing on the banks of the Yellow River, far enough away from the falls that we no longer hear its pounding. The water, which fought me only a week ago, now moves guiltlessly along. Andy shows me the remains of her bracelet, which she found back at Isaac's camp. The rock with the hole is missing. "I think Isaac took it to Tommy," she tells me.

A few days ago, Ian's body floated down the shore—well, most of him, his back broken and his belly split open. Later that same day, Angus followed, missing his head. I don't care to think about the details of his condition. Just as with Ty Yorkshire, one day I will have to answer for my role in his death, whether in this world or the next, and I can only pray that God will be merciful.

For now, I am content that God saw fit to keep my own body intact. Perhaps He has carved out a path for me whose general direction is up, despite troublesome corners, and perhaps luck is not a sticker in my boot after all. After a thousand miles of trail, it seems to me that good luck is always just a few steps ahead of bad, and maybe the amount one receives of either simply depends on the distance traveled.

We didn't find Isaac. I imagine that, like the falcon, Isaac flew away faster than death could reach him.

Cay holds a bouquet of wildflowers as we all stare at the river. "Dear God, I'm sorry I never knew the man, but he must have been a good one, since you cut him from the same cloth as Andy here." He studies the bouquet. "I s'pect one day, when we do meet, he'll knock me sideways for risking his sister's neck during that stampede, and when that happens, I'll remember I had it coming." He plucks out a single stalk of freesia and throws it into the river, then hands the remainder of the bunch to Andy.

Andy puts her nose into the bouquet and inhales. "Isaac, I know you's with Tommy now." She sniffs and her eyes brim with tears, setting off my own. "The only reason I can figure you's up there and not here is 'cause Tommy needs you more than me." Her voice breaks and a fat tear travels down her cheek. "Well. Take care of each other, boys. Amen." She casts the whole bouquet into the river. The stems separate, and the river scatters them.

Peety enfolds her under his arm. After a moment, she shakes him off. "I think I'll go for a ride."

"I'll come with you," I say.

"Not a good idea," says West, following so close he nearly collides with me when I stop. "The two of you pick up trouble like bad habits."

"Agree. Plus, Chinita's wrist is broken. How she going to ride?" asks Peety. He sweeps his arm as he bows to Andy. "It will be my pleasure to accompany you."

As he begins to whistle for Lupe, Andy tugs his fingers away from his lips. "Sammy and I will double ride on Lupe. I do know how to ride a horse, you know."

"Well then, we'll follow you," says West. "This is the Haystacks. You ain't the only criminals up here, you know."

Andy throws up her hands. "We might take a bath."

"Even better," says Peety, elbowing West. The two of them start hauling up their saddles.

Groaning, Andy shakes her hat at them. "All right. But keep a hundred paces behind."

Cay raises his hand. "I volunteer to be *le chaperon*."

West swats him in the chest. "Sit down and watch the camp."

With a grumble, Cay plops down into the grass and leans his cheek against his fist. "There's something wrong with this picture."

The great Andalusian carries Andy and me toward the grass-covered hills. I twist around and see Peety and West following, small as ginseng roots. A family of bison grazes peacefully near a shallow slice of water with steam rising off the top. Their bodies are twice as big as longhorn cattle, tufts of blackish-brown hair sticking out in patches all over their hides. They don't even lift their heads as we pass.

A week of being waited on hand and foot has been good for both of us. Andy pulled a shoulder muscle wrestling me out of the pool behind the waterfall, all by herself. I don't remember any of it. She used a sweetheart knot in the rope that saved my life.

"Told you that knot was good for catching sparrows," Cay had said.

"The boys showed up a few hours later," Andy told me. "West wouldn't let you go, kissing you all over your face. I was afraid you was gonna suffocate. But I couldn't do much about it. I had my own *problemo* to deal with." She didn't bother holding in her smile.

Lupe takes us to a pond surrounded by fir trees. The water sparkles like a sapphire brooch pinned to the earth. We dismount.

"This is one of those bubbly pools I was telling you about," Anname says. "Come on, let's get in."

I step out of Peety's new boots, which Andy had stuffed with socks.

She helps me undress. The rope tore up my hands, but they're slowly healing. We keep on our underthings just in case our two bad habits decide to check in. The pines stand guard and a swath of blue sky covers us.

We slip into the water. It's warm, almost hot. The steam rises in wisps the way down feathers do when you fluff the pillows. I haven't had a warm bath since, well, the day I first met Andy.

Her clear eyes focus on the ripples around her, like she's reading tea leaves. The bruises on her neck have turned yellow, and beads of water spread across her nose.

My chest tightens as I think about my guardian angel with the die branded on her arm. When God took away my father, he gave me a sister. She taught me how to be strong, how to thump my tail.

"That West grew a few inches," she says. "Though he forgets how to work his feet when he's around you. I'd be careful." Under the surface she goes.

I laugh. West *is* a new man, walking taller and whistling a lot. Every morning, I wake up tucked under his arm.

Andy reemerges and slings water off her head. "Peety asked me if I'd like to be the wife of a wealthy *ranchero*. Told me I wouldn't have to lift a pinkie 'cept when I drank my *chocolate*. Also said he didn't want children. His horses are his *niñas*."

"What'd you say?" I ask.

"I said, it sounds boring." She laughs, and the beads on her nose drip down to her cheeks. "Then he says, 'You'll never be boring with me.'" She leans back and closes her eyes.

"And?" I coax, wanting to splash her.

She opens one eye. "And I said, 'Okay, then.'"

I let out a yelp, and this time, I do splash her. She dishes it back, even though she knows I can only use one hand.

Then we float, side by side, and watch the animal clouds chase one another across the deep blue. I point. "Look, a dragon."

Andy squints. "Looks more like a frying pan to me."

She never did embrace her Dragon heritage. The dragon stretches out until it's two separate pieces, and soon it's nothing but ghostly wisps. "Just like life."

"What?"

"The clouds. They never hold still. Sometimes you think you're seeing one thing, and a second later, the whole picture changes."

"But we don't have to let the clouds change us for the worse. We can just let them roll over us." She frowns and her nose begins to twitch. "If those Scots hadn't come along, you think Isaac would've jumped?"

"I think..." I say slowly, "'God makes our bodies want to live, no matter what our minds want to do.'"

"Yeah," she breathes. In a sassier tone, she adds, "Those are some pretty wise words. Musta been someone ingenious told you that."

For our final meal at the Yellow River, West catches a fat turkey, and Cay plucks it. Then we all sit around the fire while our vaquero puts Cay and West to work pounding cornmeal and water into dough.

"Making tortillas is ancient craft," Peety says solemnly. "Roll, then pat"—he demonstrates—"and *he aquí*." He holds up a flat circle of dough.

Andy and I are back to sitting with our legs together and not burping out loud, though I think I'll wear trousers for the rest of my life, even if I don't have to dress like a boy. I can run, tumble, and jump onto a horse in them with no problem at all.

"So if you knew the whole time, why'd you make that wager on the Little Blue?" I ask no one in particular, remembering how close Andy and I came to an unshucking.

Cay waggles his eyebrows. "Why do you think?"

"He didn't know until you fell in," West says with a wry smile, picking a piece of gravel off his dough and flicking it at Cay. "Fool's gold is made for people like him."

"Well, at least I knew before Peety." Cay casts a glance to the vaquero.

"Sorry, hombre, I knew since the first night. I grew up with sisters, remember? Andita tried to button her jacket the wrong way. Sometimes, women's clothes have buttons on left, but men always wear them on the right." With a hand sticky with dough, he gestures to the silver fasteners running down his jacket, then looks up at us. "You're not very good *chicos*."

"And you told me you were starting to see face hairs on me," Andy grumbles.

Cay pinches off a piece of his dough and pops it in his mouth. "Ain't that something. Turns out West and Peety are the real perverts in this bunch."

West chucks a piece of dough at his cousin. "We didn't see a thing."

"That we haven't seen before," Cay smoothly adds.

Peety tries not to grin. West shakes his head. "Why don't we just make these tortillas before we have another broken hand gang."

Andy snorts, but we both let it go. We *did* win the fishing bet, though I'm beginning to suspect that was more than just luck.

"Traveling with a wanted criminal won't be easy," I say, with an eye toward Cay. "There may be more trackers, more lawmen, delaying our journey even longer—"

Cay cuts me off. "This is the frontier. Criminals are a dime a dozen. I'd say, if you weren't traveling with one, something's wrong with you."

"We got some good-looking criminals on our side, eh, West?" says Peety, though he's looking at Andy.

West trots out a dimple. "We coulda done a lot worse."

"All right, lover boys." Cay groans. "Let's have a contest to see who can make the most. One, two, three, go."

Dough starts flying.

"Takes many years of experience to do right," says Peety, eyebrows flexed as he plies his next piece.

"I think you just stuck your thumb through yours," I comment.

"Speed it up, blondie," says Andy. "This ain't pat-a-cake. And you, the one named after a direction. Don't you know shapes? That ain't a circle, that's a square."

Before someone throws dough at us, Andy and I fall back onto a stack of horse blankets laughing. We gaze at the horizon, a sweeping canvas of color and texture. The sun drops like a magic ball into a hat, leaving behind a trail of glitter in the blushing sky. It takes my breath away.

"The socks are back in the drawer again," says Andy.

"Isaac and Tommy?"

"No. The remuda." She smiles at me.

Yuanfen, the fate that brings family together. My Snake weaknesses get the better of me, and my eyes grow misty. I never knew there were so many socks in my drawer.

But maybe you did, Father.

The trail's cold now, but I don't lose hope of seeing the man in the red suspenders one day. *Even if Mr. Trask and I never meet again, I will still open that conservatory for you, Father, for us, with or without Mother's bracelet.* After all, I flew off a waterfall. And the view at the top was so wide, and the outlook so handsome.

ACKNOWLEDGMENTS

THIS BOOK WOULD NOT HAVE BEEN POSSIBLE without the support of my dream team, and for them, I am forever grateful. To my agent, Kristin Nelson and her team at Nelson Literary Agency. Thank you for your tireless work, especially finding the perfect editors for *Under a Painted Sky*. To Jen Besser and Shauna Fay Rossano, for being those perfect editors.

To the talented Evelyn Ehrlich, Caitlin Swift, and Mónica Bustamante Wagner for whom the term "critique partner" falls woefully short. You are my kindred spirits, and both my book and I are better for knowing you.

Special thanks to beta-readers Abigail Wen and Ana Inglis. I am also deeply grateful for my dear friends Alice Chen-Hsi, Susan Repo, Angela Hum, and Jennifer Fan for keeping me sane, Jodi Meadows for her infinite wisdom, and Adlai Coronel and Bijal Vakil for keeping me laughing. To Mimi Chan for her amazing technical wizardry, and David Huang for his vast knowledge of antique guns. A big group squeeze for my fellow debut authors in the Fearless Fifteen and my girls at the Freshman Fifteen. A humongous thank-you to Eric Elfman, whom every writer should have in her back pocket. And to all the other folks who generously took the time to advise me on this book, in part or whole, my heartfelt thanks, as well.

To my big sister Laura for reading my book when it was just an awkward toddler, and to both her and her husband, Bach, for taking my kids camping so I wouldn't have to. I mean, so I would have time to write. To my little sister Alyssa and her husband, Tony, for supporting me in so many ways. To Dolores and Wai Lee, who put up with all my questions about Chinese philosophy and language.

To Avalon and Bennett. Every time I look into your sweet faces, I see the person I want to be. (And I also see a little bit of chocolate on them, so wipe that off, please.) And last but not least, to Jonathan. Thank you for encouraging me to do what I love, and more importantly, for keeping the remuda watered and fed, so I have time to write stories like this.

To my parents, Carl and Evelyn Leong, who always believed that I would be a doctor, but weren't surprised that I turned out a writer. Thank you for playing songs from the Old West for me, fostering in me a love of books, and showing me the right way to live a life. Finally, thank you to God, through whom all things are possible.

Stacey Lee is a fourth-generation Chinese American. A Southern California native, she graduated from UCLA and got her law degree at UC Davis King Hall. Now she plays classical piano, wrangles children, and writes young adult fiction. Stacey lives outside San Francisco, California.

Visit Stacey at: www.staceyhlee.com
Follow her on Twitter: @staceyleeauthor